Th

"Though merely a cousin of the lowly toadstool, the Cordyceps fungus lives a life that could hardly be imagined by even the most creative science-fiction writer. Cordyceps lies quiescent on the forst floor, waiting for its unsuspecting insect prey to pass. When a bug wanders by, the fungus attaches itself to the insect exoskeleton. It then secretes a chemical that burns a hole in the insect's body armor. Next, Cordyceps inserts itself into the insect body and proceeds to devour all of the host's nonvital organs, all the while preventing the insect from dying of infection by secreting an antibiotic and a fungicide (as well as an insecticide to deter other insect predators). Once the nonvital organs are consumed, the fungus eats part of the insect brain, causing the insect to ascend to the top of a tall tree in the forest. At this point, Cordyceps devours the rest of the bug's brain, thereby killing the insect and causing its body to split open. At that point, the fungus can release its spores a hundred feet above the forest floor.

Ironically, scientists usually refer to fungi as 'lower organisms.' "

—Dr. Mark J. Plotkin, *Medicine Quest*, Penguin-Putnam, 2000

DAVID DUN

UNACCEPTABLE RISK

PINNACLE BOOKS
Kensington Publishing Corp.
http://www.kensingtonbooks.com

ACKNOWLEDGMENTS

Professional Acknowledgments: To Ed Stackler, my friend, editor, and inspiration meister; to Anthony Gardner, my agent, for being a great advocate and a terrific advisor; to all the creative people at Kensington Books: Publisher Laurie Parkin for making it all happen; to Editor-in-Chief Michaela Hamilton (and for editing my first book before it was sold); to Ann LaFarge for her editing and thoughtful editorial assistance throughout the process; to Gary Goldstein for his great and enthusiastic support and editorial suggestions; to Dr. Michael Kinsella (a fun guy with a great imagination) of Benaroya Research Institute, Seattle, Washington; to my guides in Ecuador, Roland Balarezo and Jorge Vasquez (both of Iquitos), whose information about life on the Ucayali and Marañón was invaluable; to the guide Javier Chung of Iquitos, whose knowledge of the reserves and remote tribes was of great assistance, particularly his knowledge of the Matses peoples, and whose personal support and diligent effort were very much appreciated; to Dr. Scott Sattler for his fascinating thoughts on meditation; to Ruth Johnson for her extensive research efforts and word processing; to Joanne Stevens for all manner of help including research, travel arrangements, and word processing; to Justin Kirsch for great moral support and computer wizardry; to Scott Brown for his invaluable assistance with the Web site and editorial comments on the manuscript; to Ravenna Candy of Seattle, Washington, licensed psychotherapist, for assistance with character profiling.

Personal Acknowledgments: To all of my friends, family and coworkers from whom I have received a large measure of encouragement and inspiration, some who helped with a few words, some who devoted themselves to many hours, even days, of thought and helpful editorial commentary, not all of them are listed here. I thank you all for your generosity, support, and hard work. I will undertake the risk of naming a few of these fine folks (in alphabetical order): to William Bowen for all things French; to Mark Emmerson for his penetrating analysis, editorial comments, and plot points; to Russ Hanley for action scene comments and character points; to Miles Hay for technical information on weapons and firearms; to David Martinek for his thoughtful comments about plot and my various characters; to Missy McArthur for editorial attention to those all important details; to Bill Warne, a source of encouragement and all manner of thoughtful commentary on plot and characters; to Donna Zenor for her insights into plot points and characters.

To my wife and companion, Laura, for her love and support expressed in countless ways—all my love.

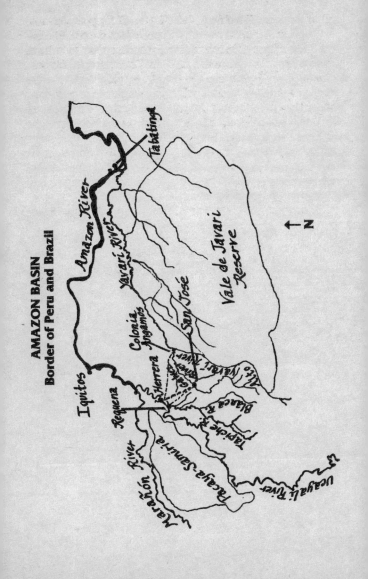

Chapter 1

To watch bees swarm, stand in the smoke.
—Tilok proverb

A pair of spotted owls roosted in an old, dead fir tree in a dense thicket of the forest. On this night, the owls hunted wood rats quietly. Sam, familiar with their ways, listened to their occasional calls and wingbeats above him until suddenly they began hooting with more vigor and coming down to the lower branches. Next they moved away, flitting from tree to tree and calling to each other. There was a certain recognizable pattern to these antics. The spotted owls had been fed live mice by so many biologists that they had developed an affinity for people. Their response to a creeping person was typically to come closer and and make a dinnertime call, looking for a mouse on a stick. It sounded very much as if Sam had human visitors. If so, they were moving away from him, and that was not what Sam expected.

Sam clicked his radio and Paul clicked back. The wind moved through the trees, rustling stiff yellowed leaves. Clouds blew past, alternately veiling and unveiling a gibbous moon. On the forest floor it remained black. Grandfather had taught Sam to look from the corner of his eyes for improved night vision, as well as to "see" with his other senses. Despite Sam's efforts, only the owls had announced the visitors.

Grandfather had taught him as well as he could. On Sam's first night in the forest with Grandfather some twenty years ago, he had grown impatient after a minute or two. Now, after two decades of sporadic practice, Sam could remain still and alert for many hours.

To show Sam how to make himself a part of the forest, Grandfather had told him a story. A friend had kept a blind horse. It lacked even eyeballs, hide covering the eye sockets. When a man approached its paddock with an apple, the old horse could easily find the hand that held the fruit. In fact, the horse acted much like a horse with vision. The average person, looking from a distance, would never know the horse couldn't see. Grandfather told Sam never to allow anyone to suggest he couldn't see, even on the darkest night. To this day Sam resisted the temptation to fall back on the obvious and wear his night vision goggles without interruption. Instead, he used them at regular intervals, and the rest of the time he spent straining to discern.

Sam lay in a grove of Douglas fir near an ancient incense cedar, most of his body tucked inside a hollow pine log and covered in a down sleeping bag that kept the late-October cold and damp at bay. He breathed in the mold smell of the forest and the odor of old fire, and this night the musk of a distant skunk. It all blended and swirled, creating a place of comfort because it felt familiar. Thirty yards distant stood his log house, built seventy years prior by a timber baron in this most remote corner of the state of California. As precious as the house to Sam were its contents, among them an eight-foot-high fireplace with iron log stands forged in the 1890s in Boston; handmade feather-cushioned couches and chairs passed down by his father's Scottish ancestors; the grandfather clock that had come across the United States in a covered wagon. Most of the furnishings, even the throw rugs, had a story. But the best stories existed in no book, living instead in the land itself.

Here in the northern California coastal mountains, among the old-growth conifers shrouded in winter mist, even the greatest of men seemed small. The timber baron had chosen well, building his house on a bench on an otherwise steep mountain, surrounded by government land and adjacent to the Tilok Indian reservation and tribal grounds, home to the other half of Sam's family heritage.

From his position, Sam could see through the bay window to the fading glow of the coals from the fire that had earlier played over the Douglas fir floor and paneling. Next to him on the ground lay Harry, a mostly Scottish terrier, snuggled in his own heavy blanket. Sam had one last doggy treat for Harry, but he was waiting for the dog to ask for it. Out of sheer boredom Sam looked at Harry and licked his lips in a fashion commonly canine. Harry gave a quiet groan of belly-felt desire, knowing exactly what was on his master's mind. Sam reached beside his sleeping bag and into the doggy treats bag, removed one, and held it under his own nose for a languorous sniff, as a man might do with a good cigar.

Harry thumped his tail. Sam held the treat in front of Harry's nose and Harry sniffed it in dignified silence as Sam had taught him. Then Sam tossed it into the air and Harry snatched it with a quick snap before it hit the ground. Harry rolled over on his back for a good belly rub, which Sam obliged. Then Sam put his finger to his lips and made a slight *shhh* sound, at which Harry lay silently on his blanket. Harry was a master at both shush and stay. Although Harry was truly Sam's buddy, he also played a practical role. As difficult as it was to sneak up on Sam, it was nearly impossible to sneak up on Harry. The terrier's senses of smell and hearing were acute and he was fundamentally a paranoid dog. Given his brushes with death, he had a right to be.

Sam fingered the braided rawhide necklace and its gold medallion, which opened like a locket. Inside was a picture of Stalking Bear, his grandfather on his mother's side. Stalking Bear had been a full-blooded Tilok North American Indian and a Spirit Walker—a spiritual leader that came along, at most, once in a generation. Although Sam was already eighteen years old when he met his grandfather, he had learned what he could in the next twenty. And on nights like this he was grateful.

Sam was every bit as tough as he looked, a long-muscled, swarthy-skinned man, an exotic admixture of his two family lines. It had taken some doing to trace his father's lineage back to the Highlands. His clan had been big, fierce, ruddy-cheeked people, brave to the point of fighting every superior force. From them had come the curl in his dark hair, which fell down over his ears. His face was more angular than round, though; the fine features were smooth and unblemished except for two scars, a line over his right eye and a small nick at his chin. His eyes were amber. As a job-related precaution, Sam did his best to conceal his features with raffia hats, sunglasses, and nondescript clothing.

Tonight it had dropped briefly below freezing, leaving the intermittent precipitation somewhere between rain and sleet. The wind whipped up a nasty chill factor. At the mouth of their log, Sam had placed a small lip of camouflage material to direct the flow of water away from their shelter. Harry was careful to keep his nose back behind the rain line. Sam hoped this small concession to comfort would not call attention to their hideaway. He looked at his watch: 5:10 A.M.

It was peculiar, he thought, how, at this moment, out of the billions of people on earth, only one man really mattered. Sam knew that every time the man called Devan Gaudet closed his eyes to sleep he felt hunted. A small comfort, but comforting nonetheless. Perhaps Gaudet retained enough humanity to realize that Sam hunted him for good reason. Still, for all Sam's efforts to focus on his side of the battle, there remained the sobering realization that he hunted a man who in turn hunted him and all those dear to him. It was a game that would end only when one or both of them were dead. As part of the game hunt Sam had decided to give Gaudet a shot at killing him. When Sam found the radio locator beacon in his car, no doubt affixed by Gaudet henchmen, he had led Gaudet and his people north from Los Angeles and into these mountains.

Although the struggle between the two men had been professional in the beginning—Sam was a contracted antiterrorist expert and Gaudet an assassin and international criminal for hire, the subject of one of Sam's investigations—it had turned personal when Gaudet began killing people Sam cared about.

After a time Sam clicked the radio again; this time he got nothing in return. Next he did a radio check. Nothing.

Silence was trouble. Men retreating into the forest were trouble because he didn't understand it and the worst sort of enemy was one you didn't understand.

Pulling himself out of the sleeping bag into the cool air brought him to full alert.

Sam straightened Harry's blanket, getting half of it under him and half on top. "Shush and stay."

Harry scrunched down.

Sam took three steps back, put on his field pack, his special forces MSA Gallet TC2000 helmet complete with night vision and headlamp, and then hefted his M4 combat rifle fitted with an underbarrel flashlight and an M 203 40mm single-shot grenade launcher. On his hip he wore a Heckler & Koch .45-caliber MK 23 SOCOM pistol, twelve-round clip, with laser aiming module and sound suppressor. "Stay," he whispered again, adding a hand signal. He knew the dog would not move.

Sam forced himself to walk slowly into the forest. If

Gaudet were active, he would expect Sam to check on Paul first, so Sam made instead a giant circle in an unexpected direction, following the spotted owls.

He donned the night vision goggles, which created a world of strange and subtle shadows. Branches hung everywhere and in places logs crisscrossed into windfalls, but Sam managed to pick his way around them. He stayed low to the ground, looking for signs of other men on foot, until he saw a lowland area ahead. It was wet with slow-flowing water in the rainy season. Traversing it without sloshing and making sucking sounds would be difficult, so he moved up toward the steep-sided rock-strewn canyons until he reached a hardscrabble path that he could use in silence.

Once on the other side he moved back down the canyon, taking only a few steps at a time. He had been moving for nearly an hour when he stopped to study a small opening near the place he imagined that the owls had gone. At that moment he heard them calling, getting closer, until they perched right over his head. He ignored them and scanned the forest. Unbelievably, he saw the glow of a cigarette well off the ground—apparently in a tree. An old road that served as a main trail ended here. No doubt the man in the tree served as a rear guard in a position so far from the expected action that he thought he could safely smoke.

Sam began a major sneak, dropping to his belly and moving inches at a time. To remain quiet in a slither meant that speed was out of the question. His father had insisted that he learn to stalk deer on his belly well enough to kill with a bow and arrow, and Grandfather had insisted that he improve his technique to the point that he could come within a few feet of a deer's flank unawares. Men were not as perceptive as deer, especially a man foolish enough to smoke when it could cost him his life.

Near the glow of the cigarette Sam made out the vague silhouette of a hunched figure pointing a rifle at the sky.

Stickery vines of wild blackberry were beginning to get hold of Sam's clothing and he had to extricate himself. Remaining silent was frustratingly difficult and he had only the wind as his ally. When he was within thirty feet, the man put out the cigarette and adjusted himself, flapping a branch in the process. A slight opening in the canopy allowed moonlight in, creating an enhanced silhouette of the armed man. After several more minutes of slow crawling, Sam lay within twenty feet. From this position the figure had disappeared altogether. This was dangerous. If they detected Sam, then a flurry of bullets from an automatic weapon could kill him before he could react.

He made out a large tree three feet distant; he crawled to it, stood, and plastered his body tight against the trunk. He needed the man to give him a final confirmation of his motive. Searching at his feet, he found a sizable chunk of wood. He further searched and felt a stone protruding from the soil under the forest duff and patiently worked to remove it from the ground.

Before tossing the stick, he removed his old Zippo lighter from his coat pocket. He threw the branch, which landed in the bushes with a soft brushy splash. He imagined the sentry tensing and straining at the night, then pointing his rifle. Sam lit the lighter and tossed it in a gentle arc. As Sam glanced around the opposite side of the tree, a burst from an automatic weapon lit the night. Sam now threw the heavy rock as hard as he could at the shooter and heard a slight smack followed by a low groan. There was a little luck in the throw, but Sam was good with a rock and the target had been close, albeit above him. Quickly he inserted a hand loaded rubber bullet into the chamber and another in the magazine. These were the only two rubber stun rounds that he carried and for that reason he had first tried the stone. They had a light charge allowing a safe hit to the head or jaw. After those two bullets he would be shooting hollow points and armor-piercing rounds called talons in an alternating sequence.

He waited for a moment; then the forest lit with the blast of the automatic weapon firing blindly into the night. The muzzle flash illuminated the man like a spotlight. Sam fired the two hand-loaded rubber rounds. He heard a crash followed by complete silence. Sam picked up a stick and tossed it. Nothing. He stuck his gun around the tree and fired a single lead round well over the man's head. Still nothing. In his pocket he carried a small but powerful NiCad light. He removed the night vision. Trying to stay hidden as much as possible, he shone the light around the tree and drew no fire. The bark of the tree was uneven enough for him to pull back a flap and wedge the flashlight in place so that he could leave it and scan from the other side of the tree. He saw bushes and ferns, but no person in the deep shadows. There were not many men in this attack group or the place would have been swarmed by reinforcements.

He quickly belly-crawled to within several feet of the man. A glance at the man surprised Sam. He seemed to be sitting on a stick or small tree stump and slumping against the larger tree from which he'd fallen. Sam got hold of a rock about the size of an egg and threw it hard at the figure. The thump of its impact sounded promising, but nothing moved.

Sam knew it could be a trap, although few men could sit still and take that kind of punishment. The body's position still seemed strange, almost like an animal shot in the gut. He took down the flashlight and drew closer. On the side of the man's jaw there was a nasty bruise. It was a mixture of luck and skill that the rubber bullet had struck him in the head, rendering him unconscious. Sam shone the light downward: indeed, the man appeared to be sitting on a narrow tree stump.

The man's head lolled to the side and then straightened and he let out a moan. Suddenly the man screamed and at the same time sounded as if he were being strangled. His scream-ing became more robust, then took on the tenor of someone crying. Confused, Sam shone the light down again, illumi-nating the man's buttocks. Blood ran freely from the seat of his pants. As Sam moved closer, he could see that the small sapling's trunk, perhaps the diameter of a quarter, disappeared up and into the immediate vicinity of the man's anus.

He was impaled.

Sam broke out in a sweat as he realized what had happened. On the ground lay a machete. Obviously, the man had whacked off the sapling to build a platform or blind in the larger tree. That had left a sharp, angled surface. When knocked from the tree above, the unfortunate soul had landed ass first, with the entire weight of his body driving the tree deep into his rectum.

With two quick strokes of the machete Sam cut off the of-fending trunk and laid the man on his side. From his pack he took a syringe with morphine and gave the man a quarter of a dose.

"I'm going to try to save you."

"Help me. Help me!" The man sounded nearly incoherent with pain.

Sam guessed that there was more than a foot of tree trunk inside him, perhaps two feet, if it followed his spine behind his vitals.

"I am going to build a stretcher as fast as I can."

Sam moved quickly to his pack, pulled out a satellite phone and his GPS. He called the sheriff, gave the latitude and longitude coordinates off the GPS, and let the sheriff call the chopper from Mercy Medical Center in Redding. The police put him on hold, then returned to tell him that they could not arrive anytime soon and that the helicopter was al-ready en route to an accident. Sam called the reservation, his mother's sister. A rescue party would arrive within hours. He told them to bring guns and to be extremely careful and to move slowly, expecting an ambush. It bothered Sam to ask for their help because he knew Gaudet and his capabilities. Sam dismantled his pack and used the heavy synthetic material and a swatch of fabric, designed for this purpose, to build a travois.

"Who do you work for?" Sam asked.

"Oh God, I'm dying. It hurts. Do something."

Sam worked on the stretcher while he waited for the initial dose of morphine to kick in. "Who do you work for?"

"Girard."

"Does he have another name?"

"I don't know. I only know Girard."

"I found the tracking device on my car. Did you follow in cars or what?"

"Cars and a helicopter. Ahhhh, it hurts. I knew it was too easy."

"More morphine?" Sam said, then inquired, "Where did you find my car?"

"Followed it from your office."

"My guy Paul thought he saw sun flash from a telescope. Did you stake the office?"

"Mmm-hmm." He moaned again.

"Where is this Girard from?"

"More painkiller." Sam pushed in a little more. "France? Quatram?" The man seemed uncertain.

"Why are you here?"

"Waiting for the neighbors to shoot a guy called Sam. If they don't, we will." The man's words were guttural and barely comprehensible.

"The neighbors?"

"I don't understand it."

"What's your next assignment after that? Anybody else to kill?"

"Amazon. Find Bowden."

"Bowden who? Who's Bowden?"

Sam thought he recognized the name. It was right under his nose, but he couldn't place it. Something about Bowden and the jungle went together. It would come to him. He snapped back to the present.

"I don't know! Help me."

He gave the man a bigger dose of morphine.

"Why Bowden? Why the Amazon?"

"Medicine. I think. They don't tell us much. Pharmacy company."

"Where in the Amazon?"

"Peru? Maybe Brazil. The border."

"How do you communicate with Girard?"

"Computer."

"Access address."

"Pocket."

Sam found a small black book. He flipped through it.

"Where?"

"Look under *u*."

Sam looked under *u* and found uaeromtioneb.net// exchange. He recognized the name spelled backward. Cute. He stuck the book in his pocket.

"What's the password to get into the site?"

"More morphine."

"The password."

"It changes at least every ten days. It's too long. Can't remember."

"Listen, my friend. I'm going to try hard, but you are probably going to die. Why not do the right thing while you're dying. Tell me how to stop this man who calls himself Girard." Sam gave him more morphine.

"It's in my computer."

Sam knew it was probably true and that the password would be very long and he took a guess about how it might be stored. He also figured that Gaudet only posted things for

a very short window of time and then only when he had
tipped off this man to look for something. Still it was worth
a try. Maybe Grogg could break through the fire wall.

"In an encoded document?"

"Yeah."

"What's the password to the document?"

"Birthdate 12/24/61, then Independence Day 07/04, my
Social Security number backward, plus the words: 'laughing
out loud' run together."

"In what file is the document?"

"I don't know."

"When you open your computer, where do you go to get
to this password for Girard's site?"

"My Documents."

"You on a server?"

"Yeah."

"Home page?"

"Irishmanandleprechauns.com."

"Do you have an ISDN line, DSL, or a cable connection
to the Internet?"

"ISDN."

"You leave your computer on?"

"Yes."

Sam got on the sat phone. At last he may have found a
weak link in Gaudet's fortifications. Gaudet was smart but
had a dummy working for him. He got Jill, his number three
in command, on the phone. Putting her in a management
role had been a logical choice. She was smart, had the most
experience next to Paul, was the most critical, and had the
best instincts of anyone he knew. On the other hand, she had
been his lover, never quite letting him forget it, and perhaps
still loved him. He had a severe mental thing about risking
her in any kind of a fight, which meant he did his best to
keep her locked away in the office, and that was a source of
contention. In her mind she was a soldier.

"Jill, go to Irishmanandleprechauns.com." Then to the man, "What's your name and the password to your exchange server? We're going in right now."

"Rollin and Rollinstrolley for the password." He spelled it slowly.

Sam gave it to Jill. "Go to the C drive. My Documents. Find an encrypted document, password as follows." He read it to Jill, up to the Social Security number. "What's your Social Security number, Rollin?"

He got it and told Jill to type it in backward, then type the words, "laughing out loud."

"Tell Grogg to use everything he's got to get into a site called by the name Benoit Moreau dot net, but Benoit Moreau is spelled backward. Use the password in Rollin's Word document at Irishmanandleprechauns.com to get in." Sam rolled Rollin onto the travois and the pain of the movement caused the man to scream himself hoarse.

As Rollin quieted, Sam heard something and jumped into a bunch of huckleberry. Quickly he circled with his .45 drawn. Whoever was coming was unskilled. Inside a minute he saw a man walking heavily through the brush. He appeared panicked by the way he moved. Sam hit him with the light.

"Freeze."

Holding an automatic weapon, the man whirled and shot, one of the bullets just grazing Sam's cheek. Before he could think about it, Sam fired back. A solid hit in the chest knocked the man off his feet, and as the man rolled, Sam realized his foe wore body armor. When he came up again, Sam blew off the side of his face with the second round.

Sam paused for a moment, feeling his bleeding cheek and allowing himself to process the fact that he'd nearly lost his life. Then he tried the radio again.

"Paul?"

"Yo."

"Where you been?"

"Might ask the same of you. Don't you usually come when a man doesn't answer?"

"I was getting around to it. You seen anybody?"

"Killed two."

"Just a minute."

Sam went back to his patient, who had begun groaning again.

"What's Girard look like?"

"Different all the time."

"Is he here tonight?"

"Yes."

"How many with you?"

"I think five. I don't know. Please help me."

Sam gave him more morphine, amazed at the fact that a giant stick up the bowel worked better than truth serum. Of course the finger on the morphine plunger was not to be underrated.

Sam picked up the radio again. "At least two left."

At that moment a massive explosion came from the direction of Sam's log house.

"You know what I think that was?" Paul said.

"Uh-huh. It means he's given up for the moment. Maybe Gaudet's losing his touch."

A pause, then a click from Paul's radio.

"I don't know, Sam. Someone seems to have a gun at my head."

Sam felt tired. It was an uncommon reaction to a colleague's imminent demise.

"I'm a dead man," Paul said before he was cut off.

"Gaudet," Sam said.

The response was garbled.

The radio on Rollin's belt came to life, a barely audible voice saying something Sam couldn't quite hear.

"Girard. Whoever. I can trade you Rollin for Paul. And I

know you don't care about Rollin, but you might care about
what he could say to the authorities."

"No!" Rollin cried. "He'll kill me."

"Just a minute." Sam turned off the radio. "Then you better help me figure how to trick the bastard."

"There are seven of them," Rollin said. "Not five."

"What else did you lie about?"

"Nothing. They'll be coming here now. They knew my
GPS coordinates. God, I need more morphine."

Using all his strength, Sam dragged the stretcher up the
side of the canyon a hundred feet and parked Rollin in a
thicket. At the hilltops it was growing light. He placed two
syringes full of morphine in the man's trembling hands and
kept the last two. He rather doubted he would see the man
alive again. As he turned away, he remembered one more
thing he should ask.

"Did you ever hear of a Frenchman named Georges
Raval?"

"Never."

Sam ran along the canyon wall, and as it started to flatten
near the house, he slowed down. They would be coming
without lights so as not to make themselves sitting ducks.
Paul had been halfway around the house; Gaudet would send
the others and stay with Paul, his ticket out.

Sam went straight toward Paul's hiding spot, slowing
when the GPS showed him within fifty yards.

Then he realized the flaw in this approach. Gaudet always
left when his plans went awry. That meant he would send his
men to kill Rollin and then order them to leave because they
had lost the element of surprise and their odds had worsened
considerably.

Damn. There was nothing he could do. He had to try to
save Paul even if the chances were nil. With a sense of utter
futility he continued on until he found Paul's dead body tied

to a tree. The Kevlar vest was on the ground indicating he had probably been held at gunpoint. He had also been eviscerated, a method Gaudet had used once before on one of Sam's men. Gaudet's process was a shadow of one taken from medieval times where they went beyond merely piling intestines on the ground and actually cooked them in a fire while the victim lived. Sam forced himself to study his friend's body. The incision was unlike the one other similar job performed by Gaudet. This time the incision was high and long and began at a partially disguised hole in the sternum. Judging from the edges it was a bullet hole. A wave of relief went through Sam as he realized that the bullet had no doubt hit the heart or the aorta and would have caused near instant death or at least unconsciousness. So the evisceration was a brutal afterthought like a calling card or a cruel attempt to convince Sam that his friend's suffering had been without parallel. Paul was dead or unconscious when they did this.

Gaudet had left him a one-word note: *ventouse.* As best as he could recall from his times in France, the word meant "sucker."

Sam moved away, his movements stiff as he processed the horror. He could not hide from the agony of losing Paul by pushing it from his mind. Such things needed to run their course or they would return in unexpected ways. He allowed the feelings of deepest disappointment and despair, followed by incredible, careless rage. Like all such feelings they would pass in time and give way to determination. Pure and simple he had to kill Gaudet.

In what he knew would be a vain effort, he ran back to the hillside where he had left Rollin. Even at a distance the man looked like a corpse. Sam felt unsettled and knew not to ignore his instincts. It would be a mistake to assume Gaudet was gone, even though that fit his pattern.

He made his way up the hill with great caution. The duff

was sodden and dense and a little like mulch, making for quiet footsteps. Then he heard someone coming fast, charging through the brush rather than coming around it. It wouldn't be the Tilok rescue team, not yet, and not that noisy. Sam squatted and raised the M4, flicking the switch into the automatic fire position.

A hat became visible and, amazingly, he recognized it. It was quite distinctive, festooned with fishing flies that in the predawn light looked like blurred dots. The hat belonged to Matt, his neighbor and friend down the road, a naturalist sort of a fellow, big into the outdoors. He killed a deer now and then for meat, gathered a lot of edibles from the forest, and smoked his fish the old Indian way. He was a good man, helpful with his neighbors on the mountain, and personally rugged. In this situation Matt could be a real asset, although Sam knew he wasn't a soldier. But Sam also remembered Rollin's strange remark about neighbors. Sam kept low in the event Rollin was right or in case Gaudet's men remained in the vicinity. As he waited, he scanned Matt with the starlight scope on his rifle.

Matt's expression was unusual, his mouth in a flat line, tense and determined. Perhaps he'd already had an unpleasant run-in with Gaudet's men. Or maybe he was a murderer in the making. Indeed, he carried a rifle of his own. When Matt was perhaps fifty feet distant, Sam heard a second person also moving fast.

Apparently, Matt heard the same footfalls and stopped moving up the hill, dropped to one knee, and assumed a firing position. He made no attempt to find cover. He raised his M14, looking prepared to shoot whatever emerged.

A bald head appeared, moving in and out of the trees and cover. It was another neighbor, James, also a good man, although Sam didn't know him as well. He lived a few miles away. James also carried an automatic weapon, which was stranger still, since James was strictly a fisherman and not a gun enthusiast. James carrying a combat rifle seemed more than suspicious.

Matt aimed at James as he emerged from the brush, finger on the trigger.

What the hell?

"Matt!" Sam shouted. Matt whirled and fired from the hip, peppering the tree that served as Sam's shield. A couple of the bullets made it through the edges of the trunk, causing Sam to pull in his elbows and squat. More shots came from below.

"It's me! *Sam!*" The bullets came faster and closer. Both men were shooting, but the bullets had stopped slapping the tree. Sam risked a peek around the tree only to find Matt and James shooting at each other. James was down and wounded, but still firing, and trying to crawl up the hill. Matt had found cover behind a black oak.

"Stop it," Sam shouted. "Let's talk."

Immediately they redirected their fire at Sam.

Bad idea. As they advanced on his position, Sam ran straight through a patch of huckleberry and behind another tree—lucky he hadn't caught a bullet. He ran back up the hill, figuring he would outrun them.

Passing Rollin, he saw that someone had shoved the stick all the way into his innards and shot him in the head.

Sam moved on and climbed to a small bench where large rock formations offered better cover. There he waited to see if his neighbors would follow. In minutes they were a hundred feet below him. Once again he turned and ran, moving farther up the hill, knowing he could get away but wondering what the men would do if left alone together. They were acting like men possessed. Sam couldn't imagine restraining or capturing them in this unnatural mind-set.

Sam would climb the mountain, then circle back, find the Tiloks, and determine what to do next. With a group of clever trackers they might trap and disarm the men before they hurt somebody. For just a moment he listened to make sure they were following, but now there was silence. He waited for minutes, but nothing moved.

Perhaps it was a trap. He made a gradual arc, descending the hill until he came opposite from the spot he had last heard his neighbors. Slowly he crept forward on his belly over slimy leaves, moving inches every minute. He knew to be patient. It took him half an hour before he caught a glimpse of the spotty camo of Matt's hunting clothes. Matt was on the ground, on his back. Sam crawled closer. Open-mouthed, the man shook in convulsions. Quickly Sam approached and found blood seeping from the corner of Matt's mouth and his body still convulsing. Sam checked his pulse: racing. Then it slowed and the convulsions ceased. Matt continued to breathe on his own, so Sam secured his hands together, left him, and found James several hundred feet down the hill. He'd been shot multiple times and crawled until he'd died—a great waste of a good man.

Chapter 2

Beware a gift of winter meat in spring.

—Tilok proverb

Sam climbed out of the Blue Hades, his rebuilt and enhanced Corvette, stretched his legs, and walked Harry across the warehouse and into a beige Ford Taurus. Harry sat on the floor of the passenger's side, having long ago learned the drill. On the passenger's seat lay a black leather bag that had originally belonged to Sam's son. Sam reached inside and removed something that looked vaguely like a Halloween mask but much more sophisticated. He pulled it on, smoothed it, used makeup around the edges, and brushed up the silver gray hair on top of his plastic pate. Then he donned an old hat with a broad brim and heavy black glasses.

"How do I look?"

The dog whined.

Sam pulled out of the warehouse, checked the sky for helicopters, and drove a twisty route through the commercial area, constantly checking for tails. It had been a week since they tried to kill him at the cabin. There was evidence that Gaudet had gone to Mexico and on a long shot Sam had tried to catch him.

He picked up the phone and called Jill.

"I'm back."

"How was Baja?"

"Big. Are we set to travel?"

"Grady's on the research. The arrangements are made. But you gotta rest, Sam."

"I would if I could, believe me. The way to find Gaudet is to beat him to Michael Bowden."

"We lost Paul. You're shaken. We all are. The only way to get your edge back is to rest, reflect, all that."

"A mental-health discussion in the middle of a war?"

"Maybe more than one."

"Where's Anna?"

"You have good instincts."

"Is she there? I hope she did the whole procedure for tails."

"She's not here."

"Where?"

"The show condo."

"Why is she there?"

"That's where she thinks you live, Sam. And she's very proud of her sleuthing. She wants to comfort you. It's normal after what has happened."

Sam said nothing while he considered his options.

"Your mother and I think you should come clean. Let Anna in, for God's sake."

"Go get her, if you can. If she'll go, take her out for lunch and—"

"Sam."

"I'll sort it out and call you right back."

There was a long pause, followed by a sigh that meant "yes."

He hung up. Jill would think of something truthful to say while he decided how he wanted to handle it. Anna Wade was his girlfriend and a mega–movie star. His anonymous life and her celebrity caused them nothing but grief. He wondered if Anna could ever be happy with him. All she knew of him really was the outer layer, the tough antiterrorist expert, the man of the shadows. Sometimes he asked himself how someone with her fame and wealth could be happy with a more or less ordinary person. A half Indian person. He had never uttered his concerns to Anna and he doubted that he would. For the moment, he shoved it out of his mind.

He'd taken the transmitter off Blue Hades several days ago and had his mechanic check for others. It would be like Gaudet to install two of them—the second one much less conspicuous. After making sure that nobody was following him, he proceeded down along the waterfront to a two-story house. This was a terrible time to have his situation with Anna come to a head. The nature of the problem was that she didn't know where he lived but thought she did. Actually, it was slightly more complicated than that. She knew the place he lived now and then, the place he had taken her when they wanted to go to "his place."

The house that actually contained reflections of his life, aside from his now-ruined mountain cabin, stood just across the street from the ocean. The mask he wore wouldn't fool anyone within ten feet into thinking it was natural skin and a real beard, but then he never stopped outside the garage and he had never met his neighbors. They had taken to peering out their windows in curiosity, but that was about it. He was in the place at most two or three nights a week, a function of traveling and the fact that there was a sleep room at the office. No one but his closest family members and Jill, his ex-lover and office manager, and the occasional maintenance man that she hired had ever been inside this house.

The condo known to Anna was tastefully decorated by a professional and it took some doing to make it appear lived in, but it really contained nothing of himself. Walking through, a person could learn only about the fictitious man the decorator had in mind. Sam felt slightly guilty that Anna had never seen his real home, though she knew his real name and had regularly been inside his offices—something few people had done. The current focal point of their relationship was his insistence on anonymity. Whenever they went someplace together in pubic, which was rare, he played the contract security man, an Anna Wade bodyguard, and seldom looked much like himself. The secrecy his work required was becoming a serious irritation for Anna, but Sam didn't have a ready solution.

At the heavy metal front door to his house Sam placed his finger on a small opaque window and his eyeball before another. It was the same security he had at the office. With a slight buzzing sound heavy bolts opened and he entered his house. When he was inside, he repeated the process to reset the alarm to the "stay" mode.

Indoors it was the usual 68 degrees Fahrenheit, cool enough to work out. He waved at Jill through the closed-circuit TV monitor in his living room, then turned it off. The place was comfortable but decidedly male. The furniture was soft leather with the exception of one embroidered rocker with a handwoven outdoor scene.

A stand with seven pipes stood on a small coffee table between two chairs and one cigar humidor. Once in a while he filled a pipe but usually preferred cigars.

A wooden case the size of two large refrigerators held photos, mostly of his late son, Bud. One showed Bud alive and athletic and triumphant on the face of a mountain of rock known as El Capitan in Yosemite; others were of him climbing at Castle Crags, parasailing in Mexico, and taking part in quieter activities, many with Sam. Most of Sam's past girlfriends were there, including Suzanne, now also dead, and Jill. The shots of Jill and him were hugging-and-giggling shots that told of a different day and a different relationship. But Jill was still important to him, so he left the photos in their place, figuring that they didn't need to go in a box until a permanent companion came along—an event that probably wasn't too far off. The tough decision would be whether to leave them in their place the first time he brought Anna Wade here.

But there were some photos that would definitely remain. They included photos of Chet, Jill's high-school boy, whose father was her ex and was now dead from alcoholism. Chet had suffered from a nerve disease, but aside from an impediment to running, the boy was all there. Chet was smart and an encyclopedia when it came to weapons. Sam wasn't much interested in guns except as an occupational necessity, but he was interested in the boy.

Sam picked up the portable phone and pushed memory.

"Hey, Chet, how's it goin'?"

"Sam."

"You haven't told anybody about me, have you?"

"You ask me that every time. Of course I haven't."

"I'm obsessed. You wanna go shooting on Christmas break?"

"Yeah. I wanna try the Desert Eagle Fifty caliber."

"Huh?"

"It's all in the grips. You said so yourself. I can do it."

"What are we gonna do? Tie you to a refrigerator?"

"It has ports to reduce the kick."

"My arms are an inch shorter since I shot that. You want arms an inch shorter?"

"I've already got short legs, might as well have arms to match."

Sam laughed.

"Okay. But if I go shooting, you gotta promise to go fishing."

"Fishing? You mean it?"

"Absolutely. And we'll invite the girl next door."

"Oh no. That would be too embarrassing."

"Hey, I can't turn her down now. I already told her that

your mom and I would take her fishing when I take you. Man, was she excited."

"Are you kidding me? You never talked to her. You wouldn't do that."

"Well, I looked about seventy years old at the time—with a beard. I'm your new god-grandfather for this trip. That's like a godfather, only old."

"Can I call you Sam so I don't forget like before?"

"You bet. Sam the god-grandfather. Absolutely."

"Sheees."

"How's the homework?"

"Good. Real good."

After a little more chit chat, Sam hung up, smiling at the boy's zest for life.

Off the living area was a hall to the two bedrooms and a large kitchen. Sam cooked slowly and with great deliberation. For him cooking was art and he liked to replicate things he'd seen in restaurants, but with his own twist. Cooking with a woman in this kitchen, for the first time, would be like making love on his bed.

Suzanne had been only the second woman he'd loved to the point of commitment, but they'd been together in France and the relationship had been cut short by her death. Rachel, his first and only wife, had long preceded Sam's purchase of this house. He sat down in his leather chair and called Anna on her cell. No answer. She was no doubt in the shower at his showplace condo. Sometimes she liked long showers.

Sam knew he was crazy and that most normal people came out of their inner shell in their late teens. He told his close friends that this terrible aloofness didn't worry him, although lately he was beginning to feel a bit like a middle-aged woman whose biological clock was ticking. From day to day his feelings seemed to change on the subject of fatherhood, and if Sam had a source of conflict that wasn't associated with the mess of his father's suicide, then this was it.

Built-in cherry bookcases contained Sam's personal book collection, weighted toward true-life exploration and adventures of all sorts, including the classics like Darwin's *The Voyage of the Beagle.* Sam liked reading about presidents. He didn't want the job but had plenty of books on the subject. His favorite topic was Indian history and that was evident both in the books and the storage cabinets on the other wall. Along that wall, also in cherry, were numerous drawers of the sort that one would use to store large nautical charts or maps that one wished to keep unfolded and flat. In Sam's case they contained maps and parchments of historic and modern Native American villages and ceremonial sites along the Pacific Coast from Alaska to Mexico and inland throughout the western states. It was one of the best private collections in existence.

Everywhere hung Native American memorabilia. One of Grandfather's ceremonial headdresses hung in the corner. There was the Cherokee blessing on the wall and likewise the Tilok blessing. He had all manner of ceremonial peace pipes and pictures of famous Native American leaders, from Chief Seattle to Geronimo.

Near the coffee table lay Grandfather's favorite moccasins. Sam's mother, Keyatchker, aka Spring, teared up every time she saw them. Sam's regular and favorite chair was a big leather affair with an ottoman sitting under a massive lamp whose base was made of carved oak. Grandfather had carved it on one of his pilgrimages to the caverns in the mountains. Sam cherished it because so much of his grandfather was in the wood that had been held in his hands and molded by his knife. It was an eagle with its wings spread. Sam's Indian name was Kalok, which meant "eagle."

Sam sat in his chair and Harry promptly jumped in his lap and settled in. On the coffee table was a baseball mitt that had belonged to his son, Bud. Some days Sam would pick it up and put his hand in it. Today he studied the old leather mitt and noticed that it needed oil. There was still an ache in him that felt like it would split him open when he thought about Bud. It had been four years. Today he would not put on the glove and feel the leather that his son had touched. It seemed unholy to mix love with the rage he felt at Gaudet. Attachments were hard because the world carried no guarantees of their permanence. Bud was gone, Grandfather was gone, and Suzanne was gone—and now Paul as well, one of his best friends.

Sam also kept memorabilia from the period before he had learned that he was a Tilok. There were pictures of him with his father in Alaska, a long-ago life that ended with Sam's discovery at age twenty-one that he was half Tilok with a living mother he had never met. All his life he'd been told that his mother was a mestizo, a whore, a drunk, and dead.

The phone rang, the display indicating it was Jill.

"You know he loves it so much when you call."

"What? Have you got that boy's phone bugged?"

"He calls me all excited."

"How are things with Anna?"

"I think you lead a charmed life. Right at the moment of truth with Anna, the CIA calls. First they say nothing all week. Now they demand we take the French as a client on the Gaudet case."

"As in, France?"

"Yep. And you'll never guess who the French have hired to represent their interests in this matter?"

"I suppose Figgy wants to meet immediately."

"You're a mind reader."

"Tell Anna I'll meet her at Forbes for dinner." He wondered if the subject of his house would come up at dinner. Actually, he wondered whether the world would be the same by dinner.

Grady Wade sat at her desk with a stack of Michael Bowden's books and a letter from his publisher. Her half-full coffee mug read: IF IT'S NOT OUTRAGEOUS, IT'S BORING. From what she'd read—and she'd now read all of Michael Bowden's books—he seemed anything but outrageous, but far from boring. A welcome surprise for a young woman who found little in life that invigorated her.

At the end of her career as a stripper, Grady had told Sam that the major problem in dancing naked for a living had been the truth in the coffee mug inscription. In the end that had been what frightened her most. Perhaps a life of kids and family and an old oak tree in the backyard would leave her listless and drive her to constant excess. The irony, of course, was that her cure, working for Sam's organization, was undoubtedly more outrageous than dancing naked. Actually, Grady did two things at this desk: work for Sam and study for college, and which activity received her attention depended on the demands of each.

Anna Wade, Grady's aunt, had a profound need for Grady to become "self-actualized"—a normal person would say "succeed"—and Sam did his best to play godfather to Grady, determined that she make herself into something that she would eventually approve of. The catch there was that Sam claimed unique insight into what it was that Grady should approve. Many days she felt like a social-conditioning project, but even that felt better than working in a strip club and coming down from a coke addiction. And so Grady studied, worked, slept a bit, and had little time for boys. Perhaps she had overloaded on men in her former occupation. For a time she had dated a man named Clint, who had fallen over-whelmingly in love with her and wanted to marry. The free spirit in Grady just couldn't do it. Not at age twenty-one. Now she saw Clint only on occasion; like most men, he wanted to see her more often.

To top off her complicated life, she lived with Jill, her immediate boss.

Researching scientist/author Michael Bowden came as a blessed relief from her normal work and schoolwork. In just a couple of days Grady had made copious notes on Bowden and the Amazon jungle, and in doing so had made one promise to herself: when Sam went to the Amazon to find Michael Bowden, she would use her best moves to ensure she boarded the plane with him—Devan Gaudet notwithstanding.

Her work area was in a large room with over twenty cubicles, each with at least an eighteen-inch computer screen, some with two or even three. Most of one wall was glass and beyond the glass was a large array of computer equipment. In addition, the complex held a large conference room, a lunch-room complete with cooking facilities, and a dorm-like sleeping room.

The place was a self-contained fortress. Indeed, all the office's perimeter walls were lined with Kevlar beneath studs laid over a heavy concrete wall. The windows in the outer walls—small openings above head height—were covered over with a so-called bulletproof plastic material. The place didn't have a true name; the people who worked there just called it "work" or "the office."

It secretly pleased Grady that Harry often picked the corner of her cubicle as a parking spot when Sam was in the office. He'd returned less than an hour ago, and she'd not seen him yet.

Her phone rang. That would be Sam, ready to be briefed on Bowden.

"We have some people coming in and I want you to brief them."

"Really? Nobody ever comes here."

"Sometimes the CIA does. Scotland Yard does."

"*Sheesh*. When?"

There was a long silence.

"I know. It's a secret and it'll happen when it happens."

* * *

The sound of cell doors slamming had become common-place for Benoit Moreau. She did not live in squalor or mis-ery, but the modern, antiseptic prison felt desolate. On her cell walls she'd hung art torn from magazines: photos of the Swiss Alps, the Pyrenees, and a picture of the Tour de France. There was also a picture of herself so that she would not forget what she was supposed to look like.

Benoit mostly lived in her mind and not in her cell. She had an exceptional ability to visualize what was not, but what might be, and consequently she never gave up. In the words of a writer of the New Testament, with which she had become familiar as a child, she knew both how to be abased and how to abound. It was a tribute to her otherwise ques-tionable character that she did not allow the trampling of her personal pride to dismantle her psyche. She had thought long and hard about how she'd gotten here, and she dwelled particularly on the men she had bedded and duped along the way. Of them, she was really interested in only one, and she determined that she would find her way back to him. Life, she decided, was the sum total of many small choices and she had made many bad ones to get to this place.

Before her life with DuShane Chellis and his company, Grace Technologies, she had been a rising executive, before that a student with many honors, including being named *prenièr,* graduating *avec mention particulière du jury,* and having her examination paper published in *Le Monde.* A se-ries of jobs in the computer industry and related medical ap-plications had resulted in her rapid rise. She had acquired a reputation as a smart, aggressive young woman who could get things done. Born Bernice, she called herself Benoit, a man's name.

On a bright full-moon night in December she met DuShane Chellis at a party. Attending the event had been an after-thought, and when she arrived, there was a buzz—people were talking about the consummate executive who was building a conglomerate faster than any businessman in French history. Some called him a savage because of his corporate takeover practices, but to Benoit, on that first evening, he was a charming savage. At the party, the first time he saw her, he kept his eyes on her. People noticed and opened a small path so that he could make his way to her. His attention and intensity were infectious; after a few minutes all those around him were glancing at her.

Within a few days she was hired as his assistant and within months a vice president. In six months the relationship became personal.

Benoit remembered him in the early years as uncompromising, determined, passionate, and seemingly without weakness. He could always concentrate and was never distracted, or so it seemed. He was a large man in every way, and when he walked into a room, he seemed to fill it. He knew how to relate to the man on the street and a prime minister. He seemed to Benoit to be the perfect corporate personality.

Like others who have lost control of their ego, as Chellis's success increased, he changed, became self-absorbed, abusive, and paranoid. For Benoit the day came when the thought of being near his power was replaced by the thought of taking it.

That day did not start out bad. Reports from Malaysia regarding the genetic technology—vector technology it was called—were never more optimistic. A brilliant young French scientist by the name of Georges Raval had discovered something amazing. He had taken two macaque monkeys and traded their hearts in simultaneous heart transplant surgeries. Both monkeys accepted the new heart without rejection and without the use of immunosuppressants. They had reprogrammed the immune systems of the two monkeys using a process familiarly known as "Chaperone." They expected that it would work on humans as well and would allow doctors to alter a patient's cells genetically in ways that made the expressed protein fundamentally different, and then allow the immune system to accept the altered tissue that resulted from the gene therapy—a genuine medical miracle.

She had walked into DuShane's office with two of the staffers that helped her administer the program. He was alone but on the phone yelling at a banker. He was in fair condition for age fifty-two, and he kept his salt-and-pepper gray hair impeccably groomed, swept back with natural waves. His face was unrounded by fat, more distinguished than pleasant. With his serious, dark eyes and the flat line of his mouth, he appeared to be a man who counted his conquests, a predator.

"I can always go across town. Don't ever forget that. And don't you dare ask me for more fees again." He slammed down the phone and looked at Benoit, then at her assistants.

"I have some very good news from Malaysia," Benoit began.

"Have you received Boudreaux's budget yet? The costs over there are out of sight."

"I mentioned that the budget will be here day after tomorrow. You agreed."

"I ask for a simple thing and I can't get it!"

"Well, we wanted to share with you the great news concerning the research of Georges Raval, a young scientist."

"I already know about it. You were supposed to have those reports. I ask for things around here and people pay no attention."

"We discussed it and you agreed. . . ."

"Then all I get is goddamn arguments. How can you do this and call yourself an executive? And why do you bring your damn toadies in here?" He dismissed the two assistants with a wave of his hand.

"That was rude and embarrassing."

"Don't fucking tell me what is rude. Rude is not getting the damn reports in on time. I have to run this whole company myself—do it all. Nobody else gets anything done. I have to watch, watch, watch. A bunch of damn children still shitting their pants."

"If you would not like to hear about—"

"Don't ever bring your flunkies in here unless I ask," he shouted.

"I am leaving. . . ."

"You are not leaving. Ever since I promoted you, you have been building a little empire. You think you're really doing something over in Malaysia. Well, I will tell you I started that when you were still a snot-nosed intern over at a bullshit company. So, now you want to run in here and tell me the good news as if you had something to do with it."

"We know it was your idea. I just thought it was important that—"

"Get on the couch. We're going to do what you're really good at."

"We're working."

He slapped her hard.

"I made you," he said. There was blood on her face. He continued to work himself into a rage. She did not deny him the sex he demanded and during the days to follow continued to offer it under less violent circumstances, and for that as much as the other bad choices, she still loathed herself.

It was that same day in the evening that she first responded to Devan Gaudet's entreaties. He was the most sinister man she had ever come across. Chellis hired him for things that he seldom talked about, but she knew that Gaudet was shrewd and ruthless. That night she went to bed with him and thus began the long plot to dethrone Chellis. Thereafter she learned that there were men even more ruthless than Chellis, and Gaudet was one of them.

Chellis had been unwise in creating trusts to hold the stock of Grace Technologies, making his wife and Benoit trustees if he became incapacitated. Benoit, Chellis's wife, and Gaudet saw to it that he was incapacitated, using the genetic brain-altering technology developed by Grace Technologies in Malaysia to turn him into a quivering mass. Although it certainly wasn't the purpose for which the technology was developed, the personality transformation was astounding.

When Benoit and Gaudet got control of Grace Technologies, the world was their oyster—except for a man called Sam. Unfortunately, Benoit didn't know that this Sam fellow hated Gaudet as much as she hated Chellis. Sam, she learned, lived in a shadow world of spies and treachery. When Sam built the case that put her in prison, Gaudet did what he always did—protected himself and killed his enemies. Apparently, Sam was the exception to the formula since Gaudet had never been able to carry out the second half of his equation.

Benoit blamed herself for her lot in life and had carefully traced the bad choices. The difficulty was that making only inherently good decisions, if indeed she could recognize them, would not get her out of this pit. To escape she would have to resort to the more troubling of her talents and then, like a caterpillar that transforms itself into a butterfly, she would use her dark side to produce the light. Her task would require more cleverness than was common even for her, more guile than she had yet displayed, and in the end more goodness.

Circumstances would soon make the transformation a possibility. The French government had shown signs of beginning an all-out campaign to solicit her assistance. She had started the process by giving them a meaningless hint, disclosing that the key to the riddle was nicknamed Chaperone, a protein molecule with a number of anomalies. Predictably, this had sparked their imagination, and for good reason: since Louis Pasteur, the French had not been good at anything except wine and women. On this point she knew she was perhaps a bit jaded, but it seemed that her countrymen were possessed of a kind of brilliance that enabled them only to do stupid things faster. As the government realized that mastering the vector technology, and particularly Chaperone, would quench its thirst for greatness, its representatives would come to her. And she would be ready.

The familiar sound of the hall door slamming preceded a set of footsteps.

"They're coming," said the girl from the next cell.

Benoit gathered herself and waited obediently by the cell door.

They threw the switch and the door slammed open. As she walked down the corridor, some of the inmates called out greetings; a few unleashed curses. There were three more sets of doors and two corridors before she arrived in the long hall where prisoners usually waited for the visitation room. There were tables and one could sit with visitors under the watchful eyes of the guards. But this time there were no lines, no other prisoners. Her cousin Colette worked for important people and could arrange special visits.

Colette was the chief of staff for Charles Montpellier, a well-known member of France's Senate, *le Sénat.* Although Colette did not approve of Benoit's chosen course in life, she nevertheless acknowledged that Benoit had a heart that seemed to draw those who loved life and some of its excesses. Benoit was the rascal that people liked despite themselves. That would include a fair portion of the French legislature, where she was well known to several members.

When she entered the visitation room, Colette managed a slight smile. Benoit knew her cousin hated it here. All the tables were bare metal, likewise the chairs and the walls equally stark and heartlessly mechanical.

Benoit sat down across the table from her cousin and, for a moment, they just stared as if looking across a gulf. And indeed they were. Two different worlds would collide and then, after a few short minutes, separate.

"I have a plan to change my life," Benoit began.

"Too bad the men who put you here aren't around to help."

"Well, they aren't and they wouldn't. I've got to do this myself."

"Does it involve committing more crimes?"

"I am in a bottomless pit. To get out I must climb over certain people."

"Speak plainly."

"I will use the greed and the lust in others to further my own advancement, but I myself shall not be taken with greed or take any ill-gotten gain. When I reach my goal, I will have love and a law-abiding life."

"What about before you reach this goal?"

"I cannot promise perfection in a world of flaws. I need your help, Colette. I will not endanger you. I will ask you to do things that will enable me to catch demons, but I will catch no angels because I have no angel bait."

"You speak in metaphors. I think Americans would say bullshit. But so far you have never dragged me into your problems. You have destroyed only yourself."

"You know that the French government, now that they have taken over Grace Technologies, must be desperate to understand the genetic research that I helped administer before they put me in here."

"I know very little about it really, but what if that is true?"

"If I helped them get it—if I did a great service for the government, could I get a pardon? This technology is very valuable. There are the parts Gaudet has. I can get those. There are the parts even Gaudet doesn't have, the part called Chaperone. I can get that as well."

"We have gone over this. I think there is no way for you to get a pardon."

"I hear the SDECE is paying me a visit."

"That is not about a pardon. It is because they desperately

want your help. It is the beginning. Maybe years from now if things go well with them, you could get something. House arrest they call it, or something like that. Don't think about a pardon, you will only be disappointed. Many French shareholders lost a fortune when Grace Technologies went under and they are angry. And I am telling you, do not try to fool the government."

"I will tell the SDECE the truth. From you I want to know Admiral François Larive's prospects for political advancement. I want to know where his strengths lie, what position he might next hold, and who would be responsible for getting him there. I want to know the same for an agent, Jean-Baptiste Sourriaux. In the not-too-far distant future I may want you to send certain e-mails to America."

A guard came in.

"Time to go back."

She would wait for the Service de Documentation Exterieure et de Contre Espionnage, commonly the SDECE, and she would hope—for without hope she would die.

Grady was dressed in her gym shorts and sweatshirt and was ready to go out the door for a late-afternoon workout in lieu of a lunch break. She was taking a last look at her desk; then she looked up from her cubicle to see Sam walking toward her with a gray-haired, mustached man. Her gut tightened. Never had she met anyone inside this building that wasn't part of the company. And certainly she had never met visiting dignitaries while she wore her gym clothes.

Harry growled a low growl.

That was even rarer.

"Grady, I would like you to meet Figgy Meeks, officially Alexander H. Meeks. One day I will have the pleasure of telling you how Figgy got his moniker."

"I'll blow you to hell, Sam," Figgy said.

"This is Harry, he kind of adopts Grady when I leave and he's my pal and he's smarter than most people."

Figgy nodded at Harry, but Harry left the cube, most likely for Sam's desk.

"Figgy here, as you can see, is a cursing, uncouth man who can't make breakfast taste good without the *f* word, but he helped teach me the spy trade."

"The private spy trade. We could never persuade Sam to become a government man, although it wasn't for lack of trying."

"He was good enough to teach me and they don't come any better than this professor emeritus of the spy business. He's here on behalf of the French government."

At the mere mention of the word "French," Grogg stuck his head up from a nearby cubicle, his quarter-inch-thick glasses hiding his eyes but not his emotions. Grogg couldn't stand the French, but his feelings were based on nothing more than a nasty divorce to a rotund and mouthy woman of French descent.

"The French are the only human subspecies actually capable of fitting their own nose up their own ass," Grogg said.

"This, as you know, I'm sure, is Grogg," Sam said. "He no longer drinks French wine and he's given up French women altogether." Before Grogg could say anything, Sam said, "Come on. Let's go to the conference room."

As they turned to leave Grady's cubicle, they ran into Jill. "Well, well," she said. "Figgy Meeks, the legend himself."

He kissed her hand, continental style, and she joined the group.

On the way down the hall Figgy stopped. "That must be the infamous 'Big Brain.' " He stood at a large glass-walled area with racks of computer hardware.

"Officially it's called the Common Object Repository for the Enterprise," Sam said. "And Grogg here—our expert on French ex-wives—helped me conceive her."

Grogg nodded.

"Bet she's some kind of memory hog, huh?" said Figgy.

"Anything we download is in there forever," Grogg said. "It's amazing how much we use old stuff."

"What kind of stuff?"

"Oh, we have investigators trained in what to feed Big Brain."

"From people's garbage cans to your computer," Figgy said.

"Yep. We're good at collecting garbage and other things. But it's how you query the database that really matters."

Figgy nodded, feigning interest for Grogg's sake.

The conference room was large enough to seat thirty around the massive table. It was a room with character, collectors' items in a bookcase, pictures on the wall, heavy wood moldings, quite out of sync with the high-tech cubicles in the rest of the office. Sam had a cubicle like everyone else, just a little bigger. When he wanted complete privacy, he worked in the conference room.

On a sideboard stood a jug of coffee, juice, soft drinks, and Danish pastries stuffed with a combination of cream cheese and blueberry preserves. Sam wanted two, but dutifully he passed on the pastries and high-calorie juices, poured himself some water, and thought about whether defined abs were really worth it. The prior day he had suffered through the sight of Grogg wolfing down a Reuben sandwich. Sam had turkey on whole wheat, mustard, but no mayo. He was still thinking about the Reuben. Somehow he sensed that Grady was watching him and the Danish to see who would win and, of course, it was imperative that he be a rock. When alone, Sam had no problem with food, but there was something about watching another man expressing his satisfaction that tested Sam's steel.

"So, let's start with what I've got to know." Figgy sat and took a giant bite of a Danish. "Fill me in on this technology."

Sam leaned back in his chair. "Let's not be disingenuous, Figgy. You work for the French, and they know the score. Better than we do. So don't ask me—*tell* me."

"Actually, the French are in the dark about this technology."

"According to the French, Grace Technologies never made any successful gene-altering discoveries. So what do they have to be concerned about?" Sam pressed.

"They know it's a gene-altering technology that can induce violence or tranquillity in people. The French want to stop Gaudet as badly as you do. News of your incident with your neighbors up north sparked their interest. They sent me." Figgy sat back in his chair, hands down, palms out. "Sam, we go back a long way. I'm telling you what they told me. I have no reason to disbelieve them."

Sam looked at Grady and Grogg, chuckling. "See how good Figgy is. Now he's using old times' sake to get what he wants."

Figgy finished the Danish. "Do we have a deal?"

"First you tell us what the French know about our problem; then we'll get serious about deals and the like."

Figgy sighed. "Grace was into all kinds of research—"

"I was there, Figgy. We all know in general about the vector technology. We know your clients have it and are probably floundering around with it. They're probably torturing monkeys as we speak."

"France now owns all the assets of Grace Technologies, including this vector technology. Devan Gaudet also has it, which could mean disaster anywhere, anytime. What we can't figure is why Gaudet would use this extreme vector on a couple of your neighbors in the mountains."

"Because he's a twisted son of a bitch," Jill said. "He has history with Sam. Maybe it's a thrill to kill a guy using his neighbors."

"What kind of history?" Figgy asked Sam.

Sam tried not to think about it. There had been plenty, and it wasn't a favorite topic. "Like a lot of high-powered criminals, you tend to run into Gaudet in more than one sewer. He's killed people who were close to me. That isn't the point. The point is, yes, Gaudet possesses a powerful, poorly understood, destructive technology. But he doesn't have the whole thing, at least as I understand it."

Figgy's face was a blank. "Meaning?"

"It's an immune-system issue. It doesn't take long for the body to reject this gene-changing vector, because it literally creates foreign tissue in you. It appears that with this particular vector, when they change the DNA in your brain cells, they might as well have been transplanted from another person. Or it may be that the body is rejecting the vector, treating it the way it would a virus. So far, Gaudet doesn't have the immunosuppressive part of the technology that we think was used by Grace. Either that, or he isn't using it." Sam paused. "Tell me if this isn't familiar to you. The French know this. If they aren't telling you, you're of no use to them . . . or us."

"I know what Grace did with the vectors. Generally. Grace used the vectors on human and nonhuman subjects. The vector worked to alter brain cells and the subjects lived without an immune-system catastrophe. Some of these people, like Chellis, are still in the custody of the French government, so we're sure about this. Gaudet and Benoit gave Chellis what the Grace company staff called the nervous-flier vector—an extreme form that was cooked up just for him. The opposite end of the spectrum was an extreme version of a soldier vector called raging soldier."

"You think that's what Gaudet used on my neighbors?"

"No doubt. Best we can tell, the original vector technology, as used by Grace, included some other exotic molecule—the French have named it Chaperone, because that is what Benoit Moreau called it. Chaperone prohibits the vector from killing its host."

Sam nodded.

"Gaudet doesn't seem to have the Chaperone part of the vector. If he did, he'd have an unbelievably powerful—and valuable—tool. He wouldn't waste time coming after you and your neighbors. He'd be selling it and maybe using it, depending on whether he'd like his homicidal creations to last more than a day or two. Instead, he doped your neighbors with the raging soldier vector and, according to your report to the FBI, one of them died within hours from the immune reaction."

"Don't be sure Gaudet wouldn't be coming after me. He probably wants me as bad as I want him. But I do believe that Chaperone isn't being used by Gaudet and that he probably doesn't have it or understand it," Sam said. "And I don't understand why he didn't try a much more efficient method of killing me. Using my neighbors wasn't the best method and that is unlike Gaudet."

Figgy stood and grabbed a second Danish. "We're on the same page. We suspect that the people who understood this Chaperone technology are either dead or on the run. From Gaudet."

"And the French," Grogg added.

"Do you think this Michael Bowden knows something about Chaperone?" Figgy asked.

"Maybe. He's an ethnobotanist. In the Amazon he could have discovered an organic material that at least contains the basis for the Chaperone molecule."

"What makes you think that—besides Gaudet's interest in Bowden?"

"For a few years Bowden has sent his organic samples to Northern Lights Pharmaceuticals. They in turn had a long relationship with—"

"Grace Technologies," Figgy said.

"Before we make any deal, you have to tell me what the French want. Is it to catch Gaudet? Or to get ahold of

Chaperone? Perhaps it has occurred to them that it would revolutionize the practice of medicine and be worth a fortune."

"Both," Figgy said. "The technology legally belongs to France. I have to be sure that you and the U.S. government will recognize my client's title to the Chaperone technology, if you find it."

"Talk to patent lawyers and the State Department about that. It's not my concern. Stopping and catching Gaudet is. But to do that, I have to know everything the French know about Chaperone." Sam hated the amused look on Figgy's face. For some perverse reason the Danishes had never looked all that tempting until Figgy started wolfing them down with such relish.

"You said Benoit Moreau nicknamed the substance Chaperone. Come on, Figgy. Tell me everything."

Figgy shrugged. "I'll tell you what I know, but my client won't like it. Essentially, Benoit Moreau is not talking, although she has told us a few things and we have gotten other information from Northern Lights." Figgy took a sip of coffee. "As you might suspect, Benoit knew all the scientists. One or more of the scientists obviously understood Chaperone. Benoit knows which ones, maybe even where to find them."

Sam stood and drew a cup of coffee. "Come on, Figgy, there's got to be more."

"I'm getting to it. Northern Lights Pharmaceuticals supplied Grace with a complex protein molecule. They won't admit it, but we can now assume the material came from their client Michael Bowden. They haven't been able to fully analyze or describe the molecule yet. This is apparently typical of complex proteins—it can take a very long time. Synthesizing them is a bitch, and before you can even hope to do that, you have to figure out what it looks like or you have to know the gene that produces it. To some extent, Grace Technologies seems to have lucked into the Chaperone solution. They ordered an extract from Northern Lights, expecting an ordinary immunosuppressant like cyclosporine. It turned out to be about one thousand times more powerful and better suited to the brain in particular. It took some work, but Grace adapted it through some sort of chemical process that nobody we know understands. Instead of just temporarily suppressing the immune system, it seemingly reprograms it entirely. Nobody who's talking has any idea how that works."

Sam smiled. "And Northern Lights is fresh out of the Chaperone molecule, right?"

"Grace bought it all for a tremendous amount of cash. Bowden must know where to get more. His kind would never take all of a species. Presumably, Gaudet realizes this. So now it's an old-fashioned footrace to the Amazon. The French are willing to let you contact Bowden if you'll sign me up for your little program."

"It's a free country. I can contact Bowden anytime I wish."

"Look, Sam, the CIA owes us and they promised us we're in. And you need Benoit Moreau."

"Figgy, I know the French have influence on this, but I don't know why. Maybe they saved some poor soul that the U.S. government thought needed saving. And I see who pays my bills, so I do listen with at least one ear. But it wouldn't be the first time that I've said no to our beloved government."

"Do we have a deal, Sam?"

"Only for old times' sake, Figgy. But I'll need full cooperation and full disclosure."

"Good." Figgy held out his hand and Sam shook it. "Full cooperation guaranteed. I've gotta get on a conference call, but could I first use the latrine?"

"Sure. But to make this deal, I need to ask you one thing: when you talk to your client, ask if they'll arrange for me to talk with Benoit."

"You sure you want to meet the dominatrix herself?"

Sam's expression provided his answer.

"Sure. You bet. I'll ask," Figgy responded.

"Okay. To get to the restroom you go out of here, past Big Brain through the door, and down the hall to the right. If you find the dorm rooms, you've gone too far."

"Don't do anything exciting until I get back." The big man took a last look at the food spread, chose a soda, and walked out.

"You didn't mention anything about this Georges Raval," Jill said after Figgy was out of earshot.

Sam smiled at her, his usual way of saying there would be no discussion. "Let's talk about Michael Bowden." He turned to Grady. "What did you find?"

"Didn't you want me to brief Figgy at the same time?"

Sam gave her that smile again.

"You don't trust him, do you?" she asked.

"I trust him fine," Sam said. "But there's no sense in testing human nature when there's this much at stake."

Chapter 3

Bad spirits bring their own kind.

—Tilok proverb

Jean-Baptiste Sourriaux, occasionally called by his childhood nickname of *le souris,* "the mouse," listened to the tick of the gold clock that sat on his mahogany side table. The clock had been a gift from his wife, subtly intended to get him home on time. On this night, as most, it did no good.

Baptiste was a tall man and thin, in fairly decent shape. He had no striking features, only a high forehead leading to a nose that slanted downward so that the tip hung a little below the nostrils. He spoke crisply, more in the fashion of an Englishman than a Frenchman. His colleagues claimed he had no sense of humor, but he knew he had humor, he just kept it to himself. Besides, France was going to hell and no one was doing anything about it. It was all liberal these days and no one cared that the ghetto people were becoming lawless and propagating like rats and had nothing but contempt for their adopted country and her ways. His offices were on the Boulevard Mortier in the 20th Arrondissement in the Caserne des Tourelles; that meant that anybody who knew anything knew he was an intelligence officer (known collectively as honorables correspondents) when he walked in the building every morning.

His office was small, despite the fact that he reported directly to Admiral Larive, the head of the SDECE. It was the spook branch of the French government and was comprised of career military officers and assorted civilians. Baptiste, roughly the equivalent of a major in the U.S. Army, called Command and, but for the "special assignment" of personal interest to the prime minister, would have reported to a colonel. He expected to retire with the same rank, since he was already forty-eight years old and had no promotion in sight.

Field agents never got much in the way of an office, normally just a cubbyhole with a divider, because they weren't expected to spend much time sitting in them. Because of his special assignment, however, Baptiste had been spending a lot of time here. At the moment he was pondering the biggest issue of his career and waiting for a vital phone call.

Finally the phone rang.

"Yes?" Baptiste struggled to maintain his usual flat calm.

"We are in."

"For sure."

"Yes."

"They believe you?"

"The main man does. Others may be skeptical."

"What are you drinking?"

"A soft drink. Why?"

"Can we use the computer instead?"

Baptiste's hired agent Figgy Meeks could download a cipher code from the SDECE for his communications, each code lasting only forty-eight hours. Baptiste waited for his own download of the current cipher. In seconds the written text appeared on his screen; now written dialogue was possible, and it could be kept on file for future reference.

"*They are going after Bowden. I will stay in the States. They don't seem to know about Paul. Attribute it to Gaudet. They wonder, as I do, why Gaudet would risk using the vector against Sam's neighbors.*"

Baptiste replied:

"*I have no idea. It has gotten the attention of American intelligence. They will be looking harder. That means we redouble our efforts . . . And remember: It was an accident. You bear no moral responsibility for Sam's man.*"

"*That's wishful fantasy.*"

"*You know how to count $5,000,000.00?*"

"*Remind me again that I'm doing this for money and I may cross the ocean and shove it up your ass,*" Figgy communicated.

"*Next report when?*"

"*When I know something worthwhile. Have you learned anything more from Moreau?*"

"*They are working on it. Nothing yet.*"

"*Sam wants to talk with her ASAP.*"

"*No chance. As to Bowden. . . . Where is he, exactly? When are they leaving?*" Baptiste prodded.

"*No intel on that yet.*"

"*Remember that you are working for the French government and are handsomely paid. Get me that information.*"

Figgy's transmission died. Like all American government men, Meeks was a prick. At least he was a greedy prick who had been screwed over by the CIA in a fashion similar to what the French government was doing to Baptiste.

Baptiste thought carefully about his next move. It would be dangerous not to run it through channels. He called the admiral and amazingly got him on the first ring.

"I'm about to run," the admiral snapped.

"We have a situation in the Amazon. The Americans feel—"

"Yes, yes. You told me. A man named Bowden supplied

Northern Lights and perhaps Chaperone came through him. You have my permission to shadow the Americans. Who will you send?"

"René Denard," Baptiste replied.

"A bit of a renegade, don't you think?"

"We need someone strong."

"Tell him not to cross swords with the Americans." The admiral rang off.

"I need Bowden or Raval." Devan Gaudet spoke in French to Trotsky, his assistant, who sat on the other side of the coffee table in a rented house in Mexico, not far south of the California border. "Ideally both. I'll need better men than those who went after Sam and I'll need better men than those who went to South America last time. I don't like losing."

Men were finishing up with the boxes and loading them out the door into a truck. Most of the stuff was staying and would go up in flames when the small house burned to the ground. After everyone had departed, Trotsky would open the propane line—it would make for a fast, hot fire.

Angelina, a Mexican woman who had been tending the home for several months, was cleaning behind the movers. Even though Gaudet had spent little time here, his fastidious nature required a housekeeper.

"The team is coming together," said Trotsky. "You needn't worry. They'll be up to the job."

Gaudet's thin lips were pursed white in a rare display of emotion. "I am worried. We looked like asses in front of our investors." Gaudet closed his eyes as he forced the thought from his mind. "Let's review the video."

Trotsky turned on the TV. A huge auto parts store and fenced lot flashed on the screen.

"Sam's offices are in the back, behind the tall brick wall.

There's cut glass on top of the wall and those signs you see are posting a warning. It's got tight security and it's no doubt a bomb-hardened structure." Trotsky glanced at the maid.

"She is fine," Gaudet said. "She barely speaks English, much less French."

"Sam is like any other man. He can be killed."

Gaudet did not reply. He stared at Trotsky until he shifted in his chair and turned to the movers.

"Shove off," Trotsky told the men, who hurried to leave with the last of the boxes.

From outside, Gaudet heard the big diesel engine of the transport truck. "Angelina"—Gaudet thought through his request in Spanish and did the best he could— *"Puedes cortar esa Guayava y trerme la aquí, por favor?"*

Saying nothing, the maid went to the corner of the kitchen and removed a guava from a burlap sack. Using the knife, she skillfully cut it up and brought it on a plate. "You may have one as well," Gaudet said.

"Gracias, no."

"I insist," Gaudet said.

Angelina shrugged, took a slice, and began eating as though she had had a secret desire. Trotsky ate as well. Gaudet picked up a slice and held it while he spoke in French. "So as long as Sam is alive, he is the single greatest threat to our plan." He stopped the videotape. "But I'm out of time at this moment. Bowden is all that matters now. Later this video will come in handy."

Trotsky walked over to the TV, inserting a second video. Gaudet rose to pour two glasses of port while he watched Angelina out of the corner of his eye. Suddenly she swayed on her feet, grabbed the counter, then collapsed to the floor and began convulsing. Trotsky whirled and saw Gaudet still holding his slice of guava. Gaudet gave Trotsky a slight smile, enjoying his little joke. Trotsky looked uncertain, a little panicked.

Slowly Gaudet lifted the guava slice to his lips and took a robust bite. Trotsky's shoulders dropped and relief washed his face.

"It was only a catalyst in the guava," Gaudet told him. "I poisoned her earlier. For you and me, the catalyst is harmless. For Angelina, it will look like a heart attack. Nonetheless, make sure the fire burns hot."

Chapter 4

Cleverness in an evil man is like fire in the treetops.
—Tilok proverb

Her green eyes could have been taken directly from Mother Amazon.

Michael Bowden always felt Marita's presence before seeing the bronze of her skin catch the light. She appeared infrequently and always silently. Michael fancied her a creature of the forest, a shadow in the green, but knew there was more to her. She would reveal that aspect, or not, in her own time.

The informal alliance had been formed from the smallest subtleties over many days, though they had never been closer to one another than about twelve feet. On certain days she would come right to the railing of the large porch, though her favorite place seemed to be the giant ficus tree, where she'd perch among the vines that wrapped the limbs like braided rope. He had been preparing to draw a map for a book when he'd first noticed Marita on this hot, muggy afternoon. She had come much earlier than usual. From the expression on her face he knew instantly that something was different. Perhaps she was troubled. He would be patient, keep on with his work, and let her settle in. Maybe today they would talk.

Built on massive stilts, the entire house, including the porch, stood some eight feet off the ground, a measure taken against the coming wet season. In Peru, in the vast jungle province of Loreto, two great rivers, the Marañón and the Ucayali, came together to form the Amazon—unless you were a Brazilian citizen and then the Amazon was said to be formed by a downstream confluence that was, not surprisingly, in Brazil. Between the Marañón and the Ucayali lay the 5-million-acre lowland reserve Pacaya-Samiria. Only 1 percent of the reserve remained terra firma during the wet season. In fact, during the annual high water, from December through June, 80 percent of the Loreto Province (if you didn't count trees and floating grass mats) lay underwater.

To the south of the Ucayali the local people, called the Matses, used stilted huts near the river to weather the wet season. Historically, they had been nomadic and among the most skilled hunters of the Amazon. In modern times they remained among the more remote of the indigenous natives of Peru and Brazil, although they had been influenced by Western missionaries since the 1970s, and they had been exposed to Western culture more than the other tribes across the border in the Brazilian refuge.

Marita was Matses, though she lacked the tattoos or nose piercings common to Matses women. Westerners called the Matses "cat people" because of whiskerlike wooden pieces that the women wore in their noses as a matter of course and that men donned during special celebrations.

Michael wasn't sure what language Marita spoke, but he had heard that she had been away to school. He was fluent in both Spanish, the official language of Peru, and Portuguese, Brazil's dominant tongue.

It had been months since Michael had been with a woman—

not since his wife died—but, for him, Marita's seductive light was cast by much more than her sexuality, although that too seemed considerable.

She had come out of the vines and stood on the ground where he could clearly see her, but where she could not see his work. That alone was different.

He felt he should continue with his map, let her decide whether to come closer. The map concerned a group of animals (people thought of them as plants) that he believed were closely related to a saltwater sponge—in this case a previously unknown freshwater species. He'd found them during a ten-day walk, Matses time, through the jungle and across the Yavari, into Brazil, where Matses had led him to another tribe that in turn led him to a *quebrada,* or small, deep, black-water river. Michael suspected that like some saltwater sponges, these might have anti-inflammatory or immunosuppressant properties. Shamans from this deep jungle tribe in Brazil had used an extract from the animal, mixed with four other plant extracts, to heal what had appeared to be neurological disorders that seemed to Michael like MS. Most noteworthy, however, was the fact that such cures were an apparent medical impossibility using conventional therapy. In his own mind there was most definitely some rational explanation for this anecdotal information because the laws of nature were the laws of science, and the laws of science were ultimately the laws of the universe. It was up to the scientist to make the reconciliation between seeming conflicts. Some of this animal and plant material had been submitted to the pharmaceutical company and they were begging for more, though he had no idea why.

Returning to the site of a prior discovery was easy these days, thanks to the handheld GPS. Still, he wanted a good hand-drawn map, if not for actual use, then for his forthcoming book. A map would make the tale of the discovery of the sponges more vivid and exciting for the readers. Since the reserve was strictly regulated with a prohibition against visitors and very remote, it was unlikely that an *estranjeiro* would try on his own to follow the map. As a final precaution Michael deliberately did not draw the map to scale.

A table of pine that had belonged to his grandfather, and had been brought from the United States up the Amazon River, supported his work. A stack of notebooks, blue in color and nicely bound, stood on one corner. Directly in front of him was a computer that sucked up its power from batteries that were recharged by a diesel generator. At one time he had thought of the generator as a vile intrusion on the jungle, but now he wasn't sure. A second, much longer table formed an L with the computer desk; on it were the Bunsen burners with clay pots, retorts, glass tubing, beakers, and various other laboratory items. Michael sometimes used modern conveniences in reproducing the concoctions of the shamans, but he often found it was best to use their methods and their materials at least the first time.

Michael looked up from his work: Marita had come to the bottom of the steps. She held something . . . a book—intriguing. When he held up his paper and beckoned her closer, she seemed to ponder the idea instead of fleeing. He lowered his eyes, waiting to see what would happen next.

Marita advanced, climbing two more steps. Michael admired her tangled, curly hair and the beautiful lines of her face. For the first time he realized that this haphazard pile of ringlets atop her head might be the result of grooming and not an accident of her DNA. She had clean, delicate features with an aquiline nose that displayed the European in her genetics. Brazil and Peru were populated by an odd mix of peoples, and even among the riverine tribes any combination of hair, complexion, and eye color might pop out of a Peruvian or Brazilian womb.

The Matses, who did not consider themselves *riverinos,* had for centuries had an odd custom of kidnapping women for wives. They commonly had raided faraway villages, especially *riverinos,* and hence had introduced an especially wide variety of DNA into their gene pool. A Matses man could have up to four wives. Two was still common, and before the 1960s all of a man's wives might have been stolen from distant peoples.

So Michael couldn't guess what this strange girl's heritage might be. He had learned her name from the people of the various families living on the river down the way. On one occasion when Marita had come in the afternoon, he had followed her through the jungle until darkness swallowed her and she had left him behind to pick his way back through the blackness. It had taken all the skills that he had learned from his father and the Matses to find his way home, and as he stepped onto the porch, he had looked around to see a slender shadow retreating down the path. She had followed him.

He looked down at the map again, wondering how he appeared to Marita. Michael had curly blond hair and light skin. The blue of his eyes matched the blue of the extravagant morpho butterflies, his face lean like his body. Some *riverinos* thought Michael Bowden to be a pink river dolphin in disguise, and therefore he was rumored to have great seductive power with the native girls, who in fact flocked around whenever he entered a village. It was said that under his hair was a cap and that if you pulled it off, the dolphin head would be exposed down between his ears.

Eight months previous, after his wife died—murdered, actually—Michael had become deeply depressed before he became angry. He barely ate for a month and, for the first time, began questioning his life in the jungle. One day, lying on his porch watching the bugs crawl over his pots and burners, he'd seen Marita appear. She had thrown him some manioc bread. While he ate, she watched as though he might disappear if she didn't pay close enough attention.

This evening she wore a white pullover blouse of cotton

livened up with some hand embroidery. Her legs were bare and she wore brief shorts fashioned from faded blue jeans. Unlike most of the clothing worn by the natives, her outfits were always clean.

When next he looked her way, he saw a forthrightness in her stare. He had the feeling that she was working up to something, although he couldn't imagine what it might be unless she intended to venture onto the porch. Just as he thought it, she walked up the stairs and stood at the top, hesitant and small like some delicate creature of the wild.

There was a chair on the opposite side of the table. Using his foot, he pushed it out and angled it, making it easy for her to sit. Then he nodded.

"Have a seat if you like." He said it in Spanish and then in Portuguese. He had overheard a conversation and had gotten the idea that she might have been in Brazil for her schooling. He was reluctant to say or do more, since direct attention on his part would send her skittering and he very much did not want that to happen.

Sometimes he thought of going to the city, maybe Manaus or Iquitos, to meet a woman, but he seldom ventured there. He knew that apart from the science that he read about in a myriad of periodicals, the world was leaving him behind. It had been pulling away since he was nearly twelve years old, and he left Ithaca, New York, with his father. Michael knew the names of a few movies but had seen only one in sixteen years. It was a good enough experience, but it just wasn't as compelling as his writing or his research or the poetry and literature he read before sleep. He had a clear recollection of television, but even as a child he hadn't been particularly enthusiastic. Growing up in New York State and California, he had been studious enough to be teased by other children, except he also excelled in wrestling. That seemed to make his disdain for frivolity acceptable. By twelve, when his father took him to the Amazon, he was an apt home-schooled pupil learning easily everything from mathematics to physics and biology. Only the social sciences lacked interest for him.

Michael graduated from college by correspondence and had since been awarded two honorary Ph.D.s in absentia for his research and writing. Before his wife died, he had viewed his world as expansive and as much a feast for the mind and soul as a man could ever need. Science was exploding in all directions. Sometimes he read in a frenzy, moving from one article or paper to another, never able to keep up. People from all over the world sent him things, most of which were interesting, some of which were vital. The balance of his time he spent writing of his experiences and work in the Amazon, its tribes and flora and fauna. Exclusive of his purely scientific articles, all of his writing incorporated stories. He never wrote just about a creature or a plant but rather always told the story that led him to it, and about the people he encountered along the way. He deliberately chose a plain style so that even a mind numbed by years of television might partake and find an adventure worth consideration.

Such a tale might come from today's experience. Michael watched as Marita slowly lowered herself into the chair, placed her book in her lap, and folded her hands on the table. It appeared in his brief look that the book was one of his. On the table near him lay an unpublished manuscript. He put it in front of her, then dropped his eyes as he saw her begin to read. It was in English, but she appeared fascinated. He couldn't have been more shocked if she had said, *"Hi, I'm Dr. Marita from Harvard."* Next to him was a portable cassette player. He turned on the tape, which played soft *quena* flute music, floating, lilting. Michael was the instrumentalist, a dedicated member of the Red Howler band in Angomos. He would now go on with his work as if all this were perfectly natural.

Marita kept reading. Michael wished his scientist friends

could see this Matses girl reading English. Had she read magazines? If she went away to school, to the city, Western publications would be available. Had she seen a car? Western-style makeup?

He wondered what she knew of the outside world and immediately wondered how much he really knew of what was happening outside the vastness of the Amazon jungle. Occasionally he thought perhaps he should go to New York and meet Elaine, his agent, and Rebecca, his editor, at the publishing house. He liked them both. They were creatures of the corporate world, but when they communicated with him, it was all about the Amazon—he the expert and they the novices. Their relationship had been cast in that mold. He wasn't sure he wanted that to change.

When he looked at her again, Marita held his gaze. "It is very good. Like all your books," she said in workmanlike English.

"You are astounding me, you realize. You come here and never say a word. . . ."

"I am shy. I like to watch people first."

"It is still strange to go that long," he said.

"Especially when visiting pink dolphins."

He laughed. "A tale you obviously don't believe."

"Blond men from America are blond men from America."

She placed her book on the table next to the English manuscript: *The Ramparts of the Amazon* by Michael J. Bowden. It was a Portuguese-language edition.

"Ja leis-te?" He asked her. *"Fala Portuguese?"*

"I speak Portuguese fine. But I wish to practice English. I want to go to New York. At least to see. If I like it, I want to have my children there."

"Is that why you came to see me?"

She hesitated. "I desire that you come with me. Now." Somehow her grave expression didn't match the words she spoke.

"Your English is remarkable."

"I have been to missionary school for twelve years. Catholic. On the Brazil side of the river. In Tabatinga. They say I learn fast. They give me many tutors."

He was beginning to get an inkling that she was older than she appeared. Girls normally went to school from about ages six to twelve, maybe fourteen, and then they began bearing children. In Peru early education was compulsory except for the indigenous tribes. Obviously, Marita was not fitting the mold of limited education and that told him that she must have an unusual aptitude for learning to attract such attention among the Catholics.

"But you have never spoken to me. You stood and watched."

"I explained the best I can about that. Now I need your help. You will need a gun."

"A gun?" Michael didn't like them, but he owned plenty.

"A long gun," she said, gesturing with her arms in the manner of someone firing a rifle.

She looked dead serious, even a little fearful. Without questioning her further, Michael walked to a cabinet that held his rifles. He removed a .300 magnum, Winchester Model 70. Returning to the porch, he said, "This is a big gun. Why do you need it?"

"Do you have a small gun? I think we'll need both. You can show me how to shoot."

"Why? What's wrong?"

"To protect us from the bad men."

"Que homens? A gue distancia? Como e que sabes que sao maus?" He spoke rapidly in Portuguese to make sure she understood his questions.

What she said next nearly stopped his heart.

"One of the men is the man who killed your wife."

Before he realized it, he had sat back down at the desk,

dumbfounded. After a moment he opened a side drawer, removed a .357 magnum Ruger GP 100 pistol, and placed it on the desk. "I need to understand how you know this."

"They are one day's walk from here . . . for a *estrangeiro*." She seemed stuck on English now.

"How many?"

"Six. Matses hunters saw them on the Blanca."

He tried to picture the terrain. It sounded like they had come up the Ucayali and Tapiche river system, then overland on foot. It would only make sense to do so if they sought to remain hidden. To think the Matses wouldn't see them was foolish. That would make them foreigners.

"I saw them this morning," Marita said.

"But you're here."

"They are *estrangeiros*. I am Matses."

"Do you know why they have come?"

"The same reason as before, when the man killed your wife. They are looking for your experiments."

Michael stood again. "You're sure this man killed my wife?"

"Yes. He took your things too."

"You saw him do this?"

"I did."

"Tell me."

"It's better not to talk about it. She fought and they killed her. They were trying to . . . hurt her."

"But only one of these new men is the same."

"Yes. They call him Cy. The other men . . . I think they are very bad too."

"What do you think you can do?"

"I want to kill them."

"We have police."

"Where? These men will break the police like little sticks. And the police won't follow if they go into Brazil."

"Soldiers?"

"These men will be here and they will kill and hurt Matses and they will be gone before the soldiers arrive."

"We could leave and try to get everyone out of San José."

"Matses men? Run? They already think I am unruly and crazy. They will say I have bewitched you."

He thought for a moment and nodded. He had never seriously considered killing anyone. Even when he found his wife's brutalized remains, killing did not become his dream. His first rule of life was to do no harm. But then to kill this kind was to prevent harm. Perhaps his first rule of life could use some rethinking.

"Did they hurt you?"

"No."

He was surprised at the almost physical sense of relief he felt at her answer.

"They hurt my sister, and killed my child," she said. "Before my sister escaped . . . ," she trailed off. "She is different now."

His throat thickened and he hesitated. He still did not know for certain if there was a connection between his wife's death and this group. Or if so, who exactly was responsible for Eden's murder. He looked to Marita. Her eyes said what he scarcely dared to think: one, at least, among these men was a murderer and rapist, and that was enough.

He stood. "How will we find him?"

"They will walk along the small creeks. The way the land lies they will eventually find the trail from Herrera to San José. Like any *estrangeiro* they will stay on it because the jungle is thick."

"Probably." Quickly he went back inside and pulled two military M-16 rifles from a footlocker. He had bought these guns only after Eden's murder. He grabbed a backpack already loaded with the basics—knives, lighters, water, and the like. He stuffed all the ammunition in the packsack.

Back at the footlocker, he removed a Glock 10mm model 20, with fifteen-round clip, and for her a Glock 9mm model 17, with a seventeen-round clip. As much as he liked any gun, he liked this one and he had plenty of ammunition. Then he considered that they should both be using the same ammunition, so he grabbed a second 9mm and took the 10mm as a backup. He got her a pack for her ammo and water, then threw in some more supplies. Normally, she would need only matches, salt, a fishing line, and a knife to survive in relative comfort for lengthy periods, so she would be traveling in relative luxury. In the packsacks were a number of individual flour sacks that had been dipped in liquid latex, making them waterproof and buoyant, allowing the backpack to double as a crude flotation device. Anything that needed to remain dry went in a latex-coated sack.

"We may die trying. Is this worth it to you?" Michael was tempted to revert to Portuguese for the philosophical aspects of this question.

"It is worth it."

Before they left, they practiced with the guns for half an hour, and when they were finished, she could use the M-16 to obliterate a stump in seconds. Her facility with the guns was almost unnerving.

They gathered up their things and began walking toward the Tapiche. Somewhere between the Tapiche and the Galvez they would find the trail of the men who came to steal again, perhaps to rape and kill. And they would kill them.

Baptiste made his way to a small holding area where informants, witnesses, and prisoners could be interviewed by the government. He did not want to speak to Benoit Moreau in her cell or in the regular visiting area. By bringing her out, he hoped she would begin to feel what was possible and to build in her soul a yearning so deep that she could not resist the generous offer of the French government.

She waited in the holding area, a neat and clean room with a fresh coat of paint, sitting in a nice chair, such as the kind that might be used by an executive secretary. There was even a desk for her to sit behind; in a way she could imagine that she was interviewing him. These were props of pride and position, luxuries that would never again be hers . . .

Unless.

He had come up with the idea himself, like a car salesman who puts you behind the wheel of a brand-new Citroën. There was a glass window in the office and blinds that were partially open to let in light and to allow her to see snatches of what was going on outside the door of her little office. She sat in the chair in chains. That was different from the Citroën and the unctuous salesman, but necessary for the time being.

He started by offering a friendly smile. He was not good at them, as his wife often pointed out.

"I'll get right to the point," he said when Benoit showed no reaction. God, she was beautiful. He knew it, he had seen her, but still he wasn't quite ready for it. And for just a brief second he wondered whether he might ever have sex with her, and then he blew the notion out of his mind, knowing that it was incredibly weak and incredibly dangerous. Straight-backed and lithe, she projected a cold sexiness even in her prison suit.

He sat, determined to let her see nothing in his eyes. "I called you here to begin a discussion regarding an offer from the French government."

"Aren't you going to greet me? How are you, mademoiselle? How do you like the office, mademoiselle? Nice weather we're having? No small talk or chitchat? Amazing for a man with a big plan."

"What big plan is that?"

"Whatever big plan you have to lift yourself from obscurity in a job that is going nowhere and a future that is only slightly less dull than this office."

"I like my job. I take it very seriously. You are the one with no future."

"Really?"

Something about her unbelievable confidence was unnerving.

"You think you have a big future? You can go back to your cell in your chains and rot."

She rose, completely unperturbed. "I'm ready. I'm sure that the admiral will be wanting to see me, so give him my best regards and tell him I am looking forward to our meeting."

She was ambling toward the door in her chains. A wave of panic washed over him. *Could she . . . ?* The admiral was reputedly a womanizer like many Frenchmen in positions of prominence.

"Unfortunately, you won't be seeing the admiral."

"Uh-huh."

"Get back there and sit down," he said.

She sat and smiled. "It's true that I've only seen him once. He was curious like all men. He lusts, but he is too smart to ask for sex. Just as you are. But, just like you, he was tempted."

"I am not going to waste time on your games."

"What, then? Will you physically abuse me? Are you going to rape me as well?" She studied him with bright appealing eyes. "You want my help with the genetic science of Grace Technologies, particularly Chaperone, but of course at the same time you're wondering if we might one day have sex. Don't deny it and we'll get along better. I hate men who lie to me."

"I am interested in making an arrangement where you can do France some good, instead of sitting on your ass all day. In exchange you would be released from prison each day. Of course you return here at night. And there would be security to and from and at work. The key is that you earn our trust. Which you are not doing right now. For example, you could start by telling me what the name Chaperone means. Why did they call it that?"

"For me your offer is a way out of that hole at least for the day, to see the pigeons on a windowsill, to watch it rain, to walk outside, to be with normal people instead of lunatics, maybe to have sex in the copy room. And by telling you about Chaperone, God knows what little extras I might get. I got it. But I'm not interested."

"Why?"

"Because it's not good enough. I can touch and hold, but I cannot take a bite and cannot really taste. No thanks. My imagination does the same for me here. I'd rather rot."

"But there are possibilities. Real possibilities."

"Yeah? Like what?"

"If your work were good enough. If you were reliable. Maybe, who knows, a sort of house arrest? You weren't convicted of actually pulling the trigger on anyone. There were a lot of charges for conspiracy, and of aiding and abetting, that sort of thing. Nobody, though, said you shot anybody or poisoned them, except of course Chellis, but he didn't die and he mistreated you, I am sure. An argument could be made."

"I'll think about it."

"You do not have long."

"I want to talk to the admiral before I make a deal." She stood and her chains rustled. On her, the chains seemed nearly elegant.

"He is too busy."

"No. You are too afraid. Tell me what you are afraid of?"

"Nothing. Absolutely nothing," Baptiste responded.

"Then we have no deal."

"Do you know now if Chaperone is actually one molecule? Do you know how it works or where it came from?"

"I know more than you," Benoit challenged.

"I am offering you something. If you don't want it, just say so."

"Fine. I say no." She stared at him with confidence born of resignation. Even though she didn't like prison, clearly she could stand it. The question was: could he?

She shuffled toward the door, not even bothering to look at him.

"I've got to move quickly. You and I are going to come to an arrangement or I will find a way to make your life hell."

"My life is already hell. But I'm listening."

"What do you want?" he demanded.

"Before we do business, you have to make love to me. Take it or leave it."

He was stunned. Oddly, he didn't know what to say.

"With a c-condom?" he stammered.

"No condom. I am clean."

"How would I know?"

"Recently I got myself tested. You read the records. Who in here can I have had sex with since? No one. But maybe you assume a guard. How dangerous is that? They're all married and their wives are like coal mine canaries."

"You're insane."

"You aren't man enough to take a woman? So be it. I don't do business with eunuchs."

"Where would we have sex?"

"I go on outings when we make a deal. Remember? Sex in a government lab wouldn't be bad. When the glory of France is at stake, something can be arranged. You'd like that, wouldn't you?"

"No. We can't be intimate. Something else. Choose something else."

"I want you. And I insist on you. But there is something else as well that you can do right this minute."

"What is that?"

"Tell me about this Sam man, who put the case together that sent me to jail."

"You want revenge?"

"Hardly. I want to know if the two maniacs have had any success trying to kill each other. I will need them both alive to help me solve your problem—after you sleep with me."

"I don't understand," Baptiste answered.

"Simple question: are they both alive?"

"Yes. As far as I know. And Sam, whoever he is, still hunts Gaudet."

"Where has Gaudet set up his operation?"

"We think he travels. The man is completely elusive. He could die and we would never know it."

"I am ready to help you get all of the technology for the glory of France. The rest is up to you."

She reached for the door and turned the knob. The door wouldn't budge. Outside, a guard seemed to have a large foot placed as a doorstop.

"You aren't going anywhere until I say."

"Big man with no balls, huh?" she countered.

"You slept with Chellis. Now he's crazy and locked up."

"Chellis hit me. Chellis humiliated me. He became a murdering, bellicose asshole. It is the explanation for his failure, not an excuse for mine. I chose Devan Gaudet. It was wrong to go in league with Gaudet, but he's rich and on the loose. Now I choose you. Think about your pathetic pension. I'm here because you already contemplated your retirement. It's written on your forehead. I can do it for you and for France. I can cut you in for a piece and we can both get out of this sewer. Think about it. You know what Chaperone is worth. You've already thought about what you could do with that kind of money. Now all you need to do is make it happen for France."

"I thought I was a cold bastard."

"You're tough. With me you'll be tougher. You'll get

Chaperone for the greater glory of France and we'll get a piece for ourselves. You will retire a hero."

"How in the hell are we going to share in what rightfully belongs to France?"

"You're not getting my ideas until we make a deal and I get what I have coming."

He needed time to think. He had behaved like an amateur. Benoit Moreau had controlled the discussion. At that moment he wanted to kill her and he knew that in matters of the ego there wasn't a lot of difference between doing that and ravishing her.

Afterward, Benoit was satisfied with her meeting with Baptiste, although waiting to get to the admiral was a major frustration. Knowing that Gaudet was alive was a huge relief and knowing that he had not killed Sam an even more encouraging confirmation. Already the admiral had sent an emissary, indicating that she might call him if she wished. Of course she would not call him. It was imperative that he be the first to initiate contact. Carefully she wrote down the name of each person she would communicate with and their motivations. She tried to crystallize in her own mind what would be driving them and how they would react to the situation that she expected to create in concert with history. Her list was six long:

- Baptiste
- Admiral Larive
- Gaudet
- Georges Raval
- the man they called Sam
- Michael Bowden

Next she wrote down the themes that she would stress with each and she tried to picture the world as that person would see it as the critical circumstances unfolded. Finally

she imagined leading them to a certain vision in keeping
with her plan.

Being stuck in the cell while she waited for Baptiste and
the admiral was agonizing beyond words. Her only relief
was thinking about the man that would one day be her lover.

Chapter 5

The fat fox waits by the right rabbit hole.
—Tilok proverb

They came up the river at thirty miles per hour, Sam at the bow of the twenty-five-foot boat, watching the mud brown Yavarí River disappear beneath him. Even a quarter-mile distant, the giant trees that created the highest layer of jungle canopy seemed immense. It bore no resemblance to the conifer forests of northern California. Here, one experienced layers upon layers of green, things growing up and down the enormous trees, things flowering, things sprouting, things dying in a never-ending cycle witnessed by few and understood by no one.

Sam's party had come down the Amazon from Iquitos to the Yavarí and from there up the Yavarí and finally to Angamos, where they refueled before proceeding toward the black water of the Galvez River. Two hours later, they were forty miles up the Galvez.

Sam waved for the guide Javier to stop.

Grady announced her intention to use this opportunity to run into the jungle and pee. Yodo, a big Japanese man whose body was about halfway between a sumo wrestler and a professional basketball player, with a round cherubic face and hair drawn back tight to a smidgen of a pigtail, followed at a discreet distance. At the moment his job was to protect Grady, and he was a man who took his job seriously. Javier grabbed a small fishing pole and some chicken bits for bait and proceeded to pull in piranha and toss them in a plastic tarp.

Sam called the office on the sat phone. They connected him to Jill.

"Where are you?"

"Not far from Bowden's. About ten miles downstream."

"Well, you may want to hurry. We have word that a boatload of white men is headed up the Tapiche, one of them traveling under a French passport. I'm convinced that Girard is really Gaudet. Figgy says he's not so sure. The Tapiche would be the back way to the Galvez if somebody didn't want to be detected. They could walk from the Tapiche near where it joins the Blanca. That would take maybe two or three days."

"Damn." Sam consulted a map of the region.

"The spooks are getting their Brazilian general friend to turn 'Big Eye' in your direction. Nothing yet."

"I sure didn't expect this."

"Neither did we."

"I have Grady. I can't go all the way back to Angamos. And even if I did, I can't just drop her off on the beach. I'd have to leave Yodo and the guide as well."

"All true. But Grady can fight."

"Yeah," Sam said without enthusiasm. He could handle dying in a firefight with Gaudet, but he wasn't sure he could deal with watching Grady being tortured. There was a conspiracy of feminine minds in the bowels of his company. They believed in women in combat and he couldn't quite admit that he did not, so he flirted with it, allowing female fighters when he was reasonably certain there would be no fight. So far, he had been right more than he had been wrong, but there was a dead woman to commemorate the occasion when he had misfigured. It had left a hole in his soul that would never be filled and no amount of ethical reasoning would change that for him. It didn't feel like normal war, if there was such a thing, when a woman was being abused.

"We could travel with the spotlights and be to Bowden's in an hour. We'd have to go slower in the pitch dark."

Jill stayed quiet and Sam thought.

"I'm gonna go. As you say, they *should* be at least a couple days getting there. We'll figure out a reception."

"Okay. We'll be sitting here with our fingers crossed."

It took only forty-five minutes to get to the landing, but finding the house was tougher. It was set back a bit in the jungle and the palm thatch roof came down low over the porch, so at night it blended with the jungle. Sam led the way up to the porch and found a note written in Spanish. Javier explained that Mr. Bowden had gone off with a Matses girl to locate a group of criminal intruders headed to the Galvez from the Tapiche. They went into the house and found handmade furnishings and a shortwave radio. Sam found a sheet of paper on the floor. It was another note in Spanish and he handed it to Javier. According to the note, trunks containing notes or papers from Bowden's work had filled part of this room. The note asked a fellow called Ramos to take the trunks and to use Bowden's boat in order to deliver them to the scientific group at Pacaya-Samiria and then to have them sent to a professor at Cornell University. It listed a Professor Richard Lyman and his address.

"Obviously, he suspects the men are after his work. Now he's going after them? Unbelievable," Sam muttered. Grady and Yodo were standing at his elbow, just behind Javier. "Bowden can't know what he's getting into. We'll put Figgy on the Cornell professor, so we can get to the journals."

"What now?" Javier asked.

"Go after them. Fast. If it's Gaudet, Bowden's a dead man. Unless Gaudet needs him alive."

"If he's with a Matses girl," Javier said, "things may go better than you think."

A day after the last debacle, Baptiste had another meeting planned with Benoit Moreau that he hoped would go better than the prior. He had just spent a half hour talking to his doctor about AIDS and other sexually transmitted diseases. Benoit had had a test recently and was clean, but according to the doctor, the results would not be accurate as to AIDS for any recent sexual activity. The woman was a terrible risk for more reasons than AIDS, but the logic of the situation was not taking any toll on his loins, only his brain. Even though it was more dangerous than trying to strangle a Paris whore, he couldn't abate his desire nor could he reason with it. He had never even really considered being unfaithful to his wife because in the area of intimacy he was paranoid. And he was a Catholic from a Catholic family, even if it was more in name than in deed.

For the paranoid, such as Baptiste, sleeping with Benoit would be a terrifying dance with chance. He pondered whether she might claim rape and retain some of his semen to prove it, and he obsessed over that one. Other problems in life did not have this effect on him. Figuring all this out took an incredibly large chunk of time and a bigger chunk of emotional energy. Asking the questions made him feel demeaned. He supposed that is what Benoit Moreau had in mind.

If he didn't obtain Benoit's help, he was placing all of his hopes in René's race against the Americans to find Bowden first. That wasn't a good enough bet.

Before he went to see Benoit, he had a meeting with the admiral. Waiting outside the office at the end of the line was agonizing. He wanted nothing more than to get it over with and get on with Benoit. It took about five minutes to get his turn. Sitting in front of the admiral, he concentrated on remaining calm and unflappable.

"How are we doing with Benoit?"

"I think I'm getting closer."

"'Closer' is not your assignment. The minister is on my tail, and the prime minister is calling me every day. I'm making things up to say—things that sound like real progress. We need success, and we need it now."

"Our man is in with the Americans. René's in the field. We have good men in New York. We're in a good position," Baptiste confirmed.

"So the Americans have to wipe our ass. Don't misunderstand, it was smart to get in with them. But we have to beat them, not catch their crumbs. As for René . . . you know my feelings about him."

"Yes, sir."

The admiral took a drink of his very black coffee. "I know that this American, Sam, is well connected." Baptiste wondered if his boss was nervous. They both were familiar with the rumors surrounding Sam. Few knew him, but nobody claimed he was anything less than shrewd. "Do you really think Newton or René can outmaneuver him?"

"So far, we are clean. I'm waiting for a full report from both."

The admiral nodded, his eyes distant. "I wish we could play rough with Benoit Moreau, but she knows too many politicians. Carnal knowledge, I mean. Even in prison she gets more favors than a round-heeled laundress."

"I did not know this. She has it good?"

"She's behind bars—but aside from that, they treat her

like someone would be treated if there were a steady stream of discreet inquiries from parliament. If you get my meaning."

"No wonder it is hard to bribe her," Baptiste affirmed.

"You're talking about the job offer?"

"Yes. She has not bitten."

"On the job or your cock?"

"I would never—"

"Of course you wouldn't. Make sure you don't. Maybe I should talk to her. Discreet inquiries or no, she's still in a cell. The work deal should appeal. Go see her again, and if she says no, then I will see her. If you have to promise her a possible pardon, then do it. It won't be possible anytime soon, but she won't know that. Whatever it takes to get her cooperation is what you should do," the admiral stated.

Baptiste swallowed and nodded. *Indeed.*

"The admiral wants to come and see me, doesn't he? He's looking for excuses." Benoit Moreau gave Baptiste a level stare when she said it, and for some strange reason he wanted with all his soul to give in. He wanted to be in league with her, to be her partner and confidant, even her subject. There was a strange titillation to it. Somehow she knew what he wanted better than he did. So strange. But he was not ready to accede to her demand for sex. Not yet.

"My boss wants the job done."

She smirked. "I'm so grateful you don't actually believe that. Okay, let's do a test. You pick up the phone and call Admiral Larive and ask him if he would like to see me. Just a simple question with me listening. We can share an earpiece."

"I can return you to your cell. I can find an excuse to throw you against the wall. Break your ribs, knock your teeth out—and you just don't get it."

"Knock my teeth out. Go ahead. Great career move."

"What the hell do you want?"

"I will deal either with you or your boss. Which will it be?" Benoit challenged.

"Let's talk about the deal. You go to work. You get out of here for the day, every day. You help us and we make your life a lot better."

"Okay. It will be your boss. I will make your deal and take care of the admiral myself. When I am in my new office, I will ask him to come and see me. I will tell him all my secrets and you will be rewarded because you made the deal."

"You will never seduce him."

"Then that is not your concern. Besides, I said nothing about seducing him. Let's make the deal."

"The deal is, you go to the lab starting tomorrow. As long as we like your cooperation, you keep going. That's the deal. And on your first day there you will tell me everything you know about Chaperone," Baptiste explained.

"That is not the deal. A deal is a negotiation. That was no negotiation."

"You are a criminal. The French government does not negotiate with criminals. They impose conditions. You will not see the admiral and we will not be manipulated."

He was angry and knew he shouldn't do what he did next, but he could not lose face now. He yanked her from the chair, dragged her to the door, and threw her out of the office so that she tripped in her chains and landed hard on the linoleum. The guards looked mystified and a little nervous. She looked up with pure superiority and he knew he wouldn't like whatever she was about to say.

"If the Americans get Chaperone before you do," she whispered, "you will look like an idiot."

He kicked the door shut and felt for a fleeting moment as though he had reclaimed his manhood. Then her words sank in and he knew that she knew.

* * *

The place was a green-leafed steam bath. In some places the visibility in the beam of the flashlights narrowed to a few feet. Dawn had just arrived, revealing highland jungle: terra firma. It actually tended to have thicker foliage than the lowland jungle because it was not underwater for six months out of the year. There was no visibility above to the sky even in the daylight except in natural openings and thin spots in the forest canopy. GPS signals were often weak, maybe one good satellite signal and one faint. In the rare clearings five good satellite signals were common.

Sam was getting the hang of this jungle, although navigating was extraordinarily difficult. Javier managed to walk generally in the appropriate direction according to the intermittent GPS readings, but it was obvious that they traversed nothing like a straight line, making the journey longer than the map would indicate.

Sam used a GPS to find the approximate coordinates of a spot on the Tapiche closest to Bowden's house. As they went, they meandered, looking for the sign of a small group of men. They traveled into the early afternoon and then looked for a natural opening in the canopy and once again used the satellite phone. Sam noted that he had a good signal. He dialed and got his office on the line and soon was talking to Jill.

"Where are you?"

"About twenty miles from Bowden's as the crow flies. We've been wandering, looking for a sign. We'll go no farther toward the Tapiche, unless you guys know something we don't."

"Give me your latitude and longitude."

Sam gave it.

"Yeah, we have you. We are almost sure you have bad company."

"Yeah?"

"I don't know if you want the particulars or just the conclusions." She was referring to Big Brain, which must have correlated far-flung data to make the conclusions.

"What do you have?"

"We have Girard and company traveling to Brazil, then into your area. We have a confirmation of that from French intelligence as communicated to Figgy."

"Why is French intelligence mucking around in our business?"

"Just trying to be helpful, I guess."

"So Gaudet or whoever it is didn't come through Lima?"

"For some reason they flew from Manaus to Iquitos. We have confirmed they hired a boat in Iquitos, went up the Ucayali. We have six bodies leaving the Tapiche on foot."

"That from Big Eye?"

"Yeah, the on-foot part."

Big Eye was a surveillance system built at the urging of the United States by Raytheon for the Brazilian government at a cost of about $1.4 billion and consisting of nine hundred listening posts, five airborne jets, and three remote sensing aircraft. From a height of 33,000 feet and a distance of 125 miles, the radar systems could detect a human being under cloud cover on the forest floor. Brazil had not yet consented to share Big Eye information with the United States, but the CIA viewed that issue as a diplomatic technicality. Somehow U.S. spooks had hotwired the thing, and since Sam's project was of some interest, they ran a data pipe over to Big Brain, which did its usual voracious data guzzle.

"You could be watching any six people. You don't know they came in a boat, right?"

"Right. Could be Matses people returning from a rare trip to Requena. Maybe European types on holiday. But I doubt it. What are the chances?"

"How close are they?"

"Very close. Under a mile. And there is a lone somebody even closer and another single a little farther away."

"Two alone?"

"Natives probably. Especially one of them—from the way he moves. Fast."

The sat phone's connection fizzled.

Sam told Javier what he knew. The guide nodded and they began making a slow circle, using their flashlights. Staring at the forest floor, they walked for what seemed an hour in constantly widening circles. Since they were not paying attention to natural pathways, they had to claw their way through tangles and vines, which were dripping with ants. Even seeing the ground was difficult at times.

"I found them," Javier said at last, surprising Sam, who hadn't even realized that Javier had disappeared and traveled some distance.

"Six pairs of shoes." They all gathered around and looked. In the soft mud next to a small deep river of black water— that no doubt ran into the Galvez—the imprints were obvious. "By now they could be several miles distant."

"Next clearing we'll try the sat phone and find out."

Nothing about the trek was as Sam had envisioned. Most significant, of course, was the fact that they were now following six pairs of shoes, one of which might be Devan Gaudet's. From this fact flowed many other unanticipated eventualities, such as Sam's decision to stalk these killers, which added the prospect of a deadly encounter. Walking in the same general direction as the six men, they would not literally follow each footstep because the process of tracking over a leaf-littered jungle floor would slow them down. Instead, they would travel on their own and make sure they located the track every fifty feet or so; failing that, they would backtrack to the last-known location and try again.

Sweat poured down Sam and the heat baked through him. For reasons he couldn't quite grasp, he was drawn to this place, perhaps to the utter wildness, and so it seemed was Grady, although there was no hiding her physical discomfort. Perhaps the anticipation of meeting Michael Bowden kept her going. Yodo never seemed to feel much of anything about his surroundings. He was pretty close to immune to environmental influences except when someone was trying to kill him or one of his charges.

They tried not to use machetes to cut a trail because it made noise and left a memoir of their passage and, more significantly, because to actually chop enough to do any good required great effort and much time. So they slithered past everything they could, all the while unable to imagine how any human without a GPS could find anything or anyplace in this jungle—ever. They came upon a toppled tree that opened a vine-tangled spot in the forest that was maybe thirty or more feet across. In this stretch of jungle the open space seemed like a mall parking lot.

As they made their way across the opening, Sam glanced down and saw something protruding from the base of a small tree. He stopped to retrieve an arrow, which no doubt missed one lucky monkey. Grady stepped around him, apparently walking on automatic. Just as she was looking for a likely spot to reenter the green wall, Sam noticed a brown face with interesting tattoos around the mouth. He stared at two brown eyes. The young man's body was partially obscured by foliage, but his face was clearly exposed. His hair fell below his shoulders. The fellow seemed to be naked above the waist. He was quite thin and Sam wondered if he saw hunger in the eyes.

Neither Sam nor the native moved. There was a wicked-looking, stone-tipped arrow about fifteen feet from Sam's nose and it was poised for release, but it was not aimed at Sam. Grady was standing immediately in front of him, so it was her forehead that would take the shot.

Very slowly Sam put a hand on her shoulder and gently eased beside her, and then around her, all the time watching the native's eyes. It took a full minute to make the switch.

The arrowhead wore a deep red stain that was smooth and had a sheen like fiberglass. That would be a neurotoxin made with excretions from a dart frog (Grady's research had indicated it was the Matses version of curare and more effective) and mixed with various venoms.

"If I need mouth-to-mouth resuscitation, it's your job," he whispered, unable to resist the wisecrack.

"You can count on me."

"Tell him we're friends," Sam told Javier.

Javier spoke Spanish, but the man appeared not to understand.

"He isn't so wild he doesn't speak Spanish, is he?"

"He looks Matses and he is in Matses territory. In these parts the Matses speak Spanish," Javier said.

Moving very slowly, Sam removed a knife on a string from his pocket and demonstrated the folding and unfolding of the blade and then hung it over a branch. Doing his best to look at ease, he stepped back, signaling for Yodo, Grady, and Javier to move back as well. Grady needed no encouragement. The gesture of giving the knife was called *atraccao* and meant luring. Early contact with pure jungle natives was normally accompanied by the presentation of gifts. With luck he would win reciprocity and more contact.

There was good muscle in the young man's shoulders even if the cheeks were slightly gaunt. Sam noticed a slight relaxing across his chest and the hand came forward, slowly reducing tension on the bowstring. As Sam watched the man, their eyes locked. The native was watchful. *I am a friend,* Sam repeated in his mind as if it were a mantra. Then, *I want to hunt with you.* Sam now saw three hairlike wood strands protruding through the man's nose—the "cat whiskers" characteristic of the Matses. Around the man's mouth was a tattoo.

The cat man put his bow to his side and studied the knife. He opened and closed it with familiarity; Sam was sure that

Cat-man had seen others, perhaps even owned one. Sam sensed that the man wished to make a return gift.

"Tell him that I am traveling, so I cannot carry any gift that he might wish to give."

"Good thinking," Javier said; then he tried to communicate that idea in Spanish.

"He doesn't understand. He doesn't speak Spanish. The Matses have their own language, but they all speak some Spanish. That's not all that's weird. Normally, the women wear the nose whiskers unless it's a special deal, and the men are dressing for dinner, so to speak."

Reaching under his shirt, Sam removed his braided rawhide necklace with the gold locket. He opened the locket, walked forward three paces, and in the beam of a flashlight showed Cat-man a picture of his grandfather Stalking Bear. Cat-man studied the picture for a moment, then ran his fingers over it before turning his attention back to Sam.

Sam slowly squatted and cleared away leaves and vines on the forest floor until he came to dark soil. He waited a minute and then began patting the ground in a ritualistic fashion and smoothing it. When he had smoothed a three-foot-square area, he stopped. The native stepped out from behind the bush that had partially hidden him, squatted down, cleared the leaves and vines over a similar size square, patted the ground smooth, then stood next to the patch and stomped his feet. Then he stepped back.

Sam took a stick and drew a winding line in the ground, then drew a number of intersecting smaller lines. He was intending to depict the Yavarí River and its tributaries, as well as the Blanca, Tapiche and Ucayali. If he were local Matses, the man would know the geography. Sam stood and stomped on the ground, then pointed with the stick at the crude lines, attempting to indicate their current location between the Galvez and the Tapiche and their direction of travel toward the Galvez. Then he pointed at the sky low on the horizon and circumscribed an arc to the opposite horizon. He pointed to a spot on the Tapiche and made two full arcs, indicating two days' journey.

"For him it wouldn't take two days," Javier said.

Cat-man took the stick, went to his own square, and drew a river system similar to the Yavarí, then drew what looked like a mound and made two arcs with his arm for two days. Then he put a round mark on the map and stomped his feet.

"That explains it," Javier said. "It would take us at least three days to get where he is indicating. Maybe more. It looks like he's saying he's from the Brazilian refuge. Probably Rio Lobo. Totally unusual because they don't cross over the border just to hunt or wander around."

"Why is he alone?" Sam asked. "I would think they would hunt in groups."

"They would not come over here just to hunt."

"Fala Portuguese?" Javier asked.

"A minha lingua e Portuguese."

"There is your answer. He speaks Portuguese. I don't speak much."

"Interesting challenge," Sam said.

"Tu nao deves de estar aqui."

"What's he say?"

"Something like . . . that we are trespassing here. I will say that I know the people of San José."

"Ask for his help in following the white men."

"Too complicated," Javier said.

"Eu consiou uma mulher dos Matses neste lado do Yavarí e ela e muito boa e ela vai ser a mulher," Cat-man said.

"What's he say?"

"Something about a woman. Maybe he's over here courting a wife."

Sam opened the locket and once again showed him Grandfather's picture.

"Tell him this man was my grandfather."

"I know the word for father."

"That won't work."

"Why?"

"Because I need the force of the truth. I want to take him back to the sandbar."

"Vamos ao rio," Javier said.

Pointing, Sam indicated that Cat-man should lead the way back in the direction Sam had come. The group went a couple of hundred feet through the jungle and Cat-man stopped. Without waiting, Sam kept going and broke through the jungle onto the sandbank of a Yavarí river tributary. On the river bar there were the footprints of the six booted men.

"Do you know the words for my son?"

"Meu filho."

Sam said the words. Then he took Cat-man's arrow and pantomimed a man being shot, falling to the ground, and dying. Again he said the words: *"Meu filho."* Then Sam took Cat-man's hand gently and clasped it to his chest. *"Meu filho,"* he said.

"Your son was killed by the men we are following?" Javier asked.

"Yes. That is the truth."

Cat-man opened the gold medallion hanging around Sam's neck and took another look at Grandfather.

Sam pantomimed following the tracks in the sand. Again he repeated the pantomime of his son's death. Without any other communication Cat-man started off after the six men. Intermittently as they walked, he pointed out a footprint or two. It appeared to be a cautious, disciplined group they were following; they didn't leave signs like normal civilians would.

Now the men they followed were not far and Sam knew they were confident, even overconfident. He wondered if they could be beaten.

It occurred to him then that there was something not good

about using Cat-man and his skills. No reasonably certain recipe had yet been found for bringing indigenous peoples into the modern world without bringing them onto welfare rolls to stagnate until they died. Cat-man was already in the netherworld between his natural state and civilization. An experience like this would carry him farther from his roots, if it did not kill him outright. But Sam balanced that against his desperate need to find and stop six men bent on harming and probably killing Michael Bowden and likely many others. All he could do was hope this walk through the jungle would not bring harm to Cat-man.

Sunlight came down through the top layers of the forest in cascades that exhausted themselves before they hit the ground and were gobbled by the largest leaves in the world, soaking up the rays and breathing in the carbon dioxide and exhaling oxygen—the lungs of the earth. Sam had read that the Amazon basin produced 40 percent of the world's oxygen and pumped out 20 percent of the earth's flowing fresh water. It was late afternoon under the thick of the jungle canopy and in spots Sam couldn't even discern if the sky was overcast or clear.

Yodo followed behind Grady, who walked behind Sam, Javier at his shoulder; Cat-man led the way. After they had walked a half hour with Cat-man barely studying the ground, they came to one of the tributaries of the Galvez. It looked to be nearly seventy or eighty feet across and on its near bank stood a half circle of abandoned huts. Matses often made small fishing camps, such as this one, which they'd leave when the fish stopped biting or the floodwaters came.

This camp had one unique feature: dead tribe members lay between the huts. It was astonishing because the bullet holes indicated they were killed by westernized people, and it was almost unheard of for *ciudadanos* to sneak up on natives. Devan Gaudet, if it were indeed his work, never ceased to amaze Sam. It was, however, apparent that not all of the natives in the village had been killed. There were five bodies and, judging from the huts, there could have been as many as fifty in the group. Two of the bodies were prepubescent girls. Three were young women; none were men. The men had probably been away fishing; perhaps others had escaped. It mystified Sam that Gaudet would allow his men to slaughter natives, especially before his main mission was complete. The young women had obviously been tortured, probably raped, so Gaudet would have watched while his men distracted themselves from the discomfort of the jungle. Sam had a hunch that a man like Gaudet would not free his baser instincts in front of his men. He might watch, but he wouldn't participate. For that, he would need to be alone.

Could this really have been purely for his troop's morale?

Grady began to retch. Sam quickly pulled her away.

"It's him, isn't it?"

"We don't know. If I thought he would get here this quickly, I would have left you home."

"I hate that bastard. Evil isn't a big enough word."

Cat-man displayed no emotion and made no attempt to communicate. He seemed as immune to the smell of death as to the muggy air.

Sam kept his arm around Grady as they skirted the huts, following Cat-man to the place where the killers had exited the fishing camp. Within a couple of minutes they were deep in the jungle.

Sam noticed a new purpose in Cat-man's stride as he slipped more quickly through the vines and undergrowth, but still he left no visible record of his passing.

At nightfall they hadn't yet caught up to the group. Cat-man came to Sam and pantomimed sleep for the group and continued tracking for himself.

"When Matses go to town, they will walk all day and hunt at night. Cat-man wants to move at his pace and find the bastards. He'll come back for us when he locates them . . . would be my guess," Javier said.

It took twenty minutes of machete work to create an opening large enough for five hammocks in the thick jungle. Cat-man set about gathering fruit and within twenty minutes had a pile large enough for everybody to get a good taste if not a full meal. Then he hung his hammock and left.

"They aren't like you and me. They see in the dark," Javier said. "He'll find those gringos fast, and they'll never see him."

"Don't suppose he'd tie them up for us?"

"I don't think so. Cat-man understands guns."

Everybody but Cat-man had a rain slicker to pull over them to provide minimal protection from any nighttime rain, which was fairly likely even at the end of the so-called dry season. It also helped with squirmy things that might be falling or unreeling on spider silk from above. Around them the vines and undergrowth were thick and full, so that in the soft camp light it appeared that the machetes had created four walls. There were heavy fragrances, some like rotting eggs, some like whore's perfume. Sound emanated from every direction. There were many sorts of noises: rustling of branches and leaves; a steady intermingled chorus of frog sounds that were bass violas; singing sounds that were the cricket violins; birds that sang melodious and flutelike; raucous birds that squawked and chirped, chief among them the horned screamers, also known as donkey birds, that sounded like a jackass at hell's gate; there was a clicking sound like those made by street rappers; and finally the eerie calls of howler monkeys, similar to the big, breathy hiss of a mountain lion or a child instructed by his mother to make quieter monster sounds.

Sam could tell that this jungle cacophony wasn't Grady's favorite night music. He stepped away to take a leak and reached into the zippered pocket of his jungle pants, where he found a pack of cigarettes. He didn't smoke, he reminded himself. And it could be dangerous if they were being stalked. He squatted down facing a large tree and cupped it in his hands. Just a few puffs. He took three deep drags, put out the smoke, and returned to camp.

"There is a certain primitive flavor to this place. So much life and so much death all jammed together," Grady said.

"You know you wouldn't have said that when I first met you."

"Do I make you proud?" She laughed. "All that college?"

"Sometimes."

"Funny thing," Grady said. "With all these damn smells something reminds me of cigarettes."

"Probably something like a tobacco leaf," Sam said.

Grady turned to Javier.

"Do you smoke?"

"No. Maybe there's been a fire nearby."

"Let's get some sleep," Sam said.

After a few minutes Javier stepped over to Sam.

"The exact truth is not always important?"

"The truth is always important," Sam muttered. "Full disclosure is another matter. . . ."

It was something of a puzzle to get four hammocks hung in their small hole in the foliage. Ultimately they ended up with Sam's hanging over the top of Yodo's. Finally they all managed to slither onto their hammocks, pulled on their mosquito netting, and doused the lights. Sam was falling off to sleep when he felt Grady reach for his hand. He patted it in what he deemed a fatherly touch and whispered that everything would be fine. He could sense that the slaughtered natives and the image of Gaudet were haunting her. But she still seemed to cope. That was up until the jaguar screamed and shortly thereafter a rather large snake came down one of the trees. First they heard it and then Grady's flashlight lit the beautiful mottled skin.

"Sam?"

"Uh-huh."

"I'm sleeping with you in your hammock."

"It's not big enough."

"Oh yes it is."

She brought her slicker and slipped rather neatly beside him, even getting under his mosquito netting. It took a little doing to get both slickers over the top of them. Anna, being Grady's aunt, would probably understand about the single hammock. In fact, if anything happened to Grady, Anna would have his ass.

With Anna had come Grady, a wild and beautiful young woman whom Sam had salvaged from drugs and a booming occupation as a stripper. It had been one of those family interventions, where Sam had swooped in, paid Grady to leave the club, and delivered her to a Tilok Native American spiritual leader who happened also to be a psychologist—and Sam's mother. Grady graduated from his mother's drug counseling with honors.

Using her formidable powers of persuasion, Grady had talked her way onto the staff of Sam's business, and lately her smiles and the way she flashed her eyes were stirring his soul. There was a freshness to her youth and an exuberance about her that dug deep in a man. When at work in his offices in LA he noticed that he looked forward to chatting with her in the morning on his way through the office complex. But the side of him that he inherited from Grandfather made sure that he never crossed the line.

He didn't really know if his feelings were limited to the sort of affection that a man has for a niece or a daughter, or if maybe it was something more unsettling. On most days, when he and Anna weren't arguing, he realized that he had something special with Anna and that helped him with Grady. Just as significant, he knew that a forty-two-year-old man would take something from a twenty-year-old woman the minute she committed herself to him, and it was something that he could not give back. The way he figured, to love Grady would be to let her go, and if he didn't love her, he had no business taking her. *Mentors do not have sex with the mentees,* he advised himself as he put a fatherly arm around her shoulders and clenched her hand.

"Thank you," she whispered. Then after a minute or so: "Sam?"

"What?"

"Do you believe Gaudet's in this jungle?"

"I guess my gut is starting to tell me that he is. If he is, he won't touch you. I promise."

She moved closer.

The sleeping arrangement made him uncomfortable. And it got worse. The hammock was too narrow and he spent the night rearranging her so as to maintain decorum. None of it seemed to bother her; she just kept on sleeping and moving.

Chapter 6

When a man loses a woman, the year loses the spring.
                                                    —Tilok proverb

Michael Bowden and Marita zigzagged through the deep jungle, looking for the trail of the six men. Marita thought their quarry might be wary enough to stay off the trail. This meant a laborious and slow tracking process that had yet to turn up any sign of the group.

That night they built a tiny fire and ate roasted piranha. They were easy to catch and reasonable to eat, although they had a bit of an oily taste. Another appetite suppressor was the macabre appearance of the piranha's teeth. Although he cut off the heads before roasting them, Michael could never quite get the picture of those little razors out of his head.

Sitting by the fire, Michael began looking at Marita with a new sort of gaze. No longer tentative, he deliberately sought eye contact. To his delight she looked back and they sat unabashedly studying each other. It was so novel for them that he burst out laughing.

She lowered her eyes, and Michael could see that he had embarrassed her.

"Why are you laughing?"

"Because I am happy to be with you and I guess I questioned whether I would be happy to be with anyone again."

"You are not laughing because you think I am what . . . weird?"

"I am laughing for the reasons that men the world over laugh with women they like."

"You are handsome," she said after a time. "And you are a man with many ideas. A smart man."

"And you are beautiful," he said. He found himself wondering if perhaps his amazement was reflected in his gaze. "I am continually surprised at your English. And at my uncertainty."

"You are uncertain?"

"Some loquacious poet of the eighteenth century said that uncertainty is the steed on which romance rides into the heart."

"I am proud of my English, but I do not understand. . . . The steed is?"

"A horse. . . . In those days English people rode horses."

"And romance comes to us on this horse of uncertainty. . . . I think I understand. Then I like this uncertainty."

"I know that the Jesuits are amazing educators, but I am stunned that out here in the jungle I have a girl who is so . . . I don't know . . . Western."

"We had toastmasters night at the priests' school. I have read *Moby Dick, The Great Gatsby, Tom Sawyer, Huckleberry Finn, Gone With the Wind*—the priests didn't know about that—and all of Jane Austen. She is my favorite. And I have read many others."

"I can tell. You're practically a hometown girl."

"What is a 'hometown girl'?"

"I don't know anymore. It used to be a girl like you, I think. I came from a college town in America. It was far from the big city. I was twelve when I left and things are a bit hazy. I remember the big things, but it seems like the jungle has swallowed many of the details."

"I want to go to New York City. Would you take me?"

"Just like that." Michael chuckled. "I have not been to New York since I was a little boy and I don't remember it."

"Your books are published there, no?"

"Yes, but my father had an agent and an editor and I have the same people. I talk on the phone and write them letters. That is all."

"Still, you could go."

"I could."

She paused awhile and they listened to the night sounds. The howler monkeys had bedded down, finished warning off other bands with their calling. But the other night creatures were anything but silent.

"The priests said you cannot be with a man until you are married."

"Yes. That's what they say." He studied her.

"That is not the custom here."

It was under 70 degrees Fahrenheit and there was a little nip in the air. They had already set up their hammocks. The firelight played off her face and she smiled at him, then looked away. Michael stood up, went to his pack, pulled out mosquito netting, removed a blanket, and draped it over her shoulders. She sat on a chunk of a downed tree and there was space next to her. She took his hand and pulled him down beside her and they draped themselves with the netting, only inches between them. He wanted to touch her face. His eye followed the contours of her body. It was so lithe . . . maybe ninety pounds. Her arms were toned and beautiful and her waist small enough that it seemed he could encircle it with his hands. Her face was smooth and only slightly round. She had full lips and gorgeously shaped eyes. Her hair was thick and curly. It had a natural sheen, black as a raven's feather. He touched it. Between his fingers it felt soft. No doubt the Catholics had taught her to bathe daily.

"Do you have shampoo?" he asked.

"Of course."

"The priests?"

"Everything is from the priests. Books, magazines, wine, newspapers, cheese. Even my boy was from the priests. Nobody knows and he is a nice man. So don't tell."

"The boy is the one who was killed?"

"Yes." She sighed. "I cannot talk about it. I am sorry."

"It's understandable. None of the other Matses read much about the outside world?"

"It is true. Except for the Protestant missionaries at Buenas Lomas Antigua. They bring in things on the planes, but it is very limited compared to what we have in Tabatinga. I miss the Western things, the magazines."

"How old are you?" Michael was intrigued.

"I am twenty. I have had one child, but I plan to have more. I would have more, but the priests taught me birth control. Isn't that funny?"

Only her age surprised him.

"It matters?" she asked.

"You have a man?"

She turned toward him and engaged his eyes.

"I did. I had more than one. I do not now. I am too educated."

"And unruly." Michael laughed.

"My family agrees and my mother would not give me to a man unless she warns him. But I do not seek a native man."

Michael nodded again.

"I am going to manage the workers for the house and garden for the priests in Tabatinga," she explained.

"You are leaving the Matses?"

"I am in love with books. We do not have any. The anthropologist is just now getting our language in written form."

Michael was getting a whole new picture of this young woman. "If you have children, they will not be Matses."

"I know. Maybe there will be a new Matses."

Michael thought about that and the wreck that the civilized world was making of their culture. But who could say that the young woman should not have her books? Or that she should not explore Western culture?

"I want to kiss you," she said. "Like in America," she added, and leaned toward him. He met her lips halfway and kissed her gently. "Is that how you do it?" she asked.

"That's one way."

"Show me another way."

This time he used his tongue and she giggled.

"I like this more. This is how I do it too."

With the next kiss, his hand moved to her waist of its own accord, as if detached from his will.

"You are sure?" he said.

Her answer was to kiss him long and deep.

Under her shirt her skin was moist and hot and it was a magnet to his fingers. She kissed him again, thrusting her tongue against his, while she flattened herself against him. His hand finally found her breast full and firm and his fingers began playing at her nipples. They hardened and he moved one hand to her leg, letting his fingers drift. When they reached her inner thigh, she began to quiver and to cling to him. For a second he paused, trying to fight his desire, to think about their mission and her relative innocence and the myth of the pink dolphin, but he couldn't. He knew that his willpower had fled. In the morning he would have to sort out what it all meant—assuming they survived.

*　*　*

Outside the holding area Baptiste told the guard that he needed the keys to Benoit Moreau's shackles.

"That would be highly irregular."

"I know. But we are under something of an urgent time constraint. You can call the colonel or even the admiral if that makes you feel better."

The man withdrew the key. He had been tipped off or was smart enough to know that this was no ordinary situation.

Once again Benoit waited in the office, only this time he had instructed the guards to put her in the chair facing the desk, reserving the chair behind the desk for himself. It was not a subtle message.

When he entered, she looked at him pleasantly, showing no sign of fear, relief, or the false adoration of a sycophant. The woman could give lessons to Machiavelli.

"I thought I would take a few minutes to see if you are ready to discuss our conditions before I have you thrown in the hole."

"How would you justify throwing me in the hole?"

"I don't need justification."

"Well, then I am ready to go in the hole."

"You know what it is like in the hole?"

"Don't waste your valuable time telling me. You need to spend your time learning about Chaperone for the glory of France. I am sure I will be there until your admiral pulls me out, makes love to me on a soft bed somewhere, and hears all my secrets."

"He can't take you to a soft bed."

"With the glory of France at stake, of course he can. The guards will be just outside and I will make a great furor during my orgasm to let them know that the admiral has the power of a bull and the finesse of Michelangelo. Then he will quietly brag that I just needed a man to get headed on the straight and narrow, a real man, and he will have the secrets to prove it. And no one will reprove him, absolutely no one, because this is France and, after all, her glory is fading, and to reclaim it, well, it is a small price to pay. They will nearly give him a medal for being the greatest cocksman in all of Paris. And you, of course, will appear. . . . Well, actually you won't appear. . . . You'll just be shuffled off to another job."

Baptiste rose from behind the desk, walked over to her, took out the key to the cuffs, handed them to her, and told her to unlock them.

She did so, but for the first time looked slightly uncertain.

He drew out his Manurin 9mm service revolver, got down on one knee, and pointed it at her throat, the muzzle only a foot from her chin.

"Here is what I am going to do. I am going to call the admiral and tell him that you have tried repeatedly to seduce me. That you've claimed you could seduce him as well. You have also claimed to me that members of *le Sénat* are under your control, that you are blackmailing them because they had illicit sex with you. Although I regret it, I will have to file a report on all of these matters. The report will reach the parliament, and I will ensure that it is copied to the media. True, my mission will have been a failure. But what do I really lose? I will get my pension and maybe an early discharge. You, though . . . will be a pariah. They will never leave you alone with any man, especially the admiral. You will never get a deal. You will lose all your contacts and your leverage in *le Sénat*. I will do this. I swear it."

He stepped back to the phone and began dialing.

"Perhaps my boss will tell me to shoot you and claim that we fought over the gun. On the other hand, that would probably be too easy."

He put the receiver to his ear.

"Wait," she said.

Yes, he definitely saw a crack in her affected nonchalance.

"Look," she said. "I will trust you where I could not trust others. I will not use my lawyer and I will tell you all my secrets. I shall be at the laboratory at your suffrage. I will put myself in your hands. But I must have one thing from a man such as yourself. I must have you. I want to feel you inside me."

Baptiste was within microns of complete victory. Or was he? She could flit like a bird and be off, call his bluff. Would sleeping with her to make her happy be unpardonable? Many agents would do it and brag about it. What was stopping him?

He set the phone down. "All right. We have a deal. You report to the lab in the morning. I will find a soft bed. But I want to know—why do they call it Chaperone?"

"After the soft bed that you promised."

Devan Gaudet did not like the jungle, but he understood it. Here the strong ate the weak, the large ate the small, and no one paid attention. There were no eulogies, no tears, not even remembrances—only birth, death, and more death. For Gaudet, there was something warm and familiar about death. He had killed many and knew he would kill more, so it wasn't the dying that offended his sensibilities. Other than death, the jungle offered torture, his own, and he didn't care for pain unless the suffering was someone else's.

There were six of them seated around the fire. Except for Gaudet, who at all times retained the appearance and air of civility, they were a ragged group with dirtied shirts, mud-caked blue jeans, and partial beards. They stank. And now that they were through dining, they belched and farted with abandon.

The five members of his group spoke French, English, and Arabic. The local guide spoke Spanish, English after a fashion, and a smattering of Portuguese, which did none of them any good. The local was Carlos, the other hires found by Trotsky and imported from France. Gaudet had no regulars and never worked repeatedly with anyone. Whenever possible, he worked alone, and if he needed men, he directed things from a distance. This group scene was not his cup of tea. All of this crowd, but the guide, were unused to the humidity, the bugs, and the heat.

"It's hotter than a whore's cunt," Cy said, not for the first time.

"Wetter too," John said, giving the obligatory response.

"Right now I'd like more of what we had back at the huts."

This was becoming tiresome. "That was a distraction. We'll waste no more time," said Gaudet.

"She was a tight little spinner," John said.

"This trip we pay attention to business. Last time we failed." That closed the discussion.

Gaudet did not believe himself a sociopath, but rather a man of business. At the moment his one business goal depended on finding Michael Bowden and obtaining all the information on one kind of plant or animal tissue that Bowden had collected and first located in 1998, most particularly its identity and where it might be found. He knew that it would be a powerful immunosuppressant but that it also would do far more than merely suppress the immune system on a temporary basis. From this organic molecule had come Chaperone and he desperately needed it. It was distressing that Bowden himself probably wouldn't know which material it was, or why it might be useful. Bowden discovered hundreds of new plants and other organisms, large and small, each year.

Gaudet estimated they were about twenty miles from Michael Bowden's place. Of the six in the party, only Cy had gone with the group sent for the initial visit. They hadn't gotten what he needed and so this time he had come himself. It would be important that Bowden did not make a connection between the two visits.

They had managed to disguise the last intrusion as motivated by looting and rape and had left the authorities with the impression that it was the work of ordinary criminals. Unfortunately, Michael Bowden had left his wife at home but had hidden all his journals, including the one for 1998. Gaudet walked to the edge of the jungle and ignored the men at the fire while he listened to the night sounds. He had a feeling and he always paid attention to his hunches. And maybe it wasn't just a hunch. The American, Sam, was hunting him and was getting close. People had shown up recently at his old home site in Polynesia, his beloved island, and they had conducted a thorough search. Was it Sam's people? The pursuit had grown wearisome.

Gaudet stepped into the darkness away from the fire and watched the men as they joked about women and sex, the same topic as always. After a time he heard a symphony of bird cries in the jungle.

"Carlos, what is with the birds?"

"Could be anything. But there are no warring tribes around here."

"I'm the nervous type. Go check."

Carlos groaned but made his way into the jungle and did not return.

Gaudet went to his pack and removed a Beretta 9mm model 92 automatic pistol with a fifteen-round magazine that was a twin to the gun in his shoulder holster; then he retreated farther from the fire and squatted, watching and waiting. The birds continued with the noise and a nearby troupe of howler monkeys started their breathy calls.

* * *

It had begun to rain, but in the heat they didn't bother with rain gear. Wet or dry didn't really matter because even when it wasn't raining, it felt wet. However, the rain did affect what they could hear. Little droplets popped like tiny bullets as they bounced down through the leaves blending to form a sort of pimpled and dimpled wall of sound. Whispers or movement through the brush were much harder to detect. It was good for sneaking, but not so good for finding. Marita was a wizard in the forest and Michael followed her closely, knowing that some inner sense guided her in a way he'd never understand.

"We will need to stop for the night," she said. "I cannot feel the river."

"How do you mean?"

"Whether it is there or there," she said, pointing in two directions that were ninety degrees apart. "I am not used to the flashlight and it confuses me."

"Which river?"

"Galvez."

"Ah." He now realized that she knew the location of the Galvez from her position in the jungle and that sense served as the basis for her navigation. Interesting, though it explained nothing about the source of this strange instinct.

Michael pulled out the GPS. He could only get one satellite signal strong and one weak. Three were needed to get a firm location. He showed her the electronic map.

"We are probably here. And the river is probably this way." He pointed. "But the signal is not good here because of all the trees overhead." They had gone a little farther, looking for a spot to make a clearing and hang their hammocks, when she stopped and sniffed.

"There is a fire. I can smell it."

Michael sniffed but could detect nothing. He took hold of the pistol grip on the gun and continued following her. He seldom shot at animals, even with his bow, and had never shot at a human being. Even now, despite his anger and fear, he could not imagine shooting to kill. He felt only the certain knowledge that he must try to capture the man who had killed his wife.

They walked farther and the rain abated, although some of the dripping continued. Then he detected the charcoal smell and soon after they saw a faint glow lighting the forest canopy. At some time past, the birds had seemed to increase their night calls and the howler monkeys began. It was eerie.

"They will know we are coming," she whispered.

"Probably."

"What do you want to do?"

"I will go to the edge of their camp. You stay back with your gun, Marita. I will tell them to raise their hands, and if anybody tries to shoot you, shoot them. Hopefully, we can take the bad one and scare the rest out of the Matses territory."

"That sounds difficult. I intend to shoot."

"But only if they go for their guns. Otherwise we talk. We need to make sure we have the right men. We cannot shoot men we don't know."

"I will tell you when I see him," she said.

Michael wondered how close they would have to get before she would be able to identify the man.

They moved ahead quietly, inches at a time. He found his knee shaking and his hands unsteady.

Perhaps fifteen yards from the fire they stopped. It was a yellow dancing flicker through the trees. They could see no faces despite their efforts to find a clear line of sight. After each deliberate step they paused for seconds. The men were speaking in French, joking and not particularly wary.

They were screened by some small trees and brush, but no large trunks. A giant kapok grew to Michael's right and a Brazil nut to his left.

Suddenly one of the men rose and said something in French.

He came right toward Michael, who held his breath and studied the man, trying to guess his intent. He could see the man's reddish whiskers growing far down his neck, heavy brows and a face molded in a cold stare. Dried blood caked the man's pants; Michael supposed it was from the native girls. The man bent over and reached in a pack and pulled out a small bottle of liquor. Whiskey, by the look of it. Then something rustled the bushes behind Michael. The man leaned forward, staring. It seemed a certainty that the man was looking right at him. Michael waited, knowing he couldn't start a war until Marita confirmed the man's identity.

Turning, the man shrugged and sat back down.

The others quieted. They were nervous. Then one of them joked and the others, still looking a little uneasy, began to converse. After several minutes Michael and Marita were a mere twenty feet and all the faces were visible. She tugged on his sleeve and pointed at the man who had been staring in the brush. Michael motioned for her to move behind the broad trunk of the Brazil nut. For one crazy moment he wanted to ask her if she was sure about the identity.

She motioned for him to step back. Fear flashed through him. They couldn't stand around where they might be seen. She motioned again. Carefully he stepped back behind the tree; in response to her beckoning he put his ear to her lips.

"The others are not there."

"But that is the man?"

"Yes. The big one. I watched him rape my sister. He killed my child."

Michael willed himself forward.

"Help, help me!" Michael shouted.

The men jumped for their guns. Faster, though, Marita began shooting. Michael ducked back behind Marita's tree and began firing himself. The gunfire from Marita's M16 automatic nearly severed the redheaded man's arm at the shoulder. It hung by a thread, and the man stared openmouthed as the next bullet knocked him over backward.

Michael shot a second man, square in the chest, then continued firing at flying bodies. The others quickly disappeared into the forest—how many wounded, he did not know. Michael turned to Marita and saw her facing a man who held a gun at her head.

"Put down the gun," the man said to Michael.

"No," Marita said.

He knew she was right. There would only be death if he put down his gun. He calculated which part of Marita could best suffer a gunshot that might get to the man. Maybe a shoulder.

"I came peacefully," the man said. "I saw what you did. You shot at these people first."

"The big man over there killed my wife, raped Marita's sister, and killed her child."

"I know nothing about this man or these men. I'm looking for a scientist. Michael Bowden."

Out of the corner of his eye Michael saw the big man, covered in blood, struggling to point a handgun with his good arm. A boom sounded. Michael felt the bullet explode through the meaty part of his thigh. It was like being hit with a maul and he nearly fell over. Wavering, he shot at the man's head but missed. Before he could fire again, the redheaded man fired, catching him in the shoulder and knocking him to the ground. As he became numb to the world, he saw the man holding Marita shoot the redheaded man.

Marita whirled and swung her gun up at the stranger. He slapped it out of her hand. Quicker than thought, she grabbed for the man's gun; he pulled away, but she hung on like a demon. The gun fired, its blast muffled by her torso. Slowly Marita slid down the man's body.

Michael did not understand why she would fight a man

who was killing her own quarry. He would probably not live to consider the question.

"Goddamn it," the man said. "I didn't want to hurt her." The accent was French.

The howler monkeys increased their already raucous calls. Michael was losing consciousness.

"I wonder what's coming now," someone said. "Let's get back."

Minutes passed, he had no idea how many.

"Those monkeys will do that over a jaguar, or all the shooting, or just because they feel like it." A new man had arrived and spoke in Spanish. "We're a little late," a big, dark-haired man spoke in English, with an American accent. He came to Bowden. Quickly he put a tourniquet on the thigh and put Bowden's fingers on the shoulder wound. "Press," he said before moving out of sight. "We'll be back. You'll make it."

The other man followed him. The pain began to mount; Michael wanted to scream. He could barely think.

More time passed and then he heard cursing and swearing and crashing in the bushes. The big man with black hair had hold of a dirty, frightened man. He shoved him into the fire-light, where the man stumbled to the ground, his face pouring blood. Michael saw shackles on the man's wrists and legs.

"Don't mess with a Tilok or a cat man," the big man said, stepping back into the jungle.

A shot came from the forest and the captive man's head exploded.

A flurry of shooting followed. It sounded like a war. Then a long silence. The next Michael knew, the dark-haired man was bending over him.

"It's morphine. It'll help," he said. "We're going to get you to a hospital."

Next to the dark-haired man Michael saw a beautiful

young blond woman in the soft light. She looked terribly concerned. He knew he must look worse than dead.

"Marita," he said, hoping someone would help her. He saw pain on the blond woman's face and knew it wasn't good.

Cat-man seemed to have departed. Sam pumped his only living captive, John, full of morphine, but not so much that he went off to la-la land.

"Your leader shot you."

"Fuck you. And him." He coughed deep and ugly. Things were breaking loose inside.

"He killed another of your men, right in front of me. Why protect him? Girard—is that what he's called?" No response. "You're gonna die. You're bleeding inside. You have a few seconds to do something right, but maybe it isn't in you. I hope it is."

He retched and coughed "Yes, we called him Girard. He's from France."

"He was here tonight?"

The man nodded.

"Beard?"

He nodded again, choking.

"Uses a knife?"

He nodded hard and fluid rattled in his lungs when he tried to speak. Turning nearly purple, he rolled his eyes back and his bowels let go.

Sam kept his eyes locked on the dying man's, and for just a second they flickered.

"You want to go after him, don't you?" Grady asked.

"Just a minute," Sam said, still watching the man. He leaned over to the man's ear. "In the end you did good." Once again the man's eyes rolled and Sam knew he was gone.

Sam nodded. "The three of you can haul Michael back to Galvez." Bowden had wavered on the edge of consciousness since being shot. "It's close. Michael, you've got a fast boat?"

"Very fast. But others, my friends, might have used it to take my journals. Doubt they've returned it."

"Let's hope Gaudet doesn't know about your boat—assuming it's even there."

"He wouldn't find it. Can't start it anyway. Needs an electronic chip." Michael was breathing deeply from the pain and trauma. "Ramos my friend has one and the other's in my pack."

"Good. I doubt he wants to try to drift a speedboat all the way to the Amazon even if he does find it."

"He'll go to the Tapiche."

"He could go down the Galvez," Javier said. "But once again he'd have no boat and I can't see him paddling a stolen dugout through Matses country. They don't kill people anymore, but a thief, a murderer, and a white man might be different."

Although Sam could tell Grady hated the idea, she wasn't going to stop him. It wasn't her way to wimp out in the clutch. And she trusted Yodo as much as Sam did.

Sam took out his GPS before starting off into the dark. He had to take a chance that Gaudet would head for the Tapiche. He struck off through the jungle, trying to walk something of a straight line. Looking ahead was surreal. It felt like passing through an underwater kelp bed. Aerial roots came down from branches like taut rope and small sacropia grew up with stems twice as thick as a man's thumb. It was hard to find a foot-wide space anywhere in the first few hundred feet of the trek. Interspersed among the growing saplings and aerial roots were the giants such as ficus, saeba, ironwood, kapok, and the feathery-leafed acacia whose branches gave an appearance similar to an evergreen softwood tree. At their bases some of the large trees had a splayed root system that had formed triangular-shaped wedges in the vertical plane so that the lower trunk of the tree looked something like the foot of a coatrack.

Traveling in a straight line turned out to be impossible and dangerous, so he risked using his flashlight, hoping he wouldn't walk into an ambush. On the forest floor wet leaves made for quiet steps, but the brush rubbing on his body and pack was noisy. On any incline the clay mud beneath the leaves made the footing tenuous and every slime-covered log was a hazard. Ants and other insects were crawling over him; attempts to brush them off seemed futile. He went after the little tickles on his skin, squishing anything that got under his clothing. Anytime he paused, the raucous sound of mosquitoes filled his ears with their mind-scalding wingbeat. He had spread repellent liberally over the exposed skin and wore typical UV-screening jungle clothes designed to cover most of his body.

The heat burned into him with the exertion of traveling fast through the tangles of vegetable matter that clung and slowed him. He couldn't spend a lot of time attempting to circumvent thickets. Every couple of minutes he glanced at the GPS and observed the gnarled track that he was leaving on the incandescent screen. Sweat dripped down onto the screen like rain as the heat squeezed everything but blood from his pores. On his feet he could feel the start of blisters as he continuously worked to keep his footing on the jungle floor.

After traveling a couple of miles he came to a sizable black-water stream that barely moved. It was a tributary of the Tapiche and it meant he might be slightly to the north of where he imagined. Or the map was wrong, which was very possible because it was made before GPS was available. He ran his light along the banks, illuminating pairs of eyes of a number of black caiman. Swimming at night was not appealing. There were more gruesome parasites and diseases in this part of the world than he cared to think about. And, having eaten piranha the prior day, it occurred to him that in some sort of cosmic justice the fish might want to return the favor.

He sighed. Without waiting any longer he stepped down into the muddy water and began walking. He removed his pack, threw the strap of his rifle across his back, then replaced the pack. It was a poor choice if he wanted to shoot from the river, but it freed both hands for swimming without fear of losing the rifle. Soon it was deep and he began the breaststroke. A caiman flung his tail and splashed, surprising him and causing him to pick up the pace. He tried not to think about the stickleback fish that had a bad habit of crawling up assholes and urethras, or the leeches that in some parts of the Amazon grew to eighteen inches. He told himself the sticklebacks were probably farther north.

He was halfway across when he sensed that something was wrong. He studied the far bank and saw a six-foot shadow by a big tree. And there was movement. He went limp and quiet, then turned and began swimming back to near where he started.

There was a shocking boom and a bullet hit the water an inch from his nose. Then the night filled with reverberating booms. Somebody was going to kill him with a semiautomatic high-powered rifle. Quickly he dropped the rifle to the bottom and got rid of the pack and all its flotation. One gulp of a breath and he went under. Bullets jetted through the water and he went the several feet to the bottom, knowing it would be a long time before he could come up. Had it been daylight he would already be dead. He felt for the rifle and slung it over his head, then began pulling himself along the bottom with his hands. He felt prongs everywhere and realized they must be branches of a submerged tree.

The bullets seemed to have stopped.

Sam could stay under for more than four minutes, which seemed phenomenal to his friends until he told them of deep divers who could stay down seven minutes. Reaching out, he felt for the branches and allowed himself to rise slowly over them. It used up precious time and air. Pulling himself across the tops, he found open water when he felt nearly out of air. He did a smooth breaststroke with a frog kick. A slow burn had developed in his chest and he could feel the weakness beginning in his body. He began to count strokes as a means of forcing himself onward. He would do ten strokes, and when he got to ten, he was determined to do five more. The burning was now strong and the desire for a breath was all-consuming. Five strokes extra had pain in his mind and body. Three more strokes. With his fingers he felt the bottom rising. His consciousness blurred. He was near the river's edge. He turned downstream. Just three more strokes. His mind seemed to be floating and he knew he was about to go lights out. Gently he rose.

He suspected the shooter would have lowered his gun after about three minutes and that he would then stare into the darkness. Ripples and sound betrayed a swimmer at night. Sam rolled and came up gently on his back. He denied himself a massive inhalation, forcing himself to be quiet. Few things took so much will.

The cacophony of an awakened jungle greeted his ears and he was grateful for something to cover the sound of his breaths.

When his lungs had stopped burning and his body had partially recovered he went under again. This time he swam downriver, figuring to put distance between himself and Gaudet before he crossed and began stalking the man. Somebody was going to die if Sam had his way. It would either be him or Gaudet, except he knew that Gaudet did not think that way. The moment Gaudet felt a shift in the odds he would flee. Gaudet preferred to kill from a distance, then disappear. Reading about it in the paper was good enough.

Above, the sky was black. There was almost no light. Trees overshadowing the river were barely visible where the tops framed the sky. There was no sound but the nighttime symphony of a startled rain forest. No shots. He was back on the far side of the river and downstream. After several breaths he was able to slow the gasping. Quietly he moved into the shallows so that his feet rested on the bottom. If he stood, there might be enough of him to see or hear. With an automatic rifle Gaudet wouldn't need to be very accurate.

Fortunately, combat wasn't Gaudet's forte. If it were, Sam knew that while he had been swimming, his pursuer, Gaudet, would have been charging him, getting as close as possible. Three more kicks downriver were uneventful; at the end of the third, Sam surfaced. It was even blacker than before. The cauliflower border of the trees against the sky was no longer visible. The forest had quieted slightly but was still like a concert hall compared to the night sounds of northern California wilderness where Sam had first learned from Grandfather the art of listening.

Trying to scan the opposite bank, he used peripheral vision, but the shadows were so deep, there was no form— only void. He was barely around one bend and it would not be safe to cross. The shooter could have moved downriver. Instead of crossing, Sam eased toward the bank and crawled on his belly into deep brush, hoping he wouldn't run into a fer-de-lance, the most poisonous snake in the Amazon. Once in the jungle, he went away from the river a hundred yards or so, turned on his flashlight, and walked downriver for twenty minutes, where he made a quiet, uneventful crossing.

Going as fast as he could, he went back into the jungle, then turned upstream until he figured he was near the point of the ambush. Without a GPS or access to Big Eye, he couldn't be sure that he was even traveling in the right direction. He attempted a ninety-degree turn in his general course of travel and immediately noticed a flash from a man-made light. It was only for an instant. He crept toward the river with his light turned off. Nearly an hour had passed. Feeling for every step, he could see nothing. As he walked, he made some slight noise and wondered if it would be enough to draw fire. The constant risk of instant death taxed him. Sweat poured down him as if he were running a race. His body was constantly trying to ready itself for a fight, but there was no fight. There was only the black, the jungle, and the next step. Near the river the bank would be steep; he began to feel for the drop. Overhead, monkeys were making chirps that sounded almost birdlike.

A donkey bird awoke and let the world know its displeasure. After walking many more minutes than Sam would have thought necessary, he was able to discern what he thought was an opening. Maybe the river. Feeling ahead with his foot, he at last perceived a drop-off. He had no idea how close he was to the ambush point. No doubt the shooter had moved, and Sam had glimpsed his light. Perhaps he was there, perhaps he was hundreds of yards off. He needed some bait. If he didn't find the man soon, he would attempt to continue on toward the Tapiche.

Sam hoped that the man was not within easy earshot. Working quickly, he stacked a row of palm fronds near the river. The row was a little over six feet in length. Then he leaped into the water, splashed, called for help in an agonized voice, jumped back onto the bank, and covered his face and hands in mud. Next he lay under the leaves, not quite able to bury himself but getting himself largely covered. Then he waited.

For several minutes there was nothing. Lying quietly his wet clothes and the mud cooled him. The temperature had fallen to perhaps 70 degrees Fahrenheit. There was a breeze and he could sense the weather changing. An extravagant display of lightning lit the river and made the trees stark against the sky. It would rain, and when it did, all sound would wash away with it. The rules of the hunt were changing with the weather.

He began turning his head and even his body, trying to watch 360 degrees in the occasional flashes of lightning. It was as if a mad photographer were running about the jungle with a flashbulb, disrupting the simple passion to kill. The lightning was a complication. With rain, noise would be almost a nonfactor. Eyes would become everything.

Something moved—a branch. It was maybe ten feet distant. Perhaps a monkey, a bird, or a snake. Perhaps a man. It moved again very slightly. Sam waited, content with his camouflage. When next the jungle lit the river, it became a luminescent trough into which the sky poured the light. He saw a man. The splash and the desperate calling had drawn the hunter to the hunted.

Sam was in his element. Some part of him, a major part, was a hunter. If possible, he would use his hands to subdue Gaudet, but not for any noble reason. He simply was more valuable alive than dead.

His quarry was moving very slowly and held a gun as if ready to use it. Huge bolts of lightning etched the black in all directions, even the canopy was lit by the power of the massive electrical strokes across the sky.

Sam watched the man take a step and then search the night. After what seemed like minutes, the man was within ten feet, his light playing through the myriad vertical roots. But his hunter was thinking of a standing man and not a muddy clump of sodden leaves. Sam considered trying to jump him. Too far. Too much noise. Sam pointed his .45 at his target's midriff, tempted to pull the trigger and end it all. There were pros and cons, but the biggest con was that he couldn't be sure it was Gaudet. Living with a cold-blooded killing was not acceptable when an alternative existed. So he waited.

The man took another step. With the next step the man would pass him by. Sam pointed carefully at the now-invisible shadow and waited for the next flash of lightning.

"Drop the gun," he screamed as lightning surged in a series of pulses that lit the jungle.

The man started firing above Sam, bullets chopping the foliage and spewing indifferent death. Sam put a single bullet in the shooter's shoulder, dropping him, then rolled and charged, knocking the automatic away. Sitting on the man with one knee on the good shoulder and one knee on the mangled side, he caused the man excruciating pain to the point he was screaming with near incoherence. He released the pressure.

"Tell me about your leader. Girard? Gaudet?" This was not Gaudet. Gaudet would have fled by now, and this man seemed taller than their best descriptions indicated.

"Girard. No Gaudet," he said in broken English.

"Tell me about him."

"Six eyes. Nervous like a cat."

"Did he watch you do the women in the little village?"

"He watched. But the others did the women. Not me."

"Is he in this jungle?"

"Yes."

Suddenly something gripped Sam's chest.

"Where did he go?"

"I don't know."

Sam prayed that Yodo was with Grady.

"GPS? Map? Electronic?" Sam said.

The man nodded and Sam pulled the man's packsack out from underneath him. Inside was a handheld GPS.

"Girard?" Sam asked, sticking the small electronic map in front of the man's face.

The man didn't answer.

Sam pointed his pistol at his nose. "Girard?"

The man shrugged. "I don't know."

Chapter 7

Fear in the night is gone with a single torch; fear in the day must be pushed out like dirt from the badger's burrow.

—Tilok proverb

Grady walked behind Michael Bowden, who lay on the travois dragged by Yodo. Periodically he called out the name Marita, no doubt the woman they had buried in the jungle before they left. They had finally told him she was dead. Since then, he had been very quiet. Early morning light barely made its way to the forest floor but she welcomed it, as the night had seemed a harbinger of terrors too numerous to count.

They were headed for the trail that ran from Herrera to Santa José on the Galvez. Javier led the small party.

As she walked through the dripping green forest, Grady fantasized about a simple room with a chair, a bed, a shower, and an air conditioner. She wore lightweight nylon-polyester jungle pants and a shirt like every other yuppie who went to the Amazon. The clothes dried fast and afforded UV protection—it was space-age stuff. On her back she carried a pack bulging with Yodo's things so that he could remain as unburdened as possible for the task of dragging the crude stretcher.

It seemed that Michael was nearly delirious from the morphine, but when he wasn't pumped full of the painkiller, his suffering (albeit silent) was so great that they hastened to remedicate him. Even so, he frequently asked Grady if she was all right and if she was tolerating the jungle. Once he explained that she needed to be wary of snakes and spiders, as if it might not have occurred to her.

Grady now carried a gun and was prepared to use it.

Occasionally she could see the sky and she noticed black bottoms to the clouds. They passed a large snake curled around the lower branches of a tree. It spit a forked tongue in their direction, seeming to wish death on all who passed by. A giant scorpion, surely the mother of all bugs, crunched under her boot, and nearby a foot-long insect sat like a skeleton in a morgue.

Michael's wounds were bad, but his essential character came through, and Grady found him even more appealing than she had in his books. He was intelligent, sensitive, and handsome to boot. He spoke sincerely, absolutely without guile, a rarity in Grady's experience. His constant concern for her safety won her over completely.

When they finally made the trail, it was a tunnel in the green, in places six feet wide and obviously the beneficiary of regular machete hacking. This made it a more logical place to make an ambush. That caused new worries.

Then it got much worse.

They heard something large, maybe man-size, moving through the jungle. They stopped and it stopped. At this point Grady could see only a few feet into the heavy foliage. The mosquitoes were fierce and distracting. As they waited and watched, the gun became heavy in her hand.

"Let's keep moving," Yodo said. At the same time he signaled for Grady to get down. She squatted. He signaled for her to move back so she duckwalked back down the trail, careful to make no noise. She wasn't sure what Yodo had in mind, but she assumed he wanted them to spread out for a reason. Perhaps it was a more effective way to fight with guns.

They all aimed their firearms, waiting for something to emerge. Silence. The gun grew heavier in her hand.

"Send her ahead, not behind," Bowden whispered. Then he looked at Grady. "Down the trail to the Matses."

Yodo was now signaling for her to come ahead, so she reversed and, in response to Yodo's waves, went past Michael Bowden, who touched her hand.

"Get out of here," he whispered.

She nodded without knowing why. She had no desire to head out by herself even on a trail, but Yodo seemed adamant and Sam would bust a gut if she rebelled against the leadership. Sam's lectures had had an effect. She kept moving. Down the way about fifty feet or so, the trail took a small bend. As she went around it, she knew the others would disappear from her sight.

Now Yodo was signaling frantically that she hurry. She stood and started to jog as quietly as she could. Immediately she realized how much harder it was to be alone in this strange place. Once down the trail she ran in earnest; then she came to a fork and took the one to the right. She supposed they figured that Michael was the target and she could run ahead on the trail, both to get help and to be safer.

The foliage along the edge was growing over the trail and it had narrowed to a couple of feet. As she ran, she came to more forks, and it usually seemed obvious which was the larger and more well-traveled path. Then it began to get difficult as the splinter trails looked the same. Finally she found herself walking through the jungle. She realized she should look back and mark the trail in her memory, but when she did so, the two large sacropias—and the rest of the jungle for that matter—seemed entirely unfamiliar. Looking up, she recognized nothing distinctive.

She decided to backtrack a few feet. Past the closest sacropia she looked for a trail but saw nothing. When she went to the next tree, she saw a faint pathway through the foliage that immediately forked. Her heart started to beat faster as she imagined getting lost in the vast jungle.

She had no GPS and she knew Yodo meant for her to stay on the trail. But which trail?

She decided that one of the trails was slightly more disturbed and that would be the one she had arrived on, so she took a few more steps, moving slowly, careful not to leave the track. Then she heard something rustling through the leaves at her side. It was barely perceptible. Instantly she aimed her gun and flicked off the safety. Whoever it was would be blown to the next world if they looked the least unfriendly. It stopped. She could feel her heart beating in her chest. She peered through the branches, wondering if she should walk toward or away from the rustling.

Curiosity won. She took about ten more steps down the track and stopped. Again she heard the sound. Then it stilled and she was left with only the birdcalls and the pounding of her heart. A donkey bird took up his eerie call. With great care she moved ahead, her gun still pointing in the direction of her stalker.

As she moved—he moved. Maybe it was a coincidence. She took a few more silent steps, and once again, whatever was shadowing her stopped when she stopped, moved when she moved. It had to be human because an animal could not be so synchronous. Sweat ran down her sides, back, and arms as the thought of Gaudet stole into her mind. She fought to control herself, remembering the native girls. Stories of his slow and calculated tortures began to soften her mind and made concentration difficult. The unbelievable cold of the persona came back to her now as if breathing in her face. Her knees began to shake and she bent over, knowing that she was losing control.

Then, letting Sam's reassurances echo through her mind, imagining Sam's voice instead of Gaudet's, she forced herself to stand straight and pointed the gun, thinking that she'd shoot the moment she saw him. But the lack of further sound unnerved her, and she ran back the way she'd come, moving hundreds of yards before realizing that the trail had disappeared again.

Her chest was heaving and her breathing was loud. She listened.

Branches were being pushed aside, still on the same side of the track. She ran again, heedless of direction or paths, praying she'd find Yodo before her stalker caught up.

She thought she saw the trail and she tried to maintain her speed, though the footing was slick with mud.

Then she stopped short and cursed herself. She remembered something Sam had told her long ago: fear was her biggest challenge, and it was defeating her. With absolute clarity she recalled that she must think of the forest as a home. Her home. The first thing to do was find a safe place. If cold weather was killing her, then it had to be safe from cold; if she was hunted, then she had to make herself safe from the hunter. Nearby she saw a walking palm. She went deep in the foliage and, with her back to the many branched trunk, she sat. She could see fairly well but could not easily be seen.

It felt safer. If Gaudet were following her, she would make him come and get her and make him pay with a bullet to the chest. Her breathing had slowed and her mind was beginning to work again.

Then she heard movement. This time she remained motionless and the noise stopped. She told herself again that no one could approach her without revealing themselves. Despite buzzing mosquitoes she kept her gun aimed and controlled her breathing. Off to her left she saw a scorpion, but fortunately it wasn't coming her way.

More movement. Someone was getting closer and they were straight ahead, right down the gun barrel. She let her finger clamp heavily on the trigger. She remembered the disemboweled native girl and Michael's story of his wife and the rape of Marita's sister. She had no doubt that she was about to kill. A terrible confidence grew inside her. Then she heard a faint movement behind her and her heart jumped in her throat. Slowly she turned her head, but she couldn't see more than a few feet.

Now the stalker in front of her was taking a step about every thirty seconds, but the sound was barely detectable. A leaf moved. She drew a bead about chest high. There was a white hand parting heavy vines and then it froze. Nothing moved. She considered shooting. The thick post sight on the front of the gun was wavering, even with the double-clench grip. Something bounced off her head. She jumped. Ahead of her Sam stepped out of the jungle.

She lowered the gun. "You scared the shit out of me," she cried out.

"I know. I'm sorry. I thought I was following Gaudet. Hey, don't worry. I think he's gone. You did the right thing. Stopping running was the right move."

Grady slumped, shaking and exhausted.

"You did good," Sam said. "And you didn't shoot me, which I also appreciated."

The rare praise restored her like a drug. She stood and threw her arms around Sam, holding him close, and he hugged back.

Baptiste crawled out of bed at the Hotel International. He was out of breath and covered with sweat, both his and hers, after what had been exhausting sex. Except for the guilt that had hung over the bed like a cloud, he supposed it might have been the best sex of his life. It was hard to remember that far back. Benoit Moreau was the most sexually sophisticated woman he had ever met. For years sex had lasted ten, maybe fifteen, minutes. This had lasted over an hour. And then she insisted that they do it again.

The day after their deal was struck, they had gone straight to the hotel from the prison with virtually no paperwork. He had gotten the admiral on the phone and promised that information on Chaperone was imminent. He stood on the threshold of the biggest scientific breakthrough of the twenty-first century and the future glory of France. How could the admiral say no? Baptiste thought he heard envy in the man's voice, and that made him feel better than he would have guessed. Plainly the old man wanted to find a way to substitute himself but could not.

Even though it was highly irregular, France was desperate, and if the woman wanted "tea" at the most famous hotel in Paris, then "tea" it would be—delivered by room service along with miscellaneous pastries.

When she went for her shower, he sat on the toilet in a reverie, letting his mind wander over the case and allowing it to play with his growing curiosity over what he was about to learn. Victory was at hand. Never in her earlier interviews had she explained anything about Chaperone.

She stepped out of the shower and began applying moisturizing lotion to her body in what looked to be a long and cherished ritual. He jumped under the shower for a quick one. After he was out, he found her in the bedroom.

"Can we go to the lab now?" he said, realizing immediately that there was a new deference to his tone.

"Of course." She was nude and beautiful, her black hair tousled but attractive, her face animated and her eyes flashing. Because she had never let her body go, and gave it many forms of exercise, her stomach had the flat look of youth and the definition of an athlete. Even in prison she trimmed her pubic hair, her arms had contour and definition, her butt was like two cantaloupes, and her breasts were a mouthful—but petite and shapely. He wondered if she really had had three orgasms or if it was all feigned. Never mind; he would get his information now.

"Tell me about Chaperone," he said as she pulled on her panties. Oddly, he thought to himself that he still had not had enough.

"You are sure you can get me a pardon?"

"I have discussed it with the admiral. He said yes." Baptiste felt guilty for lying about something so important to her, but what could he do? He had a job.

"I will tell you about Chaperone on the way to the laboratory. More important, I will tell you about a man named Georges Raval. Through Raval we can know the precise details of the science behind Chaperone. I believe that he is the only living scientist that understands the technology and can teach it. He is the primary inventor. And I will tell you about Gaudet's plot, or at least its name—'Cordyceps.' Right now I want to talk about my new routine. What time do I leave the prison each morning for work?"

While he answered a multitude of questions about shackles and security and where she could go and where she could not, Baptiste watched a fascinating reverse striptease and repressed a great deal of marital guilt.

Sam and Grady sat around the hospital bed. The yellowed paint on the walls was thin with tiny cracks that splintered and forked like the rivers that seemed to drain the soul of this place. The structure was dying along with many of the patients under the ruthless onslaught of humidity, heat, and the DNA of abundant life that seemed to eat without end. The linens in the place were gray like the muggy afternoon sky, the fan whirled cheerlessly, its blades matching the yellow of the walls as the plastic became brittle from ultraviolet. Age and decay were moving with remarkable speed—the downside of life in a paradise that otherwise was a symphony of rebirth.

Michael remained mildly drugged on small doses of morphine and Sam stared with some sense of horror at the bloody bandages, imagining the infection that was sure to come. He wondered whether the IV could pump antibiotics fast enough. Fortunately for Michael the bullets had found their way through meat rather than organs. With luck all his body parts would work as before—if he could survive potential infection. As they sat there, Michael shook himself fully awake and Sam could see the strength in his face and eyes. The guy was tough. As soon as they were able, they planned to move him to a large hospital in Rio.

"You're looking better," Sam said, putting a hand on his shoulder. "Much better. How do you feel?"

"Depressed, and like a caiman bit three times as he swallowed me. I was very fond of Marita, the girl, and I'm going to miss her. Did we get the bastard who shot her?

"I don't think so. There were a few guys in the jungle around there and we didn't get them all. We didn't get the leader yet."

Michael looked dejected.

"Well, you're alive and we're going to take good care of you. That's a promise."

"You never told me how you happened along," Michael said, amazingly coherent.

Michael knew Sam as "Robert Chase." Grady and Yodo had so far managed to keep the name straight when Michael was present, but Sam knew that soon he would have to lose a little of his anonymity where Michael was concerned.

"We were looking for you," Sam said. "We knew that Devan Gaudet was looking for you as well."

"What does he want with me?"

"We hoped you had some idea."

"My work, maybe."

"We think Gaudet wants information about something called Chaperone."

"Never heard of it."

"It's one part of an advanced technology that he stole."

"How does it work?"

"Well, the technology itself genetically alters targeted brain cells in a living human being. It works quickly, in a matter of minutes or hours."

"That's pretty hard to imagine. How did it come about?"

"A company called Grace Technologies took a herpes virus from a monkey, pulled off the outer protein layer, broke apart the DNA, and discarded the portion of the DNA that made it infectious. Then they spliced in their own engineered DNA. Specifically there were two strands, a promoter sequence and the coding sequence. The promoter sequence ensures that only the correct brain cell types are altered. The coding sequence does the actual alteration of the DNA in the brain cell. Then they gave this new string of DNA a protein coat." Sam stopped.

Michael seemed to be following him fine, narcotics or not. "How exactly does this technology alter brain cells?"

"It installs DNA that adds an extra receptor to the dendrite, thus making them hypersensitive."

"I would think it's complicated to alter brain cells to achieve a particular effect."

"They were looking for generalized emotional effects, like increases or decreases in anxiety or aggression."

"How do they suppress the immune response?" Michael wondered aloud.

"How did you think to ask that?"

"I am a biologist. If you are changing the DNA in a body cell, the immune system may reject that cell if it is producing proteins that are foreign. It may also reject the vector, just like it would a virus. Basic biology. And I might add that I think there is no known way around that. Only immunosuppressant drugs, and they don't do such a good job. I can't imagine the brain functioning well after such a transformation."

"You're right. It doesn't. Except in Grace's initial trials. They were using something called Chaperone, which we think alters the immune system. We believe that you have discovered organic material that Chaperone came from. Something you sent to Northern Lights Pharmaceuticals," Sam suggested.

Bowden only nodded.

"Whatever the case, you won't be safe unless Gaudet believes you're dead. It is extremely important that we convince him that you are. So we've put out a story."

"What do you mean?"

"An account of your death. Not in the States. Just locally in Peru and Brazil. We told your publisher confidentially that you are not dead, but that you needed to appear so for your protection. They told your agent. Their publicity people will refuse to confirm it at least for the moment."

"I don't want my readers to think I'm dead."

"You'd be a lot safer if they did," Sam explained.

"I'd rather take my chances. I don't understand why Gaudet would want me dead."

"He wouldn't until after he had tortured you and gotten the information he needs. So at least don't screw up the scuttlebutt in South America. It'll be much easier to keep you safe. With two bullets in you it's easy for Gaudet to believe you're a dead man. Let's not change that."

"From what you're saying, Gaudet would need my journals. They're gone. The Matses have taken them to my scientist friends in Pacaya-Samiria. I hope that by now they'll have shipped them to New York."

"That will piss him off, all right." Sam smiled at the good feeling it created. "We know about Professor Lyman at Cornell. One of my associates will be ensuring the journals get there safely."

"I'd rather pick up my journals personally. I doubt Richard would release them to anyone else anyway. It looks like I've got to go to the U.S. Who is going to believe I'm dead when I'm walking around New York?"

"Well, that's a point I wanted to make. You have to hide, not be public at all. Go out in a disguise."

"Hide? I would think you'd want him to chase me so you could get him yourself."

"Gaudet isn't the kind of person you bait. Not unless you're willing to run a terrible risk. I tried. My friend is dead," Sam answered.

"Well, I'm not cowering."

"I'm sure Grady would be happy to go to New York with you. . . . It isn't that you could never go out. . . . "

"I appreciate what you're suggesting, Mr. Chase, but I'll take whatever risk I have to."

Sam could tell Michael needed to rest. He nodded and led Grady into the hallway.

"He seems to like you, and he's a nice guy. . . . I was hoping you wouldn't mind staying with him and the men."

"And maybe convincing him to lie low?"

Sam nodded and dialed Jill on the sat phone to learn what Big Brain was uncovering.

"For reasons that are typically convoluted, after hacking into the Hertz car rental company in Sydney and a nearby hotel, we think we have a recent Gaudet alias—Jean Valjean—a character out of *Les Misérables*. The hotel that we hacked was his last watering hole before the Amazon. We also ran the parcel delivery database and looked at all the packages from that hotel."

"And?"

"Somebody sent an express package on that date from Gaudet's hotel to a woman in Manhattan by the name of Claudia Roche," Jill revealed.

"Who's she?"

"She's Georges Raval's aunt. He's now the highest name on our list of ex-Grace scientists that might be alive and not be working for Gaudet."

"Has somebody talked with this aunt?"

"Oh yeah. Our locals in Manhattan. Raval is supposedly in the U.S. and they're wondering if he's in Manhattan near his aunt."

"What do you suppose Gaudet sent to Raval's aunt?"

"When our locals paid their first visit, she didn't admit to receiving any package. But they won her confidence to some degree and finally she said she received a promotional cell phone from some company. It had five hundred free minutes—supposedly a trial gift," Jill outlined.

"Clever. No doubt it has a very extended memory for the call log. So Gaudet knows about Georges Raval and is looking for him just like we are."

"Sure looks that way."

"Had she used the cell?"

"Yes, but she gave it to us. We looked at the call log and found nothing that helps us find Raval. And the aunt is very tight-lipped. Claims she hasn't seen him in years. We think she's lying, but what can you do? We're watching her. We don't have a great ID on Georges Raval yet. He's blond, apparently," Jill offered.

"If he hasn't dyed his hair."

"But I saved the best until last."

"Okay. Shoot."

"Grogg's got to tell you this one himself. It was a masterpiece. Here." Jill signed off.

"Hey, Grogg, you're the man of the hour. What do you have now? Jill says it's hot," Sam teased.

"Remember 'popsicle boy'? Well, we got into his computer and found an IP that matched the old Grace Technologies mainframe. Then we used our favorite former disgruntled employee of Grace."

"Jason Wade?" Sam suggested.

"None other. And he knows that mainframe intimately. It disappeared when Gaudet gutted Grace. Now it's on a satellite link in some computer room somewhere on the planet. We can't figure out where, but with Jason's help we actually broke in and found an interesting file. It's called Cordyceps. Actually, two files. One just Cordyceps and one Cordyceps/ Windows SMB/CIFS. Without Jason's old password we could never have gotten in because it shuts you out if you make a handful of unsuccessful attempts. Somebody just forgot to delete that particular password. We tried to open them both and they both self-destructed. I think the SMB file is related to a computer worm. I'm betting someone's building a computer virus. SMB files have had weaknesses that have been exploited in the past by virus builders."

"But now it's gone?" Sam questioned.

"Actually, no. Just for the hell of it we went back there again and there was the file—restored. So it actually disappears for a time, probably into some disk memory, and then it is visible again. So we get another shot and we have an idea about how to get around the password from something that Jason Wade discovered a long time ago about how this security works. With a general password we can make the document stop disappearing into memory and maybe we can download it, even if we can't yet open it. We're working on that. Jason thinks that when we open it, we'll know a whole lot more. So we'll see. The files had a silent alarm, but we were able to neutralize it. Hopefully, they won't detect that we invaded," Grogg summarized.

"Cordyceps. Hmm."

"We looked it up in the encyclopedia. It's the name of a fungus," Grogg elaborated.

"Let me ask Bowden about it. He does fungus."

In a couple of minutes Sam was back in Michael's room.

"Do you know anything about Cordyceps—other than it's a fungus, according to the encyclopedia?"

"Actually, I do." Michael looked from Sam to Grady. "Why?"

"It may somehow relate to what Gaudet wants from you. We think that they have a plan called Cordyceps."

"Ah. Well, it's not just any fungus, cordyceps. It has a fascinating life cycle." Michael explained the gruesome manner in which the fungus killed bugs and propagated itself.

Sam marveled at the black metaphor. "No way."

"Afraid so. Cordyceps was also the origin of cyclosporine, a fairly effective first generation immunosuppressant. Interesting that they appear to be in need of an immunosuppressant and they call their plan Cordyceps. Chinese olympic runners attribute their success to a diet that includes cordyceps. Asians also used it to restore sex drive in elderly people, and recent clinical studies have backed that up. It's a fungus or a group of related fungi. Five of the top thirty drugs in use today came from fungi. So, yeah, cordyceps is impressive."

"You say they make immunosuppressants from it." Sam needed to hear more.

"Yes, but I have discovered several powerful immunosuppressant molecules. One I'm thinking of is from a rare freshwater sponge. There are very few freshwater sponges and this one is unique. But I know of nothing that would reprogram a human's immune system as you describe for Chaperone. I've never heard of anything that powerful."

"Assuming the name Cordyceps is a metaphor, I wonder who the beetle is?" Sam mused.

"Now that I think about it, Northern Lights did take a lot of those freshwater sponges. And they wanted more."

"Say nothing to anyone about that," Sam cautioned.

"I couldn't give them any more, though. I'd already taken as much as I dared. For a while. We need to let it reproduce. I'd found it in only one site. As I'm sure you know, the Amazon is about the size of the continental United States. There's bound to be more of it, but who knows where?

Remember too that this sponge grows underwater in a land full of rivers. It's blind luck to find it," Michael reasoned.

Sam smiled. "When it comes to security, I guess that's as good as it gets. But if I get your journals, do I get the GPS coordinates for everything you've found?"

"Yes, you do. But you would have to know which organic tissue contains the magic molecule or whatever you're looking for."

"Making you the key to his success again. Gaudet would do anything to boil the search down to one plant."

"If it were the sponge, it's actually an animal. Sponges are one of the oldest living animals dating back to the pre-Cambrian period. A colleague has called them biological Titans. They, or the microorganisms that inhabit them, have provided us some of the most important drugs ever discovered—anticancer drugs, antiviral drugs for AIDS, Herpes, and Shingles, anti-inflammatory drugs, and immunosuppressants. But I still don't see a connection to cordyceps any more than one of the thousands of other tissue samples I have provided them."

Sam saw that Grady actually had her hand on Michael's arm. Nice distraction from the pain of the wounds.

Leaving the two of them alone, Sam went back to the phones, deciding that he would update Jill before calling Figgy. He repeated the conversation about Cordyceps, sponges, and the rest; then he closed with the observation about the touchy-feely situation between Michael and Grady.

"This Cordyceps thing is spooky," Jill said.

"Yeah, we all wanna know who the beetle is."

After their normal perfunctory "see you later," Sam hung up. Next he made a quick call to Figgy.

"How are we doing on Moreau? I need to see her," Sam reminded his contact.

"A lot of red tape. I'm working on it."

"What's their problem?"

"I'll level with you. They're trying to talk with her and having their troubles. They don't want to be upstaged on one of their own kind by an American. But I'm working on it and you'll get there and I'll get you everything they get."

"Find out what the French know about Georges Raval."

"Will do," Figgy answered.

"I want to see the French list of all the former Grace scientists and compare it to mine."

"Maybe they'll want to look at yours and tell you if there is a difference."

"I'm not gonna deal with games like that. I can always tell the CIA to stuff it and drop France from the group. Tell them that."

"Come on, Sam. The French still have some clout with the CIA. You won't bluff them that easily."

"Get me the damn list."

Sam hung up, disgusted that he had to do this dance with the French. Only God knew what they were really up to.

Then he made arrangements to move Michael to a large hospital in Rio.

As he neared Michael's room, Sam couldn't help asking himself what it would be like if thousands of people suddenly acted like his neighbors, Matt and Frank. As he thought it, he answered it—and wondered just how much time he had.

Chapter 8

Men who piss into the wind wet their own feet.
                                                              —Tilok proverb

Grady was describing the differences between Michael Bowden and Sam to Jill when she heard a loud *boom* over the phone, followed immediately by the screeching of the alarm.

"Oh shit," Jill shouted, then began talking as if recording events. "We've been hit, probably by a small rocket. Probably didn't understand the layout of the building. Sounds like it went into the auto parts store. Just a minute." Jill had obviously covered the receiver. The muffled sounds continued for what seemed like an eternity; then Jill was on the line again. "They're telling me it damaged the back wall in the men's dorm room. Tons of dust in here already. The computer room seems safe. I hear someone screaming. God . . . Sam had a plan if this ever happened. Police will be coming. Oh God, Grady, I gotta go. Have Sam call me."

Grady tried to reassure herself that none of her friends were hurt. She ran to find Sam. At moments like this he became her mother, father, and whatever else mattered. Down the hall from Michael she found him at a nurse's station.

"Sam, they've shot a rocket at the office or blown it up or

something. I think everyone's okay. Jill says the computer is safe. But it hit the dorm, I think. . . . I . . ."

Sam put his arm around her and moved with her to a private room. He called Jill on his sat phone. Grady put her ear up to his and tried to make out what Jill was saying.

"It's bad. Wounded people all over the store. Customers. I'm having them tarp the hole in the back wall as fast as they can. Big Brain is sealed and the dust hasn't gotten to it. The temperature control still works. Grogg's not letting anyone in or out of the computer room."

"Okay. Go to the safe and open it. Go to the lockbox marked Emergency. Punch in my birthday and your birthday followed by 533561298. Then follow the instructions exactly. It will tell you everything to do. You will be in the new office and running by tomorrow or the day after. All the security will be in place seventy-two hours after that. I'm coming right away."

"We think we got the people who did it. We noticed a van just driving around. I called the local police and some of your retired friends. They followed the van, put it together. The van was actually a getaway vehicle. There were two guys with a rocket launcher in a third-story window of the Grey Building. One of the offices was empty. Our guys were just a little late and watched the rocket exit the window. When the suspects came out, there was a shoot-out. The van driver and the two rocket boys are dead. They must have been shot ten times each. None of our guys were hurt."

"I'm sure it's Gaudet. The question's whether it's a diversion," Sam said. "Could mean he's setting up to grab Bowden down here. I don't know. But if he wanted my attention, he certainly got it. First thing to do is move Bowden to Rio."

While they moved Michael, Sam was constantly on the phone for updates from the office. The van was stolen and had stolen plates. There was no way to trace the men or even to determine their nationality. They were Caucasian and their photos and prints matched no record of the FBI, Interpol, or Scotland Yard.

Using a private jet, Sam moved Michael Bowden to Santa Maria Hospital, a large private hospital associated with the Universidade do Estado do Rio de Janeiro, a teaching hospital and medical school. Expertise here would be better and medical supplies more plentiful. They had run out of the antibiotic vancomycin in Tabatinga; before leaving, Michael had insisted that the doctor pack his wounds with honey, explaining that it was the first-known antibiotic and a decent substitute for modern medicine.

Sam and Grady raised their eyebrows at the idea of honey-packed wounds, but the doctor went along with the plan, saying that honey killed bacteria by sucking the moisture from the cells. Although it was unorthodox, it worked to slow infection.

The move between hospitals was accomplished so efficiently that in a matter of hours Michael lay in surgery at Santa Maria, where the wounds were debrided and the physicians removed bone chips created by the passage of the bullet through his leg. The prognosis was for a quick recovery and little, if any, permanent damage.

After surgery the staff took Michael to a private room in a corner, where he could be watched by Sam's half-dozen security people on duty at any given time. Sam and Grady sat by his bed at about the time they thought he would awaken.

After a few false starts at consciousness, Michael came to.

"I need to go back to the States," Sam told him.

"I'll be staying with you and the security team," Grady added.

Before Michael could respond, Sam continued. "Someone attacked my offices in Los Angeles, and I'm sure Gaudet was behind it. I'm worried about leaving you because there's a chance Gaudet knows you're here. I'm going to be hunting him, and soon we'll move you to a safer place. Meanwhile, you're in good hands with Yodo."

Michael didn't seem to have the strength or will to respond. He simply nodded; then, within minutes, he nodded off.

Sam was gone three hours later.

Devan Gaudet sat in a Tabatinga café near the clinic. Across from him was a young English-speaking doctor by the name of Costa. The restaurant was constructed of plywood over studs and had watermarks on the walls and in the corners of the ceilings. The furnishings were vinyl and all the surfaces pastel Formica. It was nothing to brag about in the way of cleanliness, and Gaudet was anxious to complete his business and leave.

The young doctor flirted with the waitress and wolfed down Portuguese sweet bread and linguica sausage while Gaudet spoke to him.

"If you can help me, there will be money in it. A lot of money," Gaudet said.

"I didn't know journalists paid lots of money."

"Well, I'm a writer of feature articles—series pieces—and to get what I need, I spend my own money."

"And you just want me to find a doctor in Rio who can help get you an interview? I don't even know whether Bowden's gone to Santa Maria."

"Why would Dr. Torres be calling surgeons in Rio if Bowden wasn't going there?"

"Any number of reasons. Like asking about the efficacy of putting honey in the patient's wounds."

"I think he's going to Rio. Are you with me?"

Dr. Costa leaned his bearded face forward and held out his hand.

"I'm trusting that you are a legitimate reporter with *Le Monde,* out to write good things about Dr. Bowden."

"You can count on it."

Dr. Costa met Gaudet back at the café two hours later.

"I found someone, a Dr. Ayala. He is not from a wealthy family. Like all doctors in residency, he does not make much. I don't know him well, but I think he'll work with you."

Santa Maria was large and, at least outwardly, looked like any European or American teaching hospital. The young doctor Ayala located the famous Dr. Bowden in the surgical wing fairly easily, even though he was admitted under another name.

Gaudet met Ayala just down the street from the hospital in a coffee shop. For their purposes they agreed he would be Dr. Burré, a French trauma surgeon visiting relatives in Brazil. Ayala was a good-looking man, big, probably six feet three inches, with Anglo complexion and features. Gaudet discerned the doctor's interest in money almost immediately. He played that to the hilt, asking only for a brief interview with Bowden—alone—and a similar interview with Grady, the young woman, accompanying him.

Gaudet and Ayala each wore a white coat and entered Santa Maria Hospital at eight o'clock on a Tuesday evening. They waited in a radiology section of the hospital, which was quiet at that time of the day.

The doctor left Gaudet and went about his duties. Gaudet used the time well, exploring every portion of the radiology wing and the neighboring radioisotope studies lab. When Dr. Ayala returned at one in the morning, they entered the elevator and headed for the med surg wing. His room location was obvious: no other patient had a handful of *estrangeiros* led by a mountainous Japanese man outside the door.

Dr. Ayala had done substantial preparation with the nursing staff. According to the good doctor, the preparations had included certain intimacies in the broom closet with a fairly fat chief nurse, plus chocolates for the others. The staff was allowed in on the secret efforts of a famous French journalist and agreed to look the other way, if not to help.

Gaudet had one concern. He did not like the way Dr. Ayala stared at his face. No doubt to a trained eye, the beard could be seen as part of a very careful makeup job. Gaudet deliberately made himself up to look like a green-eyed Abraham Lincoln. He wasn't a replica, but the similarity would be apparent to a Lincoln aficionado. The gray-green of the eyes was created with contacts. As they walked down the hall through the glare of the bright lights, Gaudet told Ayala that he needed a moment of privacy so they could talk. The doctor showed him to an exam room.

"You are staring at my disguise. Do you think it is unsatisfactory?"

"I didn't know you had one. Why would a journalist wear a disguise?"

"Bowden is publicity-shy. He has tried to dodge me in the past, and if he recognizes me, he might not give me the interview."

"I would have thought an author like him would welcome the publicity."

"Well, he will in the end enjoy the publicity for his books. But I believe that he's been having a romantic relationship with the young lady in his room. He worries that journalists will dwell on that aspect of his life. I come from France. I have no interest in writing about that sort of thing, but . . ." Gaudet shrugged at the silliness of the notion.

Unfortunately, Ayala appeared mildly skeptical.

"Listen," Gaudet continued. "I did not say this would be easy. If you make this happen, there is an extra U.S. three thousand dollars in it for you."

"In addition to the other?"

"In addition."

The doctor nodded. "But you are sure this will be good for Dr. Bowden?"

The young man's innocence was amusing. He was struggling hard to justify his role despite the payoff.

"Publicity never hurts an author. Your job is to get me alone with them without any guards present. With the guards my chances of getting a good interview are much less."

They exited the elevators on med surg and immediately ducked into a shower room. Nobody would be taking showers in the middle of the night. The hallways were gleaming and bright even with the lights slightly dim. They peered out through a small window in the door and watched in the direction of room 317, where the *estrangeiros* remained congregated. Gaudet slowed his breathing and closed his eyes. Getting into the room without the guards might not be so easy after all.

Sam was in heavy traffic in a Rio taxi on the way to the Rio airport to catch the 11:55 PM flight to LA. Always he had put a high premium on his instincts. No matter how he thought about it, he couldn't imagine that Gaudet had gone personally to LA to fire a rocket into his offices. Had he done so, the explosion would have been more accurate. What else could it be but a distraction? A distraction designed to move Sam out of South America.

"Take me back to the hospital," Sam said to the cabbie.

The driver looked back to indicate his puzzlement.

Sam made a circle with his finger and pointed back up the street, the way they had come.

"Ah. You . . . ahhh . . . leave . . . ahhh . . . forget . . . the suitcase?"

The driver made a couple of turns and headed back to the hospital. Sam began looking at his watch, knowing that in the traffic it could take an hour or more. Using the cell phone, he called Jill and explained his decision. She told him that they would be fine and that the move was already going smoothly.

Gaudet moved in beside the gurney, trying to determine what might go wrong with his plan. They passed through the throng of security people, the towering Japanese immediately behind Dr. Ayala, who pushed the gurney.

Grady walked on the far side of the gurney, holding Bowden's hand. They were going to the X-ray lab to perform some X-rays requested by the surgeon. It was a final check for any remaining bone fragments.

It was unlikely that Dr. Ayala, who wasn't assigned to the case, would be talking with the surgeon about Bowden's case, but no one questioned it. It was equally unusual that a first-year resident in internal medicine would be taking a patient to the X-ray lab. Normally, it would be done by an X-ray technician and the only doctor who might be present would be a radiologist and then only if it was a special study—in those circumstances the radiologist would wait in the radiology department. Dr. Ayala had told Gaudet all this, and even so, he risked it. So far, so good.

Ayala's face showed the stress he felt. He was probably wondering how he'd explain all of this if someone brought it up when the chief resident returned tomorrow.

Gaudet's greatest concern had been that Grady Wade would suspect him. So far, there had been no sign of any recognition whatsoever. Things were going remarkably well.

It was late evening in Rio. At such times people in a hospital naturally held their voices down and moved quietly. Almost all of the rooms were semidark or dark and they encountered only two nurses the entire length of the hallway. The hospital was designed with large wings and elevators in the center core. When they arrived at the elevators, Grady, the Japanese, two of the security men, and Dr. Ayala all got aboard. By his own observation it seemed to Gaudet that Grady and the big Japanese were by far the most observant. In the close quarters of a crowded elevator, they, if anyone, would discern that most of his face was a creation.

Grady held Michael's hand and watched his face in silence. When he looked back at her, it felt, as always, as if he were speaking to her, even though they said nothing.

The doctor from France, on the other hand, acted strangely. Actually, it was how he looked. He appeared to wear makeup. Was this a French affectation? And why would two doctors take a man to be x-rayed? She glanced at Dr. Burré. He looked like a man who wanted to shrink. The younger doctor Ayala from the hospital didn't seem comfortable either. It almost seemed as if they had terrible news they were reluctant to divulge.

The dark of the hallway began to make her uneasy, and the farther they went, the more they were becoming isolated. They went through a section subject to remodeling and the ceiling was partially torn out, exposing conduit and wires. This ugly wound in the building reminded her of a war zone.

She looked back at Yodo. He seemed watchful, as always. Their eyes met; now he knew that she was afraid. The gurney rolled silently over the vinyl tile and eight pairs of feet made a quiet patter as they walked. Normally, in a large group in a hospital one would feel completely safe, but Grady did not and she didn't know why.

"How much farther?" Yodo said.

"Almost there," Dr. Ayala replied.

The lights were inadequate here. It was dark enough that Grady could no longer tell the color of the paint on the walls.

They turned a sharp left, then went right through two large double doors and into a waiting area that was obviously closed for the evening. They proceeded through another large single door and into the back and then into a central working area with X-ray viewing screens all around.

"We'll need you all to wait out here," Doctor Ayala said.

"I'm going with him," said Grady, "and so is Yodo."

"There is radiation in the room when we take a picture. Normally, you would be in the waiting room and not here. We have brought you as far as we can."

"Perhaps the young woman could come as the patient's representative," Dr. Burré said.

"There is a shield," Yodo spoke up. "In the wall. I have seen them. You stand behind it. So will we."

"I also wear a lead apron. And the rules don't allow for people in the X-ray area. But you can be right here and we will be right through that door."

"It'll be fine," Michael said. "Like the doctor said, Grady can come."

Yodo obviously didn't like it but acquiesced at least for the moment. Grady and Michael passed through the door and into a large room with odd-looking machines. Dr. Ayala kept going.

"Where are we going now?" Grady asked.

"Into another X-ray room with the correct equipment." Dr. Ayala flipped a light switch.

They went through a doorway and into a smaller X-ray room. It was very bare and seemed to have been built and furnished in an earlier era. In the middle stood a large metal bed with an X-ray unit overhead.

Dr. Burré closed the door and walked over to Dr. Ayala. As he did so, the young doctor's eyes seemed to freeze. He was trying to say something. His mouth seemed to be forming an O, as if to express surprise. Then he slumped forward. Dr. Burré was holding him up and then lowering him to the floor.

"What's wrong?"

Then Grady saw it. Protruding from the doctor's lab coat, just below his chest, was a bloody wooden handle and thick, deep red blood flowing onto the floor.

In horror Grady saw the gun aimed at her belly. In that moment she knew who he was.

"*Dios mio.*" Michael sighed. He understood it as well.

"Please go through that door." Gaudet directed Grady to get behind the gurney. Tentatively she pushed it; it rolled easily. "This is going to be a mess here."

Gaudet had the gun to her back and there was nothing she could do. "Don't say a word. You understand?"

They rolled into another room that opened into a back area filled with strange-looking machines. Grady's mind flashed around the place, looking . . . thinking . . . how to escape. Having Michael on the gurney was like having her in shackles. Doorways, a hall, a gun at her back. *Think, think!*

They proceeded out of the next room and into a hall, apparently having circumvented the main workroom where the others waited. There were several doors off this hall, but only one was labeled. It was in Portuguese and Grady couldn't understand its meaning. Grady guessed it was another lab, or perhaps a back door.

"In there," Gaudet said.

Inside were three treadmills and IV stands alongside each. It was some kind of physical-fitness testing area.

"Put your hands behind you," Gaudet said.

Instead, she looked around desperately, trying to imagine some way of escape, some salvation. Anything. But there was nothing.

"If you don't do it, I'll cut your face." A metallic sound, and she saw his razor-sharp knife.

She put her hands behind her and felt the cool steel close over her wrists. She felt herself starting to cry but stopped the tears knowing it would only incite Gaudet.

"See there, Michael? She's already imagining what I'll do to her and I haven't even told her yet. See the fear in her face? You could save her from great suffering."

"What do you want?"

Gaudet took a cord from his pocket. One end was tied with a hangman's noose.

"I carried this just for you. All that time we were walking from the room to the elevator and then from the elevator to here, I was playing with it in my pocket, waiting for the moment when I would slip it around your neck. Back up," he said to her. There was a wall and there were hooks on the wall for lab coats. He put the noose around her neck and drew it taut until it bit into her neck, constricting her airway. Next he was tying something and then he lifted her and it choked her again. Her eyes felt as if they were filling with blood. She fell back. Again he tied the line and lifted her. This time it remained taut.

"Stand on your toes." Pushing herself up, she could just breathe. Sharp pains cut through her feet as she struggled to keep the noose from tightening further. She had to remain on the balls of her feet or suffocate.

"Don't hurt her," Michael said. "Tell me what you want. Be rational."

Gaudet spoke quickly and without emotion. "You discovered some organic material and sent it to Northern Lights. They in turn sold it to Grace Technologies. It had a profound effect on the human immune system. You understand what I'm saying, don't you?"

"I've heard about this substance, yes. And I believe it came from my work in the Amazon. But I collect thousands of samples each year. I have no idea which one worked in this way."

"Come, Dr. Bowden. You can do better than that." The knife tip bit into Grady's cheek. Blood trickled down to her neck.

"Depraved bastard," she said, through clenched teeth. "Don't tell him."

"Stop!" Bowden shouted. "Northern Lights showed special interest in a freshwater sponge. Maybe that's what you need. I first located it in 1998."

Gaudet seemed not to hear him. "You've heard how rape terrifies women, haven't you? It's nothing, *nothing,* compared to what a woman feels when you start cutting her face."

"I just told you what I know."

"Keep telling."

"I found it in a deep water stream in the Yavarí Reserve. Six days' fast walk from a point about thirty miles above Angamos. The coordinates are in my 1998 journal."

"Where is the journal?"

"On its way to Cornell University."

"You understand how that doesn't help me, don't you?" The steel was back at Grady's face, the point working its way into her flesh.

"Tell him something." Michael plead with Grady.

"Raval," Grady choked out. "A man named Raval."

"What about Raval?"

"A Grace scientist. He may know how the m-molecule w-works," Grady sputtered.

"What molecule?" Gaudet demanded.

She quit talking.

"Tell him," Michael said again.

"It's Chaperone."

"Do you know about Chaperone?" Gaudet asked Michael.

"I heard about it from Grady's associate. Robert Chase."

"Oh, is that what he calls himself now? Well, Chaperone is merely a word. Make it more than a word."

"I would if I could. I don't understand it," Michael confessed.

"Mmm-hmm. Do you want me to cut her face or her body first? Which will it be?"

"We're telling you everything we know."

Gaudet ripped the buttons down Grady's blouse and the yanking motion choked her. Grady lost her footing and struggled. The ceiling was starting to move. As the rope bit into her neck, she began gagging and couldn't stop. It felt as if her eyes were going to explode.

"Well, look at that, she's going to die."

His words were echoing now and she knew he was right. Her feet wouldn't support her and her legs were giving way. She felt her bladder go and the urine running down her legs. Then her body was hanging. It felt separate from the rest of her, quivering as Gaudet's hands touched her and his voice moved in circles like the ceiling.

"She pissed herself." She realized that Gaudet was propping her feet under her. In a few moments her legs supported her, but she was still on her toes.

"This can be terrifying as well," Gaudet was saying. "Hitler slowly hanged his errant generals repeatedly with piano wire. Doesn't your girl deserve better?"

Ignoring the pain in his leg, Michael rolled off the gurney and lunged at Gaudet. The look on Gaudet's face was gratifying, but a terrible thought entered Michael's mind. If he took down Gaudet, Grady would hang unsupported and suffocate.

Gaudet smiled as if reading his mind. Then the door behind Michael burst open. Michael fell clumsily to the ground, white-hot pain shooting from his leg up his spine.

Robert Chase stood in the doorway.

Gaudet was backing away, his gun aimed at Grady, who was beginning to choke as the rope tightened. Robert moved swiftly to Grady to stop her strangling. Gaudet fired a single shot at Robert, then vanished out the door.

The bullet knocked Robert to the floor, and Grady began

to choke again. Miraculously, Robert jumped back up and untied Grady, who fell into his arms. Her voice was barely more than a rasp, but Michael thought he heard her moan, "Sam."

Yodo entered, then ran out in the direction of Sam's nod. Sam closed up Grady's shirt and held her in his arms, but she pulled away and knelt over Michael, her eyes drawn to his leg.

The leg hurt and blood was seeping through the bandages, but Grady had stopped crying, indeed she was smiling at him, and that was all that mattered to Bowden.

Sam forced his mind away from the pain in his chest where the steel breastplate had compressed the flak jacket under the force of the bullet. Even experienced killers like Gaudet in the heat of the moment, and desiring an easy target, often automatically shot for the center of the chest.

As much as he wanted to chase Gaudet, his rational mind told him to stay with the targets, Grady and Michael, or risk losing them forever.

He lifted Michael back onto the gurney, and Grady rolled it back down the hospital corridor. It was still quiet; one would never know that a half-dozen bodyguards were chasing a madman through the bowels of the hospital.

One of Sam's men from upstairs ran to Sam and stopped. "If you find him. Kill him," Sam commanded.

"Roger that." And the man was gone.

They took Michael to his room, where nurses swarmed him, checking the sutures even before the doctor arrived. Dr. Ayala's death had produced many somber faces. Soon the off-duty guards began congregating and Sam began with the new instructions. Grady showed no emotion whatsoever and Sam knew it was a tour de force of self-control that would end when the danger was past. When the last of the guards was in place and Yodo had returned from a fruitless search, Grady stepped out of the room. Sam followed and found her sobbing against a wall. Without waiting for good-byes Sam walked her to the elevators and out to the front of the hospital, where he hailed a cab and took her to her room at the Copacabana Palace. Safe at the hotel, she still had a bit of a strange look in her eyes and there was terrible bruising on her neck. When he nudged her to take a shower, and he tried to close the bathroom door, she started crying. When he opened it, she clung to him—and so he waited for what seemed a half hour, just holding her. This time when he closed the door, she took a shower. When she had donned new underwear and a T-shirt, he crawled, fully clothed, in bed with her. Wrapping his arms around her back, he held her tight and taught her to breathe in her nose and out her mouth—slow, regular deep breaths. Then he told her things that Grandfather had told him when he first knew him. He told them as Grandfather had told them to him as best he could remember them. Then Grady slept.

Baptiste walked through London's Heathrow Airport to the location where he was to meet René. It was like a rat maze and didn't have the open feel of the tall-ceilinged de Gaulle International Airport. The smells from the abundant restaurants, which according to Baptiste ranked among the worst in the world, forced him to breathe through his mouth.

He met René at the gate to the flight to Turkey.

"Are you getting anything out of Benoit?" René asked without preliminaries.

"She's cooperating. I think she's dribbling out the information. I'll see her again soon. Have you found Bowden's location? Confirmed that he survived?"

"Neither, though I can't imagine the shots killed him. I'll tell you, if Sam and his people spy as well as they fight, we'll never find Bowden now."

"Don't let the admiral hear you say that. I'll expect a report when I return from Turkey. Make sure you learn *something.*"

"Shall I use Meeks?" René asked.

"No. Stay away from Figgy."

"Why?"

"Because I don't trust him completely."

"But you're basing this Turkey trip on intel he gave you," René countered.

"Just do your job."

This was hardly a typical business trip to Turkey. It started with a flight from London to another international airport, followed by a ride in a government car down a highway, followed by a descent into the bowels of a government building in the desert that Baptiste hoped never to see again. When he arrived at the building, he encountered a gate in the midst of a Cyclone fence topped with razor wire. It wasn't as secure as a prison, but, then, when people were brought to this place, they were quickly reduced to physical wrecks and it didn't take much to hold them.

At the gate the guard spoke Turkish. Baptiste shrugged his shoulders, lapsing into English.

"I am a special contractor for the CIA."

"And I am Mickey Mouse." The man smirked. "How would I know this?"

"Because if I lied to your officer, you would make me drink camel piss and send me home a eunuch. That or kill me. Look, Figgy Meeks sent me."

"Why didn't you say so?"

Inside the building they stopped at a desk manned by a sergeant and two guards. The sergeant looked up with a steady, confident stare.

"What do you want?"

"Figgy Meeks, a CIA contractor, said you had a prisoner

that I could interview. This man allegedly knows about a plot against the United States."

"We don't allow foreigners here. There must be some mix-up."

"I'll need to speak to your superior officer, then," Baptiste bluffed.

The sergeant stared at him a moment, then went down the hall and turned into a room. In a moment an officer appeared. Baptiste couldn't tell his rank from his shirt.

"What do you want?"

Baptiste repeated himself.

"I was told you might come. I can brief you. Alfawd knows nothing of significance, as I'm sure you already know."

"I still need to talk with him."

"Please, you are not the CIA. You are the French. So go to hell."

Baptiste felt a wave of fear and anger. He pulled his gun and stuck it under the officer's nose.

The sergeant jumped up and pulled his gun at the same moment the two guards leveled their M-16s.

"I am from the *C,* fucking *I,* fucking *A.* I am on contract. Figgy Meeks, retired agent of the CIA, was told by the director of the CIA to send someone here. If you want to be responsible for a bloodbath, you go ahead. I am ready to die. Are you?"

The officer looked to his men, then back at Baptiste.

"Don't think of me as French," Baptiste said, his tone softening. "Think of me as American. I work with Figgy Meeks. Figgy works with a man named Sam. Do you understand?"

The officer's eyes shifted again. "I have not heard of any Sam."

"I don't believe that."

"I need to call my commander."

"There's the phone."

The officer stepped to the sergeant's desk. He spoke rapid Turkish for a moment, then waited. There was more talk. Then they waited a long time, the officer still on the phone.

"My colonel called the CIA. The CIA called this Figgy. Figgy says to prove you are Baptiste. Jean-Baptiste Sourriaux."

Baptiste was sweating now in earnest. It was fear sweat, not heat sweat. It had finally sunk in—what he was doing here. The Turks were merciless.

He handed his wallet to the officer.

"Still, I am not satisfied," the Turk said at last. "Tell me the number of your office, Mr. French SDECE man."

Baptiste gave it to him.

"Tell me your boss's name."

"Admiral Larive."

The Turk raised his eyebrows.

"The very one," Baptiste said, sweat trickling under his collar.

The Turk dialed.

"I want to speak with the admiral." He looked at Baptiste and seemed perplexed. "They say I need an appointment."

"You will not get through to him like this."

"Tell me, madame," the officer said. "You are familiar with Jean-Baptiste Sourriaux? Could you describe him for me?"

There was a pause while the Turk listened.

"I will hand the phone to him and maybe he can convince you. His manhood depends on it. So, if you don't want him back with no balls, you better figure out a way."

"What does she say?"

"They don't give descriptions of army officers."

Baptiste took the phone.

"Marie, this is Baptiste. You need to tell this man what I look like and what my wife looks like. He has a picture of my wife to compare."

"How do I know it is really you and not a ruse?"

"Ask me something."

"Who does the admiral want to screw?"

"The new office girl. The blonde with a flat stomach and no tits."

"Put him back on."

The Turk listened for two minutes, then hung up the phone and looked to Baptiste. Faster than Baptiste could register it, he'd slapped the gun out of his hand, and two of his men had grabbed him from behind. The officer's expression remained impassive.

"If you ever pull a gun on a Turk again, I'll have you flayed alive." He nodded at the men, who released Baptiste. He put Baptiste's gun in his desk, then sat in the sergeant's chair. "We have already broken Alfawd. It was not a pretty sight. You can ask him whatever you want and he will tell you. He will suck your dick or give you his daughter if you want."

Baptiste nodded.

"Now get out of my sight."

The soldiers escorted Baptiste down two flights of stairs and past agonized graffiti on bare concrete walls into the bone-dry, gritty hell of the lower level. It smelled of blood and excrement even before they reached the small, miserable cells. Alfawd was a spindly little man with his shirt off; he was covered in caked-on blood. Unfortunately for him, he had been convicted of corrupting Turkish officials in high places. Some of them would be tried and thrown in jail forever, while the luckier ones would skate. The Turks were angry at the instruments of their own corruption, and one of these instruments was chained naked to a chair and muttering about the afterlife.

In the presence of two Turkish "investigators" and an Arabic translator, Baptiste was allowed to ask anything he wanted. The electrodes were still connected to the man's burned testicles.

"You know a man who calls himself Gaudet, Girard, Jean Valjean, and a host of other names, and who probably has French citizenship under some other name, and who is rumored to live in Quatram, and who was rumored to have lived in French Polynesia? You know this man?" Baptiste spoke in French and the translator restated it in Arabic.

Then the translator came back with the answer: "I have met with others and a man like that. I don't know if it is the same man."

"He has some science that works magic on people's brains. You know about that?"

"I have heard."

"What did you hear?"

"Not much. That he has a clever plan called Cordyceps. I have told this all before. I don't know much."

One of the guards flipped a switch. The man bounced off the chair, arching his back and screaming in Turkish, saliva foaming at the mouth. He urinated a trickle onto the seat. As a conductor it exacerbated his misery until the guard stopped the flow of electricity.

Baptiste flinched but only slightly. Alfawd choked and moaned incoherently.

"You need to tell it again, but with more details. Last time you left things out," the Turkish interrogator said. "We will need to wait a couple minutes. He will be confused now and incoherent." They all sat as if they were waiting for a bus. For the Turk it was all in a day's work.

"Tell us now about Gaudet."

"This man you are calling Gaudet had a beard, wore a hat and sunglasses even though it was indoors. There was no way at all to tell what he looked like."

Alfawd stopped for the translator and then the translator

proceeded. "His body seemed normal, maybe five feet ten, but he was always sitting in my presence. He did not move. You could not tell his age, he was in the shadows, he spoke very quietly, and you had to strain to hear."

"What is Cordyceps?"

"Some sort of disease or fungus. It kills bugs by eating them inside out. It is what he is going to do to the United States."

"How?"

"I don't know. That was for later. But the stock markets of the world would collapse. Prices would drop. He could not kill the United States forever, but for a while they would be hurt. Crippled."

"How were you and Gaudet to make your money?"

"Precise details, I don't know, but we all know that you can make money if you can predict ahead of time what the world financial markets will do. The exact execution of it, we were not yet told."

"When is this to happen?"

"I don't know. We were to hear next week. I invested."

"How much?"

"Three million. The minimum. Others invested more."

"What exactly did you invest in?"

"It is like . . . what do the Americans call it . . . I cannot explain it. I am a little guy. I go with Habib and he understands. You put the money somehow in things that do good when America does like the beetle."

"Habib got you into this? You invest in what Habib invests in?"

"Yes. That is right."

"Who is Habib?"

The man rambled about a rich Saudi family that didn't interest Baptiste.

"Who else invested?"

"Other Saudis mostly, people with big money, one Lebanese man, a couple of Turkish men, and an American."

"American?"

"Yes. He was of Iranian descent but born in America with many connections in the Middle East. He seemed very involved and the plan had something to do with computers, and of that I am certain. And then it had to do with this brain science. This American had lost a lot of money in the stock market and was hungry to make it back."

"Why were you meeting? Why get everybody together?"

"Some of the others, the Saudis and the American, they knew more than I. They were not believing so much about the science. They wanted proof. And so Gaudet, Girard, whatever his name is . . . told them he'd give them proof. There was a man who worked for governments. He is like a man hunter, maybe a terrorist hunter, and some of these investors, they are afraid of him. So they say to use this science of the brain to kill him. And Gaudet tried this but did not succeed. So then he says he will use it on a company instead. A pharmacy company. Make the executives start killing each other. He promises this."

"Just to prove to these investors that the technology would work?"

"Yes. And I believe it will."

The questions continued for a half hour, but Baptiste learned nothing more of substance, just rumors of Gaudet's exploits, many of which he had already heard, none of which were confirmable, and none of which really mattered. Alfawd, as might be expected, knew nothing of the details of the brain science. Baptiste was about to leave when he thought of another question.

"Did they talk about any other investment opportunities?"

"No. But the American told me privately that there was."

"Why did he do that?"

"He needed loans and I was going to lend him some money. He was desperate to convince me, but still he would not tell me details."

"What about these other investment opportunities?"

"He said it was in medicine. He said Gaudet was trying to get hold of something that would be like making gold. It wasn't this brain technology, not exactly. Maybe related, though. It had a name. Chaperone. A very valuable item."

Barely able to contain his excitement, Baptiste questioned him further, but Alfawd revealed nothing more, even when electrocuted until his heart stopped.

Baptiste left in a hurry. No reason to test the hospitality of the Turks. The same words kept moving through his mind, unbidden: *Markets. Investment opportunities.* And last but not least: *Retirement.*

Baptiste walked from his office down Gambetta, turned up Rue de Tourelles, until he was satisfied that he had no obvious tail; then he hopped a cab to the Saint Jean-Baptiste de Belleville Cathedral, where he took a stroll through the main sanctuary and then various hallways, then out a side door to a nearby restaurant. He made his way inside the eating establishment to a familiar public phone with good privacy except for people passing to the rest room, and these did not remain long enough to overhear a conversation.

"Are the Americans getting any closer?" he asked Figgy without preliminaries.

"Of course. They have Bowden. What I don't know yet is whether Sam has gotten with him in narrowing down the various samples he sent to Northern Lights."

"Will Sam share this with you?"

"I think he will, and I don't think he'd lie to me. But I'm

pretty much at an impasse with Sam until he talks with Benoit Moreau. I told you this."

"That won't work. I want Chaperone in my hands before anyone talks with Benoit," Baptiste emphasized.

"What happened with Alfawd?"

"Nothing. He knew that Gaudet wanted Chaperone and that Gaudet figured he could make money with it."

"The Americans aren't going to trust me after this Alfawd business. Sam will be furious," Figgy speculated.

"Make it sound like an innocent mistake. We were closer to Turkey, so you decided to send us. He was in South America."

"Don't be ridiculous. He'll know I was pandering to you and screwing him. It's not complicated."

"You've known him a long time. He may forgive you."

"Back to the money. How much will Chaperone be worth?"

"I have no idea. A lot. I can envision a heated negotiation between our buyer and the French government. France has the better legal claim, but they will negotiate a cheaper license if someone else has it as well. We sell to the high bidder in any case, but on a completely confidential basis," Baptiste theorized.

"Nice words. I hope it works."

"It will work. And you will get a handsome fee even if all we do is succeed in delivering Chaperone to France. I need your reaffirmation that you are committed to this," Baptiste prodded.

"Oh bullshit. Once I say I'm in, I'm in. You don't need me to repeat on a weekly basis that I'm going to screw one of my oldest friends."

"Just be sure you're the first one to get to Bowden's journals. Update me daily. In text. You understand?"

"Type. Type. Type. What a drag," Figgy complained.

* * *

Sam flew home while Michael continued to recuperate in an anonymous safe house in Rio with Yodo, Grady, a team of security men, and a sizable contingent of local police, whose job was to hunt Gaudet if and when he came back after Bowden. They went over the security rules and reaffirmed that Bowden would not be without his security for any reason. It seemed to Sam that Gaudet was like a building wave, every day his strength grew and every day he became more deadly. More to the point, he sensed a certain measure of desperation in Gaudet's acts, an aspect of the man that was utterly familiar and more than a little problematic.

The plan was for Sam to go to LA first, then meet Grady and Bowden in New York City. Sam's LA offices were the best place on the globe for him to direct the hunt for Gaudet. Still, for a few moments he tried to forget about Gaudet—his obsession—and let his mind rest. He drove down the freeway in the dead of night, feeling the Blue Hades, his Corvette, and its power, the way it rolled over the pavement, the suspension stiff, the turning responsive, the torque awe-inspiring—flawless—everything fine-tuned. He wondered if Grandfather had ever felt the poetry in anything mechanical. Probably not. An absurd thought, really. A few moments in a sliding turn at the racetrack could never touch his soul the way sitting with Grandfather at Universe Rock had. And yet the sliding turns were good.

He approached the massive outside door of his new LA offices buried in a gated building complex that was largely an office building and data center. Sam put his face up to a camera, aligning his brow with a molded piece of plastic. A computer identified his retina while a plastic pad transmitted his fingerprints to a different portion of Big Brain's memory. Within a split second Big Brain matched the finger to the eye and let him in. Inside, it was very close to the old office in layout, except slightly more spacious.

Harry was all over the place, dissipating his considerable excitement by sprinting around the office and culminating in a flying leap into Sam's arms. He tried to lick Sam's face, but for most of the strokes Sam held him just out of reach.

Jill started right in. "Important news, in case you haven't heard. A massive, fatal shooting incident at the offices of Northern Lights Pharmaceuticals. Two employees went berserk and started killing colleagues. No official explanation for the violent behavior, but it sounds like the soldier vector all over again. One of the shooters died from extensive seizure activity."

"That confirms it, then," said Sam.

"Just before the guy died, the medics got a brilliant idea and gave him a powerful immunosuppressant. It slowed the seizure activity and they figured that if they had administered it sooner, it might have staved off an immune reaction. A carbon copy of the incident with your neighbors."

Sam saw a certain tension in Jill's body.

"What is it?"

"It doesn't matter."

"It does to me."

"It's nothing anyone can help. Gaudet knew where our old office was and now he may discover this office. He just about killed Grady even though she was surrounded by our security. That's new for us as far as I know. And these vectors are so insidious. They rob you of your mind and all you have to do is breathe them and they're irreversible. It's ugly."

"It is ugly. That's why we have to catch him."

"I don't know why the government isn't doing more."

"Don't sell 'em short. Hiring us is something. They've got stuff all over the world and they're working on this. They just aren't telling us. Michael agreed to make himself our bait in New York. And guess what? We're probably the government's bait."

"Don't tell me that. Should we tell the Feds?"

"Oh, we'll tell them, but it won't help. Saying we think he'll do something is like saying we think Islamic extremists will blow things up. They know that. They just don't know what the hell to do about it, and they're not going to talk about it officially. *I'm* afraid to turn on the TV news."

"We found a computer worm expert," Jill said.

"And?"

"You should hear it directly. He's under contract with the government to come up with worst-case scenarios."

"Let's get Grogg in here."

Grogg came in, sighing under the weight of his considerable bulk. Sam had offered numerous times to hire the plump and balding man a personal trainer, but his Buddha belly kept growing and the muscle mass kept shrinking. Grogg wore glasses like Coke bottle glass but wouldn't consider sight-correcting surgery or contacts. Claimed it might ruin the image. Despite Grogg's quirks, Sam was fond of him.

"How goes our computer worm research?"

"It goes in galloping gigabytes."

Jill got Jacob Rand on the speakerphone. His company was called IT Defense.

"For purposes of our analysis," Jacob began, "we've assumed someone with a lot of money and a workforce of, say, twenty experienced programmers. They'd have to know security. There would be other personnel, network engineers, and the like. We are assuming a lot of money, resources. The attack we envision would require a powerful computer worm that would confine itself largely to U.S. computers and would corrupt data, and in many cases effectively destroy hardware. They would choose a widely used software application. As an example they could use Windows SMB file sharing—"

"You mean like Windows SMB/CIFS," Sam interrupted.

"Exactly. This service is on by default on many corporate installations and a lot of private ones as well. We figure they will discover a previously unknown vulnerability in this or some other common program, a weakness that has never been exploited. They are there and when they find it—bingo! At first we won't know what the hell is happening, because we won't have seen the computers go flat on their ass in precisely this manner.

"The way into a system will be via mail worm mode or an infected Web server mode that can infect a browser. The Nimbda virus demonstrated the effectiveness of a mail invasion for crossing firewalls. It didn't go into a guy's computer and use the address book application indiscriminately. It only replied to incoming mail. It was slow and insidious. A good worm would not waste time mailing to Hotmail accounts and the like, but instead would limit itself to only certain addresses—the ones that inflict the most damage. For example, if it invades a corporation's computer system, it would not send out e-mails to other computers within that system. That way you won't have twenty people all comparing notes and realizing that they all have the same peculiar e-mail in their in box. The virus only needs to get into one corporate computer to infect the entire corporate intranet. Once in, it just goes from one computer to the next, munching the data on the hard drives and/or frying the drives themselves. It would be careful to filter out IP addresses that weren't associated with the U.S. That way the bastards could work from a foreign country with impunity and unharmed.

"We figure in the U.S. there are eighty-five million computers in businesses and about that many in homes. Using these techniques with the right research, we guess they could get as many as fifty million computers. It would do at least one hundred billion dollars in damage and send the stock market plummeting."

Jacob went on to describe how the virus would systematically destroy a computer system, step by step, and the techniques it would employ. Sam got the idea quickly and, in fact, had imagined such things himself, just never with Jacob's morbid precision.

"So the upshot," Jacob concluded, "is that a good virus would in the end go through a comprehensive erase routine while it was showing the operator a virus protection screen that indicated an ongoing virus scrub—you feel good while they sodomize your computer. In about a third of the machines we examined, the motherboard would also become inoperable."

"So, they really could kill hardware that would take days or weeks to replace?"

"Afraid so."

In the end, though, Sam suspected that it was really the killing of people that Gaudet intended. The computers would be a means to that end.

He took a minute to call Jill's boy, Chet, to talk about fishing, the girl next door, the next big asteroid to pass Earth, the latest German gun, and what they might do next summer on the camping trip. It was good to think about everybody being around next summer.

Chapter 9

A maiden brings more dreams than a night in the sweat lodge.

—Tilok proverb

"I like to work alone," Gaudet said.

"We just burned down Northern Lights," Trotsky said in a rare display of impertinence. "These people aren't dummies. Stealth and brains won't be enough."

"I don't disagree. We will need more bodies. We need Raval almost as much as we need Bowden and the journals. And I'd really like to get Sam out of the game, for once and for all. If I find Bowden, I may find Sam and end that part of the matter. Raval, who knows? The aunt's gotten us nowhere. I suppose the journals are priority one. I watched Bowden's face when I had the girl. He'd trade that journal for the girl. And I'd bet the stuff about the sponge is true. But where are the journals? Cornell University? Maybe. That's the question."

Trotsky nodded and sat back.

They were in the Waldorf-Astoria. Gaudet liked traditional places such as this. All the furnishings were quality, even if older, and in the restaurants downstairs the service was ridiculously attentive. It seemed there were as many waiters as patrons. He and Trotsky dressed as a couple of ugly old women when they went to the restaurants. Normally, they used room service and only Trotsky had to play the part.

"If we are correct and Bowden will come to New York, how many associates could we use here?"

"We can't use the men involved in Cordyceps. Can we?"

"No. We can't compromise that."

"I'll make the calls."

"You have almost no accent. I need for you to do something else as well."

Although Gaudet had spent almost all his life as a contract killer, he had taken care to acquire or steal legitimate business interests and now had a small empire. Trotsky and a man who worked for Trotsky did all the day-to-day management.

Gaudet had been listening in when Trotsky, claiming to be a journalist, phoned the assistant to Bowden's editor at his publishing house. Before the call Gaudet had done his homework and had found out that a writer—usually—would know his editor better than anyone else at the publishing company. If it was a senior editor, such as Rebecca Toussant, then she would have an assistant. These helpers often knew more than they were supposed to tell. In this case the young woman, Sherry Montgomery, had stuck to the script but sounded nervous at the name Michael Bowden. The denial that she knew anything of Michael Bowden's whereabouts was casual and studied, so there was no way to be certain that they were expecting a visit from Bowden. But in Gaudet's mind it was a reasonable bet. He had heard something in that young woman's voice, and when he played the tapes, he heard it again.

Gaudet then contacted a literary agent and explained that he was a French journalist researching the American publishing scene. After a half hour or so of interviewing the agent, Gaudet learned that if a big author like Bowden came to New York, there might be a book signing at the downtown Barnes

& Noble. Such arrangements were normally made months in advance but could be made on much shorter notice if the number of books that could be sold were significant.

Trotsky called the community events person at the midtown Manhattan Barnes & Noble and advised them that he had it on good authority that Michael Bowden was coming to New York and might do a signing. The lady reported that she knew nothing of any such signing but would check with the publisher. Trotsky explained that he would call back if they would be so kind as to check out the rumored signing. Next Gaudet had Trotsky make a similar call to a *New York Times* reporter at the arts desk, who also promised to check out the story.

The next day Trotsky called Rebecca Toussant's assistant.

"We understand that Bowden's signing is on the twenty-second."

"I don't know anything about a signing. People keep talking about it . . . but I don't know . . . but he won't be here until . . . Well, if he were to come . . . Actually, I really don't know anything about Mr. Bowden's schedule. We haven't heard from him in weeks."

"Well, I appreciate that. He *is* from the Amazon."

"He certainly is."

"Well, thanks anyway and good day."

Trotsky had done well. Clearly, Bowden was due in New York and the girl even knew when. That meant Sam would be around. And Gaudet would be waiting.

Sam walked through La Guardia International Airport on his way to the taxi, having flown in from LA. Using his cell phone he called Jill.

"We have a new problem," she started right out. "The CIA wants, and I quote, 'to know why the hell you sent the SDECE to investigate a report of a plot on the U.S.' "

"What are you talking about?"

"Apparently, the Turks have a guy who thought he had seen Gaudet. According to the CIA, the reports from Turkey indicated that the informant really didn't know much. Also they suspected he had been severely tortured and under those circumstances they were just as happy to have us do the initial interview. If it turned out there was something there, they could come along after the guy was cleaned up. I guess the Turks plugged his testicles into a wall socket, among other tricks. Figuring that since we were working Gaudet, and with the low priority and the torture and whatnot, it would be fine if we went. Only we didn't go and somehow the French did. There were pissed-off phone calls between the Turks and the CIA and Figgy Meeks right in the middle of it. The Feds are a little reluctant to criticize Figgy, since he was one of their own and they sent him to us. So they've decided they're pissed at us."

"Get me Figgy," Sam said, doing a slow burn.

"I thought of that. He's waiting for our call. He's at the French place in the UN."

After a few rings Figgy picked up. "Figgy, this is Sam," Jill said.

"Figgy, what are you doing to me?"

"Well, I made a tactical error. The French were right near Turkey and, well, I figured—"

"I don't believe this. You took a call at my office from the CIA?"

"Well, yeah. I was in the office and Jill was taking a snooze, and, hell, I was one of them."

"That's the last call you're taking. You called your French buddies and sent them and then you gave them the imprimatur of the CIA. I can't believe this. I'm speechless."

"I won't make that mistake again. It just seemed efficient. They said he knew very little. It isn't like it was a big-deal interview. And if it was, Alfawd is dead."

"Figgy, you haven't behaved like a friend."

"What's that mean?"

"It means I can't trust you." Sam hung up, fuming, wondering if he could kick the French out of the group; then he realized he couldn't. Figgy would eventually sell his "tactical error" line to the CIA, and the Feds still had some irrational favor they felt they owed the French, or they were trying to buy something, or ... damn ... what a mess. Climbing into the taxi, he got Jill back on the line.

"Don't let my great friend and mentor, Figgy Meeks, back in without an escort. He does no work in our office. Take him off anything to do with the journals and make sure Professor Lyman knows that Figgy has nothing to do with Bowden's journals. Let him stay at the French digs. And get a report of what the French found. It'll be a false piece of crap. Arrange for one of our people, Jim maybe, to try to see the guy, Alfawd, assuming the Turks will talk to us. Figgy claims he's dead but let's make sure."

"Right.

Sam sighed.

"Sam, I'm sorry. I mean about your friendship with Figgy."

"I know."

He hung up and mentally worked his way through his schedule. The plan was that he and Anna would meet Grady and Michael and then take Anna's charter jet directly from Republic Airport on Long Island to her ranch. He was having misgivings about leaving headstrong Michael and Grady in New York.

Sam first saw Anna standing on the tarmac with a strand of her hair blowing gently in the breeze. But for the errant strands her hair was pulled back tight into a ponytail, her face bright with excitement. The radiance was natural to her, nothing she consciously arranged, and it was the spontaneity of it that made her so attractive. He loved it when she dressed plainly, without baubles and makeup and all the trappings, and it was this way that she too preferred to dress. But he didn't enjoy her for long, his gaze wandering over the landscape looking for killers even as they made lovers small talk. If it wasn't killers, it was paparazzi. And if it wasn't them, he had to worry about the pilots and about Michael and what they might suspect or observe regarding his relationship with Anna. If the press learned about him and Anna, life as he knew it was over. Everything about Sam depended on anonymity.

For some reason private jets made him feel uncomfortable of late. Especially when Anna brought them. Since he wasn't going anywhere, there was no sense thinking about it, so he shook it off.

"God, am I looking forward to kicking back with you," Anna said. Sam hadn't yet told Anna that he had decided minutes before that he didn't dare leave New York even for a weekend. He noticed Anna's pilots watching and the arrival of curious bystanders. Something about Anna's face or her body language was begging to be touched, maybe to have him put his arm around her or hold her hand, maybe a quick kiss.

"I think we should go riding tomorrow," she said. He knew she would love getting on Toby, her big chestnut gelding, and that made it all the harder to tell her that he couldn't leave.

"That would be so good," he said.

"I have some surprises for you when we get to the ranch."

"Well, I have some surprises for you. But before we discuss surprises, I was wondering if maybe we could spend the weekend in Manhattan and see each other in the evening."

"Manhattan? But we talked about the ranch ... the horses ... sitting by the fire. . . ."

"I know. And I really wanted to."

He let her work her way through the disappointment.

"I bought a book to read to you, it is a book of Native

American lore on the subject of love, and if that fails us, due to cultural disconnect, I have some selected Shakespeare's sonnets, and a bottle of Turley zinfandel. I'm going to give you a back rub to your favorite music." Sam offered this in a low voice, which was nearly a whisper, because other travelers stood about twenty feet behind them. He knew he sounded uncomfortable about the Shakespeare.

Despite the audience he took her hand and gave her his best look.

"You are a thoughtful man and so prepared . . . bringing things to read. . . . The forethought . . . it's so charmingly old-fashioned. Manhattan will be great. And since when did you start reading Shakespeare?" He knew she was forcing herself not to complain that he would be working.

"I didn't. I thought I would try. You keep saying he's good with words. We can always switch to Nelson DeMille."

Anna laughed now and then looked at him. He couldn't quite read her feelings, but he knew they were good.

"You know that I would like to hold you."

"I know," she said, but there was the slightest hint of disappointment. No doubt she would trade one good public hug and kiss, a sort of public proclamation, for all of the poetry.

"You know reading poetry is not an Indian thing for a man to do to impress a woman."

"Let's pull your pants down and check to see if they're shrinking," she joked, then patted him on the back. "I'm sure your status as a strong and brave man is intact. A little poetry won't shrivel them. Since you Indians don't bring ponies anymore, I suppose the manly thing would be to take me for a ride in Blue Hades and show me sliding turns. I think I'll go for the poetry. So where in Manhattan do you have in mind? My place?"

"You know I like your place."

He began to walk toward a Lincoln model Town Car cab and nodded at the pilots, who already had the idea. They began unloading her luggage. As they walked, she said: "So who are you today? Maybe you could be Kalok Wintripp? Personally, I like that name. We could have a sort of coming out of the closet party for you and unveil your real name."

It was a mild rebuke.

"How about if I leak to *People* magazine that you're pregnant with frozen semen from the chairman of the Republican National Committee," Sam bantered.

"Now that we're on the subject, it's probably a good time to bring it up."

"What?"

"I'm pregnant by you, Sam."

Sam stopped and whirled her around, looking in her eyes, and what he saw sent him tumbling into a whole new world.

"It's a new life, Sam. A natural wonder." She searched his eyes. "I hope you can be proud of it."

Grady and Michael arrived from Rio with so much luggage they took a separate cab. Sam was grateful for the privacy.

With Sam, major life events were contemplated—until now. He sat in the cab close to Anna aware that he needed to think about Gaudet, and to calculate the danger to Michael Bowden. He needed to hunt Gaudet even as Gaudet hunted Michael. Just as important he had to find Raval.

And yet there was a new life growing in the woman beside him and it was half his. Anna's eyes had that slick shining look that artists and storytellers alike portray as love or adoration or both. It was as if she were making her case for the baby, speaking without words even more effectively than Cat-man. Sam wanted a trip to Universe Rock; he wanted to speak with his dead grandfather; he definitely wanted to talk about birth control and the no-bullshit pact that he thought they shared. In the instant she'd told him she was pregnant, he had felt ripped apart, even betrayed. The whole thing was a whirlwind of complications. The child would need a father, not a ghost, and right now Sam was a ghost.

Grandfather. His mind went to Grandfather. He sensed he could be on the verge of a huge mistake.

Calmly, even warmly, she watched him and he could feel the question.

He forced himself not to mention that she supposedly took birth control pills. "I'm not sure how we are going to do this."

"The baby is coming. We'll figure it out." She settled back and closed her eyes. Then she stirred herself as if she had made a decision. "There is something you should know. I'm sure the child was conceived two months ago at the ranch. You said it was okay that I had forgotten my pills in LA, remember? You may recall that I missed two."

"At the ranch? I said it was okay?"

"Well," she whispered despite the glass partition, "I was still half asleep and you were playing in bed and driving me nuts with the foam as I recall, the mustache . . . ?"

"I know. I told myself that foam and sponges are pretty effective."

"We got the five percent. Can you think of it as a wonderful accident?"

At once Sam remembered a day with Grandfather. Sam was twenty-three, and it was the fall of 1985, the year before he graduated from MIT. He had taken a little time toward the end of September to work on his thesis and he went to his cousin Kier's cabin in northern California. Kier was a rural veterinarian who sometimes lived wild, off the power grid, nothing but a diesel generator and a dirt road for coming and going. It was in the Wintoon River Valley over Elkhorn Pass by road and between the Marble Mountains and the Trinity Alps, or maybe in each, depending on who you talked to, though most thought it rightly belonged as part of the

Marble Mountains. It was in the Salmon River country and all ran into the Klamath river system above the redwood belt, back in the mixed conifer zone. Although the cabin was marvelously crafted and an exhibition of one man's love of wood, there wasn't much there, other than one's thoughts, to keep you company.

Sam's grandfather had shown up—come down out of the mountains from the caves. Grandfather was a Spirit Walker, a *Talth,* and therefore a mystic. Spirit walkers, in addition to their communion with the spirits, were expert at surviving in the wilderness, exquisite at tracking and hunting. Mostly it seemed to Sam that Grandfather was a man who largely existed apart from his surroundings and whose sense of self and whose well-being were substantially disconnected from his earthly status or physical condition. Grandfather had genuine peace of mind, something that seemed to elude Sam and everyone else he knew.

Just sitting with the man used to please Sam. Most people who were not in the grip of their surroundings were also lacking in the essential charm of humanity—the ability to give for the goodness of giving. Grandfather was anything but inhuman. When he looked at you, it felt like the whole world was springing flowers around calm lakes. That's why he had shown the picture of Grandfather to Cat-man. He thought perhaps Cat-man would see something in the eyes, even in a photo.

The week that Grandfather showed up unannounced was warm and sunny, a time for Sam to stay in the shade and undertake his college studies—but Grandfather had insisted they should have an outing. The morning after his arrival, about a half hour before daylight, they started up the mountain with water and nothing else. Grandfather mumbled that too many beavers were shitting in the creeks. They climbed for four hours and Sam began to think the unthinkable—that Grandfather might have to slow down for him. Fortunately, the old man reduced the pace before Sam brought it up. Sam was never sure why.

After six hours of grueling climbing, they came out at an alpine meadow bordered above by a tiara of snow that melted water into the meadows and mixed with the sun to make the stuff of life. As they walked among the late bloomers of the wildflowers and passed the wizened stunted pines, it seemed they were under the eye of God. When they topped the rock knob, the earth dropped away in streaks of granite and ribbons of green trees and effervescent meadows. As the eye drifted down the mountains, the trees became larger, the greens deeper. They overlooked a valley and in its bottom the churning of the Wintoon River could just be heard, the white of its rapids imaginable as splotches, like flowers on a vine.

Grandfather took him around the rock on a tiny trail that put them on a ledge below the top of the dome, perhaps a hundred feet down the cliff. Here they sat. A hawk flew out over the abyss, giving their eyes perspective and their minds a fleeting reminder that some creatures could fly but men needed a contraption in order to soar. The grand quiet of the place and the slight breeze hushed the soul and seemed to bring them near creation, if not the Creator.

"This is Universe Rock," Grandfather explained. "We will sit and take this into our spirit so that we may later breathe it out."

Sam did not understand what he meant, but he did feel that which cannot so easily be felt with the hordes of mankind. Perhaps in part it was the scale of the place. How better to appreciate the vastness of space than to sit atop a mountain, a sort of kindergarten of the universe. Or if not a mountain, then the Tiloks' Universe Rock. Or maybe it was the solitude that was the chief ingredient. The subtleties of the soul were most likely lost in farting pistons, humming refrigerators, rolling wheels, flushing toilets, whizzing traffic, and talking toys. Maybe it was the beauty; it could be reflected in the soul that absorbed it but could not be created there.

"You must take what this place has to offer, put it within you and take it," Grandfather said. "There will come times, difficult times when people are pushing your feet out your ears. It is at those times that you must remember and quiet yourself. You must bring this place out from where you have hidden it and you must let it go out through every member of your body. And you must feel the peace that we feel here. Once you feel it, you must remember the eyes of your mother, the love that she felt when she knew you were alive. The white people call this compassion. We call it *we pac maw.* In the place of peace you surround yourself with *we pac maw.* You become the center of a sphere and around you is *we pac maw.* When the man of wrath and scorn comes and you have centered yourself in peace and put on your *we pac maw,* then you do not think of him as other than yourself. There is no them and us. There is only a wounded friend.

"When you look at him, give him only *we pac maw* and he will see a reflection of himself. If the reflection is bad and his character is strong, his shame will not poison him and he will turn away from misdeeds and contemplate his place. If his shame is too great and he cannot turn around in his path, then he is a dangerous one. If he feels no shame, then he is a very dangerous one. Sometimes you must choose the least evil."

Sam tried to assimilate everything he was hearing. It was by far the most he'd heard Grandfather speak in one sitting. "What do you mean 'the least evil'?"

"Sometimes a man must step out of his peace and leave his *we pac maw.* It seldom happens, but if he must, then . . . to fight may be the lesser evil."

As Sam brought himself back to the here and now, he watched Anna's eyes begin to cloud with tears.

"Give me just a few minutes to think about this miracle

growing inside you," Sam said. Then he leaned back in his seat, closed his eyes and tried to do as his grandfather had instructed him. He imagined himself centered in a sphere and possessed of the mountains' peace. Then he surrounded himself with the *we pac maw* of his mother's eyes.

At last he looked at Anna. He could see that she felt alone with her decision.

He smiled. "You are feeling the weight of motherhood. No?"

"I am. What are you feeling?"

"Right now I need to understand you."

"It isn't a feeling. Or maybe it is. It's more of a thought, I think. I'm scared. If we share this child, we will have to decide whether we will share together or apart. If together, we would be a family. Little families run on commitment. A man like you looks at long-term monogamy the way a thoroughbred looks at a fence. You will tell yourself the issue is anonymity, but I think it's deeper than that; it's what's inside you. . . . Anonymity isn't really the issue." She paused as the tears returned. "I think I'm afraid because I'm so very hopeful."

Sam knew his words had been right, but the little wrinkles on his brow were still betraying him. He would need to practice this *we pac maw* and figure out what lurked in the dark places of his mind.

Baptiste and René walked in the Menilmontant, in a neighborhood off Rue de Couronnes, on a small side street lined with middle-class flats. When they arrived at the Flower of Paris Apartments, they climbed the stairs to the first floor off the street and took the elevator to the third. It was a nice enough place for Paris, reasonably maintained but with tiny, single bedroom flats. Space in Paris was at a premium and one had to pay for it.

They knocked on the door of apartment number 7 and were greeted by an older woman obviously crippled from arthritis.

"Hello. I am Baptiste, Jean-Baptiste, and this is René, and we are from the government. May we talk to you for a few minutes?"

Baptiste showed his badge, as did René.

"Come in," she said, moving slowly back in small, awkward steps.

"We are here to inquire about Georges Raval. He is your son?"

"Oh no. That is my brother's boy. I'm Chloe Raval and I'm living in their apartment. Well, actually, I guess it's my apartment now. My sister-in-law and her son went off to America. Is there trouble?"

"Do you have an address for them?"

"No, I don't. It's strange. They send me letters but no address where I can write back."

"Do you have any of those letters?"

"The last one was a week ago, but someone else came and I gave it to them."

"Who?"

"Someone from his old company. They said their name, but I forgot it. It was very important that they find him right away or he might lose his pension, they said."

"What about the envelope? Was there anything on it that would indicate where he was?"

"I threw that away before the letter."

"Do you remember where it was postmarked?"

"No. I'm sorry, I don't. Are they in trouble?"

"Oh no. Not at all. In fact, they could be of great service to their country."

"How so?"

"By giving us information."

"Well, they call sometimes, and when they do, I will tell them."

"When did they last call?"

"Just two days ago."

"When they call again, would you ask that Georges Raval call this number?"

Baptiste handed her a card.

"Of course. There is one thing, though."

"What's that?"

"I have a sister who lives in New York. I think she might know where they are because sometimes she's on the phone with them."

"Where in New York does she live?"

"A place called Manhattan? Does that sound right?"

"Could be. What's her name?"

"Claudia Roche."

"Do you have her address?"

"Well, I have it somewhere. It's something Christopher or Christopher something."

"Could you find it?"

She went slowly into her kitchen and opened a drawer. Inside was a box with cards. Eventually she pulled one out that bore the address and phone number of Claudia Roche. Hurriedly they wrote it down.

"Did these men from the company leave any message for Georges?"

"No."

"If you hear from Georges, have him call this number. And you call us."

They left after going over the instructions several times. Baptiste also made sure she knew to call if she ever saw the men from her nephew's company.

"According to Figgy, Bowden is in New York, and sooner or later we'll find Raval with Bowden. It will be a remarkable coincidence," Baptiste said to René as they hurried down the steps.

"We could check her phone records."

"Go ahead. But Raval calls her and not from any place we could trace. If he wasn't smart Gaudet would have him by now."

Chapter 10

Deceive a clever wife and you will have a weasel in your lodge.

—Tilok proverb

Baptiste found himself frequenting the lab where Benoit spent her days away from jail. He admitted to himself that she was probably becoming a dangerous habit. Without really planning to, he was telling her every facet of the investigation. In return she spoke openly of her knowledge about Grace Technologies and Devan Gaudet.

After having left her two hours ago, she had just called him on his cell phone. She needed to see him right away. Benoit was allowed visitors and had recently seen a staff member of *le Sénat*, according to the log in the lobby. Baptiste was more than a little curious.

"If we want to move ahead, we need to do something radical," she began.

"We are. I have a man inside with the American, Sam, and I'm after Georges Raval. We found his aunt Chloe. She's a good start."

"That won't do it. You'll muddle around forever."

"Then what do you suggest?"

"We need to contact Gaudet, make a deal directly, and

then I need to go to the United States and see Raval. He will see me. He won't see you. It's the only way to do it quickly."

"You're out of your mind," Baptiste scoffed.

"Maybe. Maybe you need to open yours. See what the admiral thinks."

"I don't want the admiral involved."

"Look, he doesn't need to know about our financial arrangements. But think about what we have to accomplish: we need to broker a deal between Gaudet and the French government to buy everything. That means getting the Chaperone technology from Raval and putting it into a Swiss escrow. Plus we need to get the molecule from Bowden and put that in the same escrow. Lastly I'll buy from Gaudet all the Grace Technologies lab notes he stole. But we have a serious time problem. Gaudet's going to attack the U.S., and he isn't waiting for us. Do you see how the admiral could facilitate much of this?" Benoit challenged.

"He'll never let you leave France."

"You've yet to ask him."

Baptiste was still processing the details of her plan. "Even assuming you could convince Raval to give up the technology process, why the hell would we then run it through Gaudet and pay him anything?"

"First, because Gaudet already has the technology. It may be our only way, depending on whether I can find Georges. Second, your idea of how to make money is far too dangerous and it's stupid. Selling it to a foreign government? Yourself? I will tell you what works. The French government buys from *Gaudet* and Gaudet gives you a cash kickback. Likewise Raval. Gaudet is a criminal so he is our shield. Believe me, you don't want the government throwing you in jail. I can attest to its unpleasantness. Do you understand?"

"How do you work with a man like Gaudet?"

"The Swiss escrow's the key. By agreement, the government pays directly into that account. By agreement, you get your cut, Gaudet his. Gaudet doesn't actually touch the cash originally, so depending on him to pay you is not an issue."

"I don't see why Gaudet needs us at all in this scheme," Baptiste grumbled.

"He needs me and I need the French government. I can deliver Raval and probably Bowden. There is no time for Gaudet to try to find Raval and either persuade him with money or torture, so without me there is a great probability that Gaudet will fail to deliver a sellable product to the government of France. Without me France will have a hard time knowing whether they have the real goods. I am only interested in a pardon—not money, so I am the glue that holds this deal together. It's that simple."

Baptiste merely nodded, still absorbing the structure of her proposal.

"You know what we do next? If we learn when Gaudet plans to launch his operation, this Cordyceps attack, then we use the money to sell the world markets short by buying short-term put options just before Cordyceps is launched. We take positions in London, Japan, and not much in the U.S. Use twenty different brokers. The leverage will be incredible. We don't even need much of Gaudet's cut to make money, you see. Say two and a half percent on two hundred million or five million. It isn't enough money that Gaudet will want to double-cross you, and with a properly set up Swiss escrow it would be nearly impossible to cheat you anyway. The market after Cordyceps will turn the five million into more than fifty million on highly leveraged accounts. This is all if we learn the precise date. I don't even care about the money myself. You take as much as you want; I get my pardon from the French government for brokering the deal with Gaudet. Got it?"

Baptiste sat stunned and somewhat reluctant to admit that it was brilliant. It seemed to involve very low risk.

"Why does Raval cooperate?" He was fishing for any loopholes or flaws.

"To get certain money now. You have said many times, and the lawyers have said, that Grace owned the technology. Raval can't capitalize on it because the French government now owns the assets of Grace. So why shouldn't he want cash? I am his friend and I can persuade him."

"And what about Bowden? How do you get him to cooperate on the Chaperone molecule?"

"Bowden will deal with the first legitimate entity with a sound plan. That's from what I know of the man. He's in business to help the Amazon. Show him how to do that and he'll play ball."

"Even if you can do all this—which seems impossible—the admiral will never allow you out of jail. It would be his neck. And he will never go for the kickback. He would have us all arrested. "

"I will take care of convincing the admiral to let me go to America."

"How?"

"The greater glory of France. My plan is the only plan that has a chance. Let's face it. You are getting nowhere." She was very sure of herself.

"We have a partner. Figgy Meeks. We got him into Sam's camp. We have to pay Figgy a share."

"That's fine as long as it comes out of your end. Why should that bother me?"

Not for the first time Baptiste felt like a child talking to Benoit.

"You can deal with him, can't you?" she asked.

"I think so. He's in deep shit. He killed one of Sam's people. Although it was an accident, I doubt whether Sam would understand. So I have leverage, if need be."

"Good. I thought you would. Now listen closely. I will tell you how to send a message from me to Gaudet. I guarantee you that once he gets it, he will contact you."

* * *

Devan Gaudet walked into the lobby of Globe Publishing as if he belonged there.

The man at the security desk stopped him and asked for ID. He showed his passport. "Here to see?"

"Randall Crest."

"Just a moment."

Randall Crest oversaw sales to independent bookstores and to the large distributors.

"Mr. Crest doesn't answer. The girl says he's on vacation."

"Try Osterling, head of sales."

A pause followed while he tried the other number, followed by an explanation, presumably to Osterling.

"Mr. Osterling wasn't expecting you and can only see you for a few minutes."

"That will be fine."

"Ninth floor. He'll meet you in the lobby there."

Once inside, Gaudet did not go to the ninth floor. Instead, he went to the seventh and inquired as to the whereabouts of Sherry Montgomery and went straight to her desk.

"I have a meeting with Gene Osterling on the ninth regarding promotion of Michael Bowden's new title to the independents. I'm Mr. Bowden's private publicist. We'll need to get Michael on the line. I know he's only temporarily here in New York, and I'm afraid I've misplaced his number here."

Sherry looked troubled.

"I'm sorry for the inconvenience," Gaudet said. "Gene's waiting up on the ninth. Probably pacing."

"Well," she said, "all I have is this number. Let's see it's . . ." She went to a large calendar book. "You know, I just need to check this with Rebecca. We don't usually give things out. But if Gene Osterling . . ." Sherry looked tentatively at

Rebecca Toussant's open door and the empty desk. "She's got someone with her." Obviously the office was large and had a separate seating area within.

As Sherry walked to the door, Gaudet flipped open her calendar book. He flipped back a day and found Michael Bowden's name and the phone number. He flipped the calendar shut at about the same time Sherry stopped to look back at him. A look of some concern crossed her brow as she hurried back to her desk.

"I know this is important, but I'm afraid I can't allow you poking around my desk. I need permission to give you the number."

"I am most sorry. I don't want to put you out or cause you to do something you're unsure of. I'll just call my housekeeper. She can probably find the note. Don't worry about it."

Gaudet left and took the elevator to the ninth, where he met the gray-haired Osterling.

"I'm afraid I've just had an emergency call. Your cohort Randall is off on vacation anyway, so let me just not disturb you and be off. I will get hold of Mr. Crest when he returns." Osterling looked slightly nonplussed, probably wondering why he had to wait around in the lobby for ten minutes just to hear this, but he obviously wanted to get back to work more than he wanted to ask questions.

Outside on the sidewalk Gaudet dialed the number for Bowden. It turned out to be a bed-and-breakfast. The proprietor had never heard of Michael Bowden or anyone named Sam, but they were booked with a large party.

Gaudet smiled. This might turn out to be easier than he had thought.

Gaudet hobbled into the bed-and-breakfast establishment, appearing bent by arthritis or scoliosis of the spine, his face designed to look time-worn and yet nondescript.

"I'm looking for my grandson," he said to a young woman

who appeared to be the official greeter. "He's due here with a sizable group, anytime."

"His name would be—"

"Oh, he's a fine boy. If you've seen him once, you'll never forget him. He's French like me, but without the accent."

"I'm sorry, I need a name."

"Yes, of course. It's Dupre but it's a large party and he wouldn't have made the reservation."

"I'm sorry, without the correct name . . ."

"Of course. Of course. I'll return. In the meantime I wonder if I might use your bathroom."

"Certainly."

She showed him to a room down the first-floor hall, where he installed himself long enough to pull out a small remote microphone. Once he had it in his palm, he waited an appropriate time, flushed the toilet, and emerged. She had disappeared for the moment, so he moved quickly down the hall and stuck the microphone under the desk that held the sign-in book.

Gaudet turned, tottered out into the street, and was gone.

Michael rode through New York in a hired car with Sam, Anna, Yodo, and Grady. He wanted to see the area where the World Trade Center had once stood. They had arrived only the day prior and things were still new to Michael. Sam had protested getting Anna close to Michael, but she was a woman of means and willpower and she would not be deterred. Michael never seemed to deny another soul an adventure and really did not argue with Anna risking her life to ride around town with the Gaudet "bait" if that was her choice. Michael used Grady's cell phone to make his daily call to Professor Richard Lyman about his journals. There was silence and the tension was palpable as he placed the call.

After a brief hello and virtually no pleasantries, Michael popped the question. It looked to Sam like Michael's heart was sinking to his feet and so he knew the answer even before Michael reported that there was no package and no communication from Peru or anywhere else in South America. The professor took the number of the cell phone in case anything changed.

After a time of disappointed silence Sam decided to try and improve the mood.

"New York must seem strange after the Amazon."

"The people all seem to wear black shoes—like boots but with low tops. The buildings remind me of giant ant heaps. There's a sign for everything—almost as though no one has their own thoughts. The place is crawling with people."

Sam was amused at the virginal quality of Michael's observations. He had now figured out, by listening to Michael or getting information from Big Brain, that Michael had left the United States when he was almost twelve. When he was six years old, his parents divorced and he moved from the campus of Cornell University in Ithaca to Humboldt County, California, where he lived with his mother. Sam marveled at the coincidence—so close to the Tiloks. Humboldt County was not a place visited by many, about 250 miles as the crow flies north of San Francisco, in redwood country. It was green and peaceful with many more trees than people, mountains pushed up against the sea with creeks in every furrow, and wild lands for miles and miles.

When Michael was nine, his mother died and he returned to Ithaca to live with his father. From talking with Michael, Sam had discerned that most of Michael's memories of the Finger Lakes region were indistinct, as though earlier memories were crowded out of his mind by Amazonia. For an eleven-year-old boy the culture shock of the deep jungle must have been incredible.

Michael gaped at the sheer number and enormity of the buildings, the volume of vertical concrete and brick placed on more concrete and steel.

"Amazing, huh?" Grady said.

"If there is some evolutionary advantage to all of this, it escapes me. Unlike the ants or the bees, it seems to me that all this jamming-people-together in buildings would increase danger to the individual. The benefits of commerce obviously outweigh the hazards."

"We Americans are in a frenzy to do something. When we don't know what to do, we work. I guess this is the result," Sam said.

Michael found the Gramercy Park bed-and-breakfast oddly cluttered with knickknacks seemingly placed with great care. There were cookies and tea, silver urns, hushed silence—or at most half-whispered tones—and fabrics that all seemed to sleep. The place offered little for a man accustomed to trekking in the jungle, fishing catfish for dinner, and having a good chew of coca before hitting the hammock.

He did notice an unusual brightness in Grady's eyes when she looked at him. He couldn't recall ever seeing a woman with a better body. But he was confused at her relationship with Sam. (Robert had explained that his nickname was Sam and Michael was only now getting used to the new name.) He was also bewildered now that he had seen Sam with Anna. Obviously, Michael's place was in the Amazon and a woman like Grady would not last there, so any alliance would probably be temporary and he wasn't sure how she might feel about a short-term romance. Much less himself. He still was not over the shock of losing Eden and then Marita.

Still, Grady was long-legged and blond, with a narrow waist and high, firm bust. Her eyes shone with such a striking shade of azure that Michael wondered if it was some modern contrivance. But it was her glances, and her strong Slavic face, the high cheekbones, and especially the expressive lips, neither full nor thin, that piqued his desire. From the moment he had seen her in the jungle, he had concluded that she was an astonishment as females go. Even when he was half sick, he had wanted to grab her and plaster his lips to hers. He suspected that this uncommon rage to copulate was due in part to all the carnage he had just left—a coping mechanism that would enable the mind to let go of the pain and depression of death.

The desire remained in him here, but he kept it behind a controlled and seemingly placid exterior. Michael determined that in the fashion of a civilized man, this desire was best ignored, at least for the moment.

After Sam advised the proprietor that they wished to extend their stay, they made their way upstairs. Anna went with Sam, although Michael understood that she was staying at her own apartment. At the second floor Sam paused and gathered them around. They stood in a mezzaninelike area the size of the parlor with a well-furnished library. Behind a balustrade, which made a large oval around the staircase, were the doors to various rooms. Fresh flowers stood under a gilt-framed mirror.

"I'd suggest you stay around here. Let people come to you."

Michael appreciated Sam's concern but bridled at it just the same. "I have no problem with your bodyguards if they have the courage to go with me. But I will do my work. And that is the end of the discussion."

"But, Michael, we talked. . . ." Grady began.

"I said I would be careful. That is all I said." He paused. "I don't mean to be rude."

She nodded and turned toward her room.

As Michael entered his, he turned and his eyes found

Grady's across the way. It pleased him to see her eyes searching for his. They both closed their doors in a slow, synchronous movement, accompanied by an unmistakable smile. But he hadn't missed the worry behind the smile.

Chapter 11

A maiden's eyes are a club to the young man's head,
her lips a snare for his neck.

—Tilok proverb

Benoit sat at her desk in the government lab approving
invoices from suppliers and coordinating the delivery of lab
supplies, as well as supervising all of the clerical help. It was
growing to be a substantial job and she had only been at it
for eleven days, but her mind wasn't in it.

Unlike other lab offices, hers came equipped with a couple of guards, although the real security lay in the fact that
there were only two exits in the whole building and she was
not allowed through either without a full escort, and she had
to be in shackles.

Her phone rang. The admiral.

"I have grown to anticipate your calls," she began. "Have
you considered my suggestion that we meet for tea?"

"I am considering it. Baptiste certainly thinks it would be
counterproductive."

"Yes. Well, you will have to consider whether that is how
you want to run your agency—always relying on second-
hand information."

"It seems I'm getting it firsthand over the phone."

"You know what they say about looking into a person's eyes."

"I know what they say about looking into your eyes," Larive parried.

"What do they say?"

"They say that you are bewitching."

"That would be my ass, not my eyes. But, of course, you have never seen my ass."

"Perhaps one day we will remedy that."

"Not as long as you are too politic to meet me for tea."

"What can you tell me to encourage me about the project?" Larive cut to the point.

"I can tell you that if you do some hard and daring things, you will win the vector technology and Chaperone for France. I have been telling you this for some time."

"Yes, and you want to meet with me to explain it."

"That is right," Benoit acknowledged.

"And you do not want to tell Baptiste."

"That is right because he cannot approve what needs to be done. We must contact people that I can best contact. We must make deals. You will need to let me out of here in order to accomplish what you want."

"That would be extraordinary," Larive remarked.

"It would be temporary, only until I have earned a pardon from the French government."

"Tell me more of what you would do."

"With all due respect, I could think better and be much more forthcoming if we were speaking in private and I could see you and be assured that you have my interests in mind."

"In other words you once again request a personal meeting."

Benoit smiled.

Admiral Larive attempted to suck in his gut with marginal results. He was standing sideways to a full-size mirror in his office that he used to judge his suits. Unfortunately, he had quit the hard workouts and his belly sagged over his belt. Off and on throughout the morning he had imagined what it would be like to take tea with Benoit Moreau.

Five minutes before the appointed time he arrived at the hotel. That morning he had put on new boxer shorts and undershirt. Although he had wanted a haircut, there hadn't been time. He had taken extra pains shaving and cut the hair out of his ears and he had vigorously gone after his long, dark nose hairs. Outside the door there were guards and they opened it to reveal Benoit Moreau in chains with another guard.

"You may take off the chains, for God's sake, we're having tea."

"Sorry, sir, but it's regulation. We never take the chains off unless ordered, so I gather you're giving me that order."

"Yes, yes. Come on, man, she works in an office."

"Begging your pardon, sir, but it is a very secure office, much more secure than this hotel room."

They removed the chains and handed him a key, then left to take up positions in the hallway outside the room.

He and Benoit sat down at the table in the middle of the large suite near glass doors that opened onto a balcony. Green and gold draperies were pulled nearly across the doorway. On the table was a plate of French pastries, but he wasn't sure about taking one. He knew that fat in quantity could interfere with Viagra and he didn't want anything diminishing his potency.

Her hair was dark brown, and soft like a feather boa, her face unmarked by age. She looked younger than her thirty-eight years. If she slept with him, he told himself, she would need a very good reason. He knew as he sipped his tea that such a reason would no doubt be very bad for him. Strangely, he could not rise from the table and leave.

"I will get right to the point. There are things you should know in addition to the things I have told you on the phone."

She obviously enjoyed his undivided attention. "These are things that I have not told anyone, not even Baptiste." She turned in her chair and he noticed that her blouse was not buttoned to the top and with the angle he could see some cleavage. "Baptiste does not have your stature. I do, however, like him." She sipped her tea and his curiosity about her information was getting to him. "I miss the women's magazines. Baptiste brings me one or two. . . ."

"What would you like?"

"Cosmopolitan in English and *Vogue,* also in English. I like to practice the language."

"It will be done."

"I miss lingerie, you know. Do you like lingerie? I mean as opposed to just nudity. Most men, of course, enjoy a nude woman."

"I like lingerie. Yes. But I think you toy with me."

"Of course I do. That is why you came here. I am very good at it. Would you choose for me some elegant lingerie, a long white silken robe and buy it for me?"

"Yes. I think so."

"I would like that. You seem a wise man and they say you are good with money."

"Who says?"

"Friends. The same friends who say that you are going to be appointed a minister."

"These are your friends in *le Sénat?* " Larive commented.

"I hardly have friends in *le Sénat.* These are staff people of the people in *le Sénat."*

"I hear otherwise."

"Well, that is flattering. You may continue to think such good thoughts of me."

"You are an intriguing woman."

"Men find that I am intriguing. Many women find me unacceptable. Those are usually the women whose husbands want to sleep with me."

"And what do the husbands think?"

"They are attracted to any beautiful stranger. The more mysterious, the better. They cannot help it. I guess it is like a disease in a way."

"You are more attractive than your explanation allows."

"You are a very astute man. But intelligence is definitely not an antidote for what you crave. Is it?"

"No. It is nothing more than an annoyance where my loins are concerned."

"You put it very well. You can see it happening to you, watch it unfold, but still you are drawn. And I think it is not bad at all. It is just the way you feel and sometimes a person should live in the moment."

"My grandmother would have said that this is Satan's lie." He allowed himself a smile.

"My feet are cold. Would you like to rub them for me?"

"Of course."

"Let me sit on the bed and take off my stockings." She wore panty hose and pulled up her skirt to take them off. She wore the slimmest of underwear, a thong, and her butt was beautiful—even with the quick glimpse. The thong was tiny in front; she obviously trimmed her pubic hair. When she sat down, she let her skirt ride high, but he could no longer see her upper thighs and it frustrated him. Then he felt a slight sense of panic. He knew it was happening, but the reality of it was like a drug rushing through his body. This woman was a criminal. Although his reputation was immense he had been faithful to his wife for two years. An old almost forgotten anxiety came over him. When she had herself situated, he knelt and began a foot rub. The irony of being on one knee did not escape him nor did the physical discomfort.

"What is it that you were going to tell me?" Larive broke the silence.

"It is more than telling you something. It is something we can do together."

"What is that?"

"We could save the United States from a disaster and obtain Chaperone and the vector technology for France. All at once."

"Save the United States from what?"

"What Devan Gaudet is planning. He calls it Cordyceps." Benoit was full of information.

"What is Cordyceps?"

"I'm not sure yet. But I can imagine." She told him the story of Cordyceps and the beetle.

"Intriguing," the admiral said. "I've noticed that your plans hinge on your going to the United States."

"Because Georges Raval understands Chaperone and I understand Georges," she explained.

"Have you told this to Baptiste?"

"Of course. He lacks imagination, though. Would you like me to take off my skirt? It appears that you cannot see whatever it is you are trying to look at."

"You are very beautiful."

"Do you want the skirt off or not? You are a shy boy. I don't know how you ever get what you want." She stood and unzipped her skirt, letting it drop to the floor, then sat again.

He wondered about her blouse. It would be very good if she took that off as well. And the panties.

"I need to go to the United States and see Raval's aunt in New York. This must be in person. She knows me and will send a message to Georges or tell me how to find him. I will explain that France owns Chaperone, which he knows, and I will tell him how he can make some money by helping the rightful owner. In the end, though, we must go through Gaudet."

"Why through Gaudet?"

"I've been at work for a couple of days now, as you know. It's obvious to me already that our lab does not really understand the vector technology. We are altering brain cells, but not in the correct patterns. Our scientists don't understand the promoter DNA sequences. The sum of it, without getting too technical, is that we do not get well-defined and predictable mood alteration from modification of cells in the limbic system. Gaudet does much better, as we have seen. All he lacks is Chaperone, which enables the subjects to live with the brain alteration. His scientists clearly understand the technology. So I will get Gaudet to sell you his lab, all the Grace Technologies papers and research, and give you leads to hiring all of his employees as part of the deal."

"That makes some sense." Larive was impressed by this gorgeous, conniving woman.

"Now for the second reason I need to go to the States. I need to work with Gaudet and I know he is there. I can talk with him. I believe that he trusts me sufficiently to tell me about Cordyceps. He won't be able to resist bragging to me because we were lovers for over a year. He will believe I have come back to him."

"It's the right thing to do, obviously, stopping this Cordyceps. But why should we risk Chaperone when it's the U.S.'s ass that's on the line. Just to play devil's advocate," Larive proposed.

"If the U.S. markets go, Europe will go with them."

"I suppose to some extent that is true."

"More important, you need a relationship with the U.S. so you must be seen as cooperating. Appearance is everything. So are relationships. Of course, if for some reason we fail to stop Cordyceps, there is a fortune to be made."

"What?" This woman continually surprised him.

She outlined Gaudet's plan to short the market and also to invest in gold stocks and gold bullion so that money would be made when the market fell. She explained how it could be done.

"There is another thing I need to tell you." She appeared to be on a confessing jag.

"Yes?"

"Baptiste plans to make a deal for a five-million-dollar kickback from Gaudet and to use that money to short the market himself. He will make a fortune if Cordyceps goes forward."

"I don't believe you."

"Well, you'd better because it is true. Did he tell you what he learned from a Turkish prisoner by the name of Alfawd?"

"I never heard of Alfawd," Larive replied.

"Well, you should have." Then as the admiral sat dumbfounded, she told him all that Baptiste had learned about the investment group and Gaudet's tests of the technology with Sam's neighbors and at Northern Lights.

"Did Baptiste tell you that Figgy Meeks accidentally killed an associate of the man they call Sam and that he then, at Baptiste's direction, made it look like Gaudet by gutting the man, as Gaudet often does?" She was relentless in her disclosures.

"This could implicate the French government. It's a disaster." Larive nearly moaned.

"Yes, and apparently the autopsy showed the heart still beating when he was gutted."

Larive groaned.

"I could fix that too with Gaudet. I could provide testimony that one of Gaudet's men did it. A man who is now dead."

"Why would you do this?"

"I'm getting to that. One more thing: did you know that one of your agents, a René, accidentally killed Michael Bowden's girlfriend when he tried to take a gun from her? A gun that she was using to protect herself against Gaudet and his men?"

"This is true?"

"All of it. Baptiste is planning a meeting with Gaudet to make that deal. And he is going to allow Cordyceps to go forward. If you put that together with the money . . ." She allowed Larive to make his own deduction.

"That makes the French government an accomplice. Fucking Baptiste is out of control!"

"That's why you should let me go to the States when Baptiste asks. You will know everything that is going on. You will then, on behalf of the French government, be seeking to thwart the plot of a renegade agent."

"It's not that simple. I should turn him in and replace him."

"Keep in mind, first and foremost, that you want the technology. Diplomatically, you need only a fig leaf. You need complete success and not another horrible scandal in your agency. And most important of all, you may need someone to blame. Baptiste has done this on his own, but if you replace him, then suddenly you become solely responsible for whatever happens. Or am I incorrect about that?" Benoit had built a tower of irrefutable facts.

The admiral sighed—as she knew he would. "Tell me exactly what you will do."

"First I will go to Gaudet. I will be present when Gaudet meets Baptiste, but Baptiste will be unaware of this. That way the French government is spying on its own and is not acting in concert with the renegade Baptiste. I will tell you exactly what goes on. Then, in New York, I will broker deals with Bowden, Raval, and Gaudet. I will ensure that Gaudet offers all of his vector technology as part of the bargain. I know about it and am the best one to judge. We will open a Swiss escrow. The formula, notes, and so on will be deposited in escrow, along with contact numbers for ex-Grace employees and their job functions, et cetera. France will deposit two hundred million; ten million will be deposited for kickbacks, leaving a net one hundred ninety million."

"Wait, I thought you said Baptiste was getting five million, not ten million."

"I'm coming to that. There will be a period of examination to authenticate the materials. If I'm able to bring Bowden into the deal, the Chaperone molecule will be part of the escrow. Finally Raval will deliver that actual, authentic Grace record of invention for Chaperone, along with everything he knows about Chaperone. I will do everything in my power to learn the date when Cordyceps will be unleashed—how Gaudet's going to do it and what exactly he is going to do. I will deliver that information to the French government before it happens. You will notify the Americans. That will avoid any scandal. The French did their part. If for some reason it is too late to stop Cordyceps, then you, Admiral, can invest the five million I'll earmark for you."

The admiral slammed his fist in his hand. "I would do no such thing. I will not take money. Do you think I am a dog like Baptiste?"

"Calm down. You can tell the Americans the details of Cordyceps once escrow with Gaudet closes and not before. If you tell them before, then the whole deal could come apart and you will not get Chaperone or the rest of the vector technology. Once the Americans know of Cordyceps, they will go crazy. Gaudet will know that you have told them. He will cancel the escrow with immediate document destruction as provided in the escrow. And then he will unleash Cordyceps anyway."

"But we must tell the Americans."

"And you will. After escrow."

"I will tell them and that is all there is to it. And I cannot take this money."

"You need to calm yourself and think this through. Your money will be in a numbered account. You will have the number. In truth, if discovered, it will be part of what Baptiste expected to get. That will be the story. He'll get arrested for five million. The other five million will be missing. Yours. Leave it in the anonymous account if you don't want it. You can always turn it in to the French government. Say you tricked Gaudet and it would be a feather in your cap. I am putting it there in any case, and only you and I will know. The point is, you don't have to decide now. The key, remember, is making the deal for the French with Gaudet before telling the Americans about Cordyceps. Understand?"

"Benoit, I have one simple question: why would you risk telling me all this?"

"I want a pardon. Don't underestimate me, Admiral. I can do this. Not only that, I'm the *only* person who can do all of this. Without me, Chaperone will be lost to France for at least your lifetime, and you can take that to the bank. Without this deal another country or entity will get the functioning vector technology first."

"Why do you wish to involve me?"

"Because you can send me to the States. And because you are almost a minister. I need the promise of a pardon from the French government from someone who counts."

She had shifted on the bed, revealing a firm thigh.

"Would you like me to take off this blouse?"

"You know I would." His heart was beating hard as she teased off the blouse to reveal a sheer bra and a firm, high set of breasts with dark rose nipples. His throat constricted and he became fully erect.

"Where do you get such lingerie in prison?"

"My cousin in *le Sénat* staff. But your staff are not complete morons. They have to stretch the rules to let me wear it—I think that had something to do with the fact that I would be with you this afternoon."

She leaned forward and pulled him toward her, running his hand across her upper leg.

Larive swallowed. "You say this Raval is the only hope to understanding Chaperone?"

"Yes."

"And Bowden the only man to find the source of the Chaperone molecule."

"Yes."

"What does Bowden get?"

"France will have to pay him a royalty. You and I will negotiate it."

"Were you Raval's lover?"

"No. But we enjoyed each other's company. We flirted, but it never went anywhere. I was in charge of coordinating with Malaysia from an administrative standpoint, but not the science. Boudreaux, the chief scientist, kept the Chaperone research very much compartmentalized. It was even at another facility a few miles from the main lab. Boudreaux kept a double set of books for the employees there and they were lumped in the budget under R and D Immunological Pathogens and Disease Processes. Those books are long gone, of course. But Raval knew everything. It was essentially his project."

"Why would Gaudet tell you his secrets, and if he did, why would you then tell me?"

"He may, he may not. We were lovers for years, as I told you. Also, I can make it part of the deal. After he launches Cordyceps, the technology no longer has much value to him. Making a deal with France first is his best choice. He'll want that two hundred million, have no doubt. And why tell *you?* Isn't it obvious? France is my whole life. I want to live here and be free. I supposed that if I obtained for France the secret of Chaperone, I could obtain a full pardon. To me, my darling, you are freedom."

He looked at the young woman. Tactically, she was brilliant. And she might be right. She might pull it off. There would be no quick pardon, but she need not know that now. He might get her house arrest and rules, then a minimum security with work release in a couple of years.

"You will have a pardon," he said, his hand still on her leg. "If you pull off the whole thing. All of it."

"It is a deal, then? You will let me go to the U.S.?"

"Baptiste must come to me. It must be his idea that he shoves at me. That he guarantees. It cannot be my idea that I assign him."

"I understand."

"And he, of course, will know nothing of our talks. If there is a reason I will do this, it is because your fantastic ideas have very little downside and are the stuff of which great triumphs are made."

Even as he heard himself speak, he felt in a fog, all of his instincts warning him away, and yet when she rose and slipped off the bra and lay on the bed, it drew him like a mouse to the cheese. Playing with her thong, she teased him as he undressed, hurrying so fast he nearly fell over, fouled in his half-removed pants. When he was nude, she removed her thong and used her hands to pleasure him while putting a condom on. Then she sat astride him. The sight of her dried his throat. She grasped him and played with him, using her body and her hands until he thought that he had reached the outer limits of desire. Then she used her tongue. She made him feel young and, yes, powerful because she chose to have him. Even as he felt himself falling into Benoit Moreau, he knew he must be a chump. Wanting a young woman this badly was a classic flaw. In a fleeting second he wondered if this bizarre breach of ethics and good sense had undone all that was good in him. And then he was in her, and she was moving on him. The sensations of her moving against him, her butt on his thighs, her flesh engulfing his, sent him into a daze. He felt her touch his shoulder and he understood that she wanted him to roll. In a flash he was on top and she pulled her legs up and put them along his flanks and she reached and clenched his balls in her hand as he was thrusting, and he looked down in her eyes and they were gleaming and he felt as if he had conquered all.

* * *

Grady lay on the bed, procrastinating. It wasn't until her thoughts moved to Gaudet and his attack in Rio that she got up and changed her clothes and showered, ready to start the evening. Tonight was dinner with Michael's editor. The next day would be a larger lunch with the editor and various bigwigs from the publishing house.

It struck her that Michael Bowden was getting dressed in the next room. As she thought about him, she tried to convince herself that she was being ridiculous, that if he knew about her past he wouldn't want her. A straight-up guy like this—with one of the few pairs of innocent blue eyes in North America—how would he ever comprehend stripping? How could she even explain it? She knew that if she explained it and saw his face, his eyes, the expression of bewilderment and maybe even pain, this fascination that seemed to grip her mind would depart and she could become normal again and forget about him.

Even more significant, Michael would one day return to the Amazon and she doubted she could live in a place like that. She rose and stripped off her clothes. She headed to the shower when there was a knock on the door between her room and Michael's. Something clicked in her brain and she knew she should get dressed before she opened it. Instead, she wrapped herself in a towel, wearing only her thong panties beneath. When she got to the door, she thought about calling out to Michael and explaining that she needed a minute. Her hand rested on the knob for a full thirty seconds. Once again there was a quiet knock.

"Michael?"

"Yes?"

"What do you need?"

"You thought I should wear a tie, but I haven't ever tied one."

She laughed and opened the door.

"Pardon my towel, Michael. I was going to shower."

"I could step out while you put on something."

"Not necessary. Here, I'll show you how to tie a tie, for future reference."

Then she began tying the tie. It felt exciting, standing so near him, as if she were enfolded in his energy. His new growth beard was slightly rough and she liked the look of it and she felt his imposing size, the heft of his shoulders and chest. She felt an urge to spread her hands over his shirt, to touch him. As she completed the double wrap on the tie and was sliding the end down through the loops, she stood on her toes and somehow the towel began to slip. She caught it at the same time he did. His big hands were fast. Slowly he wrapped it around her and, as he did so, his fingers grazed her and she could never recall wanting a man's hands on her body as badly as she wanted the touch of Michael Bowden. Aware that he had seen something of her breasts, ex-stripper or not, she was embarrassed. His eyes now focused on hers and she could see the desire so strong in him that she thought it would come out in words. It was as if his whole body were full of sexual energy.

Her throat felt tight. So she cleared it, but it did nothing to break the tension.

"Michael, we shouldn't . . . because . . ." She found herself stepping even closer to him and looking up, and she couldn't move as his lips came down toward hers a millimeter at a time. And when his hands took her towel, she did nothing but quiver, and then his lips were on hers and his large thumbs were on her nipples, coaxing them. Suddenly she was kissing him as hard as she could and she had his face in her hands. It felt good and very natural as they kissed—like it had happened before. A large hand slid down her belly and she opened her legs, wanting him. She felt herself moisten under the ministrations of his fingers and she groaned when he pulled her panties to half-mast.

Suddenly there was a loud knock on her door and the phone rang at the same time. It was as if she had been caught at something and it was terribly wrong. She looked in his eyes, pleading for understanding.

"I've got to get that." She pushed him slowly back through the door, then closed it in a state of shock. There was a second knock on the front door. "Just a minute," she called out. Now she leaned against the inner door to talk with Michael, wanting him to understand. "God, Michael, I'm sorry. That was my fault. I am so sorry. Someone is supposed to have self-control and that's me and I apologize for leading you on. I'll be back."

Then she hoisted her panties, ran to the closet and found her robe, took her laundry, ran to the door, and missed the phone call. As she guessed, the nice young man came for her laundry in reply to an earlier request. Once that was taken care of, she returned to the inner door to Michael's room. The phone rang. It was Michael.

"No worries," he said. "The customs are different here. I know we are supposed to eat and have romantic talk first."

"No," she said. "We don't have to eat first. You have to know some things about me first and I have to know some things about you. But it's okay. Everything is cool. I have a robe on now and I'll tie your tie."

She figured this was like riding a horse—if you fell off, you had to get back on quick. The longer she waited, the more awkward it would become.

When she opened the door, she was determined to act as if nothing were amiss, so she reached up to take his tie and began again. Standing close, she once again had the over-powering urge to mold herself to his body, but she managed to show none of it. Nearly breathing a sigh of relief when she had completed the job, she sent him to his room, showered, then went to her closet and found herself pondering which of the few outfits would impress a man from the Amazon. Then she reminded herself that her purpose was to help protect him, *not* to impress him. She stared at herself in the mirror, wondering what she was about. She knew herself well and realized that a good portion of her brain was currently given over to female plotting that even she didn't understand. Amazing, given that Gaudet probably had people in New York who would kill her to get to Michael.

She had to get him out of New York. The only complicating factor was the journals and Michael could come back to Ithaca for those—if and when they arrived. Fortunately, Michael had revealed a goal similar to hers. Now it was time for her to seal the deal.

She called Michael and said she might be up to twenty minutes late for dinner. Then she called her on-again, off-again boyfriend in LA, thinking she might break it off. But as they talked, she considered how abrupt this was; she was excited but uncertain; then she thought of Sam's self-control. After a newsy chat she followed her habit and said, "I love you" to a boyfriend whom she no longer loved, then hung up.

It took Michael only a few minutes to put on a sport coat and tie. As he waited, he felt an acute sense of embarrassment and tried hard to get his composure so that he could pretend that what just happened never happened. Like men everywhere, he needed something to distract himself while he waited for the lady. Picking up one of his science journals, he read about a newly discovered painkiller that was one thousand times more effective than morphine and derived from one of the five hundred or so molecules that make up the deadly toxin of the cone snail. People with chronic-pain syndrome were being freed from their misery, and there were few things, other than Grady, that he could think of that were more exciting. The drug was called Ziconotide. At the moment he needed something like that, only effective in killing the sex drive, which at this point was becoming a form of pain.

Grady had encouraged him to look the part with his editor, although for him that meant his jungle clothes. He suspected that the traditional business garb was because she wanted him to blend in with the street crowd, but he didn't argue. Eventually she emerged from her room looking like the models he had seen in American magazines. She wore a black knit dress with an eye-catching plunge at the neckline. It certainly did not hide her figure. Michael was aware that deep within their brain Homo sapiens had programmed certain body ratios that were associated with fertility. Males seemed to equate this hourglass configuration with mating behavior and, in fact, found it quite inspirational in that regard. Clearly, the dress fully retained his sense of inspiration.

Just as he was about to walk out the door, the phone rang. It was Rebecca.

"Looking forward to seeing you tonight and tomorrow," she said.

"We are about ready to leave."

"I wanted to mention, a man was here looking for you today. He left you a letter, said he was a fellow scientist and that it was urgent. He asked if there was any way I could get in touch with you. I think he thought you were probably still in the Amazon, although I'm not sure about that. I told him I thought I might have a rare opportunity to get you on the phone and said no more."

"Good. My friend Grady is convincing me that we must not tell people that I am in New York. Bring the letter to dinner tonight if you have it. Did the man leave a name?"

"Yes. He did. Although he wanted assurance that I would

give his name to no one but you and I assured him of that. It's all quite mysterious."

"Who is he?"

"Georges Raval."

Grady took charge of the taxis. With them in the taxi were Yodo and one other. Their entourage followed in second and third taxis.

When they entered the taxi, she sat close and for a moment put her hand over his. The warmth of it traveled through his body.

"Won't it be exciting when you can get started on your work?"

"I want so bad to get back to it. And to spend some time in a new place."

"Do you know where?"

"The mountains of the Pacific Northwest, maybe. There's an almost unspoiled block of wilderness there. Well, more than one. This one's near the Salmon and Klamath rivers."

"Maybe you can satisfy Sam's concerns and get started on your work all at once," she said, and looked at him squarely for the first time since entering the taxi. "Maybe . . ."

"Yes?"

"Maybe it would be good to go there soon."

"You want me to do what Sam wants."

"I want you to do what you want. But not to die trying."

Her body was next to his and her thigh was touching his for its full length and he could sense that they both wanted the same thing.

Then his cell phone rang.

"I have your journals," Dr. Lyman said.

"Oh, thank goodness. Thanks for calling. You made my evening. I'll be right back to you. Will this number work for my return call?"

"It'll work. Be here for half an hour."

"Grady, I need to talk with you now, in private."

"Sure. Driver, could you pull over for just a minute?"

They got out onto the curb and Michael drew her away from a nervous-looking Yodo.

"You have to make a choice. I'm going to be honest with you and I expect you to be honest with me."

"Okay."

"My journals are at Ithaca. I'm going alone, unless you want to come. Nobody else."

"That's crazy."

"No, it's not. Two of us won't be noticed. This looks like a president's motorcade."

"I see. We'll dress and act like nobodies and pull in driving an old Chevy. Sam will never go for it."

"It's not up to him where I'm concerned. I guess you would be different."

"Let me ask one thing. If I go with you and we get the journals, can we meet the bodyguards on the way back and then lock the journals up in a vault, except for what you need?"

Michael thought about that for a moment. He sensed he needed to give her something or he would end up going alone.

"Okay. We meet the guards halfway between New York and Ithaca."

"I'll call Sam."

Michael shook his head and chuckled. "Always Sam."

A letter had come from Gaudet. After locking the door to his office, Baptiste removed it from the envelope. The moment he had found it in his residential mailbox, he had studied it, trying to determine its authenticity. He did not note this letter on any incoming-mail log nor did he make a copy for any file:

*France has its interests and I have mine. Time is
running out for France if you don't want to lose the
discovery of the century. Perhaps we should talk about
our mutual interests.*

Maybe there were times when one made a deal with the
Devil. It was shocking that Benoit had communicated so
easily and that Gaudet obviously believed her. There seemed
to be no end to this woman's intrigue.

It was late in the afternoon, so he locked up early and left
the building. With Benoit's instructions committed to memory he proceeded to a computer where he could not be
traced. According to Benoit, he could send the e-mail on any
day within five minutes of four o'clock in the afternoon.
Walking down Boulevard Mortier and then turning onto
Cros, he went for a few more blocks until he came to an
Internet café. There were a series of work stations, at least
twenty in all, and each one tied into the Internet. After paying the fee of ten Euros, he sat down and logged on to a free
e-mail Web site. With little effort he opened an account
under the name Sailorsea. Using that account, he drafted an
e-mail to Jvaljean@wanadoo.fr.net.

*It seems we have some issues. How do I know that
you are Devan Gaudet? How do I know that you can
help me? Why would you want to?*

He sent it at precisely 4:01 P.M., then sat and watched the
in box for his account. At 4:14 P.M. he received this reply:

*You have the confidence of Benoit Moreau or you
would not be writing me. If I am not Gaudet, I am at
least someone in her confidence. Yes? So do you believe her or not? Only a government-size entity can afford what the technology is worth. Because of Benoit,*

I am willing to work with the French. Call me at 212-555-2729 U.S.

Baptiste went and purchased a card with one hundred minutes of long-distance talk time. He then walked his route through the Belleville church and nodded at the priest as he walked down the side of the main sanctuary. Once out of the church, and certain he wasn't being followed, he went down a back alley and took a different route than usual to the small café where he had previously used the phone. Unusually concerned, he passed this phone, went down the street a block and into a video place, where he browsed around before asking his daughter's friend, who worked there, if he might use the phone. As he hoped, he was shown to the back office, where he closed the door. He punched in the number on the card and then the pin number and then the overseas code for the United States followed by the number. He assumed he was calling a recently rented cell phone.

"This is Jean-Baptiste Sourriaux," he said when a man answered.

"I am 'Traveler' and I will relay your conversation with Mr. Gaudet." The man had no discernible accent and he spoke quickly, as if from a script.

"He doesn't want voiceprints, I take it."

"That is right."

"I want a meeting."

"We anticipated that. However, it will occur on our terms."

"What are those terms?"

"It will take place in an airplane. You will bring your U.S. double agent. The one working with Sam. We will tell you where to go and you will board a jet and we will leave you off at a place of our choosing. Details through Benoit."

"That will be acceptable if I can be sure of my safe return."

"That will not be possible. You will have to trust in our greed and determine that we will be richer by bringing you back safely. After all, a French security officer is of no use to us."

Chapter 12

The Great Spirit gives the flowering plants to teach the
lesser spirits the festival of new beginnings.

—Tilok proverb

The prospects of female companionship in the Arab state
of Quatram were abysmal, so Gaudet imported women. He
paid them fairly and found replacements readily for those he
hurt more than they wanted to be hurt. Killing the biggest
complainers was a program that ensured good referrals and
easy replacements. None was as good as Benoit Moreau had
been, and that wouldn't change. But Gaudet still sought tall
and supple women who reminded him of Benoit.

New York City was another matter entirely. But he could
not afford to distract himself even for a few minutes now,
which was a pity because there were plenty of women.

Trotsky wore some stubble, which was unusual, and kept
quiet, which was normal, waiting for Gaudet to speak.

Gaudet sipped an unsweetened double espresso.

"When all this is over, I'll need a new place. Somewhere
they will never expect me—a civilized part of the world. I've
had my fill of Quatram."

"Maybe a nice neighborhood in Middle America."

"I'm not into potlucks."

The phone rang and Trotsky took it.

"They want to know if they can buy more art in Spain. They are obviously tired of the smuggling business."

"The store makes money?"

"Seems to."

"Let them, but control it. And put that business on the 'keep' list."

Two or three more calls came in during the next twenty minutes.

"You are growing a small empire," Trotsky said.

"I started with nothing but my bare fists, working for shit." Gaudet took his feet off the hotel coffee table. "Let's call them."

In seconds Trotsky had the Quatram office on the line.

"Get me 'Big Mohammed,' " Gaudet said, referring to the chief of the computer men. Big Mohammed was a short, balding man named Wilbur Hogan. With a noticeable paunch, Hogan was the type who liked big silver belt buckles on his blue jeans. He was divorced and couldn't find a girlfriend in Texas, so Gaudet had hired him one. Although the first and second girls didn't take, the third seemed to be sticking around and Big Mohammed seemed content living in Quatram, for the moment.

Gaudet sipped his espresso while the chief went to find Big Mohammed. It took five minutes.

"Our clients are pushing the timetable."

"Everything seems to be pushing the timetable," Big Mohammed drawled in his dreadful Texas accent.

"Do you have the time from release to complete invasion?"

"About two hours—maybe one. Fifty million Windows-based computers and a few million VN-based computers."

"How about the FAA?"

"We will get on the network, but not through the Internet. You know the old slogan: 'Crispy on the outside, but a gooey, soft center on the inside.' Cordyceps will overload the system and bring it to a halt."

"You don't know how long?"

"If it hits the hardware like I think it will, we're talking weeks, maybe months. Weeks for sure."

"Electrical utilities?"

"Some. Rolling blackouts all over the place."

"I'm counting on the phones. Especially long-distance infrastructure."

"Again I'll predict a significant impact. It will not all be down. But Americans will be writing plenty of letters. A crimp in the e-mail."

"Railroads?"

"Down by thirty-five percent. Just a guess."

"Pipelines?"

"Don't know. Not sure how tech-dependent they are. But don't worry. The stock markets are gonna crash, no doubt about it."

"Have we any chance of getting command and control?"

"Nothing's changed there. They'll still have full military capability, except to the extent that domestic chaos cripples it."

Gaudet hung up without another word and turned to Trotsky. "Make sure our investors aren't the only ones with put options. I want plenty, and well disguised."

"I've been buying for weeks." Trotsky seemed offended.

Gaudet didn't respond to that comment. He checked his watch. "How long?"

"They're strolling. How long we don't know."

"I want to watch the bastard die."

"I think that is a bad idea."

"I don't give a shit."

"Remote revenge is underrated." Trotsky smiled again. Twice in a day. "Think of it as a private jubilation of the imagination."

* * *

Grady called Sam, determined that she would go alone with Michael to get the journals and equally determined that she would put up a fight as necessary. There was no way Sam would agree and the odds of convincing him had to be near zero. In order to make the call, she walked down the street because she wasn't going to argue with Sam in front of Michael. They weren't far from the middle of Manhattan and there were plenty of people on the street. She supposed the thing that bothered her the most was that if he said no, she wouldn't go. The cabbie didn't seem to mind stopping as long as he had his meter running.

"Sam, we have to talk about something."

"I can always tell when you're loaded for bear." Grady tapped her foot for a moment and didn't say anything. It pissed her off that he had already put her in a neat, little box. It was the rebellious-brat-employee box.

"I want to go very low profile with Michael and pick up his journals. It's either that or he goes alone."

"You think it's a good idea?"

"It's better that I go than nobody goes. He needs a guide in this country. Surely, you've noticed that."

"If you want to, go ahead. Tell Yodo what you want."

"I want to pick them up halfway between Manhattan and Ithaca. Somewhere remote. And then I want Michael to lock the journals away in a vault when we get back."

"Good plan. Jill can arrange for the vault."

"Anything else?" she asked, unable to believe his response.

"Make a copy of the 1998 journal and courier it to the office. Jill can provide the courier. Also make copies of all the journals and have them locked somewhere else, where only Michael can get them. Jill could probably help you with that as well."

"Sam, are you feeling okay?"

"You're grown-up now. And that means I have to be will-ing to let you die."

Grady froze up when he said that. "You never said any-thing like that before."

"I respect you and, I think, to a certain degree you can act like a real contract agent. I'm not always going to be there to yank your butt from the jaws of defeat."

"This is one hell of a cold fatherly talk." Then she laughed because she didn't know what else to do.

" 'Treat every failure as a new beginning.' My mother said that. I believe in you."

Grady walked back down the sidewalk, feeling fright-ened . . . and proud.

"If we hurry, we can be back in time for lunch tomorrow," she said to Michael.

"I already called Rebecca and told her the meeting would have to be put off—maybe for a few days. She was very dis-appointed, but I have to make it up to her by taking her hik-ing in the California mountains. That woman is a negotiator."

Yodo came walking toward them. Obviously, he had al-ready talked to Sam.

"Good luck." He held out his hand and Grady shook it.

"What'll you be, a pallbearer?" Grady smiled.

Sam and Anna walked along the edge of Central Park to-ward the Plaza Hotel. Tonight he had a blond handlebar mustache and blond hair with eyebrows to match and wore a beret. Anna wore a Snoopy hat complete with earflaps. Looking at her, a person would never think celebrity. The driver of a horse-drawn carriage shivered in the autumn cold and snubbed his cigarette under a Red Wing boot. Sam could tell that Anna wanted to take a ride through the city.

The horse pawed the pavement, maybe bored, maybe pissed off. Since the horse's ears were forward, Sam banked on bored and ready to go.

"Take us on a thirty-minute round," Sam said.

In the carriage was a heavy blanket. Sam pulled it over them. He wanted to think, and it didn't surprise him that Anna knew his mood. Under the blanket she put her hand on his arm and looked off at the people and shops as they rode down Fifth Avenue. Sam knew he was at a crossroads in his life. There were decisions made at forty-two that could not be made at sixty-two. There were choices a man could regret, some irreversible, and he didn't want to make one of those.

He thought about his grandfather and a talk they once had. Sam had been trying to decide about a young woman in his neighborhood who wanted to go away to college, but she had become so infatuated with Sam that she was losing her will to leave home. Sam wanted her to stay because he wanted to hang out with her, but at the same time he believed that for her own sake she should leave and go to school and get a career. It was a struggle.

"I want to tell you a story," he said to Anna. "A story my grandfather told to me."

"Shoot."

"It may be a little corny." Sam grinned.

"Corny is good when you're pregnant. You have to make your thinking more basic."

"Back before my grandfather's time, the Tiloks had a very old chief. One tooth left in his head just before he died. Black Hawk. Called himself Jones to the whites. Grandfather had a painting of him and talked about how he kept the tribe from violence."

"I suppose the tooth part is apropos of nothing but a lack of dentistry," Anna joked.

Sam loved her sense of humor.

"So, Black Hawk was confronted with a choice of two men to be his successor. One was Charles Curtis, the other Andrew Wiley. Wiley had many enemies. He was arrogant and contentious, but also strong and impressive, and men followed him. Nobody could beat him in wrestling. Curtis was a good planner; he could read and write and he helped the widows. And he understood growing crops. He never talked of gaining revenge on the whites—unlike Wiley, who doted on the fantasy.

"Black Hawk needed to choose one of the two men. If he chose Wiley, the young men would be happy, at least most of them. There were a few young men, those more educated in the white man's ways, who wanted Curtis and would have nothing of Wiley. These men tended to live off the reservation. In his heart Black Hawk knew that for the future, living with the white man and abiding by his laws, Curtis was the best choice for the people. But on his deathbed the chief wanted also to please the young men.

"Black Hawk devised a test question to determine the best man for the job: 'Suppose the white man's government came to the village and wanted to buy a piece of the reservation for very little money. Suppose the money was so little and the land was so great that the tribe might not survive, so that the white man was stealing our future. Suppose there were two ideas. One idea was for the chief to starve himself and to tell the white man's newspaper of the injustice. The other was for the strongest braves to take a hostage, a powerful white man in the government who was known to be traveling in the area. What would you do?'

"Wiley was quick to answer: 'The men would sneak out at night and at daybreak, in the gray of the morning, they would take the government man and blindfold him so that he could not recognize them; then they would hide him in the mountains, where no one could find him. They would offer next to negotiate for their land and say nothing of the government man or his whereabouts. If they could not change the mind of the white men in the negotiation, they would at least kill their hostage and they would take more government men in the night and kill them as well, and they would have some retribution for their loss.'

"This answer pleased the young men.

"Curtis gave his answer: 'I would go out alone in the night. I would sneak up to the government man's house. If possible, even on the threshold or even inside. At first light I would show myself. I would ask to speak with the government man in front of the man who writes newspapers. I would tell him that I had come to prevent violence and to stop an injustice. I would tell him that I would take no food until the matter was resolved so that the Tiloks could survive.'

"Wiley scoffed, or so the story goes. He says: 'But they would ignore you and laugh or even put you in chains and then the people would be without a leader.'

"Curtis argued: 'That is where you are wrong. If they put me in chains or even killed me, the people would have a greater leader. Because a leader is a man who shows the way. You cannot kill the white men and go unpunished and it is foolish to try.'

"Wiley figured he had him. Turning to the crowd, he said: 'So you would give up without a fight.'

"And this was Curtis's answer: 'But that is only me,' he said. 'If they killed me, or put me in chains or merely ignored me and ignored my plea, the village could make a new plan. Perhaps another man could come and another. I would trade my life for a chance to buy peace for the people and I would teach others to do the same.'

"Wiley's view of the world was essentially that the chief must survive because he viewed the tribe as an extension of himself and saw himself as at the center of value. Curtis, on the other hand, saw himself as only one man and saw that there might be good in giving himself for something greater than himself. He saw value in other places. 'Every person has a Wiley and a Curtis inside them,' Grandfather said. 'They are always with us.' Regarding that girlfriend of mine, Grandfather said that my Wiley and my Curtis were in a struggle for my soul.

"I think that's what is happening now. There is something epic about a child—a small person with his whole life in front of him. A mind that a man could nurture and teach. But with the child would come diapers, whining, parent-teacher conferences." He decided he'd said enough and kissed her on the lips.

"What did you do?"

"Told the girl to go to college. She met a man and fell in love. I know I never would have married her."

"There are all those future potential girlfriends of Sam," Anna began, "or Robert, or whoever. Beautiful women. Beaches full of them, malls full of them, on the sidewalk, in the restaurants, tending their gardens, going about life, every one of them an extraordinary adventure and you would be forfeiting all of that. I know, Sam. I know how it is."

"But there is that child. A child that is ours together. And there is you."

He kissed her again, and this time she kissed back. People were watching, so they cooled it and went back to playing under the blanket.

He looked in her eyes and saw a calm certainty. Oddly, he was both pleased and distressed that she looked so wise. Still, he thought he should make things plain and give his little talk.

"I've decided."

"Yes?"

"I want to marry you." He paused. "So, I'm asking if you will be my wife."

"I love you." She began kissing him anew despite the onlookers. "You will marry me in public?"

"In Times Square, if you want."

"I accept. Not the Times Square part. The rest."

"I think we should become a family. I'll drop the anonymous routine."

"Can we do the honeymoon before the marriage?"

"It's a little backward, but sure. Did I surprise you?"

"I'm thrilled. And happy. Happier than I have ever been," Anna confessed.

"When did you know?"

"When you told me, of course."

"Come on. I could see it in your eyes."

"Well . . ."

"Come on . . ."

"I was pretty sure when I saw the pink spot on the little tester strip that says 'Sam has one in the oven.' "

Sam nodded.

"You remember when we met?" she asked.

"How could I forget?"

"When I saw that sailboat and a guy in the raffia hat, I knew even then that you were coming for me to haul my ass out of the Devil's Gate. And when I jumped overboard, I knew you would follow. And when I told you that I had to have your help with my brother, I was pretty sure that you would do it. And the first time we made love . . ."

"You're an incurable romantic."

"Okay, so when do you think I knew?"

"Some things dawn on us a little bit at a time."

When she cried, he told himself that it was going to be like this with all the pregnancy hormones and the lactation and the ligaments turning rubbery and all the other transformations that went along with this business of making a baby. Since there were pills for erections and pills for anxiety and pills for depression and pills for sleeping, Sam wondered if there might be a pregnancy pill. Better yet, a relationship pill for nervous Indians.

He waited for Anna's tears to turn to a mere glistening and resumed the conversation about her new movie deal. That worked for a minute. Then she got hungry for a pickle and a peanut butter sandwich.

They pulled up in front of the bed-and-breakfast in a yellow cab with a driver who spoke with his hands, fingers, and a clipboard with preprinted messages. Sam was a bit uneasy, he supposed about leaving Bowden. It seemed these days that he could smell Gaudet, and he now wondered if it was really Gaudet or simply the conclusion that Gaudet would soon figure out Michael Bowden's whereabouts.

There were gates of wrought iron everywhere along the sidewalk and it looked like a haphazard arrangement of barricades, as though made by kids for war games. Nobody seemed to agree on exactly how much of the sidewalk was public. On the street side of the cab Sam got out to go around to open the door for the new queen of his life, but she was already exiting, so he contented himself with taking her arm. His knowledge of her pregnancy had made her seem fragile.

She laughed, obviously understanding her newfound status in the hierarchy of his brain.

There were people on the street and in this part of town, as usual, relatively prosperous people; if there were holes in their blue jeans, they were the designer sorts of holes, raggedy white from machine washing. Some people needed to prove they could have holes and be cool.

A man stood reading his newspaper, no doubt waiting for his wife's nails to dry. He seemed to be having trouble turning the pages with his black leather—no doubt fur-lined—gloves, and his heavy black glasses seemed to match purposely the black shoes and the black poodle dog.

The buildings were many-storied and Sam glanced up and around as he reached out a hand for a gate. On their side of the street, in a window bay on the next building over and several floors up, his eye caught a glint of something, or maybe it was just that he suddenly supposed someone was behind the glass. It was a feeling like bricks falling to the pavement and he felt in himself a sort of startled response. Then the man with the newspaper jerked his head up, seemingly at the very second there was the sound of shooting—multiple shots in fairly quick succession. And then Sam felt himself lifted with a hit to the chest and crumpled to the sidewalk along with Anna. He was aware of the pain and thankful for the body armor, all in the same instant.

He rolled over the top of Anna and covered her, trying to get every inch of his body over hers at exactly the same instant, and once that was done, he stuffed his hand inside his partially unzipped coat, reaching for his 10mm Smith & Wesson.

People were rushing toward them, in what he suspected was the line of fire. Soon there were at least five people huddled round and he realized that whoever had fired the shot that had hit him was not likely to get another. And it was odd because it wasn't automatic fire. That struck him even as he lay on the pavement. It should have been automatic fire, but he had heard only a series of single shots and he was hit with only a single bullet. There was a reason for this, and he would work it out, and he hated himself for thinking it because he knew he should be thinking about Anna beneath him. And with that, he raised himself and looked down and saw blood oozing from the side of her head.

"Ambulance!" he shouted. "Ambulance!"

From the crowd came a soft voice: "Do you need anything?"

Sam couldn't respond. He thought perhaps he was weeping but wasn't sure.

Sam sat in a waiting area while they did the surgery. There had been flurries of activity around Anna since she arrived at the hospital, and mostly he couldn't get closer than about ten feet. Anna's mother, Carol, had come, but she had ignored him; obviously, there was an issue with her where he was concerned. Although he had begun explaining to her that he and Anna were to be married, Carol was like a cornered animal in her determination to hide from the truth. When he saw the pain and the fear in her eyes, he backed off and explained that he had been with Anna and that it was important that he stay with her at least until things stabilized. Carol had the durable power of attorney for health care and Sam was not consulted as to Anna's treatment. At the moment that was all right because he had satisfied himself that Dr. Prince, the attending neurosurgeon, was very competent and that Anna's mother truly cared for her.

Sam had made it a point to befriend the nurses—one in particular, named Lydia. He told her briefly that he was Anna's security man, that he and Anna were great friends, and that he had even grown to love her. He did not explain about the engagement or that Anna had returned his affection. Given Anna's high-profile life, he explained that he was very vulnerable to the press and that it would be a great kindness if she told no one. Normally, he would have expected the nurse to talk, but this woman was serious, not given to careless gossip when it came to her duties, and he knew she would keep silent. She would be an ally. Even if the woman let it slip, he had to conduct himself as though Anna would live and, therefore in her own time, Anna would announce their love to the world. His anonymity would be gone forever. It would be a great and wonderful new beginning, but if possible, it was something he and Anna should do together.

Exhaustion had set in for Sam, probably from resisting the depression. Sam needed to sit and experience his misery so that he could eventually escape it. But there was no time. It wasn't as if someone else could take over and carry on the work of stopping Gaudet. Anna lay in a coma and it seemed that if he could sit at her bedside, he might help her to get better. It was a torturous conflict whether to devote himself completely to the one, or try to save the many.

He took a moment to call his mother. Sometimes she was more *Talth* spiritual leader than pyschologist, sometimes more psychologist than *Talth,* but she was always Mother.

First he explained that Anna was pregnant, then what had happened, and that he was all right save for his weary sorrow. Of course he blamed himself. He should have had Anna surrounded with security so that a bullet could not have gotten to her. It was stupid to even be with her while he was fighting Gaudet and protecting Bowden. He should have made her see that. He told his mother all of this.

"I will go to Universe Rock and make prayers."

"I am trying to stop the man I told you about. I believe he has a very dangerous technology that could be used against many people. I don't know what he is doing with it."

"This is the man that you have been hunting?"

"Yes, this is the one."

"And you are sure he will hurt many. Kill many people?"

"I believe that, yes. I am convinced, although I don't have the proof yet."

"Even Anna might suffer if he is not stopped?"

"Yes. Definitely."

"But you have fallen in love and she needs you," Spring reminded him.

"Yes."

"Who else is with her?"

"Her mother. She doesn't much like me, but she is a good woman."

"She doesn't know you. You are uncertain about marriage?" she sincerely asked.

"I . . . I . . . don't think . . ." That one stumped Sam. "I guess I'm not sure if I'm uncertain." He could sense his mother's smile at that one.

"Anna has no Indian in her and I think it worries you that she will not accept you because you are Indian. Perhaps you question whether you will be good for her. You worry that you are not right for her world."

"It's partly what I do for a living. Worry. I compare myself to Grandfather."

"Grandfather's life force was very focused and it was focused on teaching young men and on understanding. Your life force is very focused as well."

"Yes. It's focused on catching assholes being assholes. Perhaps that is why I can never be like him."

"You can't conclude that you will never be like Grandfather. Each man has only so much he can give and he has to decide where he will give it," Spring advised.

"My mother drops the whole load."

"Normally, I would never drop the whole load as you put it, but you are on a cliff's face trying to decide which way to climb. You can't stop to cook a meal or build a house. This man you hunt kills your friends and your family and you are wondering . . . where has God gone . . . where is justice . . . and somehow you wonder if it is all because you haven't done it just right."

"If I felt bad before, it's even worse now. But I don't think I'm a head case."

"Your father killed himself and hid your heritage from you. And yet you are a very good man, a caring man, a strong man." Spring was consoling her child.

"But a strange man."

"You should know what you are up against. It is not just this evil fellow. It is what is inside you. I understand why you have called me. You need someone you respect to give you permission to leave Anna and to devote yourself to hunting this nemesis. You tell yourself that you are the only one that can do it. And it might be true. But maybe, you ask yourself, you are leaving her side because you are not strong enough to do the right thing. Many days from now, when Anna is better, and swollen with your child, when you look in her eyes and put your hand on her stomach . . . will you know that you did the right thing and will she know it too?" Spring counseled.

"That is what I don't know." Sam lost it for a few minutes and then put himself back together.

Jean-Baptiste marveled at Benoit's self-assurance. Although he was on top, her legs were tightly gripping his thighs and her pelvis was perfectly fitted to his and she controlled the friction of their movements and the rhythm of their sex so that her excitation steadily mounted. Sweat from her belly felt good under his, and the strain and tension in her body had a sensuous quality that magnified his lust and it was all he could do not to climax as he observed her passion building. The woman was to sex as the Rolls-Royce was to automobiles. Then her breaths became very deep and her voice high pitched as she began to moan and mutter her incantation: "In . . . in . . . in . . . in."

Her back arched and she nearly screamed and it made him feel very much the bull man as he worked his way up to his own orgasm.

They were back in the Hotel International, back in the same room with the same pastries. For a moment he wondered if it was bugged and then dismissed the idea.

When she rolled off, he lay beside her, admiring her body and wondering at his good fortune while he tried to stifle the guilt. His life was becoming ever more confusing. He was a good public servant in the service of a government that was as soft as it was inept. He was a man of talent who had been passed over and now he was making sure that he was not entirely without good fortune. Like rules about monogamy and sex, which he was stretching some, he was also wreaking havoc with the rules of his profession. But it seemed necessary and not unlike the things done by other men who had escaped doormat status—a life spent under the boots of the arrogant and wealthy.

She went to shower, and even when he was spent she fascinated him. He sat on the toilet seat and watched her, still thrilling at the sight of her lithe body. He never had enough of looking. It was possible to watch by pulling back the edge of the shower curtain and he enjoyed the water pouring over her skin and the droplets beading over her.

"So, tell me about Gaudet. What will he do after Cordyceps?"

"Plastic surgery. I'm sure he already has the new identity and no one really knows the old one. I know what he looks like, but that is about it."

"What will it be like when I meet him?"

"You won't really. You won't see him and you won't be close enough to touch him and he will disguise his voice. He will give you nothing of himself."

"I can see why you worked for the company—why you practically ran it."

"You know Thomas Edison, the American inventor? He said that people miss opportunity because it comes dressed in overalls and looks like work. That is the biggest component of success—work. But there is another component. When the Wright Brothers invented the airplane, the world was ready for a flying machine. When Edison invented the electric light, the world was ready to escape the soot. I am telling you the world is ready to master the body. I can see that you are a man with the vision to be part of that."

"You know how to inflate a man's ego."

"I can feel ambition in a man. I feel ambition in you. And you know that France will pay for Chaperone. Likewise, you know there are people who will make a killing when the market falls. You can take a big bite out of both apples. But now you need to ask the admiral to let me go to the United States."

"You think I can just snap my fingers?"

"Ask him or we are through. I will go back to the dungeon."

"Relax. I will ask him. He will say no, but I will ask just the same. Benoit? What made you dream up this whole idea?"

"Prison has a way of focusing your thoughts. Liberation is a powerful incentive."

Baptiste nodded.

"I will have to tell the admiral about Cordyceps and, of course, France will have to appear to try to stop it."

Baptiste opened his mouth to protest.

"Don't worry. The admiral can try all he wants, but he won't be playing with a full deck. I'll see to that."

She stepped out of the shower and onto the tile floor. Moving the towel over her body was like a peep show. When she glanced down and saw his erection, she reached for it and pushed him back a bit; then she settled on him and she hunkered down very tight and began to move. In minutes the tightness of her and the softness of her aroused him near to orgasm. Her back became taut and he could feel the muscles like steel bands above her buttocks as she orchestrated the level of friction with her pubic bone. God, it was as if her body were a suction cup pulled tight to his. Her breathing became strong and he tasted the new sweat between her breasts. When her nipples were hard, and the size of thimbles, he took the right one in his mouth and used his tongue so that she shuddered and moved even harder down on him. The slickness of her made a giant quivering in his thighs and he could feel her perfect rhythm, now like a galloping horse hard onto the finish line, and then she moaned deep and long and he let himself come and he felt strong. So strong.

Baptiste ordered security not to let Benoit contact anyone. He would do all the talking to the admiral that needed to be done. It was a dangerous career move, but the relief it provided him made it seem worth the risk. Preventing Admiral Larive from initiating a meeting with her would be more difficult. As he was thinking through how he would approach the admiral, his phone rang. It was Figgy.

"Somebody just tried to kill Sam and got his girlfriend instead."

"Why in the hell are we talking on an open line?"

"Because I don't give a shit, and besides, nobody is listening and it wouldn't matter to me if they were."

"There is actually a Sam?"

"I said cut the shit," Figgy barked.

"Who did it? Gaudet?"

"I was worried it might be you or your boss."

"No way. Get it straight. We want Sam to lead us to Chaperone. If someone is trying to kill him, it's no doubt Gaudet and we don't have a clue to his whereabouts."

"You're sure."

"I'm certain. Keep your eye on the ball. There is a lot of money to be made."

Baptiste hung up. Now was the time to meet Gaudet. He would need an alibi—a way of legitimizing the meeting if someone found out. He went to the admiral.

The man was smoking one of his cigars and that normally meant he was in a good mood. It was rare of the admiral to have a cigar in his office. The room was large, with a desk at one end and a more informal conference area at the other, and the office permitted a great deal of pacing on the admiral's part.

"I have a tip that Gaudet wants to talk," he began.

The chief puffed extra hard on his cigar and Baptiste could see a brightness in the eyes.

"How do you talk with Gaudet in the future?" the admiral questioned.

"I dial a cell phone number."

"Do you have it all down in the file?"

"Oh yes."

"What kind of a deal could the French government make with a man like Gaudet?"

"Offer to buy Chaperone," Baptiste answered.

"Yes, except I thought he doesn't have it."

"But he's a dog in the hunt with a lot of inside information."

"We haven't found Raval?"

"Not yet."

"And Sam?"

"Figgy says not yet."

"Sam brought down Grace Technologies so I know his organization is effective. What are they doing, then? That's what I'm getting at."

"Trying to catch Gaudet."

"We all claim to be trying to stop Gaudet. Where is Sam now?" the admiral inquired.

"New York. Michael Bowden is there too, Figgy says."

"We all need Bowden, that's sure. It alone is enough reason to go there. Now, how do you get Bowden on our side? Never mind. I don't need to know. You just need to do it. And get Chaperone. I have been told that France must win this race in the strongest possible terms. Do you understand me?"

"Yes, sir," Baptiste said. "There is one more thing."

"Yes?"

"I don't want you to think I'm crazy, but I believe we should consider temporarily releasing Benoit Moreau to assist us."

"You're right, I think you're crazy. Why?"

Baptiste explained Benoit's plan for getting the technology for France in exchange for a pardon—Bowden's knowledge of the source of the molecule, Gaudet's knowledge of the vector technology, and Raval's knowledge of the Chaperone immune system process.

"You actually think she could do all that?"

"It doesn't hurt us to let her try. The only risk is that she will escape."

"It'll be your risk, then. If you believe in her, I'll go with a temporary release on your say-so. Submit a memo arguing strongly for her temporary release in the best interest of the Republic and I will take it to the minister."

Benoit Moreau walked out of the government lab that day. Pulling a good travel bag on wheels behind her, she caught a cab for Charles de Gaulle International Airport.

Grady and Michael left the car off campus on the street after having looked for fifteen minutes for a place to park. It had taken them a couple days to recoup from Anna's tragedy and for Grady to become functional. They had remained in New York until the third evening getting ready and making one last somber visit to Anna's bedside.

Dressed like students, they carried backpacks loaded with volumes of an old encyclopedia they'd borrowed from the bed-and-breakfast. Traversing the Eddy Dam footbridge, they wound up past a tennis building to Hoy Road, until they finally found their way to Tower Road and Corson Hall, a biological sciences building at Cornell University. Michael wore a stocking cap and Grady an old fur-lined leather cap from the Salvation Army. Unless one knew exactly what he was looking for, it would be tough to spot them. Because the Kevlar under their parkas made their bodies appear somewhat full, a trained eye would note the possibility of body armor. Now that she was on her own, Grady wasn't as anxious to argue about the Kevlar. They had traveled in the night then took a hotel room and napped, without incident and without any hormone jokes. Both of them were serious and aware of the risks.

Yodo and the bodyguards were staying completely out of sight, back at the bed-and-breakfast, leaving the impression that the entire group, including their charges, had planned a couple of days indoors.

It was cold and looking like snow. Walking across campus, thinking about her aunt, wishing she could be at her side, Grady began to think about her own life, and to fantasize about actually living in a place filled with biology, math, poetry, weighty with thoughts but light on earthly responsibility. For a moment she wondered: was such an idyllic life really that appealing? If she wanted it, she could have it, her aunt would give it to her in a second, and so would Sam, for that matter. It was she who had maneuvered herself out of her classes and into the Amazon and then to New York, and now she was here with a pistol in her purse and no bodyguards.

Looking around with studied casualness, she tried to spot someone that didn't look like a student—maybe a forty-year-old with some flesh on his bones and a mug portraying the cold solitude of a professional criminal. It was a notion from the movies. Sam had explained that some of the deadliest killers were nondescript, never standouts. If Gaudet had any professional killers trailing them, they wouldn't be easy to spot.

Corson Hall was a mostly brick three-story building of nondescript modern architecture. Dr. Lyman's offices were on the second floor. They went in a small side door, feeling safer than if they had charged through one of the main entrances, where she imagined that Gaudet might have someone posted. The faculty offices were typical, modest, with personalized memorabilia according to the tastes of the occupant. As they looked from the doorway, they saw two men in bulked-up suits in chairs in the hallway. One read a paper, the other a book, but they both looked up the moment the quiet electronic chime went off—obviously triggered by opening the door. Grady suddenly knew why it had been so effortless to talk Sam into this mission. She felt both mildly pissed and quietly reassured. Sam wasn't really prepared to let her die yet. As they approached the office of Dr. Lyman, they noticed an open door to an office across the way. In it was a third man, no doubt with a Howitzer in his coat.

At the appointed hour of 11:00 A.M. Michael and Grady approached Dr. Lyman's partially opened door and pushed it a little farther to find a rugged-looking, trim man, fiftyish or so, and quite handsome. He sported a mustache that was well trimmed and Grady noticed a wall filled with pictures of this man with various graduate students and natives in a jungle setting. A field biologist, apparently.

"Pretty heady stuff sitting around with my own private army. They go everywhere with me except inside the class-room and the bathroom. My wife gave them milk and cookies last night. Different group, though, on nights. Michael, how are you?"

Michael shook Lyman's hand. "I'm fine. And this is Grady Wade." Lyman shook her hand as well. "You never mentioned your company here."

"Nope. I just do as I'm told. Very well-placed people from the FBI told me I should allow these guys into my life. They're good guys. It's great to see you, but I'll bet you want to see those journals."

"That'd be great. I really appreciate your taking care of them." But Grady could see that Michael was unhappy. Sam's presence loomed large here, even having insinuated itself with an old friend and colleague. She put her hand in the middle of Michael's back.

Dr. Lyman smiled. "Not a problem. The journals are in another building entirely, so we'll have to travel a ways to the other side of campus." He started putting on a heavy wool long coat and, to no one's surprise, the shadows did the same when the fellow from across the hall brought the coats.

Chapter 13

In Death there are no troubled waters nor is there any
need of hope for the calm.

—Tilok proverb

A matter-of-fact beep kept precise time with the tempo of
Anna's heartbeat, underscoring her fragile state, her head
was swathed in bandages. It had taken eighteen hours of
surgery to remove the bullet fragment. Dr. Prince, whose
straight back and firm jaw and head of gray hair were a fine
match for his surname, spoke reassuringly in the manner of
a decent trial lawyer or politician. But it was as a neurosurgeon
that he held a place in the top tier of Sam Wintripp's universe. When Dr. Prince said that her recovery was hopeful,
his soft, rising tones were themselves instruments of hope
for those seeking the man-made version. When he said there
could be no accurate prognosis, you knew that he was telling
the unvarnished truth. With that, his pastoral role ended as
rapidly as it had begun.

Dr. Prince didn't think the bullet had destroyed anything
vital, so a full recovery was possible. There was some explanation about the holistic nature of brains and the compensat-
ing circuitry that boiled down to: She might be fine or she
might have one of a seemingly endless number of disabili-

ties. Or she might die from a hemorrhage. Watch and wait meant just that.

She had been unconscious for three days. People all around him told Sam that it was best to assume she could hear him and he should talk to her. It was best to say reassuring things and to dwell on pleasant topics. If it felt like talking to a sleeping person he should take heart: comas were little understood, and not the equivalent of sleep.

They had shaved her head and he knew she wasn't going to like that, assuming she could ever like anything again. Nurses came and went, and at the moment one was adjusting the pillows that were part of bedsore prevention.

Sam drank hospital rot-gut coffee from the nurses' station. Tasted like camp coffee made in a can without a filter.

Anna's mother, Carol, came back in the room after finding some lunch and it was still obvious from the way she opened the door, the way she carried herself through it, the way she had the flowers carried for her, the way she cast her eyes, and the way she knew how to fill up a room with a five-foot eight-inch frame, she was in charge.

"I want to talk with you."

For the second time since he met her, she spoke to him other than with regard to simple logistics.

"Anna told me about you," she said right out. "Mystery man, no name, no identity, a creature of some netherworld that she didn't understand, but she was foolish enough to be excited about it. Surely, it wasn't you that made her feel that way."

Sam smiled a weary smile. "I was so relieved when I saw how much you loved her, how you wanted to protect her from the likes of me. And there was some truth in what you were feeling. My life has been dangerous for Anna."

Carol looked at him hard and then she softened.

"I want her so much to make it . . . and I blamed you."

"I know."

The woman turned away in her grief.

"I believe she's going to make it," Sam said. "Call me if anything changes."

"I will. I promise."

"I'll be checking in. You call if you need anything. It is right that I should leave and attend to things that would be important to Anna."

"I believe you."

Sam relied on a mother's love and the skill of the highly professional nursing staff to bolster his confidence. He left the hospital for the local FBI office. He still wondered about everything and it was a terrible indecision that dogged his every move. He tried calling Ernie Dunkin, his primary contact with the FBI, but got no answer. He didn't want to take whoever else might be on call. At times Ernie pretended not to like the hassles of dealing with a renegade government contractor, but essentially he liked Sam and cooperated as best he could. Ernie had gotten credit for some major arrests through tips and evidence provided by Sam, and no doubt those merit citations shaped Ernie's thinking.

Within several hours of the shooting Sam's team of local private investigators, all ex-cops, some New York city, some Feds, had begun their own preliminary investigation. It might be tough to prove that Gaudet was behind the shooting, but they did demonstrate to Sam's satisfaction that it was a setup and Gaudet was the man with the motivation.

Sam passed his Robert Chase picture ID to the woman in the glass booth. Chase was well known to the FBI. Under that ID he was listed as a top informant and always received a welcome reception from any agent with a computer. Without a special access code a field agent could not access any of Sam's aliases or the name on his birth certificate. Sam had seven aliases, but only three were deep aliases complete with a Social Security number. Possession of three Social Security numbers was the only illegal facet of Sam's aliases, but it was administratively approved for two of them through a slightly unusual use of the witness protection program. As to the third, Sam simply told the government to concentrate on the intelligence they received through his offices. To date that had cured their bureaucratitis.

Sam gave up his gun and his permit to carry it at the front desk.

He was ushered into the office of Special Agent Bud Cross.

The man had a pinched, narrow face, was balding, sported a bushy mustache, and wore wire-framed glasses. The blue eyes looked at him with something less than warmth.

They shook hands.

"I will be honest with you, Mr. Chase, or whatever your name really is. I don't care for special people. I like regular ones. However, the bosses in DC say extend every courtesy and so you shall have every courtesy of this office. I just want you to know where I stand. Cops should be cops and everybody else should be a civilian—that's my personal bias and not the official view of the FBI."

"I think it's the view of most conscientious field agents, and I respect it," Sam said. "I'm really here as a civilian."

"We've gone over the shooting thoroughly. DC is all over my ass because it was Anna Wade and not some chambermaid. And we can't find a thing to substantiate your theory. Two guys with a history get in a street fight and start shooting. They have some drugs in them. Not a lot, but enough."

"Very convenient. Two guys just start shooting at each other for no reason. They shoot way wide, missing each other, then go to an alley and kill each other simultaneously. Think about it."

"These nuts do that stuff all the time. They're paranoid once they get a grudge going."

"They fight, sure. But two guys don't often simultaneously shoot each other. More likely, that was staged," Sam said.

"Yeah, well, we've leaned on several gang members and everyone says these two hated each other."

"That's why they were pointed out by the leader to create the charade. Gaudet made a logical selection."

"The gang members we talked to say this isn't the first time these two have shot at each other."

"Look. Those two kids were being used. I know it was the work of the man I've described to you."

"Perhaps, but they are both dead. Preliminary ballistics tests confirm the bullets that hit you and Anna Wade didn't come from the two thugs' guns. But they got away from the scene. One of them might have had a second gun and that gun may not have been fired into the surrounding buildings. Or there might have been a third shooter involved in the melee. Of course both those options are unlikely. Ballistics supports your sniper theory, but we have nothing more at this point. Nobody saw anything except two guys shooting on the street."

Sam didn't say anything, hoping for more, for something else.

"Look, I'm sympathetic. We're doing a lot of forensic work on the bodies. Maybe we'll find someone who knew about a setup. Maybe they talked to somebody. Right now we have nothing but your instincts and a mysterious ballistics test."

"Whatever you can do, I appreciate it."

"You're not going to take the law into your own hands?" Cross was concerned.

"I'm going to do my job, nothing more and nothing less." But despite his words, there was a deadly single-minded determination in Sam and nothing anyone could say or do would change that.

When he hit the street, he called the nurses' station and spoke with Lydia, the nurse he had befriended. Anna's condition hadn't changed, but her color looked good and they were still full of hope, Lydia said. He would call back in a few hours.

"I'm sorry, Sam," Grogg began the phone conversation. It was the way everyone from the office started. It was hard to go on working and act normally while Anna lay in a coma. Sam wasn't quite sure how to deal with it, right down to the condolences. He couldn't stop thinking of her, seeing her lying there, so still.

"I appreciate your thoughts, Grogg. I'm sure Anna does too. I wish I could put the world on hold and be with Anna, but since I can't, I just keep chugging as best I can. So, tell me, have you turned anything up?"

"Yeah, something important."

Sam could hear the excitement in his voice.

"What is it?"

"Just a minute."

Sam then heard Jill pick up on a second line.

"Sam, we got an e-mail message from someone in the French government, probably their Senate, purporting to relay a message from Benoit Moreau. It says 'I can help you disinfect Cordyceps and deliver Chaperone.' "

"Did you say yes?" Sam said, absolutely amazed.

"We couldn't get hold of you, so we winged it and said 'Absolutely yes.' "

"Good answer. How the heck did she send the message?"

"E-mail. It was sent to firechiefatbluehades.com."

Sam's mind tumbled as to how such a thing could be possible.

"Guess she put one over on us, Sam."

"I gave that to Anna Wade, the CIA, a few other people. Wait a minute. The CIA. Figgy might know that e-mail. He could have told his clients, the French. Benoit Moreau is one of the best information gatherers in the world and she probably talked it out of some French agent right after she screwed him. That's Benoit Moreau."

"And why would someone in the French Senate want to relay a message from a convicted criminal? It could be a setup or a feint by Gaudet to mislead."

"True. But I don't see the harm in saying yes. Good job. Let me know when you get a response."

"There's more. We couldn't get hold of you at all, so we wrote a second response."

"What did you say."

" 'How can we help?' "

"Good answer."

"You won't believe what she or rather her friends answered."

"I am all ears."

" 'Monitor uaeromtioneb.net//exchange. Meet you in New York.' Signed 'Caterpillar.' Then we got no more."

"It wasn't easy monitoring that site," Grogg chimed in. "You have to have a password. Rollin's password quit working the day he died."

"But that wouldn't stop you, would it?"

"Hell no."

"So what did you do?"

"I downloaded Figgy's computer."

"You what?"

"I downloaded his computer awhile back and just recently pulled it up on Big Brain and hit gold."

"That's inexcusable. Actually, it's outrageous. What did you get?"

"His correspondence isn't saved and he has special software that scrambles it beyond recognition no matter what you do. But I got protocols for getting onto certain limited segments of the SDECE server. I was able to do the best hacking of my life and log on to the computer of Jean-Baptiste Sourriaux, a commandant apparently assigned directly for at least some purposes to Admiral Larive, the big tuna. For some reason Jean-Baptiste had the password we needed."

"Grogg, you are good. What's Baptiste up to?"

"Aside from the password, his correspondence and so on, it's all scrambled."

"Okay. Well. Use the password if it's still good. Write an e-mail. Let's take a complete flier. Pretend to be Figgy. Write: 'Please confirm independently the instructions for the meeting.' Can you make it appear that Big Brain is Figgy's laptop working through the SDECE server?"

"Good enough so only two or three computer geeks out of a thousand would catch the forgery."

"Give it a try. See what we get back."

"Hey, Sam," Jill said. "Why a meeting? What meeting?"

"No idea, but it's worth a try, isn't it? I presume Figgy meets with Baptiste at times, don't you?"

"Sure. Why do you think Benoit Moreau signed her note Caterpillar?"

"Maybe because she fancies she'll be turning into a butter-fly."

Michael, Grady, Professor Lyman, and the entourage made their way across the campus. The journals were stored in a clearinghouse structure, where various artifacts from antiquity were examined, cataloged, and held until their final resting place had been determined. Some artifacts were actually reburied once thoroughly studied. The building was located at the edge of the campus and was outfitted with heavy wire screens over the windows. It was a long brick building of three stories, simple but attractive with well-maintained white trim and matching shutters. It had no doubt been constructed for some other purpose, perhaps classrooms. It was mostly the province of physical anthropologists, paleontologists, and that sort, although the evolutionary biologists had a corner.

"Is there twenty-four-hour security?" Michael asked.

"Well, I don't really think so, but I'm sure it's safe."

They stopped at the front desk and each person signed in and received a name tag. There were people coming and going and the place looked occupied.

Michael picked up the pace as they walked through the door to one of the storage areas and proceeded to a spot pointed out by Dr. Lyman. There were about eighteen years' worth of three-ring binders, including the ones created by Michael's father before his death, with an average of three 4-inch binders per year totaling a little over sixty volumes. There were five trunks each about 4 feet by 1.5 feet by 14 inches. Each trunk was said to contain twelve volumes. Michael saw the trunks at a distance and literally trotted up to them with Grady on his heels. Reaching into his pocket, he removed a key. Each trunk had two locks. According to the labels affixed to the ends of the trunks, they were in chronological order. Michael started with the most recent trunk, dated from 1998 through October 2003. Grady felt the tension while she reassured herself that they had to be there.

But when Michael opened the trunk, it was empty.

"Amazing," Dr. Lyman said, sounding genuinely surprised in his own understated way.

Michael kicked the next trunk in line and it too was obviously empty. The rest were not. Someone had taken everything back to 1995, no doubt figuring they would get the volume describing the plant or animal that would turn out to be Chaperone.

Michael was visibly distraught. "It feels like it did when my mother died. Something very important has been taken away."

"We should have had somebody here during the day," the security man said.

"You mean you had someone here all night?"

"Oh yeah, sitting right there on that chair until they were fully operational in here at nine A.M., and we asked the people to keep an eye out for strangers."

"When were you last here?" Grady asked Lyman.

"Just yesterday. The time before that was three days ago—the day they were delivered."

"What time?"

"Early afternoon."

"Then did you call Michael right away?"

"Well, it wasn't right away because we brought them over here first."

"Who knew they were here?"

"Just me and your security fellows. Well, wait a minute. That's not true. I did tell Nemus Larkin, a graduate student I work with. He's read Dr. Bowden's books and was very interested. I'm afraid I mentioned to him about the vector technology. And Chaperone."

"Tell me you didn't." Michael groaned. "I told you not to."

"I know, I know, but he's like a son."

Grady knew that Michael had told Lyman, in fairness, so that he would understand the potential danger in taking possession of the journals. Unfortunately, Lyman had been unwise and overly enthusiastic.

"Where does this graduate student live?" she asked.

"In the basement of a house right near where I live."

"Would you take us to his house?"

"All right." Lyman shrugged. "But I'm sure he hasn't got it."

As they walked to the car, Grady whispered to Michael, "Could Lyman have taken your journals?"

"Absolutely not."

"I'm with you. I saw his face. He was as surprised as you, maybe more."

The entire group drove through the university and out Triphammer Road, past Jessup Field, past the fraternities into the neighborhoods, then down a side street to a dead-end cul-de-sac. Grady and Michael were in a car with two of the security people. They rolled up behind Dr. Lyman's vehicle in front of a brick house built into a hillside. The bottom story was a daylight basement and from the street level the house appeared as a two-story home.

Grady went to Dr. Lyman's vehicle, just in front of them.

"Please stay here with your security man."

Before going to the house Grady and Michael had a lengthy conversation with the other two security men sketching out a plan.

When they were ready Michael and Grady crossed over the sidewalk and entered through a gate in a well-kept picket fence. There was a concrete path that turned into steps alongside the house.

"He's probably not home," Grady said to Michael as they walked down the steps along a gently terraced rose garden. Someone did a nice job on the roses as the beds were weeded and the roses pruned back in anticipation of winter. The backyard was spacious for the crowded neighborhood, perhaps sixty feet square with a few autumn-colored vine maples and a birch.

When they arrived at the lower level, there was a tiny concrete porch for the basement door. Michael looked at Grady. "Once we're in, we play it by the script," she said.

"Why?" Michael smiled wryly, knowing it would get her goat.

Michael knocked.

"Maybe we should wait and talk to Sam."

"No, I want the journals now," Michael said.

A young man with gold wire-rimmed glasses and a fair number of pimples opened the door. His blond hair was short and stood on end. He smiled. Grady noticed that he was grabbing the material on his jeans right about thigh level. His fingers were constantly busy, kneading the pants.

"I'm Michael Bowden."

"Oh great, great. I'm a big fan."

"This is Grady a private detective."

"When was the last time you were over at the antiquities building, the warehouse on Osborne?" Grady asked.

"Let's see. When was the last time—"

"It's not a hard question," Grady urged.

"I was there with Dr. Lyman yesterday. But the last time. Let's see. That would be this morning. Why? What's wrong?"

"You signed in?"

"Did I sign in? Well, you're supposed to sign in."

"Did you sign in?" Michael interjected pushing his way past the young man and into the apartment. The young fellow gave way and turned as Michael entered.

"Your name is Nemus, right?"

"Right. It's Nemus."

"Nemus, you were telling Grady whether you signed in."

"I think perhaps I didn't. I know the girl at the front there."

"Did she see you walk past without signing in?" Grady asked.

"Well, let's see she might have. But . . . ah, she probably didn't."

"So, she doesn't know you went in?"

"Well, I don't know. Like I said, she knows me."

"Did you say hi to your friend?"

"Well, I don't think so."

"You mean you don't know?"

"I didn't say hi."

"How did you get there?"

"I borrowed my friend's truck."

"Which door did you use to leave the building?"

"Well, there are only three, I think."

"Nemus I don't recall Grady asking you how many doors there are. I think you stole my journals."

"That's crazy. Why would I do that?"

"Because they're worth a lot of money," Grady picked it up again. "The United States government wants them. The French want them. Terrorists want them. And Nemus they're all gonna know you have them. Michael's life's work."

"You're not scaring me."

"You have to deny your fear only because you're guilty," Michael said.

Nemus looked as if the blood in his face had drained to his feet. Plainly he was unused to crime.

"I don't have to talk to you."

"Think about how that's going to sound to the graduate school." Michael continued. "What kind of a man says I don't have to talk to you, to a fellow scientist who has lost his life's work? What would you think of such a man Nemus?"

"I'd think he was busy."

"Will they think you're busy Nemus?" Grady's voice was subdued but full of incredulity. "Is that what Professor Lyman will think, or the chair of the department, or the President of the University? When the U.S. government is bearing down, when French agents are crawling all over the place? They'll think you're too busy?"

Michael walked over to a bookcase and began pulling volumes out. Grady went to the nearest closet and began rummaging.

"You can't search my house."

"Any minute the people you were going to sell to will be arriving," Grady explained. "They'll have guns. And they'll search your house. They'll take the journals and murder you. You better get those journals out of here before they come or you're a dead man."

"You are crazy. They wouldn't . . ."

"What wouldn't they do Nemus? They tried to kill us. They murdered Michael's wife and killed a woman named Marita. Raped her sister. Killed her child. Tell us about these people Nemus if you're such an expert," Grady urged.

"I don't know what you're talking about."

"Call the police Nemus," Grady said. "Tell them you're in danger. Tell them about the people who bought the journals."

"You're not scaring me."

"It's possible we'll have found the journals by the time they get here. We'll turn them over to the police and send the academic community a full report. I'm sure they'll lay awake nights worried about your legal rights."

"Get out of my house now."

"We're exposing you Nemus," Michael began. "Ending your world as you know it. You'll be ruined forever in acad emia. Scientists the world over will spurn you. They'll get sick in the guts when you walk in the room. A petty thief. A fraud. A man who can't do his own work. What are you becoming Nemus?"

"I'm becoming nothing. Get out of here. Get out!"

Nemus was trembling.

Grady started in on the kitchen cupboards.

"Grady call the government man. Tell him we want the U.S. government. The CIA in here."

"They have no jurisdiction, you fool," Nemus said.

"Tell them that when you're full of drugs and they're pumping you for information about the foreign agents you're trying to sell to," Grady said. "Write a long letter to the director of Homeland Security and the appropriate Senate committee. After you look it up."

"Nemus concentrate on this," Michael took over. "Your whole life hangs in the balance. If you give me the journals and you leave Cornell we'll call it a misunderstanding and tell no one. If you don't a man who goes by Girard is going to take them and kill you. And if you escape that I'll probably find them in the next ten minutes or so and then you're career is dead forever. You got that?"

Nemus was thinking.

Michael headed toward the bedroom.

Nemus ran to him and grabbed his wrist but he was a small man and Michael merely glared at him and yanked his wrist away.

"Oh my God," Grady said. A man in a suit with a gun was plainly visible in the backyard. Nemus looked and moved back in the house as if to hide.

Grady pulled her Dessert Eagle .357 out of her purse. And stood out of sight.

"Here's the first one of Gerard's men Nemus."

Then a second man jumped the fence.

"We could call it a misunderstanding?" Nemus said.

"They're in the bedroom," Grady said. "His voice rose an octave when you headed that way. Or maybe they are on the way to the bedroom."

The window seat was in the hallway covered with cushions.

"In two minutes Nemus we're gonna be shooting at people. Now we need to negotiate with these people and give them the journals if we're going to get out alive."

Michael grabbed for the cushions to explore the window seat and Nemus sprinted to block him.

"Nemus this is your moment," Michael said almost in a whisper. "Your whole life hangs in the balance. If you give me my journals and tell us everything, I'll sacrifice my journals to get us out alive. I'll walk away and tell only Professor Lyman. You could still work for a corporation. No arrest. No public humiliation."

The men had now disappeared on either side of the front windows.

"You promise?"

"I promise."

Grady walked back to the window seat and opened it.

"Well look what we have here," Grady said revealing two full rows of binders. While Michael pulled them out she put her gun away, walked to the front door and stuck her head out.

"You can come in now gentlemen." Then she turned to Michael. "We have a deal Nemus but only if you come clean. So tell us about the copies, if you want to stay out of jail."

"I copied 1998. They gave me thirty grand and I sent the original out for copying."

"Where is it now?" Michael asked.

"I gave it to FedEx and threw the address away. They're coming anytime with one hundred grand to collect copies of the other volumes. They are just copying them and leaving the originals with me to return. I swear it."

"You copied these?" Michael said. "You bastard. You copied these volumes."

"I only copied the 1998 volume so far."

"What exactly did you do with it?" Grady demanded.

"I told you. I gave it to FedEx."

"Do you have the tracking slip?" Grady asked.

"Yeah I guess I do. On the desk."

"When did you deposit it?"

"This morning." Grady grabbed the tracking slip off the desk, got on the phone to Jill, and gave her the information. The package was sent to a street address in New York. It would be diverted and would end up in LA at Sam's new offices. They put Nemus on the phone for about thirty seconds to confirm the change. Jill would investigate the mailing address, but it would no doubt be newly established and a dead end.

"How much were they paying you for the 1998 copy?"

"I told you thirty thousand. But I don't know who they were. I swear."

"Where's the money?"

"They were going to give me the money with the rest. The hundred thousand for the copies of the others. Like I said."

Grady hated this Nemus character for putting her through the last forty-five minutes. She planned to talk to Lyman and make sure this fool was done at Cornell.

"I'll tell the guys to bring the trunks," Michael said.

"I'm gonna call the cops on you guys."

"Yeah, needle dick, you do that. We'll call the FBI. And we'll tell them what you stole, show them the FedEx receipt, and have you arrested for a damn felony," Grady shot back.

Nemus shut his mouth.

Grady went to get the security guys with the two 4-foot trunks and the Ford Explorer. They carried them up to the car like a couple of tiny caskets. After they had packed up the volumes, they left Nemus to his own thoughts and to contemplate the blessing of his intact body and his freedom.

Baptiste and Figgy sat at a table at a convenient restaurant located down the street from the executive terminal at Teterboro Airport. They were trying to be prudent in their eating and so had each ordered blackened salmon on cream-sauced pasta, but had the chef hold the pasta and substitute broccoli. It was boring for a Frenchman but perhaps more palatable to Figgy, Baptiste wasn't sure. It had been three long and hectic days since Baptiste had left France, on a flight to New York—the one following the flight taken by Benoit Moreau.

"Once we're on that plane, we've got no control."

"Wouldn't you want it that way if you were Gaudet?" Baptiste replied.

"There are better ways to meet people."

"It seems to me that we need him more than he needs us. As I see it, he makes money with or without us. He just makes more with us. Without him I don't see us making anything."

"That's not true. What about the copy of Bowden's 1998 journal you're waiting for? Is that nothing?"

"We won't know until we've had a chance to study it."

"Does the admiral know you're about to get the journal?"

Baptiste looked at Figgy as if he'd lost his mind. "No, and he won't until I'm ready. I need you to understand this. Gaudet is a shield, a . . . How do you say? A prophylactic for us. We need to convince my government that Gaudet stole the journal. Not you, and certainly not me. We're just making a deal with him."

"A deal with Gaudet?"

"It's complicated, but it'll work. Benoit will handle it all through a Swiss escrow. She knows Gaudet and we don't." Baptiste changed the subject to an unpleasant topic before Figgy could protest. "You killed Sam's man. A guy he probably liked."

"What the hell are you bringing that up for? It's old news. When he recognized me, I had no choice. The man attacked me!" Figgy's face had grown red. "Where are you going with this?"

"We need you either all the way in or all the way out. All the way in means trusting me to run this show. It also means letting Gaudet execute his Cordyceps plan against the U.S."

"You're a crazy motherfucker, Baptiste. That was never part of the deal. We were supposed to sell the technology to a foreign government. That's it."

Baptiste clucked his tongue and shook his head, and when Figgy had quieted, he explained the plan to multiply their cut of the deal as laid out by Benoit Moreau. "To really make money, we need Cordyceps to happen."

"It seems you and Benoit have thought of everything. I hope you two haven't outsmarted yourselves. You know she was Gaudet's lover—probably still is."

"And?"

"She could be with him right now discussing this deal!"

"You are completely out of your mind. I said you need to—"

"Whoa! Don't get touchy. You . . . you are in love, aren't you? Shit. In love with a black widow."

Baptiste stood and threw his napkin down. "That's enough! Worry about yourself, Meeks. Pay the bill and let's get out of here."

They waited at Executive Air at La Guardia for Gaudet to arrive. They noticed a sleek jet with large engines taxi up in front of the establishment and shut down.

"It's a Citation X," Figgy said. "A very fast plane."

Baptiste had no idea what kind of plane would come to fetch them. Several business types, men and women, disembarked, so it was obviously not Gaudet. Next a single-engine plane with a butterfly tail came taxiing up and they dismissed that as too small.

"It's a Beechcraft Bonanza," Figgy said. They waited and noted that it was one minute until the appointed time. Two men and a woman got out of the Beechcraft. Oddly, the woman wore an Islamic burka that covered her from head to toe. Her height, if indeed it was a she, was difficult to ascertain under the tentlike garment. That was unusual enough, but it seemed oddly out of place when the two men and the woman boarded the Citation X.

"Probably an Arab princess or something," Figgy said. "The pilots are still in the cockpit."

One of the men, tall, good-looking, with swept-back blond hair and dressed business casual, exited the jet and walked directly toward the lobby where they sat waiting. He came right to them.

"Gentlemen, I am Jack. I have come on behalf of Devan Gaudet to invite you aboard the jet."

Baptiste retained his poker face but immediately feared

that something was amiss with the person under the burka. It wouldn't have been necessary to put someone on in full view—it had to have been done for effect. But what effect?

Then as they walked to the plane, he reconsidered. The whole thing was a carefully orchestrated mind game to throw him off balance, to make impressions about important themes. He just hadn't figured it out yet.

"I will have to ask you to enter the plane one at a time. I regret it, but we will need to search you for weapons," Jack said.

Baptiste went first into a posh business jet that would seat comfortably perhaps ten people. There was a curtain across the middle of the jet and two armed men sat on their side of the curtain. Jack did a thorough pat down, apologizing once more for the inconvenience. They used a sort of electronic wand to check for microphones and another to check for metal. Baptiste and Figgy took seats facing the two men and the curtain.

"Welcome," said an electronically scrambled voice.

Baptiste should have known they would neither hear nor see Gaudet directly. Recording such a voice would be useless even if they had managed to smuggle a microphone on board the jet.

"Good afternoon," Baptiste replied in English.

A stewardess rose from the backseat of the plane, closed the heavy exterior door, and brought a tray of French pastries. They appeared to Baptiste to be of the finest quality. Figgy took one of the delicious-looking chocolate éclairs. Baptiste declined. The engines spooled up and the plane began the long taxi. The man on the other side of the curtain did not speak. As the plane taxied toward the runway, the stewardess and the two men went forward on the far side of the curtain.

"This jet is very fast," Figgy explained. "The fastest private jet. Something like Mach .92. That's even faster than the new Gulfstream."

"So, you are interested in airplanes," said the electronic voice.

"May I assume that you are Mr. Gaudet?" Baptiste said.

"You may assume anything you like. But I am not the man."

Then a cabinet in the back wall of the plane opened up and a TV screen appeared. On it was a man whose face was largely shadowed. He had a beard, but it was difficult to make out features.

"Please put on your headphones," said the man on the far side of the curtain. On the arms of their chair were large headphones with a microphone, the sort of headset that a pilot might wear.

"I am Gaudet," said the man on the screen in another electronic voice speaking into the headphones. "I am pleased to meet you. I regret that I can't join you, but I'm not particularly fond of airplanes. I merely tolerate them and I wouldn't actually put myself inside a heavily secured area like an airport for a meeting."

"Just out of curiosity, why the burka?"

"She is an intermediary between myself and the Swiss escrow company where we will do business if we make a deal. I understand from Benoit that the escrow is a must. Like me, my intermediary prefers not to be known and not to be photographed."

Baptiste figured it was either an escrow agent or a trusted lieutenant of Gaudet's. The rest were no doubt contract mercenaries.

"Let's get down to business," Baptiste said as they shot down the runway for takeoff.

And so the negotiations began. First it was peripheral matters and the bragging by each side of all that they were bringing to the table. They talked about the financial terms and there was haggling, but the end result was much as Benoit had suggested. A $200,000,000 purchase by France, with a kickback to everyone on Baptiste's team of $5,000,000 in cash. They agreed on how exactly they would communicate with the escrow company, security codes for the communications, and other related matters. An additional $5,000,000 in cash was to go to the Eviral Trust and various other trusts and corporations as dictated by Gaudet. For some reason Gaudet found some humor in the dispersal, but it escaped Baptiste.

"There are two more matters," Baptiste finally said. "We have heard that Benoit, acting through you, may be able to deliver copies of Bowden's 1998 journals to the French government. You will need to speak with Benoit about that. We realize that there is no guarantee for the French government that Chaperone is in those journals, but circumstantial evidence suggests it may be."

"Hmm. I am envious. How did you manage to pull off getting the journals?"

"That would be Benoit's doing. Take it up with her. You should get some additional money from the French government and we should get half."

"You're greedy bastards. You blame the theft on me and get half the money."

"Much will already be blamed on you . . . what is one more thing?"

Gaudet actually chuckled.

"The second issue is that Cordyceps must not come too quickly after delivery of Chaperone."

"Five days," Gaudet said.

"That is very fast," Baptiste said.

"That is all you get. I can't wait around. As it is, my investors won't like it. When Chaperone and related documents, including Bowden documents and all vector technology documents, are in escrow, you will have five days' notice of Cordyceps."

"What if we need time to authenticate before closing?"

"You do that on your own clock. My five-day clock starts running when I have everything you're buying in escrow. If we and Benoit working together take too long getting Chaperone into escrow, then we will so notify you and the deal is off."

"But we have no control over that."

"How right you are. But you don't have to spend your money if we don't deliver the product. And that, gentlemen, concludes our business."

Chapter 14

A hungry man will risk a bad oyster.

—Tilok proverb

"There goes our boy Figgy," Sam said to Jill on the cell phone. Sam was sitting in an FBO at Teterboro next door to the establishment hosting the Citation X. Sam doubted that Gaudet would be on the plane despite the intercepted messages that called for a "meeting." There had been what looked to be a woman in a burka and Sam's mind was churning over who it might have been. Gaudet? Doubtful. Again, he would not likely be present.

The question he couldn't answer was what they might be discussing. It had an ominous feel to it. When the plane taxied toward the runway, he engaged an entire group on a conference call. On the call were several private detectives, Grogg, and others on Sam's staff.

"How was the picture?" Sam asked.

"Better than CNN," Grogg said. "Great show."

"Anybody get anything while they were sitting at the FBO?"

"Nothing. They talked about airplanes."

"Who was under the burka?" Sam asked.

One of the private eyes spoke up. "It was a hundred feet from the Bonanza to the Citation. He or she took fifty steps to cover it. By the stride, I'd say it was a woman. He or she put out a hand when she climbed the stairs. Woman-size hand, although it was gloved. Height we guess at five feet eight inches. He or she is accustomed to airplanes because he or she didn't hesitate for even a second as would someone unfamiliar with private jets. But he or she is not accustomed to the burka because he or she slightly misjudged the added height and just touched the header on the entryway to the jet. We got just a glimpse of the shoes as he or she climbed the steps. They were upscale and they were female-size feet. So we think it's a she and not a he."

"Well, not to put too fine a point on it, but that could bring it down to a few thousand since not many woman with nice shoes and a normal build are used to climbing in and out of private jets. Assuming, of course, we're right about the jets," Grogg said.

"Did anyone notice the fingers of her right hand?" Sam asked.

There was silence.

"Play the tape again." Everyone watched. Sticking down out of one sleeve were the gloved fingers of a hand. They moved like cilia on a sea creature but very slowly.

"Get a signer who knows signing for the deaf."

"That won't take long; we have someone," Jill said. While he waited, Sam used his cell to call people in the flight control center tracking the jet. It was headed for Martha's Vineyard. Then Jill came back on.

"Got it. You won't believe it. She signed STOGETH-ERBM and I would take that to mean 'Sam together Benoit Moreau.' "

"Resourceful," Sam said. "In more ways than one. She's out of jail and in the U.S.? What game are the French playing?"

"Figures one of the French is wired into the deal, probably illicitly," Jill said.

Grogg added the punctuation: "Surprise, surprise, surprise."

Sam found Michael and Grady in a booth at a tavern in Gramercy Park nearby the bed & breakfast, apparently having sat with their beers for some time. There were six bodyguards spread around the place and their roving eyes created an odd sensation, but it didn't seem to interfere with business. Grady had taken Anna's tragedy hard, but she was weathering it in the presence of the strong calm that was Michael Bowden. It had been two days since the airport incident and Figgie hadn't said a word.

"You've got to get out of New York," Sam said to Michael, not in the mood for circumlocutions.

"What are you thinking?" Bowden asked.

The words didn't contain attitude, but Sam thought the tone did. "Look what they've done to try to get those journals. Gaudet has almost killed you, Grady, me, and Anna. What more do you need to see?"

"I know the whys. Why I should run. Why Gaudet wants me. What I don't know is what you're suggesting. I want him out of my life and everyone else's, out of commission, whatever. Dead. Right? Aren't we more likely to catch him if I'm visible than if I'm hiding?"

"You're right, and I don't disagree. But think about it first. It's not just your life we're talking about."

"Grady should not be with me until this is over. I know that."

"Don't I get a say in that?" Grady had had enough.

Sam and Michael looked at each other.

"Get used to it, Michael. Hey, you have to admit she's not doing bad." Sam drained his drink and leaned forward, elbows on the table. "Look, if you're in, that's fine with me. I have a thought as to how we might lay a trap. But you have to be sure."

"I'm not dying to be a staked goat, but it's better than doing nothing."

Sam looked at Grady, who glowed with pride at her mentor's earlier remark. Behind the glow, though, her face showed her disquiet. In her eyes he saw both the undaunted determination of a woman with a plan and a smart person afraid for her life. And Michael's.

"All right at least let's move you to a bed-and-breakfast over in Greenwich Village. They'll have to find you again."

"That's fine," Michael said and Grady nodded.

"First, I have a big piece of news," Sam said. "We received an e-mail today from France. We think they are relaying messages from one Benoit Moreau." Sam briefly explained her history with Grace Technologies and her imprisonment. "She seems to be out, and possibly in New York. Apparently she will want a meeting; an attorney ready to attend and most interesting, a fake 1998 journal copy that looks real but is entirely a forgery."

"What?"

"That is totally weird," Grady said.

"I do not know why that request and she hasn't said when she wants a meeting or why. It could be to work her own scam or it could be because she wants to help us. If they think they have the journal, they lay off you. I think she wants me to believe she is on our side. I should mention that the attorney is to be an expert in immigration."

"Should I make a journal with incorrect latitudes and longitudes and with altered descriptions of the material? Misdescribe flora, fauna?"

"It couldn't hurt. But I'm sure it would be a lot of work."

"A whole year's worth of actual data? Maybe. But if I got Lyman and some honest graduate students . . ."

* * *

By the next day, a full twelve days after his arrival in New York, Sam had set up temporary offices. Every morning that he could, he would stop by to see Anna and he called Anna's mother or the nurse Lydia at least twice a day. Here he could work the phones and brainstorm with the investigators feeding Big Brain. It wasn't glamorous, but unlike the LA office, he could be near Anna. He had a better chance of finding Gaudet from the computer room than he did walking the streets, because from the office he could greatly multiply his efforts using contract investigators. A new priority was learning why the French were having secret meetings with Gaudet and who had hired the grad student to steal Michael's journal.

Back at the bed-and-breakfast he kissed Grady on the cheek, clasped her hand, and left her with Michael. His instincts were talking to him again. Grady and Michael were assuming he'd go back to LA. He didn't bother to correct the impression, although there were various ways they might find him out. Since he always took calls on his cell, it wasn't always easy to determine his whereabouts and people were very used to not knowing.

Preferring anonymity he stayed over in Greenwich Village, in the apartment of a retired FBI agent. The man was traveling.

On the way to the office he stopped by the hospital. In mid-afternoon the hospital was getting ready for a shift change. Nurses were standing around flipping through charts and talking in low tones. Anna's room was a good walk down a long corridor filled with people with serious problems. There was a faint antiseptic smell and somehow it didn't help his mood. As he neared the door, the deep reserve of sadness that was always with him these days took over his mind. When he entered, he noticed that the monitor was now silent and each beat was only a line on the screen. Sitting by Anna's bed, her mother held her hand, and it made him feel good and it made him feel guilty all at the same time. When he approached Anna's mother, he noticed that her face was drawn and that deep fatigue had set in. The vigil was taking its toll.

"I will leave you alone," she said quietly.

Nothing had ever made him feel so helpless.

Anna's face revealed nothing and it seemed to Sam that she was very far away.

She always liked the smell of a good Cuban cigar, so in violation of all the rules he sat by her bed and smoked a few puffs. After he put out the cigar, he leaned forward and whispered in her ear.

Sam sat in New York in front of the video-conferencing monitor, talking to Jill in LA the way old acquaintances do, snacking, drinking, and lapsing into silence between broken phrases that called up a history of late nights at the office, long lunches, walks in the park, and even pillow talk. They had each ordered in some fried yearling oysters and Sam carefully dipped the end of about every third oyster in ketchup. He called the ketchup dunking "cleansing the palate." Jill liked the unadulterated oyster flavor and skipped the condiment. Harry sat on the conference table of the New York office watching every oyster that went into Sam's mouth and got about one out of four. Jill said the dog had superior taste—he'd have none of Sam's ketchup. One of Sam's staff had been kind enough to bring the lonely dog with him from LA.

For a few minutes Jill listened while Sam tried to tell her how he felt about Anna lying unconscious in the hospital. For some reason it was hard for him to speak the right words, and yet he knew she understood.

"I wish I were there to hold your hand," she said. There were a few moments of silence. Harry put his chin on his paws and looked disconsolate.

"You know the way you're leaning back with those oysters, you're going to spill ketchup on your shirt."

"Have you ever noticed how some people can't just wear their ketchup stain—even ketchup lovers like me. They have to cover it with a tie, or hold their hand on their stomach, or take the shirt off and use towels and water. In the extreme cases they have to leave the office and get a new shirt. As long as that ketchup is there, they can't stop thinking about it. The ketchup actually rules their life."

Jill said nothing for a moment.

"Grieving is good, Sam. It's not like a ketchup stain, so don't even think about comparing them."

"I was talking about hypocritical ketchup lovers."

"And I was talking about you."

Sam thought about that. For him, was it Gaudet that was the ketchup stain? Or was it something inside? Was it his self-doubt? Was it that he had Indian blood? Or maybe it was his anonymous life. One thing he believed: nothing could be normal or right until he got Gaudet. Not grieving, not life. Maybe he could choose a public life after Gaudet. Maybe he would have more confidence that he was good enough for Anna. Now he didn't know.

He thought about what his mother had said about Grandfather, about the focusing of his life force. Could a man focus his life on catching another man and have a life worth living? It was a question that he shoved out of his mind almost as fast as it came. Some things were necessary, he told himself.

"You don't think you should tell Grady and Michael you're really in New York."

"It worked last time."

"Yeah, Grady was almost strangled."

"I've gotta get this man that is really not a man. He is more devil than man."

"I guess if we're going to stop him, we better get to work."

"Title of the file in Gaudet's mainframe was interesting," Jill said. " 'Alpha Worm.' Some kind of joke."

"Uh-huh."

"You're tired."

"Not that tired. How is Figgy doing?"

"Great. If you like would-be traitors. He has a lot of contacts and he's working them. I guess we just ignore that he seems to have had a meeting with our mortal enemy and isn't mentioning it. He has gotten information about Grace from the French, who are suddenly discovering that they knew things they supposedly didn't know."

"Do you think he would betray the United States for some renegade French spooks?"

"What do you think, Sam?"

"I think we got serious trouble that I don't understand. We can't trust Figgy with anything we don't want Gaudet to know until we prove otherwise. It is possible to meet with your enemy without embracing him. We can't forget that. I would like to think that Figgy and the French are trying to trap him."

"But you don't believe it."

"Unfortunately, I don't."

"You know I was talking to our Harvard guys. They just keep saying that this would be an unimaginable medical breakthrough if Grace had a way of altering the immune system so that it would accept foreign cells. All of the diseases in which our bodies reject good cells could be cured. Growing and implanting replacement organs would be a breeze. We'd have pig farms growing human parts. Gene repair would be vastly simplified. You have to hear it for yourself. They make it sound like the Second Coming."

"It would be worth a fortune."

"And?"

"Maybe that's becoming bigger than whatever Gaudet is doing."

"Bigger to whom?"

"Everybody. All the governments. Hell of a thought. What if every government out there wanted it?"

"To own the discovery."

"Yeah. It would be an unimaginable thicket. But we better stop looking for ghosts and get Grogg in here."

"Grogg got into Northern Lights' computer. He found a Gaudet-related phone number in a Frank Grey's contacts list. He is one of the two that got the vector."

"So he was a threat to Gaudet? Maybe a falling-out?"

"Frank Grey also had the number of a man in the SDECE by the name of Jean Baptiste Sourriaux, and he is the same man that Gaudet wrote. And he was in Figgy's computer. And, of course, Baptiste was in the jet with Figgy."

"It's a small world."

"It gets smaller. Grey had a number in his directory that turns out to be the phone of Claudia Roche. But it was listed as Chaperone."

"It would not be a great hurdle to assume that Claudia Roche is the way to Georges Raval. She lives in Manhattan and is related to Chloe Raval in France, who claims that Georges Raval is her brother's son. Big Brain drew the correlation or we wouldn't know any of this. Could be something, could be nothing. Apparently, Chaperone was the name that Frank Grey at Northern Lights used for whatever he associated with Raval."

"It makes sense. Raval is the only ex-Grace scientist we haven't been able to account for."

"Fascinating. Gaudet kills Grey, and others at Northern Lights, wants Bowden, and is meeting with the French. Somebody almost steals the journals and they especially want the 1998 journal. Benoit wants a forgery of the '98 journal. Gaudet is doing something called Cordyceps; he's probably building a computer virus; and he's using the vector, but he doesn't seem to have Chaperone. I'm guessing that Gaudet is going to be interested in Chaperone and in Georges Raval. The action seems centered here in New York. Now, if only Benoit Moreau would come to me."

"You've done very good work," Gaudet said to the nameless short man who stood beside him on the street across from the entrance to Globe Publishing. Before answering, the man took a deep drag on his cigarette, then adjusted his hat. This business of waiting for words between puffs was an irritation, but Gaudet put up with it.

"How did you know he was alive?"

"Hard to keep a famous man's death a secret. On the other hand, it's easy to make him disappear and spread rumors."

"What are you gonna do?"

"That's my business. Find out where he's staying."

"Must be awful important for a Frenchman to be hanging around New York."

"If you enjoy the feeling of the earth under your feet, you'll quit thinking about me and keep on thinking about the assignment."

Chapter 15

A body will heal until the Great Spirit takes the flame of life.

—Tilok proverb

They had it planned so there was plenty of time to stop at the hospital and see Anna before arriving at the publishing house. Michael stood back by the door when Grady went to Anna's side and when she talked with Anna's mother. Without fail, there were tears in her eyes when she left, and Michael would let time pass before saying anything. He hoped she would be okay with the publisher meeting, but he noticed that as soon as they got out into the open air, she seemed to transform herself and to put the sadness in a corner of her mind.

The publishing house was somewhat overpowering, even in the lobby. It was brass and glass and wasn't like anything Michael could recall except on occasional trips to Rio. There was art on the walls that looked like splashy paint accidents. His father had told him about such art but had been astounded that the buying public opened their wallets and received it into their workplaces and even their homes. Childhood memories were of museums filled with paintings of comprehensible images.

There was a tentative aspect to his gait because of his injuries. On the phone he had warned his editor of his physical condition, claiming that there had been an unfortunate run-in with unsavory characters in the jungle. To a publisher, he knew, such a story had substantial juice and there would be an attentive audience for the lunchtime tale. He would explain Grady as a member of a scientific expedition that happened by to rescue him, and her enthusiasm as a reader. That along with the simple observation of her person and her wit would complete the explanation. All of the bodyguards save Yodo would remain downstairs and he would explain Yodo as his newfound jungle companion and assistant. He was comforted by the fact that, try as they might, they wouldn't get more than one or two sentences out of Yodo.

He produced his passport for the guard at the desk, and the man leaned back as if it required concentration to compare the photograph with the face. Michael decided to smile just to see if that would confuse him. The man nodded and called Rebecca on the telephone. Grady and Yodo received only a perfunctory glance with respect to identification, although the man's eyes lingered on Grady for other reasons.

Soon Rebecca Toussant was standing in front of him. She was a well-dressed, handsome woman, tall, with a charming smile and a firm handshake. Rebecca had a knack for being warm, disarming, and dignified all at the same time. Even on the phone he had liked her, and now he liked her even better. He wondered if it would be that way with the others. Right away she asked about his injuries, how he was feeling and the like. Of course he proclaimed that all was well and ignored the deep aching in his body. It was all he could do not to mention the letter from Georges Raval.

They made their way into the elevator, conversing as they went. Grady listened without speaking and Yodo towered in the corner. When they arrived at her office, Rebecca pointed up and down the hall explaining the layout of the publishing house, mentioning various individuals that Michael had heard about over the years. Yodo found a chair large enough to be comfortable in the small waiting area outside Re-becca's office and planted one hand inside his coat. Michael knew that it was wrapped around the butt of his gun and that he would remain perpetually ready to kill someone. As they followed Rebecca into her office, and despite himself, Michael couldn't help chuckling. Grady got the joke—the absurdity of it—and patted her purse where he knew she kept a handgun. She grinned. When Rebecca turned at her sofa, she probably just figured that she had an especially happy group.

Michael and Grady saw his books, along with hundreds of others, on her shelf. There was beige carpet, a couch, and a large wood table that caught his interest. The wood of the desk had a deep reddish hue and didn't quite look like mahogany.

On her table lay a picture book of the coastal California mountains and the redwoods, and when he laid eyes on it, he finalized his plan in an instant. He would return to the terrain of his childhood, the forests of northern California, and spend a year writing about them just as he had done the Amazon. He knew that no sane man would make such a snap judgment, but it didn't matter. He already had.

"It is so exciting to meet you," Rebecca said with utter sincerity.

She wanted him to talk, to paint word pictures of the Amazon, its people, his house, and all the little things about life in the jungle. She wanted that, even though she had read thousands of pages. He supposed there was some magic in the flesh-and-blood presence of an explorer, so he went with it and spoke without reservation or self-conscious inhibition. All the while the Raval letter was on his mind, but he knew to bide his time and to avoid seeming anxious. And he wasn't sure yet whether he wanted to share its contents.

After almost an hour of talking and questions, Grady and

Rebecca excused themselves to the restrooms. On her way out Rebecca handed him a stack of fan mail. There were about fifty letters. On top was the missive from Georges Raval.

There is a great secret in the science of genetics that is in two parts. I know the one part and you know the other. There are many who want this secret and they will do anything to get it. Together we can revolutionize medicine, unlock the keys to genetic science, replace body parts with near frivolous abandon, and probably cure the ravages of many immune response diseases forever. There are evil forces at work. Once they learn your part of the secret, they will kill you and the same for me. Be careful. We need to meet. Contact me at macaquemania@hotmail.com. Destroy this. Stay safe. Georges Raval

Methodically he tore the message into small pieces. Next he wrote a message for Rebecca to send.

This forwarded from Dr. Bowden: Received your message. Anxious to discuss your most recent research. Contact me through our mutual colleague, Dr. Richard Lyman, Biological Sciences, Cornell University. We could meet in Ithaca or elsewhere at your convenience. Looking forward to speaking.

They had lunch at a restaurant, where they sat around a large rectangular table with Grady and Michael in the middle. Michael was listening to Rebecca's boss, Henry, explain about his yacht, and at the same time he looked around the restaurant at the strange new world in which he found himself. In Iquitos and Leticia or Tabatinga everything seemed to exist in a constant state of deterioration. The instant a new coat of paint was applied, the Amazon sun and the humidity began their attack. This natural force that wanted to work against man and all his endeavors seemed more than the sum of its parts. In New York City it wasn't like that. Things that were old often seemed exquisite and, like wine, they seemed to get better with age. On the other hand, natural beauty was extinguished. There were no sweeping forests to frame the sky, no sense of myriad living things fitting together in a multitude of fascinations that could even entice the mind of God, the Creator.

They might build a pond and put a fish in it, but it was a fish without a world—save the thin veneer created by the cement makers who built the pond. There were pigeons in the park, but they were not part of anything but the pastime of the very old and the very young, both of whom seemed to like to feed them. People lived by their clocks and everything was thus regulated. Therefore, very few things happened that weren't foreordained. Each day was not an experiment but a manufactured event.

There were, however, those unanticipated eventualities.

After the boss was finished about the yacht, the conversation continued in brief flurries about the Amazon and various questions, Michael having taken a breather from the lecture format. Around the table most everyone was watching him and they seemed to be wondering how he liked his food. He tried to look pleased. It seemed to be very refined grease. It had been a mistake not to order a simple piece of fish and some vegetables. Maybe a little rice. It was billed as a seafood restaurant with something of an eclectic menu, but somehow he had ended up in the pasta section, so he had ordered what passed for food in Italy, according to its description. It was flooded with a fatty sauce that he was sure would wreak havoc with his innards. Perhaps he could order something more straightforward without embarrassing his hosts.

At what seemed a reasonable breaking point, he rose from the table and determined that he would retire to the restroom and then stop by the kitchen.

Located just off the entry lobby, the restroom facilities were at the other end of the establishment. With Yodo following, he walked past all the chefs behind the cooking bar and saw a number of dishes that looked palatable. As he rounded a corner, a man stepped out of the shadows. Yodo immediately stepped between him and the man. With a wry smile Michael peered around his large bodyguard.

"You are Michael Bowden." The stranger was just under six feet with close-cropped brown hair, a mustache, gold wire-rimmed spectacles, slightly uneven teeth, and a narrow face. Although not much to look at, there was confidence in his bearing and an intensity about him that caused Michael to take him seriously.

"Yes, I am. Who are you?"

"I am John Stephan and my firm represents a pharmaceutical interest that would like to speak with you confidentially. But it must be in confidence. I am a lawyer." He handed him a card with a phone number and Michael put it in his pocket. "Could we talk without the man-mountain?" he said nodding at Yodo.

Michael hesitated. "I have nothing to hide. What do you mean by 'in confidence'?"

"We need confidence," he said again referring to Yodo.

"Yodo maybe you could wait by the bar over there." Yodo moved about thirty feet away looking very concerned.

"We would like to speak with you privately at our law offices. We are a large Wall Street firm. Binkley, Hart, and Rove. The managing partner for this matter is Arthur Stewart. If you have an attorney, he may call Mr. Stewart. We like to think we have the highest standards and we plan on documenting everything we tell you. Everything." Then the man turned away from Yodo and whispered. "Specifically, we are concerned about the man you call Sam. We believe he may be using you for purposes you're not aware of. That is not to say that he wants to harm you, it's just to say that he has his own agenda." The man leaned even closer. "He is known to be engaged in a private war with a man who calls himself Gaudet, among other names, and that is not a concern of ours, and as far as we can tell, it should not be a concern of yours except that you have knowledge that he wants and that we want."

Michael did not reply.

"Put simply, you are being used as bait, Mr. Bowden. And in addition everyone wants what you have and this Sam is not above taking it. You notice how he keeps talking about your journals, wanting to get at them? What's his motive? Is it to protect you? Think about it. He doesn't need those journals to protect you. If they had been in your house on the Galvez River when he arrived, you never would have seen him or heard from him. He'd have what he wants."

"Explain that."

"First the bait part. Sam is hired by the U.S. government to help them find Gaudet. Gaudet needs some information. Sam has let it be known to Gaudet that you have what he needs. So Gaudet went to your house and raided it sometime ago, only he went much sooner than Sam expected and Sam failed to get there first to lay a trap and to beat him to the journals—which people erroneously thought would be in the house. As a result your wife was killed. If Gaudet believes he needs you, he will come, and that is what Sam is counting on. You're Sam's trap for Gaudet. Do you understand?"

"How would you know this unless you were being used by Gaudet?"

"I and my colleagues will explain that after reaching some preliminary understandings. We can give you references that we believe you will find impeccable. But I haven't explained the second part. There is a secret about the human immune system and how to neutralize it with respect to chosen proteins. I'm sure you understand."

"I've heard."

"And it is thought that part of that secret came from you."

"What kind of business do you have with me?"

"A straightforward pharmaceutical deal to replace or supplement the deal you had with Northern Lights."

At that moment Michael saw Yodo slowly moving closer and waved him off.

"How do you know the deal with Northern Lights?"

"We don't, completely, but we'll answer all your questions at our offices. There will be a company representative present who will have full authority to negotiate. Naturally, we don't expect you to agree to anything until you have consulted with your own attorneys."

"I need to think this over."

"No problem. But please give me a commitment that you will meet at our offices soon and that you will not bring this fellow Sam."

"I said I would think about it. Making commitments is not thinking about it."

"You will keep our discussions to yourself?"

"I will tell whomever I please."

"We respect fully your right to make your own choices, but may I suggest that you cannot choose intelligently without the facts. You are being used, Mr. Bowden, and it is dangerous for all of us. Dangerous for the security of the whole world, if you will."

"I don't like your pressure or your insinuations that now suddenly I am the threat. I threaten nothing. I am a man of peace. I will call you when I am ready to talk and not before. Now please excuse me."

* * *

Sam was methodically clenching his abdominal muscles; he had learned to work them while sitting at a table. Regular exercise was more a matter of adjusting to tedious consistency than it was dressing for exercise and hanging around the health club ab machines. He wore a hat of Scotch-plaid wool out of the 1950s and sported a carefully trimmed blond beard and sat in a corner with a glass of red wine, an old vines Napa Valley Zinfindel, and a copy of the *Wall Street Journal*. With Brie cheese and smoked-salmon salad—the salmon was very moist and lightly smoked to perfection—it was hard to beat, and as the glorious flavors mingled on his palate, he was alert to every nuance of his environment.

About one hundred feet away sat Michael and Grady and the entire entourage with bodyguards spread about. None of them would have a clue that he was anywhere near, though his dark complexion in contrast to his beard color might cause an observer to wonder just how tan an Anglo could get. His shoes were ungodly-looking saddle backs, his trousers nondescript dark wool without pleats, and he had a visible paunch with rolls like footballs. He wore a gold watch that was a cheap knockoff of a gawdy Rolex, and he looked the part of a fat, self-indulgent businessman taking it easy while his minions worked their asses off to give him the good life.

He noticed when Michael rose from the table and watched him coming toward the foyer and the restrooms at the far end. There was a long line of chefs and gorgeous foodstuffs on display and a short section that was an oyster bar for those inclined. Sam was inclined, but oysters weren't his concern of the moment: Michael Bowden was.

As he watched the man talking to Michael, Sam slipped the 10mm Glock from his shoulder holster and placed it under a newspaper in his lap. The move wasn't quite slick enough because a young woman seated nearby had eyes grown wide with fear. Quickly Sam flopped open a gold shield that he carried for just such occasions and she seemed to calm slightly. Sam memorized the stranger's appearance, the brown close-cropped hair, the mustache, the thin lips, and the lack of animation in the face. The man was probably a very linear no-nonsense type. He had a wedding ring, an expensive three-button suit, good shoes. It was no ordinary encounter, but neither did it seem like a setup for a grab.

Yodo stepped away obviously at Michael's insistence. Both men appeared intense, concentrating on their conversation. They had been talking for at least a couple of minutes.

It was out of the corner of his eye that Sam caught the most interesting action. An old man in the waiting area folded his newspaper and rose. By the way he folded the paper, two ends to the middle and then again, and placed it under his arm, and the way he rose and his bearing as he stood, Sam knew him by heart. There was a great tendency for spooks to do as Sam had done and to go the Santa Claus route. Add fat, age, hair, and a hat. Voilà.

By the time Michael returned to the table, they were ready for more Amazon stories.

"Let me get you something else," Rebecca said. "How about some salmon?"

"Sounds delicious, but I have ordered up some catfish filets."

"All this rich food must seem strange if you're used to manioc, jungle fruit, rice, beans, and fish."

"I see the things in magazines and I remember what I ate as a child. You know like pizza, spaghetti, giant hamburgers. Western food is in the large cities but I often pass on that. We have beef now and then from ranches on the Marañón and once I made a pizza for my friends on the river. Everyone loved it. They ate too much and got sick. So that was the last pizza. If I am not too busy working, I mix many fruits and make a compote and use a little pepper or curry and put it on the fish. When I get to California, I will try all sorts of what you call international cuisine for a little while. But I think I will always like fruit, fish, and vegetables. Actually, my favorite thing about the United States is its vegetables."

They talked on about life in the rain forest and what it was like to paddle around water-filled villages built on stilts. Everyone listened and asked questions until the middle of the afternoon and then the group broke up. Michael and Grady would return to the publishing house in their own cab, but for the moment they were taking a breather and standing in the corner looking at the wine. Although Michael did not know a great deal about wine, he knew he liked drinking it.

"I'm thinking I would like to go be bait in California and start my work. I thought maybe you could come with me."

Grady paused and he could tell she was thinking.

She put her hand on his arm and squeezed it. "You are one hot guy. The kind of guy girls wrap themselves around in their sleep. Right now I have some thinking to do in my life. I need to get back to California and see my boyfriend. I haven't really resolved my situation there. I think I need to be in LA to think things over and I know you want to go up north to the forests." She paused. "I know you'll return to the depths of the Amazon before too long and I haven't figured that out. Maybe while I'm in LA, you could find a place to live in California. Then maybe, who knows?"

"I see," Michael said, determined to look cheery. "Well, maybe Gaudet will come and find me and we can end all this one way or the other."

"Don't say that. It needs to end our way."

Once back in his room, Michael found a slow depression settling over him. Perhaps the man in the restaurant was telling the truth. Perhaps Grady was part of an elaborate trap. After a few minutes of mulling it over, he conceded that he couldn't know for certain about Sam, but Grady he was sure of. It wasn't hard to imagine Sam having more on his agenda than he was letting on to Grady.

All this suspicion was troubling; Michael was not used to it. Perhaps he was influenced by Grady's rebuff more than he ought to be. Not knowing what else to do, he called Rebecca, who was in his view a wise woman.

"You know the young woman Grady."

"Yes?"

"She is leaving for LA soon. I will be going to northern California, to the wilderness."

"You sound a little forlorn."

"I guess I was enjoying her company."

"She was certainly enjoying yours."

"Really?"

"Take it from me."

"You know some things are not meant to be. She is maybe for me a *Chullachaqui.*"

"Which is?"

"The natives believe that sometimes you run into a person in the rain forest that is really a spirit. To figure it out, you look at their right foot. If it isn't a hoof then they are flesh and blood. Maybe she is a product of my imagination created from a life-and-death situation." He smiled into the handset. "I know of course that she is as real as you and I, but maybe I have made of her something in my mind that she is not."

"Maybe she has done the same. Maybe she's afraid."

"Of what?"

"I don't know. Maybe you should try to find out," Rebecca suggested.

"I'll think about that. You're a good friend. I have something else I needed to speak with you about. Do you know a law firm called . . . let me find it . . . Binkley, Hart, and Rove?"

"Of course. They're huge."

"And reputable?"

"As reputable as a big New York law firm can be. You'll have to pardon my cynicism. They are very reputable."

Michael received the call shortly after speaking with Rebecca.

"Have you thought over our offer to meet? We would like to meet the day after tomorrow at six in the evening."

"I said I would call. Have I called?"

"We would like some assurance that you will be there."

"Or what?"

"We will need to do business with someone else. You will miss out. We'll wait for you at six." The man hung up.

Michael was weary of people telling him what to do, of being followed, of having bodyguards, of being the bait. It did not feel as if he were a free man. It was troubling that these unknown, undefined people knew his comings and goings even down to the restaurant selected by the publishing house. Notwithstanding the fancy law firm, he was suspicious of their intent, and their identity. Greed was a powerful force, and he wasn't sure he trusted people motivated by greed more than those, like Sam, motivated by emotion or revenge.

Michael didn't want to be part of any plot but one of his own making. It was as simple as that.

He thought about the proposed meeting time: 6:00 P.M. It seemed a little late in the day. Or was it? He considered calling Grady. He was less inclined to call Sam because he wanted to keep his options open. Although he had resolved himself to helping catch Gaudet, he wasn't sure he wanted to do everything else on Sam's agenda. This was not the Amazon and the rules were different. Still, he didn't want to change to fit somebody else's rules. For years he had made it in the jungle by himself and he had decided he would continue to live his life pretty much in that fashion. Talking with Grady, on the other hand . . . After a few thoughtful moments he decided the situation made a perfect excuse to see her.

At that moment his phone rang. When he answered, it was Richard Lyman.

"A Dr. Raval called. He was very secretive and mysterious. He asked if I thought you could meet him in Manhattan. I didn't know what to say, but I said I thought you could. Of course I didn't tell him that you are already there. He says he could meet you on any of the next three evenings at five at the Christopher Street subway station for the one or nine train. It's the side of the station that serves trains coming from lower Manhattan—from the area of the financial district. If you want to meet him there, he says he will explain through Rebecca. He says send a message through Rebecca or otherwise to confirm. I didn't understand the 'or otherwise,' but he said you would."

After reassuring his friend that everything was okay, Michael hung up. He noticed that his heart was pounding.

Michael called Rebecca.

"I need a confidential favor. Very confidential."

"Of course you have it. There is more intrigue in your little finger than in my whole life. Please don't think me gauche if I tell you it's really fun."

"I need you to write another e-mail."

"Okay. Shoot."

"Send an e-mail to macaquemania at hotmail.com."

Will meet tomorrow as per your last. I will be with a blond young woman. She is a safe friend. There will also be bodyguards. But we will talk in private, and when I approach, I will leave all others behind.

*Perhaps you have ideas on how and where to meet.
Anyplace in Manhattan is good for me.*

Rebecca sent the e-mail and within ten minutes was back
on the phone with a response.

*I will be at the Christopher Street subway station
by the newsstand near the entrance at 5:00 P.M. wearing a long coat with a white carnation. You watch from
Starbucks. When you see me, come to the doorway of
Starbucks and pause just outside. Put on your gloves.
If I remove the carnation from my lapel, then follow
me. I will go to the doorway of a large apartment
building. You follow. Leave all other persons at least
one hundred feet distant. You and I will go inside the
building for privacy. Once we are inside, your bodyguards may wait anywhere outside the building. If you
see anyone suspicious or strange who looks like they
might have an interest in our businesss, walk back to
the Lutheran church. Go inside and sit in a pew. If you
don't hear from me in twenty minutes leave and I will
contact you again. Stay safe. I believe we are both in
the gravest danger.*

"I think you should call the police," Rebecca remarked.

"No. He's only a scientist. I already have people who can
call the police."

"He doesn't sound like a scientist. And he says you are in
the gravest danger."

"He's right, Rebecca. You've done enough for me now.
Thank you for your help. Really."

"Of course. But—"

"Rebecca, where could I go that would allow me to return
to the Christopher Street station that he describes?"

"You're not going to listen to me, are you?"

"I have bodyguards. I have people who know the police. It's all taken care of."

"Well, if you're sure." She sighed, obviously thinking it over. "You're staying in Greenwich Village, I take it."

"Yes."

"You could go down to Wall Street, lower Manhattan."

"Why would I go there?"

"Oh, an excuse. I get it. Uhm, well, you're an explorer, a *National Geographic*–type guy. Abercrombie and Fitch has a store down there at the South Street Seaport shopping mall."

"Has everybody heard of Abercrombie and Fitch?"

"Most people."

"What do they sell?"

"They used to sell things for jungle expeditions. You could be excused for thinking they still do."

"You are a smart woman, Rebecca. Thanks again. I really appreciate it."

"Don't thank me. Just try to stay alive."

Grady met Michael knowing she looked a little the worse for wear. For a split second she wondered if she regretted her decision to go home and figure out her life. Unfortunately, Michael Bowden would believe that she was going her separate way and the situation would feel like rejection. Men were that way.

"You look good in that." He smiled and gave a bit of a lopsided grin.

She wore a fancy pair of blue jeans, a braided belt, and a dark floral-print blouse.

"Then again," he said, "I don't recall ever seeing you in anything that looked bad."

In the foyer she put on her flak jacket under a heavy parka.

They took a cab to Pete's Tavern, and although she wanted to take his arm or give him some other physical signal of reassurance, she forbade herself.

"You don't look so happy," he said.

"I'm going to miss you," she answered.

They sat in a rickety bench seat with an old varnished table. The bar was crowded. It seemed the place was full of people who knew each other, people who shared little pieces of their lives in this neighborhood. Even though there were millions of people in Manhattan, somehow the people in this spot managed to have a sense of community.

"There is something I need to tell you," Michael said.

He told her the story of the encounter with the lawyer in the restaurant.

When he finished, she tapped the table. She knew the veins at the base of her neck would be standing out as her face reddened.

"I can't believe you didn't tell me this."

"Well, don't get mad. I'm telling you now."

"You could get killed or kidnapped. You're practically a national treasure and I like you."

"Okay, well, I'm still here."

"Good. Let's keep it that way."

"But I've got to do my business." He tilted his head and smiled a little.

"You accepted protection from Sam and the governments who hire him. You're supposed to let us keep you alive. Don't forget that. And besides, is it all right if I care what happens to you?"

"You have a boyfriend. Responsibilities. I look out for myself. Always have."

"We have to call Sam. Do you object to my calling Sam?"

"Wouldn't matter if I did."

"You got that right."

It took a while to get Sam. They patched her through to

his cell phone and it rang forever. Quickly she explained Michael's encounter with the lawyer in the restaurant and just as quickly Sam explained what he wanted.

"Sam's coming from LA to New York. He's going to that meeting."

"What?" Michael's brain was moving but not fast enough. "He can't."

Grady just smiled.

"Okay. How?"

"To get in the door," she said, and winked, "he'll pretend to be you."

Michael wasn't at all certain he would allow Sam to attend the meeting in his stead. But at the moment he was more concerned about meeting Georges Raval.

"I'd like to go to Abercrombie and Fitch." He tried to sound nonchalant, but he wasn't sure he had succeeded.

"Huh?"

"Abercrombie and Fitch. Haven't you heard of them?"

"Of course, they're a dude store."

"You said I was a dude. So can't I go?"

"You're not *that* kind of dude." She wrinkled her nose. "All right. I'll get us some cabs."

"I want to take the subway."

"The subway?"

She called Yodo over from his corner and they huddled with one of the other guards. No doubt there would be a lot of talk about "security" and the subway. They walked Irving Street to the 1 and 9 at Fourteenth Street and went down Manhattan to Wall Street. From there they walked the few blocks to the Seaport shopping area, where they found Abercrombie & Fitch. Michael did his best to peruse the merchandise, but he was much more interested in hearing Grady's stories about growing up in LA.

At 4:25 P.M. he glanced at his watch.

"I've seen enough," he said. "Let's go."

"Let's take a cab."

"I like the subway. We take the 1 and 9 to Christopher, and it's only a short cab ride or a good walk."

"Since when did you become an expert on the subway?"

"Since I got a map. There is a saying, *'Em Roma, sê romano.'* "

"What's that mean?"

" 'When in Rome I am Roman.' "

"Michael, you are up to something here and you're terrible at hiding it."

"Huh?" It was another pitiful attempt to cover up.

"You've been, like, glancing at your watch every five minutes."

"I'll explain in a few minutes."

"Why a few minutes?"

"You'll have to wait for an explanation. You can come or stay."

"Unless this is a birthday surprise—and it's not my birthday—you're out of your depth with this shit. You gonna tell me?"

Michael just kept walking, setting his mouth in a grim line.

And, damn it, she followed.

They boarded the subway for the ride back up the West side of Manhattan. Once again he got her talking about her life in LA, until they exited at the Christopher Street station. It was 4:45 P.M., too early for Georges Raval. Michael couldn't help looking around the entrance to the south bound anyway.

"Now what?" she asked.

"We go into Starbucks for coffee."

"Who are you looking for? Your eyeballs might as well be on gimbals."

They walked past the newsstand, crossed the street from the little concrete island that was the entrance to the Christopher Street station, and walked into Starbucks.

"I'll clear all this up shortly."

"Now would be a good time," Grady said.

"What's a macchiato?"

"Italian for stained as with caramel in the coffee. You're not going to distract me."

Two of the bodyguards remained outside. Yodo and two others spread out around the place and each took a turn going to the counter and ordering. Grady and Michael were first in line and each ordered a soy latte with almond syrup.

They sat at a small table which was a little low for his height.

She unzipped her coat and got comfortable, but he kept his eyes on the subway staircase and the newsstand not one hundred feet away where he expected to see a man in a coat with a carnation.

"In a few minutes I'm going to meet a man. We will follow him; then I will go alone into an apartment building. If it doesn't look good, we go to the Lutheran church."

"You know this man?"

"Not exactly."

"No way can you go by yourself into a building."

"Get used to it."

"No. I won't get used to it. How about a compromise? How about we stand back so you can talk in private."

"We need real privacy. You must wait outside the building."

"It's too risky."

At that moment Michael saw a man in a dark coat crossing the street to the Christopher Street station. In the press of bodies he couldn't see the lapel. Slowly he rose, intent on the man and his coat. Then he saw the white carnation. The man was blond with longish hair and a beard. He walked easily—younger than he expected. And big. Could it be the right man? Then the man stopped right beside the newsstand near the subway stairs, just as he had said. It had to be him.

Michael rose, went to the door of Starbucks, brushed his fingers through his hair, and put on his gloves. With a quick swipe of the hand, the carnation was gone.

Quickly the man began walking down Christopher. Michael followed and immediately Grady was on his arm, the whole entourage following.

As they walked down the darkened sidewalk amongst New Yorkers and tourists, the cabs were jamming the streets and crowds were going home. The air was cold and the psychic intensity of rush hour was running high.

"Can you see him?" she said to Michael.

"Sometimes."

They were passing the Lutheran church.

"You'll need to stop in a minute while I keep going a little way ahead of you. I need some space."

"No way."

The tension in him began to mount. For reasons he couldn't fathom he felt danger.

"What's happening, Michael?"

"Ahead. The man in the dark coat will soon cross the street and go into an apartment building. I will need to go alone inside."

"You're out of your mind."

"Then let me be out of my mind. This is important."

"Let's talk about it first," she said, stalling for time.

They were walking slowly now past a commercial building. She thought she saw someone step out from between two buildings ahead and then step back. Quickly she looked behind to Yodo and the other two guards and then to the one in front. Immediately behind them and in front of Yodo walked two men in heavy overcoats that seemed more grim than the weather. Not feeling right, she nodded to Yodo, suggesting that they cross the street. Yodo turned and looked behind and her eyes followed his and she focused on two more men coming up through the crowd. And then two more to the side.

"I need to go alone."

She barely heard Michael. A man had something in Yodo's side. She suspected a gun or a knife, although there were suddenly more people swarming and she couldn't be sure. Sam had been teaching her to listen to her instincts.

"You really need to stop here," Michael was saying. "Is someone following us?" he changed his thought in midsentence.

"Definitely!"

Yodo nodded to cross the street before whirling and striking one of the men.

"Come on," she said, grabbing Michael's arm. Michael hesitated. She yanked and screamed, "Go." They ran across the street through a meager break in the traffic. A couple of irate cabbies slammed on their brakes, probably needlessly. Others didn't and they blocked their pursuers.

To the far side of the street, there was a building of perhaps twelve stories and a smaller one beside made of a cut stone that was an elegant off-white. There was a service entrance and a space between the buildings. Along the sidewalk were awnings and near the small building wrought iron fences, stoops, and steps, a confusing array of obstacles and hiding places depending on the motivations of the observer. Right now she wanted to escape and her eyes were scouring, looking for someplace to go. There were enough men that they could be drugged and "helped" into a car or van before the police or anyone else could do anything.

They ran down the street, dodging startled people, some of whom shouted obscenities. She headed for a side street. Glancing over her shoulder, she saw all five of their bodyguards, including Yodo, in some kind of street fight. One of the men broke free to follow across the street and was immediately tackled. A man was running down the sidewalk, pushing through the crowd toward Yodo, shouting, "Police." She wondered for a second whether he was really the police.

When she and Michael rounded the corner of the side street, Michael grabbed her arm and pointed to a heavy six-inch black pipe that went up the side of the cut stone building. It was an inch from the building held by brackets bolted into the mortar, and no doubt into the wood superstructure beneath. There was just enough room between the pipe and the building to allow space for fingers. Looking more monkey than man, Michael climbed up rapidly, hand over hand, with his feet walking up the building in an amazing display of agility. His adrenaline had to be through the roof—he showed almost no sign of the wounded thigh that had nearly killed him. His climb attracted several onlookers. Then she saw what he was doing. One story up was a fire escape ladder that he grabbed and extended downward so that she could easily climb. As she started to grab the rungs, two men came running around the corner. For a couple of seconds they slowed as if to talk and reassure her.

"Hold it, we don't want to hurt you; we just want to talk." The man had a French accent. As she climbed, they kept coming.

Banging her shins, she went rapidly and then they were at the base of the ladder climbing as well. As she reached the first landing, Michael's body hurtled past her, traveling feet-first into the lead man and knocking him into the next. Michael hit the ground on top of them and, as quick as a cat, was on them removing their guns. The two men struggled on the ground, trying to rise, obviously with broken bones. She hoped Michael hadn't crippled them. People were coming warily closer.

Michael jumped to the ladder and began to climb again.

"Wait," a man shouted. Grady looked down; the voice

was familiar. There was a blond-bearded man with swarthy skin taking off an old-fashioned hat. In his long coat there was a carnation. He had just come around the corner. "There are men headed up the inside stairs of the building. You'll be trapped. Come on down." She realized it was Sam.

At that moment another two men came around the corner. Sam clipped one on the run with a straight punch to the jaw that made an audible crack and sent him to the ground on his back. With the second man Sam whirled and struck with an elbow that took the man down, but only for a few seconds; in one smooth move he was up. The man was slim and strong in the shoulders, but Sam was fast, placing straight punches to the head followed by a roundhouse kick to the jaw. Although the man rocked and teetered, virtually unconscious, Sam pressed in with more powerful punches. The unrelenting almost balletlike attack gave Grady the shivers. What moved her was that something so clean and fluid and even beautiful could be so destructive. It was the first time she had seen Sam in an all-out fight. Four men were on the ground, two completely unconscious, the other two barely moving. Sam was going through their clothes, removing guns and obviously looking for something, maybe ID. Gawkers were starting to protest at Sam's rifling through the men's clothing. Sam showed them something, she supposed his fake badge, and that seemed to calm the crowd.

Grady climbed quickly down and jumped to the ground. At the far end of the block a group of men turned the corner running at them. From across Christopher Street men had now broken free and were running toward them, but these were tackled by the bodyguards. Yodo was struggling with two men at once, blood pouring from his nose and cuts on his face. When Grady reached the bottom of the ladder, Sam yelled to run and they began running across the street at an angle, headed toward a large corner building that also faced

Christopher Street. They ran to a door and, strangely, Sam had a key. They all passed through, slamming it behind them. Inside there was another man with glasses, maybe five feet ten inches.

"No time for introductions. This is Georges Raval. He'll meet us later. Georges, follow the plan," Sam said.

The slight man hesitated.

"They're all over the place," Sam said. "A virtual army."

"You've got to get out of here," Raval said.

"Just do the plan." Sam spoke with uncommon intensity and Raval ran for some stairs, took them two at a time, and disappeared.

Sam took the group down some stairs into a basement area with pipes and all manner of car-size blowers and duct-work. He led them to a boarded-up opening in the wall and began pulling off the boards to expose an old stairway. The sound of the subway was clearly audible.

"In the forties there was an entrance to the subway here. Now they're redoing PATH and the steam pipes and other underground conduits run all through here. Somewhere down here, Raval says, there is an old, abandoned subway station. Full of derelicts and the like, but it's a maze down there and I doubt these guys will ever find us."

"Who are these guys?" Grady said.

"French guys. Government, I think."

"When will I talk with Raval?" Michael said.

"After we save our asses, that's when. Next time, don't bring half the French Secret Service."

At that moment there was a crash and they knew the front door had been broken in.

Sam led them down a stairwell that was plugged with cement after no more than twenty feet or so. A small hole in the concrete plug had been created with jackhammers, no doubt by subway workers trying to find something in the underground labyrinth that was Manhattan Island. It was solid bedrock. The tiny passage was uninviting in every sense—just big enough for a person to worm their way through. Sam beckoned them and dove in. Grady crawled more tentatively after him. Michael came behind her.

They headed into the black of the New York underground and she wasn't sure which was worse—the men above or the hole. The concrete passage was black and strewn with the sort of gravel shed by unraveling concrete. It became very tight and she had to drop to her belly onto the sharp edges and slither. It had a vile smell, like rot and mold, dog feces, and urine. They came to sheet metal of some sort that made crawling easier, but it was even tighter. When she raised her head, it hit solid concrete. There was maybe three or four inches on either side of her shoulders. She could tell Sam was struggling to continue. It got very steep and suddenly she realized there would be no backing up. Panic rose in the back of her throat and she wanted to scream. She stopped. She was shaking.

"Keep coming." It was Sam.

As she slid forward, her chin hit something putrid. Human vomit, she guessed.

"Oh God." She groaned, but she kept sliding slowly after Sam.

She heard Sam say, "There's a huge drop." Then his feet were suddenly gone. "It's okay. I'll catch you," he called.

With that, she let herself slide down through the wet and muck.

Instantly she could feel Sam's hands on her shoulders and fell into his arms. It would have been fine with her if she just stayed there. They were in a more open area and could stand. Sam turned on a tiny light that enabled her to see three or four feet surrounding.

When Michael was down, Sam pulled up his shirt and

Kevlar vest to reveal a waistline holding two pistols. He fired into the concrete back up in the tunnel. It would be a major discouragement to anyone thinking about coming down.

They were in a concrete passage strewn with old toilet paper and bottles. They proceeded down a very steep incline that turned and pitched up sharply, only to turn down once again. The passage was roughly an S laid on its back, but without vertical drops. They arrived at some kind of a wall and there was a dim light showing through a hole. As they came closer, she could see that it was heavy plywood with bracing and that someone had knocked a hole in the barrier. Sam turned off his light. From the chamber below came the acrid smell of smoke.

In the distance roared a subway train. Peering through the hole and into the haze, she saw small fires and shadows of people in a large space far ahead. Some were hunched, as if under a blanket, while others stood with their hands over small barrels bristling with orange flame. They would be entering a dark corner of a large underground chamber. It was impossible to guess the number of occupants, as there were deep shadows and little light and had to be all manner of hiding places.

"Was I communicating with Raval or you?" Michael asked suddenly.

"Raval. We just figured out what you two were doing and talked him into some precautions."

"So you weren't fooling me?"

"No. And for all I knew, it would work fine and you and Raval would have your private talk."

"Now I don't know when I'll talk with him."

"We'll find him. Or he'll find you."

"What about the French guys? Do you think they'll catch him?"

"Probably not. At this point the U.S. government is likely

to step in. The mere fact that the French government seems to be going nuts should be enough to set our boys off."

"Well, neither government's taking me over. That much I can tell you."

"Let's fight one battle at a time," said Sam. "I think we're in an old air vent."

But Michael wasn't done. "How did you find out about Raval?"

"That is a secret of Grogg's and cannot be revealed."

"What is Grogg?"

"He's sort of like a shaman. He can look into your soul."

Michael looked to Grady, who shrugged as if to ask if she was to speak of company secrets.

"It's dark as hell down here," she said to Sam.

"To our advantage," said Sam. "Take my hand." Grady held it and then took Michael's in her other.

"The air's bad. Smells of poison."

"Yep. Tastes like it came straight out the ass end of a diesel bus." Sam was leading them forward slowly over uneven ground. In places the cement had buckled and deteriorated.

"Get out of here," said a gravelly male voice. A dog growled low in the throat. In an odd way the human and the dog had a similar snarl. A light came on, blinding them. Then the light went flying. By chance it landed at an angle to them, casting soft light over the scene.

"You bastard. I'm gonna . . ." Then Grady could see Sam grabbing somebody. There came the sound of a struggle and a series of gravelly curses.

"Let's relax," Sam said.

Grady could see that the man was huge, even all hunched over, and Sam was holding the fellow by nothing more than one hand.

"All right, all right," the big guy was saying. "Just don't hurt my dog."

"Make sure it stays put or it'll be having quite a headache."

A small light appeared in the gray and the smoke and she knew it was Sam's.

"Keep your hands where I can see them." Sam released the man and stepped back. Sam's small light shone on a scraggly, bearded man who looked like he was covered in Vaseline and lived in a dirt pit. The skin of his face shone through a sheen of petroleum and grime, maybe sweat. She wondered if he even felt the chill of this cold hell.

"We don't like your kind of strangers down here."

"We'll be passing through."

"You taking her through here?"

"With your help I'll bet anything is possible."

"Why would I help?"

"A hundred bucks."

"You're right. I'd help. You got iron?"

"Enough for an anchor factory."

"Don't be shootin' down here. Ricochets are deadly."

"We only shoot those who need to be shot."

"You got a lotta balls bringing her down here . . . these days."

The dog began barking again. "Some unfriendly city officials are coming. How do we exit?"

The man pulled out a bottle and held it in front of him. "Singe their ass with this. Molotov cocktail. Just run it up there and light."

"Got a match?"

The man produced a lighter.

"You guys should have come down on a sheet of plastic. More hepatitis up that hole than in a whore's ass," he said as he took his dog's leash. "Now I can light that rag, but you gotta run like hell with it to get it up near the old grate."

"Go ahead," Sam said.

The man lit the rag; Sam ran to the hole in the plywood and threw it.

"You should have gone all the way up near the old grate."

"I don't know the old grate. Besides, I want to entertain them, not kill them."

Chapter 16

Slay the bear before sleeping in its cave.
—Tilok proverb

Sam knew about the New York underground and the old subway stations, especially along the financial district. The city tried to keep the more obvious entrances closed, but it was like trying to keep ants out of a farmhouse.

They looked across a chamber, perhaps a quarter of the size of a football field. The old tunnel disappeared into the black, and what once had been an opulent waiting area of gleaming tile and polished wood had become like a gilded carriage left to rot in the carriage house. The base of the walls seemed to be favored for campsites. Maybe that was because if a man had his back to a wall, he didn't have to see behind him. The next most popular residential areas seemed to be around the base of the pillars.

Smoke filled the place, and to see far, you ducked down to get beneath the acrid haze. What Sam could see of the ceiling was pitch black from soot. Flame from the barrels angled toward the tunnels indicating that most of the draft came from that direction.

"What do you call yourself?"

"Lugger. Or Dog Man."

"Dog Man is pretty apparent. How do you come by Lugger?"

"When I was a kid, I played football. I was a lineman, and when I would forget myself, I used to pick up the opposing guards and carry them. Hence, Lugger."

"How do you like it down here?"

"Beats up there. You look like a Greek or an Indian or something."

"I use liquid tan. No harmful radiation."

"Is that true?"

"No. How do we exit this place quietly and far from Christopher Street?"

"You go down the tunnel if you wanna come out a long way from here. Last day or two, the tunnel's been a bad place, though."

They were near one end of the old loading platform and so, to their left, the tunnel was maybe fifty feet. To the right it was much farther because it would be necessary to traverse the entire main hall of the station to start down the far segment.

"Right or left to get out of here?"

"You're kind of out of luck. Left tunnel has the best exit and it's a long ways to daylight. But, like I said, the meanest, craziest sons of a bitches is down there."

"What are you talking about?"

"Mostly people down here live and let live. Most are too crazy or hopeless to hurt anybody. Couple days ago, some gang guys came down. No fun. Raped a girl. I think they still got her back there."

"Let's go get the girl and get out of here at the same time."

"That tunnel is one place that Lugger and Big Dog don't go right now."

"Not even for two hundred bucks?"

"Damn, you trouble my soul with that kind of money. I

came down here to get away from greed and corruption and such, and now you lay it in front of me."

"Let's go. We'll discuss greed on the way," Sam said. "Grady, you should have an extra gun." Sam handed her a 10mm semiautomatic. "Get each hand on a butt."

"I don't have a gun," Lugger said.

"I'll shoot twice as fast and that way you won't need one," Sam said.

Sam picked up Lugger's light, snapped it off, and handed it to him. "When I tell you to turn this on, give me light."

Sam used his own small light to guide the way. They walked across the old concrete floor and Sam could imagine better days sixty years ago when New York's finest made their way through a highly crafted underground structure exhibiting the proclivities of an era when craftsmen labored for hours over a few square feet of handwork. Lights in classic brass fixtures had radiated colorful tile mosaics that overlay the walls, ceiling, and floors. Signs had been created from the tile and embedded in the walls. In those days it didn't usually occur to people to mar and deface public property.

Now the place had become a haven for those left in the wake of a society committed to mass production.

There were only two or three darkened campsites in a direct line to the tunnel. Sam was concerned that soon their hunters would find a more palatable way down into the underground.

"What are the other ways in here? Tunnels?"

"Secret."

"Yeah, but what are they? It's part of the two hundred dollars."

"I'll give you a free history lesson. In the real world I operated one of the trains."

"Okay."

They came to a big drop down into the concrete well that held the track. For a moment the talking stopped as they lowered themselves off the edge of the concrete down to the crushed rock. When everyone was down, they started walking. Sam took Lugger's big light and handed Grady the smaller. The tunnel was thirty feet wide. At the sides it was packed earth.

"You have heard of the City Hall subway station. Closed down in 1945 because the curve was too tight. The cars got too long and they put the doors in the middle of the car and it didn't work on that tight curve. This station was the same thing. Happened in 1945, just like City Hall. If you look back, you'll see the curve in the track in front of the platform. The big cars wouldn't fit around the curve for off-loading. With the doors moved to the middle and the longer car length, they no longer had the right fit to get people on and off. They kept the old City Hall pretty nice. It didn't get torn up and they still sometimes run a subway on the track past the platform. But they more or less forgot about this one until it was too late, and now they don't really want to get into the fact that the homeless people ripped the thing apart. All the brass fixtures are gone. All the tile is messed up, smoked up, or fallen down. At City Hall station they plugged all the stairways but didn't plug the track. Here they did both—"

"It's fascinating," Sam interrupted, "but how do people get down here?"

"I'm getting to that. Relax."

"If we want to live, I need to understand how people can get down here, either in front of us or behind us."

"City officials, my ass. Who exactly is chasing you?"

"No one who gives a damn about Luggers or their dogs."

Despite that, Lugger walked faster, and they kept pace.

"You were telling me the ways into this station."

"Okay. Understand this principle. Manhattan is solid rock. So people like us don't dig in it. The stairs into the station are all cemented in. That part is like what they originally did at City Hall station. In this tunnel where we're walking, the overhead grates and emergency stair exits are sealed. Back at the station there is one more air vent that does go to a grate that is half covered by a building. In the past people have been able to get through the grate, but just recently they have a steel sheet under it. I wondered how you came down because nobody has had that grate open for the past few weeks. There's a tunnel from the building, but they boarded that up."

"We came through the wall of the building. I'm told that they drilled the hole in the concrete when they were looking for something. Maybe a steam pipe or something to do with the subway," Sam theorized.

"Nowadays people get here mostly by running down the live track. At either end of this side track, there's a cement wall. But it doesn't go all the way to the top of the tunnel in this direction. I think it's a dam for water when the side tunnel starts filling from heavy rain. Down the other direction the hole to get out of the abandoned track is really small. I don't fit."

"Is the other surface hole into the station as hard to travel as what we came down?"

"Harder to find because it isn't exposed to the outside. Easier to come down."

"How about ahead of us?"

"All operating subway tunnels have a grate every six hundred feet. The grates open with a bolt lock. You just slide the bolt out of the hole, but you can only do it from underneath. But like I said, this track was abandoned for good. Over time they just paved over the grates above the track or welded them up and put in a steel plate. So there's no getting out except over the top of the wall at the end of this tunnel, and then we'll be on the live track of the 1 and 9."

"Is there a hot rail in here?"

"No way."

"I thought this might be part of the PATH line."

"No, that's through the rock over there a piece and down. PATH runs under the 1 and 9."

Suddenly lights came on, shining in their eyes. Sam used Lugger's big light and shone back. There were seven men and four had metal pipes or chains. Three were fishing out their knives. No guns in evidence.

Sam waved everybody back, handed the light to Lugger, and walked forward alone with an automatic in each hand. He sized them up as a mean, confident crew with less dirt on the clothes than should be the norm down here. They were in various stages of growth on their beards. One was of good size, the others average. He wondered how often they came underground.

Behind them stumbled two girls, both in bad shape. Their heads hung. They had bulky coats wrapped around them, but their legs and feet were bare, probably nude under the coats.

"We just want to pass." Sam paused. "And we're taking the girls."

The leader looked around and grinned while three of the guys pulled guns. "We do the takin' down here. We'll start with the money and then we'll take her."

"You guys have six semiautomatics aimed at you. All you've got is a few relic revolvers, aside from the Beretta."

"Bullshit, bullshit, bullshit!"

Sam shot. Sound exploded through the tunnel. The bullet missed the leader's head by inches. Shock etched their nervous faces, everyone leaning forward at once, ready to start a war.

The leader tried to be nonchalant but put his finger to his ear as if to check its integrity.

"The next bullet goes in the middle of your forehead."

"We're gonna die right here," the leader said.

Sam knew he had a problem. "Last I heard, gang leaders still had balls. I'll fight you. If I win, you let us pass and we take the girls."

"What if I win?"

"Then you've got one less guy to deal with."

"Killing you will be a pleasure. And after that, having her."

Sam handed one gun back and put the other in his pants.

"You still got a gun," the leader said.

"How about you?"

The leader raised his hands and turned.

"Your ankle."

The leader reached down and removed a small revolver.

Sam handed back the second gun.

"You wanna come hit me with a pipe?"

"What are you, one of those kung fu assholes?"

"Nah. No kung fu. I could teach you to pronounce it some other time. But like all good martial-arts practitioners, it is now my duty to ask you not to fight. There is no reason not to let us pass."

The other men looked a little nervous and began to spread out.

"Think about it. If you win, my friends here will have a case of the nerves and they'll start shooting hollow points out of these semiautomatics and you guys will have bullets going in the front of you and blowing holes out your backs the size of grapefruits. And your intestines will probably rupture and spew shit all over your insides and it will take, say, thirty minutes to actually lose consciousness and it'll hurt like hell as you're dying. Then you'll think back to how it was that you could have just let us walk through. Of course you'll be shooting at my guys, but they have Kevlar vests, and you don't, so you'll need a head shot. So if you're lucky, you'll lose the fistfight and just suffer some broken bones."

The bangers took another look at one another.

"You gotta pay to get through. We'll take her and some money."

"Okay. Well, let's fight then, one at a time."

Sam turned to Grady and Michael. "Now, you make sure that whoever wins gets gut shot. Unless, of course, I win. Then you don't have to shoot anybody."

"I more or less specialize in the gut shot," Michael said.

Sam had been moving closer to the lead man, the big fellow, who now had a pipe ready to swing.

"Here I am. Aren't you gonna take a swing? Or can you feel that lead blowing out your backbone?"

Sam kicked in a blur right up into the man's crotch. The man bent over clutching his privates. For the moment he couldn't breathe. Sam yanked the pipe from his hands.

"If you check carefully, you'll see that your nuts are still down there, although they may have entered your abdominal cavity." Sam swung the pipe up between the man's legs, breaking the bones in his hands. When the man's hands dropped, Sam swung again and hit the testicles a second time, square on. "Never threaten a woman." With the man doubled over, he pinched off carotid arteries from behind the neck until he lost consciousness.

"Right on." It was one of the girls back in the shadows.

A man with a badly scarred face was near the tunnel wall, but he began moving nearer the others. He had a gun pointed at Sam.

"You can start a shooting war, but most of us will die."

"Especially you," the man said. Sam stepped closer, closing the distance. In his fear the man wasn't thinking about the metal breastplate in the flak jacket under Sam's coat. He was aiming right at it.

"Either squeeze the trigger or get out of the way," Sam said with remarkable calm. The hesitation was in the man's eyes and it was all Sam needed. In a fast kick he sent the man's gun hand up and then grabbed the gun hand on the way down. Sam jabbed his solar plexus, and as the strength left the man, Sam swiped his gun away. Quite deliberately he shot the man in the foot and left him screaming. One of the five remaining now grabbed one of the girls and put a gun to her head.

Grady stepped forward with her guns leveled. "Don't touch her!"

The four others were looking uncertain. Sam walked to the nearest, a short, stocky, bald man, and held his pipe low as if he meant to repeat the performance with the leader. The man moved sideways with his head down and his hips back. Without taking his gaze from the man's eyes, Sam brought the pipe up under the man's chin, snapping the jaw. Despite the fractured jaw, the man swung hard at Sam. Sam blocked it with his own pipe and struck the nose palm up with instant results.

The man with the girl was backing away and Grady was moving forward, step for step. The three nearest watched Sam with wary eyes. At that moment feet running on the gravel distracted everyone; in seconds it seemed there were blue suits everywhere. Lugger and the gang members doused their lights. Two of the suits had lights. Sam took three strides and kicked one out while Michael, already surrounded by several men, instinctively went for the only remaining light. He kicked it out of the man's hand and stomped it on the rock. Lugger's dog was snarling and men were shouting as the dog lunged at them with bared fangs.

Sam whirled, knowing that someone had been coming at him from the side and behind. Everything Grandfather had taught him about darkness would be useful in the next seconds. He stepped to the side so that any light-filled memories would be misleading. A body passed close by. The footsteps stopped. He moved to a fighting stance and stood perfectly still. There is a sense that is not touch and is not sound or sight but may be a bit of all three unconsciously applied. Grandfather had said that there was an additional sense that, working with the others, created a certain sensation when another living being came within one's personal space. Sam felt that sensation and placed the person at about three feet distant. He crouched. With his left hand he reached out slowly along the ground until he felt a shoe. At that instant he withdrew his left hand, put it to the ground, and pivoted on it, kicking hard where the leg should be. It was a knee-high kick. There was a scream as the knee popped. When the man fell, Sam was on him, first choking him, then using his left hand to line up the chin for a solid right punch to the jaw. He found a gun and threw it into the darkness. Then he found a knife, a switchblade—unusual for a suit—and kept it. He moved straight back to where Grady had been standing and discerned fighting nearby. From the sounds he guessed Michael was picking them off in the dark, much as he had done—only at Michael's location there were many more men and they all had seemed to go for Bowden.

A few feet away, the dog was in a fight for his life. First Sam smelled the perfume, then he felt for and found two hands, each with a gun.

"Grady," he whispered.

"I think they have Michael," she said. Quickly he moved her to the wall.

"Stay here."

When he turned, he heard someone nearby skidding on the rock. No doubt they were turning, trying to see. They seemed within a few feet. He concentrated, took a step back, then delivered a head-high kick with momentum. He pictured the point of impact and his heavy shoe connected with flesh slightly ahead of his anticipated strike point. But it was very solid and probably close to lethal. Whoever had been struck went down. Quickly he felt along the ground, found the body, removed and threw away the shoes, and sliced the Achilles tendon with the knife. No scream. The guy had blacked out.

Next, he belly-crawled back to the central struggle. A man moving fast tripped over him. Instantly he felt for the shoes. Ordinary street shoes. Michael and Lugger wore boots. After slashing an Achilles and eliciting a scream, he upended the man, yanked off the shoes, and threw them.

Next he crawled up the thrashing body of the panicked man, found his neck, and choked off the carotids. The man began flailing and throwing wild punches. A fist smacked Sam's jaw, but he held on until the man quieted.

He went back to the fight sounds, again on his belly, and found boots under two or three men. Knowing that Michael was on the bottom made it easy. He cut an Achilles on one man and that started the screaming. What made it even easier was that the suits wore no body armor. They weren't cops. Sam unleashed a flurry of fists and kicks on unprotected backs and flanks.

As near as Sam could tell, the man he had slashed was screaming in French that he had been cut. For the suits, castration would come to mind and fuel the paranoia.

Sam found another man trying to hang on to Michael, felt his ribs, lined up and delivered a powerful kick that broke several. Sam was careful not to puncture the lung with the free-floating ribs. The bodies rolled free now and Sam followed the booted feet to grab Michael, who still had one gun. He could feel the lethargy in Michael's body from the beating. Grabbing him and leading him, he joined with Grady.

He found Lugger by sense of smell. Like Michael, Lugger was held down by three suits. Quickly he broke ribs and left two men in misery, both with a sliced Achilles. Once he got Lugger to the wall, Lugger's dog came on a sharp whistle. In the dog's mouth hung a new plaything, a piece of bloody fabric. They moved a hundred feet down the wall and turned on the lights long enough to grab the girls. They were beat up and didn't look like they could run far. Michael and Sam each carried one. They walked several hundred feet before coming to the wall that now separated the 1 and 9 track. It was an easy jump through a hole to get onto the live track. They went only a short distance before they came to an emergency escape. They went to the platform below the grate, where Sam got a signal on the cell phone. They called Yodo, who was bandaged and functional, to bring men and surround the grate. It required a wait of thirty minutes. Grady and Michael took the girls, opened the grate, and emerged onto the sidewalk, surrounded by ex-cops with guns. Sam slipped out another exit twelve hundred feet away.

His next order of business was to find out what a powerful law firm wanted with Michael Bowden—and who they wanted it for.

"What do *you* suppose is going on, Figgy?" Sam was on the New York end of a conference call with Jill in LA, and Figgy on another phone allegedly at the French offices of the United Nations.

"The guys on the street got by the police pretty fast—that tells me it was something like diplomatic immunity," Sam continued. "The police call it a bizarre misunderstanding. They say people from the foreign service of an unnamed government saw Americans in trouble, followed them to an underground passage, and were injured by parties unknown. Which is a lie."

"Well, it could have been any foreign government."

"Yeah, that speaks French."

"Sam, I hear what you're saying, but either you trust me or you don't. It wasn't France."

"Tell me how you know that."

"I'm on both sides of the ocean. I have it on good authority from both places."

"Uh-huh. Do I have it right that your clients have you at the UN at the moment?"

"That's right."

"In New York, then. This choice of location wouldn't be because Michael Bowden is here or because you think Georges Raval is here."

"I guess it wouldn't be illogical about Bowden. Raval, I don't think so."

"You gonna tell me what your people are doing?"

"Same as you. Looking for Gaudet. Stop him before he hurts somebody."

"What's the latest from Benoit Moreau? When am I going to get that interview?"

"I'm sure any day now. But you know she's told all she knows. She can't help us catch Gaudet any more than she already has."

Benoit Moreau had moved into a sublet apartment in Manhattan's garment district—an area where there were few apartments. The usual occupant was on a trip to Europe. Benoit was calling herself Jacqueline Dupont because worldwide there were thousands by that name. From the apartment she used the phones to set up the escrow arrangements in Switzerland, kept track of Baptiste, placated the admiral. Constantly she had to keep in mind what Baptiste knew and what the admiral didn't know, and vice versa. Good news that this would be her best and last exercise in duplicity.

She called Gaudet, who was getting impatient.

"When will I see you?"

"Soon, when I've arranged everything. At the moment

I'm having trouble with Raval and trying to make a deal with Bowden for the 1998 journal."

"How do you know it is 1998?"

"All that matters is that I convince the French government that it is 1998 and tell them the page."

"Why does Bowden sell this to you?"

"He doesn't own the rights to the Chaperone process. This is his best chance to make money and be done with it."

"I am hungry for you. It has been a long time. I hear that prison has not aged you."

"Be patient. We have bigger things to do now."

"When you can come, I will need advance notice. There are many precautions."

"I understand."

Next she wrote an e-mail to Sam. Finally she dressed to meet Georges Raval for the first time in more than a year.

Chapter 17

The cougar stalks while the fawn eats.

—Tilok proverb

The law firm was a short cab ride from Greenwich Village, where Sam was staying. Instead of having the driver stop in front of the building, Sam had him drive past the front entry and drop him off a block down the street. In this area the buildings were truly huge and walking in the concrete canyons seemed like something out of a Tolkien fantasy. It was cold and he wore a dense sweater with a heavy wool topcoat—all purchased by Anna. It was hard to stop thinking about her and he made no particular effort.

The weather, like his mood, was troubled, and above the city the sky loomed pitch dark. Ground Zero was still a cavernous, empty space in the skyline. All the buildings were lit and the neon was everywhere, making twilight across the pavement and deep shadows along its borders. As Sam walked down the crowded sidewalks, he kept to the shadows and scanned the street.

Automobiles filled Broadway, taxis crept and honked while motorcycles weaved in and out, playing tag with death or dismemberment.

Sam eyed the entrance to the law firm's building and

noted that people were leaving in ones and twos, not in a steady stream. All walked briskly, no doubt anxious to get home.

There did not seem to be anyone hanging around near the doorways to the main lobby. Sam approached the building's covered portico through a break in the foot traffic. He carried a sizable briefcase with the tools of his trade. Four revolving doors were set to allow exit while, given the hour, only one was set to allow entry. As he stepped close to the entryway door, it began to move as if it had a mind, and he stepped in between the glass sections and was whisked into the building. Once inside, he went to the security man, glanced at the board, and saw that main reception for the firm of Binkley, Hart, & Rove was on the tenth floor.

"I'm Michael Bowden. I'm meeting Mr. John Stephan at Binkley, Hart, and Rove." He handed the man a fictitious Michael Bowden passport, which matched his artificially bearded face. He looked nothing like himself after an hour with makeup and the beard.

"Go on up to the second floor."

Sam looked down at the listings under the law firm, let his eye travel to S, and found no Stephan, only a Stevens, a Smith, and a Stewart. Bowden had recalled that the managing partner on the project was Stewart. The law firm occupied floors 10 through 13, not the second floor. No office number was listed for Stewart.

"I don't see a Mr. Stephan listed."

"I was told you would be meeting Mr. Stephan and that you would meet him on the second floor in the lobby of the restaurant."

"I see. Okay. Well, thanks."

Sam emptied his pockets, went through a metal detector, then walked around the corner to elevator banks for the lower floors 1 through 20, and immediately found the stairs and noted with satisfaction that they could be entered without passing through the guard's field of view, but for a scanning camera. It was an easy matter to feign waiting for an elevator and to then remain outside the camera's changing field of view all the way to the stairs. If the security had been good, there would have been multiple cameras or a hidden camera, and evasion would not have been so simple. Or perhaps it wasn't so simple and he was being watched but not apprehended. It made for an interesting life.

Sam took care not to make loud, echoing footfalls on the stairs. At the top he came to a steel door. As he approached it, he was able to see through a small window. Normally, this sort of door would be kept locked, but when he twisted the handle, it released. He opened it a crack.

There was grayish-white canvas draped around, with white wall texture material on it, and there were three men in the doorway of a darkened restaurant that was obviously being remodeled. It was a place with its guts ripped out, a skeleton of a room, and it did not provide a reassuring feeling. He listened.

"You got any more of that gum? The kind that squirts the green stuff in your mouth?" The speaker was very big, six feet four inches, probably 250 pounds, bull-necked, a round, meaty face with old zit scars, and a marine-style haircut. He spoke to a thin, smaller guy, probably just over thirty, with a jogger's body but no apparent muscle above the waist. The little guy was a sharp but conservative dresser wearing something like a Hickey Freeman suit, three-button coat with quality material, and wing tip shoes, nearly new. He sported a $40 haircut that came down slightly over the ears, had soft, white hands with well-kept fingernails, a crisp white shirt, and a red-checked power tie. He was bored, obviously hanging around with a couple of guys he deemed inferior, and he was without a doubt a lawyer—unless they had asked some stockbroker to stand around outside a gutted restaurant.

The third man was black with a mustache, the kind of guy who watches everything. He was in a sport coat, tie, and good slacks. No telling his role.

The lawyer fellow reached in his pockets and pulled out loose change, a cell phone, old receipts, an airline stub, and a wadded-up tissue.

"I think I'm out of gum. But he should be here anytime."

"Yeah. I don't know why they wanted us to go through this baloney. We could tell if he was alone down in the lobby."

"Just conservative is all. They don't want to be embarrassed upstairs."

"Yeah, well, if I was this guy Bowden, I'd get the spooks just stepping off the elevator and seeing this."

"This guy has lived in the jungle with savages, for God's sake. He tracks down remote tribes. I think he'll know we're friendly."

"Then why am I here?"

"We've gone over it, Max. You're a prop. Just a prop. Your only job is to chew your gum."

"If after talking, he doesn't want to go upstairs, he leaves?"

"Of course he leaves. Jeez, remember who you are working for. Besides, have you ever actually been in a fight after you got out of the service?"

"The rowdy client at the Christmas party. What do we do if he's like that guy, and after he listens to you, he wants to strangle your scrawny lawyer neck."

"That's not a question. And you wouldn't say that if you weren't the senior partner's pet."

Sam let the door slide quietly closed, then proceeded to climb the stairs to the tenth floor. It took between half a minute and a minute per floor, which left little time to think. For a few seconds he thought of Anna and his loneliness and his guilt and of not being with her, and the pain he would feel if he was. Then he thought about killing Gaudet, about wrapping his hands around his throat, and knew that he needed to be careful. And then he was at the tenth floor. Through the door's glass window he saw only hallway. It seemed the staff was long gone. There were still lawyers, he was sure, and there would be evening-shift word-processing computer operators. Grasping the steel handle, he slowly turned it but found it wouldn't open. That was a big letdown. He waited a moment, and someone passed by. On impulse Sam knocked. The man turned as if startled and opened the door.

"Yes?"

"I'm here to see Arthur Stewart." And then he dipped his head just a bit as if embarrassed. "I'm afraid I get claustrophobic in elevators, so I never use them."

"Ah. I see. We don't get many that climb the stairs to the tenth. Check in at reception there," he said, and then turned the corner toward the elevators and was gone.

Sam looked down the hall to the one receptionist remaining behind a chest-high granite counter. Only the top of her head, with its vivid light red hair, was visible, and fortunately she was oblivious to his presence and the discussion. Looking around, Sam immediately saw another wide hall with cubicles and offices down it. He glided down this new hall and began looking at the names beside the doors. Hinkle, Cassaway, Manchester, Warne, Thomas, Meyer, Cooper, etc., etc. But no Stewart. The furnishings in the offices were tasteful and expensive—this was a prosperous firm.

Sam decided to try the eleventh floor but didn't want to be locked in the stairwell. He wondered if there might be an inside stairway, and no sooner had he thought about it, than one appeared as he completed a tour around the outside hall of the building. It struck him as odd that the man hadn't commented that Stewart was upstairs.

He made himself climb the stairs briskly, as if he knew what he was doing. If he encountered someone, he wanted as few questions as possible. Every office seemed to have files or papers strewn on the desk, much like his own. This was hopeful. After touring the entire eleventh floor and failing to locate any Arthur Stewart, Sam went to the firm's next and second-highest floor. At the twelfth floor he discovered a library in the middle of the floor with hallways, offices, and cubicles around the outside. Just before the library there was a hall. Down it was reception and beyond that a large, glass-walled conference room in which there were four men. He moved quickly, figuring that it was the meeting arranged for Bowden. This was a group of optimists, given that Bowden had made no promise that he would show. Still, no Stewart. Finally, in the far corner of the thirteenth floor, he found the office. It was in a corner space, featuring windows on two walls. On a tripod sat a brass telescope, which was quite handsome and, no doubt, functional. There was a globe on a stand in one corner, a leather sofa, a coffee table, and, at the end opposite, a hand-carved wooden desk. Obviously, Arthur Stewart was very senior.

There was a photo of a middle-aged man and a young woman, cheek to cheek, and several other photos displaying similar togetherness. One photo, partially hidden behind a Rotary award, depicted Stewart and some thirtyish adults— no doubt the kids from the first marriage—just a little older than the new wife. He figured it was his imagination, but the young adult quartet seemed to be glaring at the cheek-to-cheek number. Sam found these happy, little families inspirational—just like Monday-night football with the boys, poker night, and other good reasons for serious caution in the marriage department.

He searched the desktop, which had a number of files stacked in the corner. One was labeled ESTATE OF MILDRED MCBETH, another TROY VS HUMBITT MANUFACTURING and still another SOUTHWAYS CORPORATION. Upon casual inspection they all involved patent rights. Looking at the bookshelves, he saw they were full with treatises on patents, many pharmaceutically related. So, this man was a patent lawyer and he did work with the patenting of molecules. It lent credence to the message Bowden had received.

Another file holder made of beautiful wood contained several more files: TRUSTEE: GRACE TECHNOLOGIES. In this file Sam found some notes:

> *Contacted by Jean-Baptiste French government. Amazonia Molecule. Uses of the molecule strictly confidential. Molecular structure to follow. Discovered by Michael J. Bowden and under development by Northern Lights. Proprietary processes claimed by French Government trustee for Grace Technologies. Need to verify exclusive rights. Need to purchase any interest possible. Need location and habitat of the plant material. Memo FPC file.*

Sam supposed that FPC meant fireproof cabinet. It would be locked probably in a secure room, so the odds of getting in were not great. Still, he decided to look. Exiting the office, he walked down the hall and glanced down a narrow interior hall, where he saw a young man and a young woman, maybe in their twenties, drinking coffee. No doubt, the junior associates burning the midnight oil. He decided to take a chance.

There was a reference to a secure file in the FPC and the date of initial contact was recent—right after they had left the Amazon. He couldn't imagine what he might find in the fireproof cabinet. He had been willing to wander around in this law firm, ostensibly lost, looking for the office of a Mr. Stewart, but breaking into a locked file cabinet was up a notch and he was still pondering the morality of that against his need to know. Borrowing the firm's copier for a couple of minutes, Sam duplicated the office file and walked into the kitchen with an air of nonchalance. The two young people barely glanced up, although the woman glanced a little longer.

He walked over to the coffeemaker, poured some black, and nodded at the woman. With a little effort he managed to catch her eye.

"I don't believe we've met," she said. "Are you a partner?"

"No. I'm from another firm. Working with Mr. Stewart."

"I thought he went home."

"He did. He's coming back and asked me to meet him at the fireproof cabinet. This case."

Sam laid the file down.

"Yeah, well, I'm not his associate and know nothing. I'm in litigation. But the file room is all the way down this hall, then to the right. It's on the short outside wall with no windows. If that's where he is, that's where you'll find him."

The logic was amusingly tautological, but he decided not to tease her. As he walked away, he heard the young man. " 'If that's where he is, that's where you'll find him'? Come on."

Sam went down the hall, turned right, and passed an office with a thirtysomething woman bent over a desk. Then he kept on to the end of the hall and found a locked door. This was the difficult part. He walked into an open attorney's office and found a phone directory. This office belonged to Norman Chapman. He was a bit of a pack rat, even had piles of papers on the floor. Using the directory, Sam determined that there were more than one hundred lawyers in the firm. He rifled through the drawers. In the top drawer he found a bunch of papers and a memo concerning one Scott Davis, dated the previous month. It was a bio, a memo with a business plan, a bunch of interviews and partner ratings. Obviously, the man had been a partner at another firm and was a candidate to come to Binkley, Hart, & Rove. On a hunch he looked in the back of the phone book to the supplement and found that Scott Davis was added as of October. Davis was brand new. He dialed the extension for Davis and got a recording.

"My first day in the office will be November fourth, but until then, I will be getting my messages, so please leave a message."

Leafing through the résumé papers and the business plan, he discovered that Davis was a civil litigator specializing in the defense of class actions. The man was from Boston and had been with the Arthur & Taylor firm. The business plan made the point that he would be bringing some large clients. On the first page of the résumé was a picture of Davis. He had a full head of hair, some graying, was clean shaven, and slightly paunchy. Unfortunately, Sam couldn't judge the man's height.

Sam took a deep breath, knowing what he was about to try was very risky. Quickly he found a restroom and removed his entire disguise. After wetting his hair down completely, he combed as near as he could to Scott Davis. He went back to the woman's office. Next to the door was a plaque with the name Martha McConnell.

"Hi, Martha, I'm Scott Davis. You probably don't even remember me—"

"Oh yes," she said. "Of course. I was in the group of partners at Grady's Bar a month ago. Actually, I stopped by for just a minute and never got to shake your hand. You've done something to your hair. It looks great."

"Thanks. Probably the Grecian Formula." He gave her a toothy smile.

"What can I do for you?"

"Oh, I was just helping out Stewart on some stuff and needed to get into the fireproof cabinet."

"Oh sure. Gosh, it's really a cabinet in a big safe and they've locked it . . . I'm sure . . . but on a good day I can do the combination of. . . . Just a minute . . ." She fished around in her top drawer. "We're not supposed to keep this, but everybody does, otherwise you have to go to Mary Weiss's desk and she always has it locked, so it's just one thing after another. They never give anybody a thing they need until a month after they've been here."

She got a key and her piece of paper and another smaller key and went back to the locked door. When she opened the door and turned on the lights, they encountered a huge file room.

"What is your kind of lawyer doing with patents?"

"I'm just a little weary of defending drug companies and car manufacturers. The big class actions require a lot of travel. Some of the patent claim litigation isn't all that technical that a guy can't learn it. Especially with Arthur Stewart around. Anyway, he thought I might be interested in this. It's about a plant from the Amazon, of all things."

"Never heard of it. But anything to do with the Amazon sounds interesting."

"I thought so."

He noticed that she was appraising him and that she wore no wedding ring. Recalling the résumé and the profile materials pertaining to Scott Davis, he recalled that he had seen nothing about a wife.

"It's normal I suppose for you to work into the evening."

"You can tell I'm relatively young and I'm a junior partner."

"What kind of work do you do?"

"Environmental litigation mainly. That's our end of the hall. The other is the estate planners. They're in another world."

"Aren't they, though."

"I guess you must be busy moving," she said as she walked toward a massive safe.

"Oh yeah."

"This is interim filing for stuff closing or just closed in

the last six months. But when somebody has the family jewels or some national secret, they put it in the cabinets inside the safe here. I think nobody ever put anything in here worth knowing, but it's fun to think about. Okay. Now for 'Big Bertha.' " She walked over to the steel door and began on the dial. It required two tries and probably three minutes, but at last she grunted and pulled open the nearly foot-thick door.

"Impressive," Sam said.

"Now we sign in. At one time this part of this floor belonged to a prominent wholesale jeweler and that's why the big walk-in safe. We would never have spent the money."

Sam wrote the name Scott Davis, the date, and the time on the sign-in sheet.

They went inside the big vault to a row of locked fireproof filing cabinets. Files were arranged by number so they located the file whose number corresponded with the one that Sam had carried upstairs.

"You will just be using the file in the office?"

"Oh yes."

"Will you be here long?"

"Just a few minutes."

"Because without Mr. Arthur Stewart okaying it, I would feel extremely strange."

"Oh, of course. I'll just be a minute with these documents."

Sam had already spied a large copier in the filing room.

"Call me when you want to lock up."

"Sure will. And thanks so much for your help. And say, I was wondering, you know, I don't want to be forward, but I was wondering if we might go out for a cup of coffee."

"Oh. That's actually a kind invitation. And I definitely would if I weren't having to get a motion out tomorrow. But maybe a rain check."

He looked in her eyes and could see that she really meant it. He felt guilty for trying to use her. Walking and talking with her as he left the building would naturally cause people not to notice him like they would a lone late-night stranger.

Sam could not recall when he had been this interested in a discovery. The locked file was voluminous and had various parts. He went to what looked like the guts of the matter. Attorney memos designed to explain in straightforward language what the hell was going on.

There were typed notes of a telephone interview, probably recorded. On the file earpiece it said: TRUSTEE: GRACE TECHNOLOGIES. On the memo header: ADMIRAL FRANÇOIS LARIVE AND MADEMOISELLE BENOIT MOREAU, REPRESENTATIVES OF THE GOVERNMENT OF FRANCE, ACTING AS TRUSTEE FOR GRACE TECHNOLOGIES.

We have various representations in this matter and a number of confidential relationships. See conflicts file.

Then there was the following:

Moreau: Freshwater sponge material was provided by Michael J. Bowden to Northern Lights Pharmaceutical in the fall of 1998. . . . I believe it was November. Jacques Boudreaux of Grace Technologies, a French Corporation, obtained a sample of a molecule isolated from certain organic material because it was said to be a powerful immune system suppressant. Boudreaux gave the material to Georges Raval, a skilled young researcher. Quite by accident Raval traveled down a path of research that led to the development of what he called a Chaperone. To understand Chaperone it is necessary to understand the underlying technology for which it was developed.

The memo went on to give a detailed and a somewhat technical description of the use of vector technology to alter the DNA in animal cells, particularly human cells—effectively, genetic engineering on live humans. In particular, it was genetic reengineering of human brain cells. Sam skipped down, since he was already familiar with the concept. In among the technical stuff there was a lawyer's explanation of the Chaperone technology that was more or less understandable.

Moreau: Chaperone gets its name from the common concept of an escort. For purposes of this explanation we will call the recipient of Chaperone "the patient." Say the patient receives a vector that alters the patient's brain cells. Once altered, they are foreign and will be rejected by the patient's body. Each cell in the body makes protein. It is the protein that the immune system either recognizes or rejects. If each new brain cell type is paired with Chaperone and introduced into the bloodstream, then those new cells will be accepted by the patient's body because his immune system will be reset by Chaperone to accept the particular proteins that they manufacture. The process of binding Chaperone to a foreign protein molecule is complex and is contained in papers of the inventor Georges Raval, former employee of Grace Technologies, to be deposited into escrow (see appendix for escrow details). There are many applications for Chaperone. Suppose a patient is to receive a heart transplant from a donor. The donor's DNA will never match the patient's and hence, except in the case of an identical twin, there is never a perfect match of the new organ from the donor with the patient. The patient's body will reject the donor's organ and the only known method of medically dealing with the rejection is to administer immunosuppressants for the life of the patient and these

*drugs have undesirable side effects. If we were to iso-
late a particular protein molecule from the donor and
bind it to Chaperone, and inject the combination into
the patient, the patient would soon accept the donor's
molecule as if it were native to the patient. Chaperone
can be bound to multiple molecules so that all of the
proteins associated with a donor's organ, such as a
heart, are accepted as native by the patient.*

*DNA altered by vector technology produces the same
proteins consistently regardless of the patient's individual DNA makeup. These foreign proteins can be bound
with Chaperone and administered along with the vectors. Hence, there is no immune reaction from the onset
of the extrusion of foreign proteins by altered brain cells.*

Sam skipped the rest of the lawyer's explanation and went
down to a section on patent rights.

*Raval was at all times an employee of Grace Tech-
nologies when this special process was developed as
was Dr. Boudreaux (per Admiral Larive).*

*Moreau states: I am certain the molecule for the
Chaperone was discovered by Bowden in the Amazon
basin in 1998. We do not know whether the molecule is
plant or animal. I was told that the properties of the
molecule as an immunosuppressant were very similar
or the same to that of a certain molecule from Porifera,
a saltwater sponge which is technically an animal as
distinguished from a plant. However, it was my understanding that the Porifera molecule would not function
as a Chaperone.*

*Grace purchased a license to utilize the Chaperone
molecule from Northern Lights. The processes for uti-
lizing Chaperone belonged to Grace through its em-*

ployee Raval as the inventor. Moreau states: Raval's
status as an employee of Grace will be verified by the
French government's bankruptcy attorneys.

A confidential communication from Northern Lights
not to be disclosed to other parties is to be to the effect
that the Chaperone is a molecule taken from a fresh-
water sponge known only to occur in the Amazon and
known only to Michael Bowden, and that Northern
Lights makes certain claims to this molecule outlined
in a confidential letter from their attorney. Those claims
seem dubious because they have not yet described this
complex molecule with any precision and parts of the
molecule are as yet not understood.

Immediately Sam focused on Benoit's comment regarding the employment of Raval. It seemed to be placed in the
interview like a bomb in an innocent-looking sack. Sam
wondered how the law firm was handling all the confiden-
tiality between all of the parties and figured they must have a
giant file folder full of conflict waivers. Looking further, he
found the "Conflicts" file, but he didn't bother trying to copy
it, since it was, in fact, massive and he was running out of
time.

There were other notes and research about process patent
rights. Obviously, Michael's 1998 journal entries would be
critical. Hurriedly he copied what looked to be the important
material and headed for the handicap stall in the women's restroom where he opened his briefcase. He spent a half hour
doing a passable job on his disguise.

As he was about to exit the restroom, he heard running
footsteps and immediately supposed that he might be in
trouble. Quickly he closed the door but for a crack.

"God, I love that show *Six Feet Under,* have you seen it?"
The girl from the coffee room. "Who's running?" There was
a pause and the footsteps grew closer. "Jeez. Who are you?"

"FBI. We've been alerted that someone has broken into your offices. They might be looking for the office of Arthur Stewart. Have you seen any strangers?"

"Bearded guy. He was looking for the fireproof cabinets. He said Mr. Stewart was there and we told him where to go." They meticulously described the route. "What's with the guns?"

Sam could see that the agents each held a 9mm model 459 Smith & Wesson. The weapon was not standard-issue FBI, and if they were Feds, they would not be running around with their guns out when there was no threat.

"Thanks. You should leave immediately. Get out of the building."

"Whatever you say."

"This guy is very dangerous."

They weren't even good imitators. Real agents would have given a name.

They left.

Sam knew that if he ran down the stairs to lower floors, he would have a good chance of fueling a gun battle and that was just what he didn't need. If he went to the elevators, somebody might watch the elevator descend and that would be a dead giveaway. If he went for the emergency stairs in the building, the number of bodies chasing him might increase geometrically as he descended. This was feeling like a trap resulting from a tip-off.

He followed the two men, figuring they would end up in Martha's office. When he got to the right turn leading down Martha's hall, he stopped and listened.

"You're sure you haven't seen any strangers, no bearded guy?"

"No. Only a new lawyer by the name of Scott Davis. That's it."

"Where is he now?"

Sam quickly stepped into the first open office before hearing the answer. He closed the door, locked it, and stepped behind the door. There was a window to the hall with blinds and he saw their legs move by in a blur.

After waiting a minute, he opened the door and went quickly to Martha's office.

When he walked in, she jumped and looked frightened.

"It's me again."

"What in the hell? The beard?"

"Be calm. I'll explain."

"The FBI is here. They said to leave."

"Obviously I'm not Scott. I'm Sam. Those men are impersonating the FBI and I am a government contractor of sorts."

"Oh, my god. Why are they pretending to be the FBI?"

"Here's what I want you to do. Get the number of the New York FBI, Manhattan office."

"Okay."

She grabbed the phone and dialed, still looking frightened.

"Please don't be frightened. In seconds you'll have real FBI agents on the phone and on the way."

"I'm beginning to hope so."

"You got them?"

"Yes. Tell them you want to be put through to the Washington field office. Tell them you are placing the call for Agent Silverwind."

"She says just a minute. She says she doesn't know what you're talking about. She says she's new."

"Tell her that she should have a list of FBI agents on her computer. Tell her to look up Agent Silverwind."

"She says, 'What now?' "

"Ask her what it says by the asterisk."

"She says that it says to put through all calls and gives a number."

"Ask her to do it."

"Please put the call through."

"She says, 'Why didn't you say so?' "

"It may take awhile. It's running through relays to the cell of whoever is on call."

"Hello. I'm standing here with a guy named Sam who says he knows you."

"Tell him I need to prove I'm a government contractor." Sam said.

"He says he needs to prove he's a government contractor." Pause.

"You have a locket?" She looked genuinely perturbed.

They waited and she reached out for the locket, which was still outside his shirt. "Let me see." She studied it.

"I see the locket. It's gold and has a picture of an old Indian gentleman. He says to take off your right shoe. There is a red birthmark on your instep."

Sam quickly took off his maroon dress shoe. It had gum soles in keeping with tradition.

"I see the birthmark. He says now to ask you how the earth smiles."

"In flowers," Sam answered.

"He says you're a good guy, but not an employee of the government. He says though that he would trust you with his own mother."

Sam took the phone. "Who have I got?"

"Ernie."

"Thank God it wasn't your hard-ass partner."

"You lucked out. What's going on?"

"Long story, no time. I'm at Binkley, Hart, and Rove on Wall Street. We have guys with guns over here impersonating agents and hunting me."

"Are you clean?"

"No, but I think I'm onto a big one."

"As in terror?"

"Terror for profit."

"Okay, so maybe we aren't so concerned about you being dirty. But don't use the term government contractor. You kill anybody?"

"Not yet. I've got to get out of here, though."

"I'll get people there as fast as I can. But this is Manhattan and there's traffic."

"Hurry."

"Do you look like yourself?"

"What difference would that make?"

"Good point."

"At the moment I may go with the full beard. Not sure." Sam hung up.

"Make a copy of these." Sam held out the Chaperone papers.

"These are documents from our law firm. Client documents."

"I have reason to believe the people who want these are on the verge of committing a massive atrocity that will make 9/11 look like child's play. It is a crime in the future, not in the past. The attorney/client privilege doesn't cover it, and if it does, then damn the privilege."

She looked at him with hardened green eyes.

"You want a lot of trust."

"I think I'm looking at someone who has the courage to be a hero."

"Or is a damn fool." She took the papers to a copy machine, copied them in about two minutes, and handed the originals back to Sam, who put them in his briefcase. She went to a file folder full of papers as thick as a couple of New York phone books and placed them in the stack.

"If you don't hear from me tomorrow, make sure these go to the man you just talked to. He's Ernie Dunkin, like Dunkin' Donuts. FBI. Call him and tell him to show them to Jill. He'll know."

"What if you don't call, how will I find you?"

"If I don't call, things are bad. I'll have to find you."

"How did you sign in?" Martha asked, obviously thinking.

"As Michael Bowden. But I had this beard. In a minute I won't."

"If I say you're Scott Davis, who is going to argue? There's probably not many partners around."

"If they know what I look like, they won't argue—they'll just shoot."

"With witnesses?"

"You die just as fast if people are watching. I gotta go."

"I'm coming with you. I can help get you out."

Sam thought of a lot of things he could say, and perhaps should say, but he had a feeling about Martha. She understood the danger and was determined to help, and standing around discussing it could be more dangerous than moving.

"Let's go up five or ten floors on the outside stairs."

"Isn't that the wrong direction?"

"We'll pull a fire alarm up there. Those guys who want my ass will have to wonder if it's real. The firefighters will come."

"I know someone up there. We'll need someone to open the door this time of night."

They slipped into an office near the exit to the stairway to use the phone. Sam pulled off the beard and got the makeup off as best he could.

"My friend always works late." Martha said. "Let's hope this isn't the only night she takes off this week."

Her friend was in and agreed without much explanation to open the stairway door. They went through the exit to the stairwell with their shoes off to keep the sound down and began climbing fast. After a couple of flights they heard someone running up from a few floors down. By the seventeenth floor Martha was breathing deeply and slowing a bit.

"One more," she said.

At the eighteenth floor a woman was holding the door open a crack. She was young like Martha, dark and Latin-looking.

"Go pull a fire alarm anywhere on this floor," said Sam, pointing at the door.

"But what about you?"

"I'll be fine. Please do it."

In his stocking feet Sam resumed running up the stairs, leaving a fretting Martha to disappear with her friend into the eighteenth-floor warren.

Sounds of foot strikes on the concrete floor began reverberating up the stairwell. People were coming down.

"You're going the wrong way, buddy," the first guy said. Others tried to be more forceful, even grabbing him by the arm.

"My family" was all he said. He put on his shoes because noise no longer mattered. When he got to the twentieth floor, he found what he was looking for—another fire alarm. He pulled the alarm and stepped behind the door, hoping there were still some late-night stragglers. There were. When the door opened, he ducked inside. No doubt men in the control room would instantly speculate that he might have pulled the alarm and thereby deduce his possible location. Once inside, he went diagonally across the building and found the stairway on the other side. The place was empty now. In his briefcase he kept a lighter. He moved about a large office area full of cubicles and gathered wastebaskets which he clumped together under a smoke-and-heat sensor. Quickly he lit the contents of each on fire and ran to the stairs. The sprinklers began pouring water down from the ceiling. The fires would be out in seconds, but somebody was going to be pissed. He began descending the stairs. There were not many people now, a couple or so that he could hear above, and a few more within earshot below.

There would be men posted at the stairs probably looking

for a bearded guy, but there might be those who would suspect a disguise. If it was Gaudet, his men might have his picture from their surveillance of the LA office. There was no good explanation for how Gaudet's men might have tracked him here, and that was a serious concern. He suspected that Figgy had somehow figured it out and passed it on to the French. Suddenly he knew he had to have the office checked for microphones. The betrayal was a miserable feeling.

He heard sirens outside and knew that both the FBI and the fire department would be arriving. As he descended to the fifteenth floor, a man in a tailored blue suit with expensive shoes exited, obviously unconcerned.

"There's no significant fire. Wastebaskets on the twentieth. Some asshole practical joker getting his kicks."

"Yeah," Sam said. "Think I'll wait right here for the elevators to start again."

"Suit yourself," the man said, electing to walk down the stairs. Sam walked into a hallway to find locked doors to a computer-processing facility. On a lark he went and knocked on a door. Soon a curious-looking Asian woman opened it.

"Yes?"

"I'm just checking that this floor is cleared," he said as officially as possible. He stepped past her, gently pushing through when she tried to stop him by holding his arm.

Then, Sam had a minor epiphany. Gaudet and the French were in league—for the moment, at least, they were the same. The men on the street and in the tunnel were Gaudet men acting on French information.

Chapter 18

A man is distinguished by his strong spirit in a great storm.

—Tilok proverb

It was a bone-chilling, misty November evening and it felt like snow. At the bottom of Central Park, just off Fifth Avenue, there was a duck pond, and at its northern corner Michael stood in the dark waiting. After he and Grady said their good-byes, he had finally collected all his journals and sneaked away to California, taking only a couple of days to find a piece of property that was to his liking. There he waited with Sam's men, hoping to lay his hands on Gaudet and anyone else who had the tenacity to chase him to his hideaway. He had returned to Manhattan just for this meeting. It was 6:55 P.M. Time did not pass easily when the adrenaline flowed. The place was mostly quiet, except for seekers of solitude and lovers walking hand in hand, or the occasional homeless person. Michael had learned to recognize these wretched souls who slept in bushes, and fled the foot police.

His nerves kept him alert, but he wished for a stash of coca leaves to chew, here in the urban equivalent of the jungle.

From quite a distance he saw a man and a woman coming from the Fifth Avenue side of the park. The man wore a beret and had on a long coat. According to his verbal description, that would be Georges Raval and the woman on his arm was as mentioned in the e-mail.

As the couple approached, he looked warily about, determined that if he saw others he would flee, but he saw no one this time. The man wore a bulky coat and he wondered if he too was wrapped in body armor. The woman wore a hat that looked to be of fur, or a look-alike material, and a heavy, stylish, long dress coat.

"Georges?" he said quietly as the man drew close. This was the man he had met briefly in the apartment building.

"Hello, good to see you again."

The man's features were hard to make out in the dark; he still had the mustache and was a little under six feet, give or take. Even in the low light the woman seemed beautiful.

"Shall we walk?" Michael said.

"Yes. As you can see, I brought a friend, but you can trust her. Let me introduce you to Benoit, the love of my life."

"I am very pleased to meet you both."

"Benoit knows everything I am about to tell you."

"Are you married?"

"No. She is a prisoner in France, let out to find me. How's that for a shocker?"

"That's a shocker."

"We should do this quickly. You know about the work of Grace Technologies, yes? Altering brain cells to achieve personality changes."

"Yes, I know generally."

"You have heard of Chaperone?"

"Yes. You created this miracle?"

"I believe I'm the only person alive who understands it. Although the knowledge is incomplete. The molecule has not yet been fully mapped and therefore it isn't ready to be synthesized, although it can be used if a supply could be obtained."

They were walking in the park and Michael led them into a darkened area and into some heavy brush and out the other side to an old bench in a small clearing on another path. "Let's sit here."

"Are you sure it's safe?" Raval asked.

"I'm sure," Benoit said, taking a very large pistol from her handbag.

"God," Raval said, "I hate guns."

"Let's continue," Benoit said.

"My only regret," Raval said, "is that I don't know you better."

Michael interpreted that as a need to trust him before divulging more. "I understand." He had a book bag, from which he removed three sandwiches. "Would you like something to eat? When you've been in the jungle as long as I have, it's hard not to carry food around with you."

"I don't need much." Georges broke his sandwich in two and gave half to Benoit. He thanked Michael, then spoke of science generally. He seemed interested in the Amazon and all that it spawned. In moments they were eating and laughing like friends, and they hadn't mentioned Grace Technologies again or vectors or the like.

When the food was gone, Michael turned the conversation serious once more. "You've been through hell. Perhaps afraid for your life. As for your friend, she seems to have an iron constitution. Perhaps she fears nothing."

"All of the above," he said.

"I fear French jails," the woman said.

"Why don't you come with me. I've moved to the mountains of California, where it is lonely and beautiful. I have bodyguards you can trust."

"Bodyguards?" Georges said.

"You saw them in the Village, when we were attacked on the street. They are good men, and I'll be able to work there."

"First we must be about other business," Benoit said.

"What is that?" Georges seemed puzzled.

"You are good scientists. But the rest of life escapes you both. It's part of your charm. There is a man, Sam. You both know him?"

"Yes. He's the one with the bodyguards."

"Well, Mr. Sam?" Benoit spoke loudly all of a sudden.

There was only silence.

"No one knows we are here," Georges said.

"One of the reasons I love you is that you do not understand what we are dealing with. We probably could have a UN convention with the people in these woods."

"Right here," a voice said. Michael recognized it as Sam's.

"So, at last we meet." Benoit said. "I would enjoy seeing the man who put me in jail—or at least this man's current disguise," Benoit said.

The bushes moved. "Yep. That'd be me."

"This better be good," Agent Ernie Dunkin said. "I have half the French Embassy and various mercenaries or emissaries or diplomats or spooks or whatever handcuffed to trees in Central Park. I can hardly wait to hear the screaming in the morning."

"I promise you that this will be interesting." The group was in several cars headed to FBI headquarters. Ernie and Sam shared a backseat. A young man was driving. Normally, Ernie drove his own car, but Sam didn't ask about the unusual arrangement.

"Let's not go to the FBI. I have a meeting room at the Park Plaza."

"A meeting room?"

"Bear with me, Ernie. None of this is going to be orthodox. None of it."

"I don't like this."

"Look, I really needed you to help get us out of Central Park without a gunfight. But we have to be free of you to solve this case and then to put it back in your lap."

"You're telling me that you just needed a babysitter in Central Park and now I get nothing?"

"Ernie, you're going to get everything on your doorstep. Without the CIA."

"Without the CIA? Then it's overseas too."

Sam nodded.

"I never really liked your shit. I prefer to solve my own crimes. But for some reason I put up with it."

"You like getting all the glory. It's no mystery."

"Yeah, well, there better be glory. This is post 9/11 and we don't screw around like we used to."

"Come on. You stretch the rules even more and you have much looser rules. You're just a hell of a lot more tight-assed about appearances."

Ernie fell silent and Sam knew he was vacillating between rage and intrigue.

"This could be the biggest one of the career?" Ernie finally asked.

"That's right."

"Delivered right in my lap?"

"Have I ever failed you, Ernie?"

"Don't give me that crap."

They lapsed into silence again.

"Take us to the Park Plaza. Drop these gentlemen off. Take me home." Then Ernie got on the radio and had the guys in Central Park released so they could go make their protestations of outrage. He chuckled, which at times like this was uncharacteristic.

"Let me in on the joke," Sam said.

Ernie got back on the radio.

"Listen up all you loyal agents of la-la land. You be sure and let it slip that you are the New York City Police Department."

"We already said FBI," a voice came back.

"So, be creative about contradicting yourself."

"Ooh," Sam said with a smile. "You're good."

The room in the Park Plaza seated ten. Benoit, Georges, Sam, and Michael sat inside along with the attorney that Benoit had requested. His name was Stan Beckworth and he specialized in immigration. Outside waited a dozen of Sam's hired help, spread up and down the hallway.

Benoit spoke up immediately when they sat down.

"I need to speak with Sam and the attorney alone."

"Why?" Georges asked.

Benoit turned to him. "I have told you that this is the one thing on which I will not compromise."

It was clear to Sam that the woman meant it.

"All right." Georges sighed.

"Why am I here?" Michael asked.

"You were the source of the original material that went into Chaperone," said Benoit. "What we need from you now is a counterfeit version of your 1998 journal."

"It was more work to make the phony journal than the real one, even using real journals as a template," Michael said. "The fake set includes a previously known salamander in place of the sponge. Now, what do you want all this for?"

"You'll know soon enough," Benoit said. "I will appreciate it if you get that journal here right away. Thank you, gentlemen."

Michael and Georges left the room.

At that moment Sam's mother, Spring, Tilok *Talth* and psychologist, entered the conference room. Sam had fifteen hours to figure out if Benoit Moreau was for real and, if he and his mother drew a favorable conclusion in that regard, to make a plan. Or perhaps they would just be fitting into Benoit's plan.

Without preliminaries, the session began.

The meeting place could have been anywhere, but Benoit began as instructed by Gaudet at Grand Central Station, where she boarded the # 7 to Flushing, Queens. Dressed in the clothing that had been sent by Gaudet, exactly according to instructions, she wore a beige London Fog overcoat over a camel St. John knit dress, with a light brown hat that supported a matching net veil. On her feet she wore cream-colored flats and thigh-high white nylons with a garter belt. The undergarments were vintage Gaudet. On the tips of her curled fingers she held a tiny locator transmitter that was not part of Gaudet's proscribed accessories. She stood midtrain, midcar, and waited for events to unfold. Around her was an assortment of people, all seemingly going about ordinary business. There were no shifty-eyed men in trenchcoats. Among the many passengers was, however, a young man dressed in a conservative three-button business suit and wearing a woolen overcoat reading the *Wall Street Journal*. He looked exactly like a commuting lawyer or investment banker, and he never looked up until the Vernon Boulevard/ Jackson Avenue stop, the first in Queens. There he folded over his newspaper in the fashion of a delivery boy and placed a rubber band around it. Even before the train halted, he rose, walked past her, and effortlessly placed the folded *Journal* under her arm. She slid her hand inside the paper and felt what she determined to be a small, rectangular box. It turned out to be a tape recorder with an earpiece. She inserted the earpiece and pushed the play button.

A male voice instructed her to exit the train and she managed to make it out of the car, just ahead of the closing doors. The next instruction was to board the next train heading back to Grand Central Station. When she arrived at the appropriate track, she stopped, caught her breath, and then smiled.

Before her stood at least twenty women dressed exactly as she, all approximately her size. It struck her as quite an accomplishment for Gaudet, given his security requirements. She couldn't imagine what the women had been told. All of them acted as though nothing untoward or unusual was happening, but the other commuters were commenting and nodding at one another with perplexed smiles as they all entered the train. The other similarly dressed women also had earpieces and a tiny cord disappearing into purses or pockets. On the train they all stood and she was instructed by the voice on the recorder to stand in the middle of the herd.

It was an eerie ride to Grand Central surrounded by look-alikes. They had standing room only and heard plenty of comments about the matching outfits, but none of the women responded. One know-it-all gentleman asserted with great confidence that the Daughters of the American Revolution were having a convention.

The male voice on the recording instructed Benoit to exit at Grand Central and to follow the man with the cigar. She looked around among all the brown hats and finally in the far corner of the car spotted a man with an unlit cigar in his mouth. They made eye contact. The next time she looked, the cigar was gone. His clothes—dark suit and dark, long coat—were nondescript, so she would need to watch him closely. The train came to a stop, the doors opened, and all of the women exited and seemed to explode in various directions. In front of Benoit was the cigar man, who once more made eye contact and then moved off at a brisk walk. Benoit followed and others of the women were moving along with her. They rounded a corner and headed down a wide hall to what Benoit knew to be the great hall of Grand Central Station. Not twenty feet away, three of the other brown hats hurried off to various destinations of Gaudet's choosing. There were shops along either side and the man veered into a jewelry shop and then stepped through a door that was opened barely a foot, allowing entry into the side of a boarded-up storefront. About twenty feet before reaching the door, Benoit brushed a display and purposely dropped the transmitter. Sam had warned her that at the first enclosure they would probably check her for transmitters.

After Benoit had entered, and before the man closed the door, a woman dressed exactly as Benoit slid past her and then backed out through the same door Benoit had just entered, yelling, *"Je dois juste aller pisser."* Benoit was amazed at the resemblance.

It would look to an observer exactly as if Benoit had stepped into a closed-to-the-public area and then backed out.

They stopped and a man with a wand went over her body checking every beep. They took the gun from her purse. Cigar man led her back through a construction site that was at the moment without any workers and through a back door into a narrow hall that ran behind all of the shops. They walked down the hall about two hundred feet and came out in the back of a store in a tiny office area. There the man left her, but not until he had shown her into a small bathroom. There were fashion magazines here that Gaudet enjoyed. Unlike some men, he liked looking at women in clothes, unless he had his knife and was able to cut them off personally. She was grateful that they had chosen a bathroom as the waiting area. She began to flip through a magazine, but the tension in her broke her concentration; her mind always went back to Gaudet and her upcoming encounter and the words that she would use, and the way she would use her body. After an hour had passed, a woman came and opened the door.

"I'm sorry, but I need to search you for transmitters."

Benoit was used to being searched and even the rubber gloves and the body cavity search did not irritate her. But it worried her because she wouldn't have anything in a body cavity unless she had done it intentionally, and that was a strong indication that Gaudet no longer had complete trust in her.

"I need to search the handbag," the woman said. Benoit pulled out the lipstick and other cosmetics, credit cards and cash.

She wondered if the woman had any inkling about Gaudet. Maybe she had met Trotsky, but probably she dealt with a contractor who had never met or even spoken to Gaudet. The woman left and Benoit returned to the bathroom and waited another hour. At the next knock on the bathroom door, she found a small, slender man in a rumpled sport jacket, with shaggy brown hair that hadn't been trimmed in a good while.

"For the next part of your little excursion, you will need to get in this," he said, pointing to a large crate mounted on a dolly. He seemed grim; she decided he would make a good undertaker.

There was a ladder and she assumed correctly that she would need to enter the crate from the top. Fortunately, there was another ladder down the inside and a chair, and she found that she could sit inside the crate with about the legroom of an economy-class airline seat. There was even a light to read by and another array of magazines.

The man closed up the crate while she flipped nervously through these fashion magazines. For about ten minutes there was complete silence and then the crate began to move. Then it stopped. She surmised that they were making a final check for any sign of a tail.

The stress was a pressure inside her that felt like it could explode. Trying to undo evil, it turned out, was much harder than doing it. There was a suspense in reaching for the light that did not exist when wallowing in the darkness. Sam had warned her about that. Always she had relied on her own strength plus nothing and rejected any spiritual dimension to life as the invention of the crackpots who wanted to exploit the weak. It was one of the few things about which she and Karl Marx could have agreed. The opiate of the masses was a perfect description. But since her time in prison, new possibilities had begun to occur to her. Spring had hit a body blow to her mind and spirit.

She had never been to the Tiloks' Universe Rock, and nothing in her family's Catholic past had ever melded with her soul. The Catholic tradition was barren for her, perhaps because at age twelve she had been required to attend as a means of occupying her time. But in her childhood there had been a beautiful valley down which the Loire River flowed. An old orchard grew there. It was quiet and fragrant in summer and near the castle of Villandry. Although Benoit knew the castle had been built by a sixteenth-century finance minister, she imagined that royalty would have taken picnics in the nearby orchard and perhaps fallen in love there.

Spring had asked if she could visualize it to the point that she could feel the experience of it, and she had said she could. Once she felt the peace of that valley, she was told to remember the eyes of her mother in a close moment. Even though her mother died when Benoit was nine years old, there were many such moments with her mother and she could place herself back in those times. Spring told her that if she could concentrate totally on the peace of that valley, and if she could remember the eyes of her mother and feel that love, then that was the beginning of her *we pac maw*. As she learned to explore it, she could take in more than her valley and more than her mother. She could eventually take in all valleys and all mothers, and she could be at peace in the gravest adversity. Spring told her that when the threat was the greatest, she could become the center of a sphere of that energy so that she could be surrounded with her *we pac maw.*

This was the beginning of Tilok meditation for the sweat lodge as taught by the Spirit Walkers of the Tilok tribe and now the *Talths,* since Sam's grandfather had been the last Spirit Walker. Benoit wondered whether, after prison, she needed such gimmicks to survive the coming experience with Gaudet. Sam swore to her that the Spirit Walker meditation was sufficiently powerful that she might survive, even prevail over, a man like Devan Gaudet.

A year before, Benoit would have instantly dismissed this exercise as the purest form of religious bullshit. Then she had begun examining her life and its value. She had explained her inner pilgrimage to Sam and he seemed to understand—at least to the extent that he believed her.

Although engrossed in her meditation, she was aware that there were about twenty minutes of jostling of the crate and then about a forty-minute ride in a truck, followed by another twenty minutes of jostling before it seemed that she had arrived. She could tell by the talking and the work on the top of the crate that she was about to be let out. When she climbed out, she saw small glass panes, dark woods, and older but elegant-looking draperies. She was obviously in an upper range courtly hotel with old world styling. There was a man beside the crate who had the appearance of age.

"Is that you, Devan?"

He nodded. "You will recognize my voice, as well as my eyes."

When she climbed down from the crate, she pressed herself to him without hesitation and gently stuck her tongue in his mouth, being careful not to kiss vigorously in order to ensure that she did not disturb his makeup. She put her loins to his as she had commonly done more than a year previous. But Sam's cautions were heavy on her mind.

Don't compromise yourself. Try everything else and something will break.

Still, it was hard not to slip back into ways that would make Gaudet comfortable, put him at ease, and then fill him with desire so that she could begin to persuade him, and to loosen him up. It was hard to be a butterfly.

"God, I missed you so."

"You were never this enthusiastic," he said when she let him up for air.

"Absence makes the heart grow fonder."

"So does abstinence."

"I can't believe that you involved yourself in this charade."

"Occasionally I'm like one of those gamblers that can't resist a chance. Besides, I never really taught you disguise well enough that I could be sure that you would do it to my satisfaction. We have to work fast."

Gaudet went to work laying out a silver gray wig, makeup, glasses, and a change of clothes.

"Where are we going?"

"To what they call upstate, the forests, there is a lake. . . . We have a little time." She could sense his eagerness for intimacy and his weird kind of sex.

"Devan, there is something I want more than anything. Temporarily I want it even more than I want you." Gaudet stopped with the hairpiece.

"What is that?"

She tried to draw herself into the peace of her *we pac maw.* "I want real freedom. I want a pardon from the French government."

"Trust a government?"

"I'm not like you, you know. I can't run from the law my whole life. If it means being pardoned, then, yes, I'll trust them. But not blindly."

"You can't run with me like we planned?" There was just a hint of irritation in his voice and it gave her a sick feeling in the pit of her stomach. She found herself losing her confidence and she wanted to be intimate with him as a means of reclaiming it. *Don't compromise. Keep trying.* She could feel the tension of the great inner struggle over going the old way or trying the new.

"Being with you isn't the problem. It's being hunted by France. I want to be able to walk around downtown Paris without fear and without a disguise. I can have both."

"It sounds like a fairy tale to me."

"I have to try. I can have Chaperone to you the moment after we pay for it. You can then deliver it to the French along with your technology. I can get Bowden's journal, the one that identifies the source of Chaperone—and the location. That is the whole pie. For that, the French will pay you the two hundred million, less the kickback."

"You brought the Chaperone formula with you?"

"No, but I can get it quickly. It'll take money, though. Same with Bowden's journal. This will all be done through the Swiss escrow."

Gaudet did not disguise his surprise.

"Just like that?" He snapped his fingers. "You were with Raval no more than a couple of days. Now he's yours? Did you have sex with him? And what about Bowden?"

"No to both. But I hinted there might be some in the future."

"Would you enjoy it?"

"No. Of course not. This is a job." She could not read him now. Sometimes reaching him was like trying to climb a glass wall. "Perhaps you do not need to wait long to close. How soon can you have Cordyceps ready?"

"Before, I thought you said it would take a little time to get Chaperone, to make deals with Raval and Bowden. I thought you and I would have a brief respite in the country. A couple of days, just you and me."

"I am very anxious. I admit it. I cannot relax."

"You are like my investors. Always in a hurry. Don't worry: my people are preparing Cordyceps."

"It's the tension—I find it suffocating."

"I find you enchanting." His eyes changed, grew harder. "Why don't you want to fuck me?"

"My period. It just began. Now isn't the time for making love, Devan. Let's get this deal done."

"I don't know if I believe you. I can feel you, Benoit. I don't think your body ever really craved mine. It was the scare, the thrill, the power that you liked in me. I represented a way to escape Chellis." He paused and studied her. "Now you have escaped Chellis and it is the French government you must escape. So back you come." She felt him studying her more than at any time in her life. But she had to pull it off. "Tell me, how is it that you can bet in the markets on Cordyceps and still get a pardon?"

"I have the French government involved at the highest levels. I can twist off their balls if they betray me."

"Not if they kill you."

"They won't. They fear nothing more than scandal, and they're too far in with me already. They'll hunker down and say nothing. Mark my words. I know our brethren."

"They are your brethren. I was nationalized by birth, not genetics. What is your plan?" Gaudet asked.

"When you are ready, I will give you Chaperone and you pay Georges Raval two million dollars. Bowden another two million."

"I can see Bowden. Without him nobody makes more Chaperone. For that, he's cheap. But Raval doesn't own anything. Why two for him?"

"They've met, Bowden and Raval, so now they are more or less together. Each wants what the other gets. It's human nature. And remember: Bowden doesn't own the Chaperone molecule itself. He knows the source, which is critical, but Chaperone has to be synthesized and you have to know how to use it—the process. That's Raval's piece. No one else understands it, even the French. They own the process but don't know how it works. You see?"

"Somehow it seems a little too simple, but I'm listening. What does Bowden guarantee? What does Raval guarantee?"

"That's a snag. Bowden guarantees nothing, because he says he doesn't know for sure which material the molecule came from. I can get his 1998 journal, Devan."

"Does he guarantee the journal?"

"No. Georges says the molecule came from a salamander. I will obtain the salamander journal page. You and I will guarantee the journal."

"The French will accept this?"

"Probably. Raval guarantees that the official Chaperone documents from Grace Technologies files will be delivered to escrow. Part of the deal with the French is for Raval—they get both unquestionable legal title and the secret to Chaperone technology; he goes to work in their laboratories at agreed terms. Part of those terms is the two million, which you are to pay to him. But it is peanuts compared to the two hundred million and the way that will be multiplied in the markets with Cordyceps. Now I still have to work out the other terms of the employment contract for Raval. I plan to finish it quickly, in the next couple of days."

"I will say this, Benoit, you seem to have all the angles figured for everybody."

She could see that he was getting restless. Something was bothering him. A lesson from Catholic school came to her: *what fellowship has the darkness with the light?*

"You don't want to go with me," he said. "Do you?"

"Of course I do. But I have work to do. I can't go off to the country in the middle of a job that will determine my whole life—my freedom. I have many things to work out."

"So you say. Your period never stopped us before."

She said nothing for a moment, working on the tears she'd need for the next step in her explanation. "I did not want to tell you this, but . . . I was raped by a guard in jail. Thank God I'm not pregnant. My period proves that. But it's been awful. I am afraid I may have caught something. If I did, then my blood could infect you. It's a dangerous time, my period. I would not hide that from you."

Gaudet's eyes widened. His fastidious nature seemed to appreciate the threat. "What did the guard have?"

"Hepatitis for certain. Hopefully, not AIDS."

"I can't believe a guard raped Benoit Moreau."

"Actually, it was two guards. They handcuffed me to a bed, feet and hands."

Gaudet studied her. He reached into the pocket of his slacks. It was the right pocket where he kept the knife. When he displayed the pearl-handled instrument, it did not surprise her. With a flick of his wrist he snapped it open. He walked forward and held it under her chin, the way he used to do in sex play. But his eyes were hard and unwavering. She felt weakness in her knees, remembering the stories she had heard of the disemboweled enemies of Gaudet. Most recently it had been one of Sam's men. More than one woman had been cut in the face.

As if daring her to do something, he began to cut the buttons down the front of her dress. Quickly she reached under her dress, pulled aside the crotch of her panties, and withdrew her bloody tampon. She held it in front of his face and stood very still, not wanting to trigger him into a bloodletting.

A smile broke across his lips. "I was sure you were lying about your period. When will it end?"

"Four, five days."

"One can be vaccinated against hepatitis. I myself have received the vaccine because of my travels. But AIDS . . ."

"I know. I'm scared, Devan. And I'm sorry."

"You make it difficult. I want to see you in five days."

"Good. Me too. By which time the deal will be done. All except for Cordyceps."

"I will wait five days from the sale of Chaperone to implement Cordyceps and no more. When is the soonest you can deliver Chaperone?"

"Tomorrow, if I go back immediately. I need to be with Raval when you deliver the money."

"Why should I trust you?"

"Because I have never failed you. And because I am too smart to cross you. Raval will deposit into escrow, as will you, and as will the French. Nobody has to trust anybody."

"We all have to trust the escrow holder."

"Come, come. The Swiss are impeccable. Everything closes at once—you, Bowden, Raval, the French government. Everyone is paid directly out of escrow pursuant to identical countersigned instructions."

He watched her for maybe two minutes, saying nothing. She did not like her dress open where he had cut the buttons, but she knew better than to pull it closed until he was through with his ritual.

"Everything is too smooth."

"I have thought about it for months. That is why. I have waited to work with you. I have plotted and schemed."

"There is no one so blind as a man who wants to believe a woman, unless it is a woman who wants to believe a man. But you never had that problem because you never had a weakness for any man. Not like I have a weakness for you.

You're lucky I don't pull your entrails out on the floor and watch you die. I hate that you weaken me!"

Benoit didn't move a millimeter. She knew that it would take almost nothing to drive the man to murder. He stepped close and touched the tip of his knife just beneath her sternum. She knew it was the place that he made the incision when he wanted to unravel the intestines.

"Tell me everything you and this Baptiste get out of this."

"I get to be with you. I get a pardon from the French government. And if Cordyceps goes off as planned, I get to be rich. I still have funds from Grace that are hidden and I will invest heavily on the short side just before Cordyceps. Baptiste and the admiral will get five million each in exchange for my pardon, Baptiste splits with others. The admiral says he won't take the five million for a long time, if ever. Maybe, he says, he will turn it over to the French government. You and I know that if he would consider it, he will take it."

"Admiral Larive will be involved with this?"

"He will not say that he will do it, of course. I told him the money would go into a Swiss bank in the name of a Swiss trust. We would invest. He never has to claim the money. He said nothing at all. A man like that cannot agree—it just has to be done."

"So he agrees by his silence. You amuse me."

"That is how it has to be. When he gets up in the morning, he tells himself he will not take the money, that it is blood money. It is how he respects himself even a little bit. And who knows, maybe he will never take any."

"Bullshit. He will take it. Maybe when he is old. How does the French government explain this to the Americans?"

"They notify the Americans on the day of Cordyceps, but, of course, they will say that they thought it wasn't to happen for weeks."

"It could affect our execution of Cordyceps if the Americans have advance warning."

"They won't." She gave the knife a deliberate glance. "I am betting my life on it."

"They cannot tell the Americans more than a few hours in advance."

"I understand. But we will have to know the date for a few days in advance in order to make our investments."

Gaudet stopped talking. She couldn't tell what he was thinking.

"Come here," Gaudet said, stepping to the bed. He touched the tip of the knife to each of his fingers as if he were counting them. His pallor was white and he seemed to have no life in his face. The lips were tight.

Fear swept through her; she consciously tried not to shake.

He cut the bra down the middle between her breasts so that she wore only her panties, shoes, her garter belt, and thigh-high stockings under the dress. He ripped it open.

"Turn around and bend over. I don't believe the diseased guard story. . . . I want it like it used to be," but he was not acting like before. She knew their reunion was not going like his dream. It frightened her.

What fellowship has the darkness with the light? Sam did not understand. She turned and leaned forward, caressing his thigh, but she envisioned the Loire Valley, and the hope in her mother's eyes when she talked of better days to come. And she remembered Spring's insistence. She bit her lip to make herself think. What was worth dying for? After a moment she took her hand from his thigh. Slowly she straightened herself, forcing slow, deep breaths. She felt Gaudet's hand on her shoulder and the point of his knife at her spine, knowing at any moment he could paralyze her forever. Kill her.

"You deny me?" His breath was in her ear.

"I only advise you. When we have finished our business and after I have tested clean, I will give more than you have ever dreamed." *Her mother's eyes. The valley.* "But it must come from my heart and not the point of your knife."

His breathing was heavy and she knew he wanted her not just for the sex, but for the power. The knife bit a little deeper. She turned her head slightly and leaned back, putting her cheek next to his. "If you wait, my body will reward you. I'll give you every assurance you need."

His breathing stopped and she could feel the tension in him. She summoned all her *we pac maw* and tried to find her peace. She left the tension of his indecision behind.

He exhaled long and slow and dropped the knife hand to his side, but he did not put it away. "Waiting is hard."

She smiled and kissed him. "And I'm the one you said is in a hurry. Tsk. Tsk." She reached for the outfit that he had brought for her as part of his disguise and turned away while she removed the ruined dress and put on the new. His eyes followed her, but he made no move to stop her.

"Tell me about Raval. I never met him in Malaysia."

"He is a bit obsequious for a tall man. His mind never leaves the science. He knows nothing of the world. He is very naive. There is not much to tell."

"You sound like you don't think much of him, Benoit, and yet you are getting him two million."

"Even weak men can find strong friends. And he is very valuable as a scientist, if not so impressive as a man."

"You're trying too hard."

"What do you mean?"

"To make him sound like an insect. But just know that if you ever touch him, I will turn him into a eunuch—should I happen to let him live."

"I must go now and speak with him to be sure he's ready for the exchange."

"No."

She looked at him, at the phone he held in his hand.

"You are not leaving. Use this and stay with me. That is the end of the discussion." Gaudet had spoken.

Chapter 19

Calamities come like the blizzards, never the same,
and never a man's choosing.

—Tilok proverb

When Sam heard Raval's voice on the phone, he knew
that something had gone terribly wrong.

"She says she's not coming back right now. She says I
have to get ready to give her the materials."

"What else did she say?"

"We spent almost no time on the terms of my contract
with the French government. But then she had told me before she left that I would not be working for the French government. And she winked. I don't know how she winks
about such grave matters. I hope she is not making promises
she cannot keep. I am supposed to print out and sign documents at seven tonight. We are faxing signatures. I will e-mail
the documents into escrow. I am to provide the official Grace
documents via FedEx to escrow. You must know from Benoit
that they are phony records because Chellis was so paranoid.
He made sure the official records were false and the real papers privately held. Now I have them all."

"We should talk," Sam said.

He met Georges at the Plaza Hotel in the same conference

room where he had met Benoit, only this time they were alone. Georges always wore a blue blazer and tonight was no exception. Although he appeared worried, he also appeared collected. He was a strong man. It was 5:00 P.M., two days after the meeting in the park.

"I will send the Grace documents and the contract from the attorneys, like she asked," Georges began.

"She knows what she is doing, we have a plan."

"You know the real Chaperone document is in the safe-deposit box."

"Yes. I know. Benoit knows it as well. She knows what we're doing, Georges."

"I don't want to endanger her in any way."

"We passed that point when she went to Gaudet. We have to stick with the plan."

"What in the hell is the plan? I thought she was coming back."

"Georges, we were going to keep it between ourselves—Benoit and me—but things are changing. So, I'm briefly going to give the broad outlines of what is happening. She's going along with Gaudet because we're trying to stop a terrorist attack on the United States. This attack is for money, not for revenge or ideology."

"What kind of attack?"

"Using the raging soldier vector on millions in the streets of major U.S. cities. Gaudet calls this plan Cordyceps."

"Oh, my God, that will be a disaster."

"We know. Georges, to get the information about Cordyceps, we need to go along with a sale of technology to the French government. But as you've figured out, it's a fraud. We intend to stop the sale before it closes. Rogue French agents are involved. We are risking France's two hundred million, but as I said, we'll stop the sale before money changes hands, if we can. We will halt the escrow immediately after we get all the information on Cordyceps. But if Benoit can't get away from Gaudet, or if we don't get the info on Cordyceps, then the deal will close and France may release their money without getting all they've bargained for."

"So then I will be involved in a swindle."

"Not exactly. You will have no legal problem, but we will explain that later. You just need to know that Benoit is going to try to leave Gaudet, and if Gaudet holds her, we are going to try and get her out."

"What if you can't?"

"That's a problem. I won't lie to you."

"This is not comforting."

Sam put his hand on the scientist's shoulder. "We are going to do everything humanly possible to get her back."

Sam left a stunned Georges and stepped into the hall, where he found a pay phone to call Jill. He wasn't completely certain the cell would be free of tapping.

"What do you think?" Jill said.

"It wasn't supposed to go this fast. She was supposed to come out. I'm guessing Gaudet doesn't trust her. Either that or I misfigured her, and if that's the situation, I don't know where this thing is going."

"We don't dare tell the Feds to warn the French and stop the deal."

"No way. It will totally compromise Benoit and it will ruin our chances to get information through her."

"Yeah. It is hard for dead people to talk," Jill pronounced.

Benoit and Gaudet were in the St. Regis Hotel, near Central Park. They had been there two days with adjoining rooms, and Benoit's outer door came complete with a couple of guards. Her room was equipped with a high-speed Internet connection and an Inspiron 8500 laptop provided by Gaudet and an "assistant," by the name of Big Mohammed, who watched every move she made. Gaudet was in an easy chair in the next room and didn't come into Benoit's room unless Big Mohammed was absent. Often Trotsky was present; that plus Spring's magic had kept Gaudet at bay. She wondered how long it would last.

Unfortunately, the laptop computer left whenever Big Mohammed left. Benoit had opened the double escrow with Credit Suisse. Pursuant to contracts between Gaudet's company in Quatram and the French government, Gaudet acknowledged in the documents that his company had no claim to the ownership of the Chaperone technology. Raval attested that he was the primary inventor of the technology and that the official Grace Technologies record of Chaperone would be deposited into escrow. For political and legal reasons Raval's attestation was critical because France's claim to the invention came through the bankruptcy of Grace Technologies, which owed massive sums in back taxes. Grace's ownership in turn came through Raval's employment by Grace, since for patent purposes he was the inventor. The entire transaction would be handled over the Internet, except for the physical signing of escrow instructions. In Gaudet's case it was agreed that an electronic signature would be acceptable. Benoit, on behalf of Gaudet, deposited electronically into escrow all of the manuals and information that he had obtained from the original laboratories in Malaysia, and even more critical, the Grace document provided by Raval, explaining Chaperone. Much of this material was new to the French laboratory, which had received only information from Grace labs in France.

France deposited the $200,000,000. The moment it was in the account, Benoit advised Gaudet. Returning to her room, she discovered the following message from Baptiste.

You need to return to France immediately. We need to work on your pardon. And we need a week for our scientists to verify the technology. Seven days from today should suffice. We will then need seven additional days in order to close.

Benoit printed the message and took it to Gaudet.

"This was not part of the deal. They are reneging. You know that the Chaperone document is correct. . . . Hell . . . you have staked your chance for a pardon on it. That has to be good enough for them. Write that. Tell them no way. It must close now."

"It is like the government. They are used to making demands," Benoit said. She went back in her room and composed a message consistent with Gaudet's directive.

Big Mohammed was asleep with his chin cupped in his hand. Working fast she put the message into an e-mail by making it an attachment and sent it off to Baptiste. Next she went to the sent items, then re-sent the message to Sam's e-mail address. Then she double-deleted the forward to Sam.

"The government will not close without a chance to verify," came the almost instant response from Baptiste.

At that moment Gaudet stuck his head in the room and saw Big Mohammed asleep. "Wake him up and tell him to get out. Leave the computer." Gaudet stepped out of the room. She woke Big Mohammed and explained that he had been sleeping in front of the boss. The man sprang instantly awake and tried to explain.

"Forget it. He'll cool off, but just leave for now. We'll call you." She was hoping for a break like this.

"You should see this," Benoit said when Gaudet returned.

Gaudet came and read over her shoulder.

"Bastards. They never said anything about this. Tell the bank the deal is off and they are to permanently delete all documents immediately. I can live without the two hundred million."

"Let's give them one more chance."

"How?"

"I propose the following response."

We'll send the following message immediately to Credit Suisse if you do not retract: To Credit Suisse escrow holder—Permanently delete all documents as per escrow agreement clause 17.

They waited. Benoit could imagine Baptiste on the phone with the admiral. Baptiste would be taut as a bow string, his retirement on the line; Admiral Larive would be cursing, imagining his career, his honor, sliding into a garbage pit.

"I will kill that bastard if he backs out on me. I have done harder things than kill an admiral," Gaudet said.

"He is not just an admiral, he is the head of an intelligence agency. Don't worry. They will not back out. They want this too badly."

"Even so, they won't get their five before Cordyceps. I'll give them three days maximum."

"Wait. You can't do that. Baptiste must believe I am playing ball with him and that he will be rich and we will be lovers. The admiral must believe the same. I need my pardon. I can't change the play."

"Damn the pardon. You will be with me."

"Of course I will be with you, but I will not forsake the pardon. That was our agreement."

"You'll stay with me. I will protect you."

By force of will she did not argue with him. In fact, with the power resting in his hands, it was the perfect moment to ask: "How will you bring down the United States?"

Gaudet's eyes were shining. Her heart beat in her ears as she stood on the threshold. She was looking at a man energized by intrigue, a man who got high on risk.

"Cordyceps is a perfect analogy. We will first eat away at their innards and then take the brain."

"The U.S. is such a large place, though. . . ."

"I have men already in Chicago, New York, Los Angeles, and Washington. They have enough of the vector to transform a million people in each city. Imagine a total of maybe four million people, all driven to kill, all for no reason. At the same time, imagine fifty million computers dying during the crisis. Police, fire, transportation, FBI, CIA—all crippled, sodomized with a baseball bat."

"But how will so few men spread the vector?"

"Helicopters that have been made to look like police helicopters." Then Gaudet's eyes seemed to regain their focus. "Now you'll have to sleep handcuffed to my wrist."

She studied Gaudet. Even through his disguise she could see the energy in his body.

With no preliminaries he stepped back behind her chair and lifted her hips so that she was bent over the computer. He put his hand under her dress. She put her mind in the faraway place of her meditation and then straightened herself up. Deliberately she turned in his hands until she faced him and looked in his eyes.

"You have changed," he said. "Not nearly as much fun as you used to be."

"Maybe I've changed my ideas about fun."

"I haven't changed mine."

He ran his hands up under her shirt. When she grabbed them, anger flashed in his eyes and she struggled to put her mind at rest and to draw strength from her *we pac maw.* Any moment he would pull out his knife and that would be the end of resistance. For a second he looked like he might really hurt her. Gradually she loosened her grip on his hands so that he was free to continue while she held his gaze. He said nothing while he pondered what must have seemed like a new Benoit Moreau.

The computer made an audible tone and broke the ten-

sion. She turned away from his hands, sitting back down to
the computer.

"Baptiste is responding," she said.

> *We will do the deal with only a 24-hour review win-*
> *dow, but only if you first send us Benoit so that we can*
> *receive appropriate reassurances.*

It was an unexpected shock.

"I've got to think." Gaudet stepped away and paced
across the room. "I wonder what I can offer them?"

"I have to go back," she said.

"Now that you know about Cordyceps? Out of the question. So now what?"

Benoit wrote a message.

> *You may have 24 hours for your review of the vec-*
> *tor and Chaperone documents, but you must view*
> *them in escrow. No documents may be removed from*
> *the offices of the escrow holder until closing, no copies*
> *made while you are determining their authenticity. I*
> *cannot come immediately. Gaudet wants the same as-*
> *surance that France wants. For him, proof of straight*
> *dealing means holding his knife to my throat. Close*
> *the deal and release the funds in 24 hours. Or I cannot*
> *consummate a transaction at this end.*

Gaudet read it.

"Tell them five days until Cordyceps. Tell them four P.M.
EST, on the fifth day."

She wrote it.

"They will never give me a pardon."

"You idiot. They won't give you a pardon anyway."

They waited for Baptiste's reply.

* * *

"How are we doing with the scan? It should be a simple matter to trace the IP addresses on Benoit's last e-mail." Jill stood over Grogg while he typed with amazing speed, running through all manner of queries on Big Brain. Sam was watching as well over the video monitor in New York. They were working on two vital puzzles at once. One was the whereabouts of Benoit Moreau.

"I can't believe I have to ask a computer where Gaudet has taken Benoit," Sam said.

"Oh, come on, Sam, give me a break. We did the best we could. Besides, the idea was to get her in with Gaudet, not keep her out." Jill was unusually tense because, like everyone else, she was afraid for Benoit and she knew the stakes.

"I'm sure we did that. She's in him, he's in her . . . in out, in out."

"Grogg, don't be such a prick," Jill snapped.

Grogg smiled wickedly, and Sam shook his head.

"You two have almost achieved domestic bliss," Sam said. "Next you start marriage counseling."

"Forgive a guy a little levity, huh," said Grogg. "You know if this goes bad, it's gonna be hell. You think your portfolio sucked after the last attack. . . ."

"People are gonna die," Jill said.

"I know that, damn it. Shit."

There was silence for a while as they waited. No one was saying a word about the second item on their minds. Sam and Jill were waiting to see if Grogg's latest attempt to break into Gaudet's Cordyceps Windows folder would succeed.

"Damn, it disappeared again."

"Oh crap," Jill said.

"I gotta try the next idea," Grogg said.

"How's the work on the antivirus coming?" Sam asked.

"I've got twenty people in a contractor's shop working on

it, along with four of our own. It's based on the assumption that they get in through Windows SMB/CIFS. I have made a lot of other assumptions. Like what I would do if I were an evil genius."

"Instead of just Grogg?" Jill patted his head.

A phone rang in LA.

"It's the FBI," Jill said, putting the call through to Sam in New York.

"This is Ernie."

"The director isn't into this yet?" Sam said.

"I'm the designated Sam expert. Around here they think you're a little crazy. They do take the threat seriously, on the one hand, but on the other, there isn't any evidence that anything is going to happen. Obviously, Gaudet is selling out to the French government, but maybe the Cordyceps thing is a hoax to hold the price up."

"Maybe. Let's hope so."

"But you don't think so."

"I think it's real."

"Our scientists don't think this can be delivered as easily as anthrax and the DNA in the vector would be damaged in the irradiation of the mail."

"Nobody says he has to send it through the mail."

"The CIA is considering destroying Gaudet's entire facility in Quatram. Defense, of course, would love to lend a missile or two," Ernie commented.

"Good idea. That way you can destroy Gaudet's main server, thereby making it impossible for Grogg to break in and read the Cordyceps files." It was a rare moment of sarcasm for Sam, but he was losing patience with the government's nonsense.

"Yeah, well, the State Department will like that argument. They aren't as fond of blowing things up. Arab countries tend to take issue."

"Tell them to wait until after we hack into the computer."

"When I tell them this, they'll want the CIA to try hacking in."

"That'll be good. They hire us to do that sort of thing, but now with millions of lives at stake, they want to learn. Tell them to do their hacking and rocketing after we access the computer."

"You gotta understand, Sam, this Cordyceps is like a bogeyman that's everywhere and nowhere. We have no intelligence on it except what you dig up. The French claim they don't know anything about it. They're just buying technology that they already own—that's according to them."

Sam thought briefly of Figgy, whose voice had been oddly absent of late.

"I understand the frustration. I guess you can tell we're not too happy either."

"What do you think we should do?"

"Check every delivery system for the vector that you can think of. Check everybody coming into the country. Especially Mexico and Canada. Look for mercenaries, not terrorists. These people are not likely to be Arab or French. This is a money deal."

"How in the hell do you profile people like that?" Ernie was exasperated.

"You're the expert on that. Not to mention that you have the invaluable assistance of customs and the border patrol. While you're at it, you might consider shutting down all private aviation until we sort this out. Also look for phony government aircraft that could be used as a delivery mechanism. Lastly, if you'd like more good news, I'm guessing that the people who will deliver Cordyceps are already in the country."

"You know we don't have enough evidence to shut down private aviation. People will go nuts if we don't find anything."

"You are exactly right. If we don't find anything, hundreds of thousands of people are going to go nuts and start killing people. So let me get back to what I'm doing. If we find out anything, I'm sure we'll need all the manpower of the federal government. Until then . . . I've made my suggestions."

"They want you at a meeting."

"Put some Tilok war paint on your face and go in my place. Either that or arrest me. I'm busy."

"Sam . . . the government pays you. . . ."

"So put a stop payment on my check." Sam sighed. "We can video-conference if you must."

"Fine. One more thing. I ran this antivirus thing up the flagpole, and even though they are paying to build it, they think releasing gazillions of antiviruses on the Internet is way too risky. The cure could be worse than the disease. It's never been done. It's not tested. Off the record, they are going to say no. And whatever you do, don't release it without permission from Homeland Security. I think they have their own ideas."

"Hey, look at it this way, Ernie. We're on orange alert. What could go wrong with such vigilance?" Sam didn't bother commenting on the fact that the government was now apparently paying for an Internet antivirus that they were certain they would never use. It didn't matter, because Sam figured he might use it anyway.

"Our government does a good job," Ernie said.

"For a government it does. But it is a government."

"I've heard enough."

"No, no, Ernie, don't go away. I need your help."

"Sam needs the government?"

"Uh-huh."

"What for?"

"I want to go talk to Benoit Moreau and you could be of assistance."

Jill's mouth dropped at that one.

"And how might you do that if neither you nor the U.S. government has the faintest clue where she is? Somewhere in the U.S., I believe you said?"

"Well, actually, I've narrowed it down a little. Let me off the line for just a second." Sam put Ernie on hold. "Jill, I know you like to hear things first."

Even on the video monitor Jill looked like an egg would fry nicely on her forehead.

"I also had a team following Benoit."

"I was in charge of that," Jill responded.

"You were. And you did an excellent job. But I had a radio locator device."

"You said that was too dangerous."

"It was. That's why she had to drop it shortly after she left the train. But we had her long enough. I wanted both teams to be completely independent. This way, because they didn't know about each other, they were. Can I do something to win back your goodwill?"

"I'll give it some thought."

"Now that I've told you, I guess we better tell Ernie because we're a little tight on time." They conferenced Ernie back on the line: "Ernie, I believe I've narrowed it down a little, but you have to promise this is off the record."

"There's no such thing anymore."

"Okay. I'll call a rent-a-cop."

"You can't do that."

"Where in the Constitution does it deny me my right of free association and free speech?"

"All right, all right. It's not off the record, I just didn't hear it."

"I need you to call the St. Regis Hotel, the housekeeping department, and tell them I'm a government contractor and whatever else you have to tell them to get their full and silent cooperation."

"Just tell me one thing and, of course, I never heard it."

"And how's that different than off the record?"

"Quit being a wiseass. What room?"

"2004."

"Is that a joke?"

"Coincidence."

"Damn," Ernie said, and hung up.

Jill still looked pissed.

"Grogg thought of dropping the transmitter."

"Don't blame Grogg, you dirty rat bastard," Jill said. "I knew there was a reason I never married you."

"There was. It was my stupidity."

"So, tell me what happened!"

"We knew she went behind some small shops. They took her out of Grand Central in a crate. Once we knew about where she was . . . Well . . . how many huge crates come out of small shops in Grand Central? The crate was one of several suspicious activities that we checked on. We followed it to the hotel and used off-duty cops to check it out. They narrowed it down to a particular floor from staff who saw a crate, and then we got a match for Benoit with a description of a woman in one of the rooms from one of the maids."

"And that's it? Why were we trying to trace the e-mail?"

"Confirmation never hurts."

"He could be torturing her, Sam. Millions could die. Why confirmation? Why not storm the place and see what she knows?"

"Because she doesn't want to come out until she knows enough about Cordyceps to stop it. She signed up to be a hero. You take her out too soon and we may lose the whole war."

Chapter 20

A departed lover is worse than a rotting tooth.
—Tilok proverb

The gray mist hung in the trees and lay over the water, just fitting in the channel as if cotton placed by loving hands. The mountains were steep and sprinkled with oak and mixed conifers. Michael had read about them but had not seen them since childhood, and his fascination was keen.

Although it had been only three days since the meeting in Central Park he was disappointed that he had heard nothing about any capture of Gaudet.

Frederick, a mule on loan from a local hunting outfitter, seemed bored with the mountain and clearly wanted the oats that were his due every time he made the bottom or the top. It was a bit of mule psychology that Michael had learned from the owner.

Yodo was in a good mood this morning and had actually made a little conversation on the way down.

"A very good place," he had said, followed by a few comparisons with the Hokkaido Forest in Japan. It was a speech for Yodo. Yodo's succinct approach to communication suited Michael fine. The best thing about Yodo was not what he said but the way he occasionally smiled. It carried a hint of irony that Michael found appealing.

This morning it helped in only a small way with the melancholy inside him. The disappointment of losing Grady would linger and he was still affected by Marita's death and the loss of Eden, his wife. Things could come together in the mind like ocean waves that mount one upon the other.

He had seen the desert in summer and it seemed a very tired place and he thought of it now. When his father had taken him, it was parched and had become like an old face, the deep lines in the clay running out everywhere and nowhere, for good reasons, but not according to any predetermination that a man could explain; the moisture of it was blown away, leaving only grit and subtle shadings of warm colors that blended easily with no line between the brown, the tan, and the gold. His soul had become like the desert, and Grady had become the white cloud forming against the incessant blue—she made him see promise of an end and a beginning; new rain that turned the soil alive and the air sweet, the restoring of the arid terrain.

Now she was gone.

They were down in a deep canyon on the Wintoon River in northern California. One thousand feet above them ran a two-lane asphalt road and at their feet, two hundred yards below, the river frothed in a deep rock canyon. Michael pondered the cable stretched across the river, a good one hundred feet off the water at its lowest point. On the far side there was a bluff and a flat two-acre area with two log houses, one with several rooms and one a cabin.

The bluff was bordered on two sides by the intersection of two rivers at right angles, the Wintoon and Salmon rivers. There was no feasible way to access Michael's new home except a white-water trip in a kayak or a long, torturous hike down the mountain and then a boat ride across the river or a hand-pull on a cable-suspended cart. Unless one crossed the gorge suspended from the cable, any other access across the river entailed scaling a cliff to Michael's plateau. To Michael, this meant protection, but Sam had been concerned about the sheer number of hiding places and the difficulties of security in any forest environment. Still, it was much better than New York, and since Michael was a free man, he decided that this would be his home. For now. It was a primitive place. Michael could feel the wildness here that he loved so well. California, even some of the remote parts, could get a bit crowded, but this area was not well traveled once you moved more than one hundred yards off the highway. Michael's home's location eliminated all but the most determined. Tourists wouldn't make it down the trail, much less across the river, unless they wanted to try their hands at white-water swimming in a cold river.

This place was called an inholding. It was surrounded by national forest and the government had wanted to buy it. Their only problem was that the white-haired gentleman who had owned the place cared only a little for money, loved his land, and hated the government. It was a formula that brought Michael his new home. Old and tired, the owner had been hauled off by his only child, a daughter, more or less against his will—even if his shackles were the bonds of love. Now, a few days after first laying eyes on the place, Michael was moving in.

The cable car was actually a flatbed with no sides. Michael and Yodo loaded his stuff and Michael tried to summon his old enthusiasm. The donkey had carried his two hundred pounds and Yodo, about 125. Michael's wounds were still healing so he carried only his camera and notepad. They hobbled Frederick, gave him oats and hay, and Michael climbed aboard the flatbed of the cable car to pull his way across the two hundred feet. It was easy to see why the realtor refused even to consider making the trip and had listed the property without ever setting foot on it.

Once on the other side Michael sent the cart back for Yodo and began hauling the two hundred pounds of stuff into his new home. He would make twenty or thirty such trips to move in, but he didn't mind. Solitude was worth a great deal. He realized that he had become a bit of a recluse. In the Amazon, in recent times, silent visits from Marita had been plenty, so long as he had his weekly trips to Angamos to play his Quena flute with the Red Howler band. Around these parts a car went by every five or ten minutes, but they were a thousand feet above him. On his side of the Salmon River one had to ascend over five thousand feet and travel a good distance back to get to the nearest wilderness area trail—all perfectly satisfactory.

For a while Sam's men would be keeping him company. The revelations concerning the law firm had brought disturbing news about the lengths to which some would go to have the secret of the Chaperone. He had delivered the phony journal as promised, mainly to help Georges and Benoit, of whom he'd quickly grown fond. He had invited Raval to come and stay here once his spy days were over. Evidently, Raval's spy days were short-lived, because he had already arrived. Michael looked forward to the day when the technology entered the public domain and they would no longer have to wear Kevlar.

Although he was volunteering to be the bait, he wondered if Sam hadn't happily shuttled him off to a secret life in California to get rid of him and to keep him safe. At least here, he and Georges could pore over the Chaperone papers in relative safety. One day, perhaps soon, Raval would tell him everything he knew. It would be fascinating to understand. In the meantime, Sam said, focus on staying alive.

"Your chin is practically on your desk," Jill said.

Grady was nursing a cup of coffee. Jill pulled up a chair.

"I'm lost. I broke up with Clint last night."

"You only told him last night? You left him long before that."

"Why am I this way?"

"The reason now lives in the north of our great state, back in the mountains on the Wintoon River."

"I want to be with him."

"The problem is that Gaudet may be watching him. He must know that you're important to Bowden. Do you want to go through that all over again?"

"I understand the reasoning. But I don't have to like it. I just wonder if Gaudet would be right about the 'important' thing. Michael hasn't called or written."

"For God's sake, he thinks you have a boyfriend."

"So what do I do?"

"Sam would say suffer for the time being, but maybe you could write him."

"I want to see him just for a day or two. That's all. Then I can write. I could disguise myself as a boy or whatever."

"Where you gonna hide your chest?"

"Very funny."

"I'll talk to Sam. Maybe a short visit, hair under your hat. We're trying to get a government helicopter to scour the mountain with infrared so we'll know if someone's watching. If Sam says okay, take everything you could conceivably need. It's miles from nowhere."

"I'm not just gonna say howdy and have sex," Grady said, catching Jill's drift immediately.

The okay from Sam came more quickly than Grady could have imagined. Sam liked the effect she had on Michael and that, she was told, was the only reason. This was the one time in Grady's life that she had packed in fifteen minutes. It was because the flight departed in two and a half hours. She landed in San Francisco at 7:00 A.M. and took the 8:30 A.M. flight to Eureka. There she rented a car and got soaked in a gray rain that seemed dismal enough that even the dogs looked wet and depressed with their hair plastered to their ribs. The sky was everywhere and nowhere, blurring the green of the trees and reminding her that this was also a rain forest but in the cold, without the womblike warmth of Amazonia.

She drove into the town of McKinleyville and bought a poncho, some gloves, and a stocking cap. She already had a warm coat. Then she drove into the mountains. Nothing had really prepared her for this, having spent most of her life in LA. She had gone on family vacations but they stayed at resorts and recreation areas in the south of the state or they went back east with money from Aunt Anna for what her mother called cultural experiences. Camping was never suggested or undertaken, so she knew the vast stretches of mountains and forests that were in the West only through books and television, and they did not convey the feel of the place.

From the plane it had become apparent that California had far more trees than people. Behind the so-called redwood curtain lay miles of rugged, mountainous forest land that was largely unknown to the public. To go there from anyplace that anybody ever heard of, you had to fly in small planes or drive winding two-lane roads.

From Eureka she drove nearly an hour and a half into the mountains, past rivers that cut gorges thousands of feet below the mountaintops. She noticed that the water was crystalline, clean enough to scrub the soul. Trees were massive along the road and there were mosses and vines and all manner of green that she could not name. She had never seen anything like it and she found herself stopping the car and looking into the forest. There were bracken ferns like those she had seen around rural areas, one of the few plants she recognized. The conifers felt so strong and ancient that she got out of the car almost without thinking, as if drawn by sorcery. It was now near freezing and rain had turned to heavy mist, so she grabbed a GORE-TEX parka.

She walked to the forest's edge and looked, straining to see like a child peeking in a stranger's house. She stepped in among the trees. There was brush, but not much. The forest actually looked fairly open. Back nearer the coast, she recalled, it was more dense. Here the lower trunks were clear of branches and grayish green brush had grown up. Moments ago she had been in a rush, intent on being with Michael Bowden, but in this place of quiet and wild, where things were more timeless, it seemed a few minutes wouldn't matter. For a while she wandered down a gentle hill, enjoying the unfamiliar mystique of the forest. When next she stopped, she heard a stream and walked on to investigate. What she found was a series of beautiful pools a few feet across and vigorous cascades running between them.

The moss was almost effervescent and the grasses lush. The rocks were white and speckled and, even in the deep of the pools, the water was translucent and small green trout were vividly outlined, the black speckles of their backs plain. Something about the place made her shiver, but it wasn't the cold. Nor was it fear.

A very large tree attracted her attention and she walked to its base. She wondered if it might be a Douglas fir. Sam had told her long ago how the species was named after a Scotsman, a Mr. David Douglas, who was the first white man to publicize its existence. Instead of asking the Indians the tree's name, it was named after Douglas. The forest floor all around looked soft and thick with old needles.

She sat and watched the pools, and in a few moments there was a *whirr* sound and she realized that a large bird had landed in a nearby tree and she could just see the branches bobbing. On the tree that might be a Douglas fir, there was a giant fungus that looked mushroomlike. She wondered at its age. Something made her suspect that such a fungus would grow very slowly. She wondered how big the tree was on the date of her birth and realized that it had probably changed very little in the last twenty years. She couldn't imagine how old it might be. She imagined bringing Michael to this place and having him explain about the tree, the fungus, and the creatures. Surely, if he had been in these woods only a few days, he would know more than she might ever learn. She knew he was like that.

Near her shoe she spied a small salamander and farther away a chipmunk running over the litter on the ground like a picky shopper at a fruit stand.

Things were so different in the world of men than in the world of giant trees and quiet streams. A couple of weeks earlier, she thought, she might at least consider spending the rest of her life with a working stiff making babies. Then something strange had happened: Michael Bowden had come along.

The tree was not like her life. It never moved.

For a moment she thought she might be nuts sitting here in a forest several hundred miles from her home. This trip could leave her feeling very foolish. She was in love with a man who lived in her mind and now she was on a mission to discover if something in this world, one Michael Bowden in the flesh, might roughly match the man in her head. Of course she realized there was another possibility and that was that maybe he was different from her fantasies but nevertheless destiny's truly intended. Where love was concerned even the most cynical corners of her mind had to yield to a little magic. Looking at the fungus and the tree and the enchantment of the stream, the barely visible sky above, she felt truly insignificant. Still, somehow, people and their thoughts of her and her thoughts of them made her life important because most of mankind seemed bound by some metaphysical strangeness sometimes called consciousness or love, and if there was anything else out there in the great beyond, it might also be subject to this same love and this same self-awareness.

When she turned around, she had to think a moment where the road was and then realized she could just listen for the next car. She stood and waited. Nothing came, or at least she heard nothing, until she heard a snapping of branches off behind a thicket of trees.

This was a lonely winter road.

Listening again for cars, she still heard nothing. It could be anything in the forest, she told herself. She reached in her purse and removed the Desert Eagle .357 magnum semiautomatic that Sam had given her to supplement the less potent, but much more compact, SIG Sauer P232 that she still had in the car. Pointing the big gun in the direction of the sounds, she began backing toward the highway. Maybe the stream drowned out the road noise. Then she considered. On one side of her, she had a stream, on the other a road. It should ensure that she wouldn't get lost. Or would it? The road had been making a giant U of sorts and wasn't running straight; so if she missed the U, she would actually be walking parallel to the earlier stretch.

Looking back toward what she supposed was the location of the road, she didn't see any parting of the bushes to indicate where she might have come. Unfortunately, she had walked through something of an open forest and paid little attention to landmarks. Again there was movement in among a thicket of trees. Fear surged through her and she turned and began to trot. She thought of Gaudet and imagined his cold eyes as he watched his men torture the Matses girls and realized she could have been followed from as far back as Los Angeles.

She began to run even as she told herself that if Gaudet was here and armed, he would have confronted her. After maybe a hundred feet she heard the whisper of a car, breathed a quiet sigh of relief, and vowed to tell no one.

There didn't seem to be anyone following. Perhaps her fear had been silly.

She emerged on the road, jogged to her car, and drove on, the mountains becoming progressively steeper and the deep canyons deeper. Rocks left scars down the hillside where they flowed like rivers and abutments had been constructed to keep them off the road. Often they failed and she had to be careful, lest she high center the rental car on a boulder. Again Grady felt small in this mammoth-size wilderness.

She used her odometer to find the wide spot in the road where, according to the realtor, the trail to Michael's house began. Jill had been smart about discerning how to find the place. Since it had just sold, Jill knew that the real estate community would have some vague idea or description of how it might be found. And they did. They said if you kept going two hundred yards past a mile marker on the highway paralleling the Salmon, you could look down the cliffs and see the cabin. At the trailhead there was nothing but a forest and a slight incline that obviously led to much steeper terrain. Slowly she drove up the deserted two-lane road and was struck with the grandeur of the walls of rock and the velvet of great forests that rose into the clouds and looked as if conjured by one of the turn-of-the-century landscape artists she had studied in art history class.

When she came to the next wide spot in the road, she got out into the chill of the mountain air and looked over the side. Almost straight down a thousand feet she saw a large, cascading river intersected by a smaller one known as the Wintoon River. Where the Wintoon River emptied into the larger Salmon, a series of magnificent cascades churned white. In the whole of the giant canyon there seemed one level spot and that was on the far side of the Salmon, at the confluence with the Wintoon. It was a plateau a slight distance above both rivers, tiny, mostly wooded, and utterly isolated. On the large bench of land stood two cabins, one fairly large with a gray plume of smoke and a light in the window that created a sense of humanity in the valley.

Looking through her binoculars, she saw various works of stone about the place. They resembled walls and wall segments and cone-shaped structures that she couldn't quite figure out. Who would have built these rock creations? Why would they bother? Grady could make out two rock piles that appeared to be small fortifications of a sort and it seemed as though she could make out a man inside one of them, for there was the barrel of what looked to be a large gun, judging from its location and the posture of it.

Ah. Of course. Sam's men.

Gaudet had the point of the knife under her chin and Benoit was backed into a corner. Her mind struggled to remember all that Spring had said. Everything was starting to be a jumble in her mind.

"Hold still or you'll be cut. Making a deal makes me hungry for Benoit. Somewhere beneath this sanctimonious bullshit that you seem to have picked up in prison, there is the old Benoit, my playmate, and I am going to find her."

"But, like I said, it's—"

"I don't care."

He pulled a condom out of his pocket and stuck it in his teeth.

"Let me unzip the dress, you can cut the rest," Benoit said. He let her turn around and then he slid the zipper down. She was near panic. Sam had come up with real blood from a blood bank and she had used a speculum to pour it inside herself before inserting a tampon. When she removed the tampon in her charade with Gaudet, she lost all the blood. If Gaudet discovered she was lying, he might kill her. The French might or might not require her release before they closed the escrow in forty-eight hours.

"I am going to use the restroom."

"That's not necessary. I like what you have on, having selected it myself."

"No, I mean I really have to go to the bathroom."

"Hurry up."

She went in the bathroom and closed the door. She was shaking. They were on the twentieth floor and escaping out the window was not possible. Besides which, she didn't yet have enough information. She turned and looked, not knowing what she was looking for; then something struck her—the makeup in the drawer provided by Gaudet. She pulled it out. There was red fingernail polish. Mixing it with water, she created a solution that looked like menstrual blood. She turned on the water and began filling the tub. It took her only seconds to strip and climb in as it slowly filled. She poured the fingernail solution between her legs creating tendrils of red in the water. Then she lay back with her eyes closed.

"What's going on?" Gaudet opened the door without knocking and came and sat on the edge of the tub.

"The presentation isn't bad. I always loved you nude."

"Have you seen the Loire Valley?"

"Of course."

"In the summer, when I was a girl, I went there to my grandfather's place. The flowers were amazing in their variety with marvelous colors and so many translucent, delicate petals. I remember particularly the beautiful blues. There were trees a thousand years old, and there were creeks and the river, and grass as green as Ireland, and butterflies. Even the snakes were beautiful and it was so peaceful in the buzz of the hot afternoons, everything seemed at rest and in its place, and there was no discord. Can you think of a place like that for you?"

"It's pure illusion. The frogs eat the bugs, and the birds eat the frogs, and the foxes eat the birds, and the men hunt the foxes down with hounds, and the dogs tear them to pieces while their hearts still beat, and the men laugh and feel strong. I don't live in illusions."

"But the flowers are beautiful."

"They are deceptions. Flowers persuade bees to fuck and men use them to persuade women to spread their legs and incur the misery of childbirth. That is all they are good for."

"Tell me about your mother."

"My mother and father died when I was young and probably never gave a shit about me anyway. I think my mother was an adulterous bitch and my father well on his way to being a drunk. I have no soft memories. I am a realist. As a young man I drove away my boss's competitors in the laundry business with my fists. Then I killed my boss and took his business. That was about as good as anything I ever felt."

"I have some good memories and I want at least a few people to be grateful that I lived."

"I want to make bad days for others before they make bad days for me. Now how can I take you in a bathtub?"

Unable to think of anything else, she slipped away into her *we pac maw,* and after sometime she heard him say "shit" and leave.

Gaudet had left the hotel by the time she dressed. Trotsky and the guards had replaced him in her room.

"He wants you when he gets back," Trotsky said. "If I were you, I'd stop toying with him."

Later, when the maid came, Trotsky disappeared into Gaudet's room. The two guards remained while the woman cleaned. All of a sudden, Benoit was shocked to see a hand emerge from under a linen drape covering the side of the cart. It waved. Glancing at the guards, she could tell that one was absorbed with his sporting magazine and another with pornography. She rose and walked to the desk, picked up a pad of message paper and a pen. One of the guards looked at her and at the paper. She ignored him. Promptly she wrote the following:

Escrow closes at 4:00 P.M.. Cordyceps in three days. French believe five. Gaudet's men to release vector with fake police helicopters. NY, Chicago, Wash., LA. Computer virus at same time.

Then she walked past the cart back to the desk, dropping the paper on the floor. The cart stood between the paper and the two guards. In a flash the hand snatched the paper and dropped another on the floor. When she went to the desk, she picked up the TV remote, turned, and dropped it by the cart, scooping up the paper when she knelt.

Do you want out? it read.

Trotsky walked into the room. "Gaudet wants you now."

"You're just in time. We should be getting the e-mailed closing statement any moment."

"Never mind that. We're leaving." He shooed the maid and her cart out into the hall. "The escrow closed. You think we would sit around waiting for an e-mail? Devan has been on the phone with Credit Suisse. We're out of here. Now."

Trotsky grabbed her arm and rushed her into Gaudet's room. They put her in a trunk and two big men wheeled her out.

Baptiste was sweating as he stared at the screen. Escrow was to close in minutes. The admiral had retired to his office to await Baptiste's call. Apparently he couldn't wait because Gaudet's phone buzzed and the electronic readout indicated it was the admiral.

"Just about to close," Baptiste said.

"The scientists are screaming that they didn't have adequate time to verify Chaperone. Raval's lab notes don't reveal the source of the Chaperone molecule. Apparently, Northern Lights kept that a secret. Bowden's journal shows a salamander discovery of all things and Gaudet says the

Chaperone molecule came from this salamander. I'm sure he's relying on Benoit. Apparently, Raval told Bowden and Benoit which of his submissions yielded the molecule, but we have nothing in writing from Bowden. There is a lot of puzzlement among the scientists," the admiral concluded.

"Well, it's too late to worry about it now. E-mail just arrived this second; it's closed."

"It's done then."

"Yes. Our money is gone and we have the goods."

"But verification of Chaperone's nowhere in sight. It could take days, or if we have shitty luck, it could take weeks! This thing is like a runaway train. We just better be right." The admiral slammed a fist into his open hand.

"Benoit is betting her pardon on it," Baptiste insisted.

"We've got to inform the Americans in enough time," the admiral said.

"It's five days. Let's warn them in four or sooner if we can verify that we have Chaperone. By that time we may know for sure."

"What if we find out tomorrow that we don't have it? Then what?"

"We still have a card to play with Gaudet and Benoit. We tell the U.S. about Cordyceps immediately if Gaudet and Benoit don't get us Chaperone."

"But then maybe Gaudet pulls the trigger early anyway," the admiral said.

"Maybe he does. But we lose all of our leverage with Gaudet once we tell the U.S. All hell will break loose and he'll know we've told them."

"So, it's really a matter of French national security that we verify Chaperone before sharing our theories with the Americans, and that's all they are . . . theories . . . about Cordyceps."

"Exactly," Baptiste agreed.

"When, ah . . . the financial arrangements . . . Gaudet's, I mean—"

"Of course if the Americans stop Cordyceps as they surely will, there won't be much of a drop in the market. I guess maybe just a small drop because of the scare," Baptiste said.

"Maybe no drop if the Americans stop it completely."

"Absolutely. No question. We're working hard to verify that Cordyceps is real and to determine how the plan would be carried out. So far, I must admit, we have been unable to gather any information on that aspect."

Chapter 21

A man who climbs a cliff cannot stop to build a ledge.
                                        —Tilok proverb

Sam jumped out of the laundry cart as the guards were putting away the laptop. One guard was big and the other was bigger.

"I could use that computer, if you don't mind," Sam said.

Their mouths looked like they belonged to sucker fish.

The mustached fellow went for his gun at the same time Sam was kicking him with a square-on strike to the jaw that broke facial bones on the corner of Sam's boot. For a second the man swayed, unsteady; then Sam hit palm up to the nose and the man dropped, completely slack. Preferring to fight, rather than go for his gun, the second man swung on Sam and hit a glancing blow across Sam's cheek. Sam kicked to the knee and they both grabbed for the man's gun as he was going down. Grasping the gun atop the barrel, Sam twisted it toward the man's thigh when it discharged the first time. A second bullet just missed the man's genitals and again punctured the thigh.

"You better quit pulling that trigger or you're—"

Judging from the guard's shrieking, something vital was hit by the third shot. At that point Sam got control of the gun and the man concentrated on grabbing his genitals. The first guy was shaking himself awake but was not ready to take on the 9mm semiautomatic.

Sam came prepared and put cuffs on the one who didn't need to hold his testicles. Then he got on his cell phone.

"Ernie, they are going to spray vectors—I told you about those—over New York, Washington, DC, Los Angeles, and Chicago. They are probably going to use dummy police choppers, but you can't count on that as the only method of application. You have three days maximum. Next get guys over here to the St. Regis, room 2004, and take custody of suspected terrorists. Deep-six these guys for three days. Make sure nobody knows where they are or if they are alive or dead. Gaudet can't know we have them or his computer, or he may change the plan."

"Got it. Did you say computer?"

"Yeah. I know you'll want a dozen G-men around Grogg when he's playing with it."

"You got that right."

"The French know about Cordyceps. They think it will go in five days. It's really going in three. Verify that they aren't telling us. I have what I think will be proof of the electronic communications. Certain French officials want to profit personally by not informing the United States." Sam explained again how the French officials could make a huge windfall profit even though the CIA had already been briefed.

Next he received a message that Figgy called. He asked Jill to call back. That way he could find out what the French wanted and avoid any questions about the transaction. No doubt they were calling everybody they knew to determine if anybody had any good reasons for canceling the escrow. And that was a call he didn't want to take.

Sam picked up the computer to take it to Grogg so that they could download every byte before turning it over to the government, along with an application by Benoit Moreau for political asylum in the United States and for protection from a hostile power—the French government. Sam had the attorney, Stan Beckworth, help her with the application the night of their meeting.

Admiral Larive was shaking. Baptiste had never seen him this angry, although it was hard to think about it given the sick feeling in the pit of his stomach.

"Scientists can be wrong," Baptiste argued.

"Tell that to the prime minister and the president. The rest of the government is convinced that we were swindled. It took them only two hours past closing. The molecule's not a match, and if that's wrong, then the description of the technology is no doubt wrong as well."

"I will get to Credit Suisse," Baptiste said.

"What good will that do?"

"They may be sending the two hundred million out in batches. Some of it may be left." Baptiste got on the phone and screamed for five minutes.

"What do they say?"

"They called us names in German. But they are holding fifty million, which has not been sent."

"Excellent. You won't have to call Gaudet. He will call you. Get agents over to Credit Suisse and threaten them with everything you can think of so they don't release the rest of that money," the admiral strategized.

"We will make Gaudet pay."

"We need Raval, and Moreau, and we need them fast."

"We tell Raval, we'll hunt him down and kill him if he doesn't come through."

"We are the French government, Baptiste. Don't forget that. What we can say and what we do may not be the same. Write an e-mail to Gaudet. Tell him that we have been cheated. Tell him that he's going to pay unless he makes it right."

"Shall I say it that explicitly?"

"He's a criminal. Be as explicit as you like, short of threatening murder. Most won't believe a thing he says and those who do will think he deserves it."

"I will have all of our people attempt to locate Benoit, Raval, and Bowden."

The admiral picked up the phone and called in his second in command.

Baptiste knew they were about to pull out all the stops. The admiral's career was on the line.

They let Benoit out of the box. It hadn't been long—maybe forty minutes. Green floral-print draperies of good quality and fine furniture surrounded her. It was not a hotel. Someone lived in the place and it was similar to a large Paris apartment. Instantly she knew that it would be very difficult for Sam to locate her again, unless he had somehow managed to use a tracking device on her crate—that was doubtful. Hotels were obvious hiding places, whereas private apartments were not. One look at Gaudet, the slight leering smile, the way his eyes locked on her body, told her that he would be in no mood to be denied.

"I need to put on my special things," she said.

"I don't care right now."

"You always let me get ready for you. It makes me feel good."

"I will let you play your game one more time if you promise me you will be your old self."

"I promise. I swear it."

"Then you can even have a bath. I know how you like them. I will wait, but don't be long. Be sure you get dressed after your bath." Benoit wondered if he was capable of sex without cutting off a woman's clothes and playing with his knife.

Benoit went in the bath, turned on the water, then went through the bedroom into a library with a doorway onto the living area. She was ten feet from Gaudet and Trotsky.

"Did you make sure they destroyed the computer?" Gaudet asked Trotsky.

"I was very explicit."

"Get the computer going. I do not like being cut off from the world. I want to make sure we are on schedule. Some of the atomizers were not working properly."

"Buying more atomizers now would be dangerous. And keeping Benoit Moreau alive is dangerous."

"The French may be pissed if we kill her. You never know who that woman is screwing."

"With all respect, that is a rationalization. They wanted Chaperone. They got it."

"I want to use both the cement trucks and the helicopters and we need some new atomizers to do both."

"Why did you tell Benoit about the helicopters?" Trotsky was perplexed.

"If somehow she can communicate with the outside, I want them to think that half the plan is the whole plan. The cement trucks by themselves would do enough damage. More than the helicopters."

"It is crazy to keep this woman alive, even as you think she might betray you. We must kill her."

"I thought that was my decision."

True to form, Trotsky said nothing more.

Benoit was convinced she knew enough and that she had to get out. Quickly she went back to the bathroom. Within seconds Gaudet was knocking on the door to make sure she was indeed taking a bath.

Then she heard Trotsky's angry shouting at Gaudet. The

tone was completely uncharacteristic of Trotsky. Immediately she sensed that he had opened the e-mail. True to his word, Sam had not stopped the transaction because she was not safe. By now the French had probably figured out at least part of the puzzle—the part where they get ripped off for two hundred million dollars.

Sam was on a video conference in the New York office of the FBI and they were set up with Jill at Sam's LA office. They had downloaded the laptop C-drive to LA to Big Brain over the Internet. Both the CIA technicians and the FBI technicians would be present while Grogg worked his magic. Grogg went to a government facility and connected to Big Brain online. Sam wasn't going to have government people he didn't know anywhere near his company. Ernie, in New York, was petting Harry as Harry sat in the middle of the conference table and took in the big screen and watched every move that Sam made. Although Ernie tried, Harry didn't look all that happy with the attention.

"Harry is worried you'll leave again. I don't make a good substitute dad," Ernie said.

"Harry doesn't like police dogs. Maybe somehow that rubs off on you, Ernie. I don't know."

Assistant Deputy Director Dennis Wagner, of the CIA, was seated next to Jill. He'd been to Sam's LA offices before and was one of the few on Sam's approved list. Dennis cleared his throat, undoubtedly certain that such banter in the face of national security risks was out of place. An anti-terrorist task force and Homeland Security were also on the call.

"We're here to discuss the French government, Benoit, and the threat—the so-called Cordyceps plan," Dennis said. In true bureaucratic fashion Dennis went on to summarize what the government already knew. Although they were confused about some important details, and didn't have a clue as to what Benoit Moreau was up to, they seemed to have the rest of the big picture fairly well in hand. Someone had obviously made them eager about Chaperone. Sam was happy to see the government's high level of interest.

"So far, we know that Gaudet tells Benoit that they are using police helicopters—that's of interest to the FBI and Homeland Security," Sam said.

"We've got thousands of people literally from all law enforcement agencies checking out every conceivable means of delivering a vapor spray to a populated area," Ernie said.

"Good. Of interest to the CIA: Benoit says that France has been told that Cordyceps will be unleashed in five days, but, in fact, it will be three. I have asked Figgy Meeks, the representative for France, if he has any new information and he says no," Sam said. "What does the SDECE say?"

"Well, of course that's classified, but they are saying nothing," Dennis replied. "Simple stonewalling, if your Benoit Moreau is right."

"She's right about Baptiste and Larive, that's for sure."

"Those are serious charges she's making," Dennis observed.

"She's a serious woman. She wants asylum in the United States."

"Asylum from whom?"

"France. She doesn't like the butter sauce and says it's hell over there."

"I thought she wanted a pardon from the French government."

"Woman is full of surprises. Actually, she thinks that Larive and agent Baptiste are eliciting her cooperation by lying about a possible pardon. At the same time they're stonewalling us and investing in the markets to take advantage of the coming disaster. I'd call that being accessories to attempted mass murder," Sam pronounced.

"Let's pray it remains 'attempted.' "

"Amen. Now it's Ernie's turn. I promised to put this right in your lap, Ernie. Are you ready? I want you to ask the president of the United States if Benoit Moreau can have protective asylum, if she is a major factor in successfully stopping Cordyceps."

"Are you mad? I've met him once for two seconds."

"Maybe, but the question is uncomplicated. Will you ask?"

"The president?"

"You can start with the vice president. He has a lot of suck. And I suppose you can go through your boss's boss, or whatever."

"I don't know the law."

"Damn the law. The president can pardon any U.S. crime; he can refuse to extradite. We could give her asylum."

"We'd be flying blind. We don't know all of what she's done."

"It's better than losing a few million Americans. If that happens and you don't prevent it, when you might have, you'll be having a reduced pension—goes with disgrace and early retirement."

"Don't be an asshole."

"Dennis, now it's your turn for some glory. Actually, the entire administration. Call Dr. Carl Fielding at Harvard University. Ask him how badly he wants Chaperone to be owned by a United States foundation, with Harvard on the board of directors?"

"I can well imagine. But it's moot. Grace Technologies was the proper owner; now the technology belongs to France. The French are all over it."

"You're not listening to me. Think about it. Would I be saying it if it wasn't possible?"

"For me, 'possible' means 'legal.' What you're saying is contrary—"

"To everything you thought. But it's only what you

thought and it's only what the French government *thought*. You ask the vice president of the United States if hypothetically Benoit Moreau could deliver Chaperone . . . and be completely legal under international law . . . to a U.S. foundation and deliver us from Cordyceps; then could she have asylum and a complete pardon?"

"She can do all that?"

"I'm betting the farm on it."

"So, this is really about the redemption of Benoit Moreau."

"And the beatification of the careers of Dennis and Ernie. Don't forget that."

Benoit Moreau was losing her faith. *We pac maw* would not save her from an enraged Gaudet. Once the French discovered the truth, it would take Gaudet only minutes on the e-mail to find out that the French were after his ass and assume that she was up to something. Trotsky's suggestion that she be killed sounded appealing in comparison to what Gaudet was capable of.

This bathroom had a window that was latched with rubber-handled, L-shaped locks. Quickly she experimented—they opened enough for her to crawl out and jump, but it was twenty stories down and there were no ledges. She pressed her face to the glass and looked up for a ledge of some sort. What she saw shocked her. A rope led upward to a horizontal surface, apparently the aluminum carriage of a window cleaner's platform.

"Is anybody up there?" she called.

"Yeah. Sam's window washers."

Oh, thank god, she thought. "Hurry!"

After the video conference Sam walked out the door of the FBI building and took a cab. In the cab he placed three calls. One was to the vice president's staff to grease the skids and to get them reaching down the chain of command, even as Ernie and Dennis were crawling up. The second was to Dr. Carl Fielding. Although he was a Harvard applied mathematician whose expertise was modeling brain function, he was familiar with the technology in question and was Sam's go-between with the internal medicine people interested in Chaperone. Never in Sam's career had he so seriously risked his reputation. If this didn't work, he would be finished with big government contracts. And the world would have even greater concerns, he reminded himself.

The third was to Jill.

"Benoit and Gaudet have now moved to a Trump condominium complex. I had probably twenty men around the St. Regis."

"Sam, you—"

"In three minutes, call Whalen for all the details. He knows more than I do." He hung up.

Sam dialed Whalen.

"The guys were hanging just above the bathroom window like you said, about to put a mike on the window, and Benoit Moreau called to us. Then somebody grabbed her and that was that."

"What do you mean somebody grabbed her?"

"Someone inside the apartment. We couldn't get in touch with you, so we just took a chance and sent everybody out in the open and one team right through the front door."

"What happened?"

"They were gone."

"Did you check for laundry chutes, under the floor, the walls? They gotta be there."

"We're checking. I'll call and mention laundry chutes and the rest. Shall we rip up the floor and the walls?"

"Tear the place apart."

* * *

"Who the heck is that?" Chandler, one of the guards, asked Michael on a handheld radio.

Michael was looking through the binoculars.

"A tourist?"

"Who goes sightseeing in November?"

"The way he moves, I'd say we're looking at a she," Michael observed.

"Yeah, she looks like a kitten in a toilet. Never seen anything so miserable in my life."

"How long you think she's been there?"

"Not long, maybe ten minutes."

"We'd better send the car over."

"It would be a dumb-ass kind of trap, but just don't forget Mr. Gaudet."

"How could I forget him?"

"I'll see if I can make the satellite phone work," Yodo spoke up. "Before you move, we need to tell Sam."

Yodo went out the door to a small fortification, where another man sat hidden, caressing a BAR .30-caliber machine gun. In seconds he had Sam on the phone. Sam advised that Grady was due to arrive, but they should trust nothing and take all due security measures in bringing her across.

There were eight guards at the compound, all armed and trained. They had four outposts fortified with sandbags and rock, and each bunker contained handheld rockets, grenade launchers, and a BAR machine gun. They created a square around the cabins and they were the first line of defense. But they were not always occupied. The men moved around the perimeter and watched, keeping in mind the location of the nearest fortification. There was always one man within twenty yards of each outpost. Although the houses were used during the day, at night they were quietly abandoned for camouflage tents hidden in the dense forest against the mountain.

Welcome to paradise.

Chapter 22

When the bear leaves its cave, the village hides its
food.

—Tilok proverb

Trotsky nearly dislocated Benoit's shoulder when he
dragged her out of the bathroom.

"You've probably killed me," Gaudet said in an even tone
that chilled her more than the most hysterical cry. "The
French have held up fifty million dollars. Now they'll hunt
you and me both, you fucking bitch."

"We've got to go," said Trotsky. His pragmatism immediately affected Gaudet, who turned away without another
word.

Trotsky pushed a hidden button in the library and a panel
opened. They entered a sizable room with vanity photos of
the apartment's owner and all manner of memorabilia:
books, wine, signed baseballs, various sabers, as well as
cigar humidors by the dozen, each carefully labeled. Trotsky
closed the panel just as they heard a crash at the front door
of the apartment. In one corner of the room there was a solid
wood panel. Trotsky pushed another hidden button and a
spiral staircase appeared. On the floor below was a large
wine cellar with wine in glass cases and adjoining the wine a

large room full of old books. Obviously, the man who owned the place was a wealthy collector. Quickly the two put on white hazmat uniforms. There was a very large cart labeled HAZARDOUS MATERIALS. When they opened the bin, it was full of white material that had the appearance of old bandages. However, when they lifted up a wooden piece, the bin was actually empty, the bandagelike material having been affixed to the wood. Inside the small compartment Benoit recognized a scuba tank and regulator. They handcuffed her hands in front of her.

"One word and I will kill you instantly." Gaudet showed her a pen. "It shoots a pellet of ricin that is instantly lethal. I promise you, Benoit, one small sound and I won't hesitate."

They put the oxygen regulator in her mouth and closed the lid.

Despite nearly overwhelming panic, Benoit felt the cart rolling forward and imagined they left the room and entered a hallway. After a minute or two they stopped; she supposed to wait for an elevator.

"Hey, would you mind showing me your credentials?" a voice said.

"Hey, why don't you show us yours?" Gaudet said with unflappable confidence.

"We asked you first."

There was silence and she couldn't discern what was happening. Perhaps Gaudet was showing them something.

"Can we look in there?"

"Hell no. Can't you read? It's asbestos shavings. You wanna die?" That was Trotsky, his accentless voice sounding absolutely authoritative.

More silence.

"I think we'll just take a look."

The board didn't move, so they were obviously deterred by the white stuff.

"You are breaking the law." Trotsky paused and clicked

open a cell phone. "We are a hazmat team, contractor's license number 9859432d, and we need a squad car at the Trump International. We are being accosted by civilians who are endangering themselves and everyone in the vicinity. . . ."

"Keep your shirt on and hang up the phone. You can go. We just had to check."

They clicked over the metal threshold of an elevator. She heard the doors close and they were going down. When the elevator opened, there were more men. The same procedure was repeated, only this time Trotsky was even more indignant and she didn't hear him purporting to call the police. With a heavy sigh she resigned herself to the fact that they were leaving the building. She felt and heard the lift on the back of a truck and soon she felt the vehicle moving slowly ahead in New York traffic.

Desperate, she pushed up on the lid. It wouldn't move. They had somehow locked it. In a way that was good. They obviously didn't expect her to get out, so they might leave her alone. The container was heavy plastic. She lay on her back and used her feet to push on the lid, but even with all her strength she couldn't budge it.

"Only a few people have left the building. We found one room off the library hidden behind a panel, but it goes no place. One way in and one way out. On the floor below there was a hazmat team with asbestos. We saw credentials and looked in their hamper and it was full of asbestos. They left in a truck. Just to make sure we have somebody on their tail."

"How do you know the hamper was full of asbestos?"

"I see what you mean. The guys said they took off the lid. But I don't know if they reached down inside."

"After being told it's hazardous? Give me a break. They're not gonna put their hand in that stuff if it looks official. They wouldn't know that it's not that easy to get mesothelioma."

"I'll check already."

"Fine. Get me to that truck. I think they're in it."

"But it was the floor below."

"Tear the walls apart."

"We pretty much have."

"The walls of the secret room?"

"Jeez, it's got display cases."

"Keep looking. You'll find a way to the lower floor. How about windows?"

"Shit, Sam. You can imagine anything . . . but okay."

"Have the guys on the truck's ass call me."

It wasn't a minute until Sam's phone rang. It was nearly dark.

"They're headed down Wall Street toward the water."

"I'm Jack. I'll be with you as fast as I can."

"Roger that, you with Whalen?"

"No. Whalen sent me to assist."

"We're doing fine."

"Talk to Whalen. I just follow orders." Sam stayed on the line and moved through traffic as fast as he could.

"Hey, Jack. You're not gonna believe this. They just drove onto State Street down to the new construction at the ferry terminal, crashed the barricades, and then went plunging into the river."

"I believe it."

"What do we do?"

"Watch me."

Sam drove up to the smashed barricades, then followed the course of the truck on foot, stopping at the end. The truck was a bit downstream, sixty or seventy feet out from the pier—sinking fast. A boat was coming up the river. Taking off his shoes and overcoat, Sam dived in and felt the full force of 50 degree Fahrenheit water. The shock was so great it was a clamp on his chest and it stung his face and put an ache in his bones. When he surfaced, he swam hard toward the truck. Just as he arrived, the truck went under with a large burst of bubbles. He descended and could see nothing in the murk. When he surfaced, he found a trail of scuba bubbles headed downstream. Swimming just ahead of the bubbles, he dived and swam down hard. The boat was approaching. After dropping, perhaps twenty feet, he hit bodies. One of them erupted in a flurry of activity, grabbing for his throat. To even the odds, he reached about the person's head and grabbed for the regulator hose, ripping it from the diver's mouth. Sam's foe made for the surface and Sam followed, but not before he yanked on the regulator hose. It broke free in an incredible stream of bubbles. Just as he broke the surface, Sam saw the gun. The man was ten feet away and coughing badly. As the first shot went wild, Sam went under. The boat propellers screamed. If the shooter hadn't been half drowned, Sam knew he would be dead. Swimming toward the man, but deep, he made a guess as to his exact location. When he came up, he was behind and to the left. With two strokes he managed to grab the gun.

As he fought for the gun, Sam saw the boat and two people being pulled over the gunwales.

The man who fought him was strong and determined. Grappling, they went under. Both of Sam's hands were on the gun. It went off, but the bullet hit no flesh. Sam flipped head down and frog-kicked toward the bottom. He sensed his adversary yearning for the surface and kicked harder. When he felt the man start to weaken, Sam increased his determination and told himself he would swim to hell. Above, the boat props wound up and the boat went screaming away. Sam's lungs began to burn and he felt woozy from the cold and the lack of oxygen. Thoughts became jumbled. They rolled under the water, and up became almost indistinguishable from down. Finally the man released and was gone.

Sam had the gun. He started up and suddenly realized his lethargy. It was hard to kick. Shoving the gun in his pants, he tried to swim. His arms were rubber. With great effort he thought his way through each stroke. When at last he took a breath of air, he was too weary to lift the gun. It didn't matter; the man was nowhere to be seen. Sam took great gasps of air, trying to recover, trying to survive the cold. He turned and the man appeared facedown. Grabbing the man by the hair, he lifted his face, rolled him over, and breathed into his lungs.

The shore was far off. There were large boats passing, but none close enough. He tried to pull the unconscious man toward shore, but it was too much. Sam could barely move his arms and feet. He knew to be still and not to thrash. He bobbed and breathed and then made gentle strokes. Someone was swimming toward him. They were trying to help but obviously didn't know how. Soon his rescuer was sputtering.

"Lie on your back," Sam said. "Put your legs around my waist." The man did it. "Now you do the backstroke." When the man complied, Sam did the breaststroke and they moved together, with Sam on his stomach and the man on his back, held together by the man's legs. It wasn't clear who was saving whom, but they made steady progress toward the dock. Another couple of men jumped in and helped them the last fifty feet to the ladder, where there were several hands to help them up. Sam lay on the dock, staring at the sky, wondering whose body was floating in the river, but knowing in his gut it wasn't Devan Gaudet's.

Sam sat down for just a moment to escape the frenetic phone calls of the last few hours. Resting was not, however, what it was cracked up to be. It was all too easy to sink back into the gloom he felt over Anna, when he wasn't obsessed with Gaudet and Benoit. Anna remained in a coma, no real changes.

Jill had come to New York, to their temporary offices, and had moved from her table over to his and he welcomed the company.

Harry lay in the middle of Sam's table, looking generally depressed despite their reunion.

"I swear, if I wanna know what you're thinking, all I have to do is look at Harry."

For the first time he noticed Jill watching him.

"I found out today that when Anna recovers, we won't have a baby. How do you think about anything, even saving the lives of millions, when you find out your baby died? I know it was a fetus, but to me, in my mind, it was a baby that I was ready to welcome into the world. I guess I was already planning trips to the zoo and wondering what it would be like to be a regular person with an identity and a child in a stroller. It's like I've been holding her on my knee. For some reason I thought it was a girl. Isn't that insane?" Sam got up from his desk, feeling that he was going to weep.

"I'll be back. I have to use the restroom."

He had lost Bud, and now this. After about fifteen minutes he called his mother.

"As we feared, we have lost our baby."

"It is a great loss for all of us. I am sorry that now is not a time for you to make your peace with this."

"No, it isn't. I don't know if I can go on."

"I wish your grandfather were here."

"What would he say?"

"Catching his mind is like trying to take a handful of wind. I'm afraid I don't know. Besides, words were different when he said them."

"That is so true."

"There might be another child, but the other can never

make up for the loss of the one. We love the one, even though it was a soul that we never knew. Perhaps our love is both our pain and our consolation. When next you come home, we will express our love for this one. I will think about that and I will put flowers at Universe Rock and tell this child of my love."

"I will too."

It took thirty minutes before he felt ready to go back. He knew that Jill would say nothing. She understood him. In order to enable himself to function, he imagined how many children might die if he didn't get Gaudet; he imagined their parents and their trips to the zoo. It was sobering and it allowed him to give himself permission to put off grieving. It was even more effective than the other emotion that he felt—anger and the desire for revenge.

There was nothing to do but swing back into action on all fronts. Grogg and the government people were still trying to pry something out of Gaudet's laptop or get into his main server. Now that Gaudet had driven a truck off a pier and damaged the pier, the cops were looking for him. They would have had a better chance finding Jimmy Hoffa. The Feds were examining every helicopter in the pertinent cities, looking for atomizer equipment.

"You remember that new program for homeland security, where we screen the incoming passengers on the international flights?" Jill asked. It was a kindness that she went on with business as usual.

"Uh-huh."

"I think we've got something."

"Great. What is it?"

"Well, we struck out on the rental-car front."

"Too bad. It was a guess. So where are you now?"

"We performed a query on flight reservations, national and international, using a certain mileage-plus number."

"What number?"

"The number once assigned to one Benoit Moreau."

"So?"

"Well, everyone who worked for Chellis had a lot of mileage-plus miles. Benoit used some of hers to fly one Gustave Flaubert to Malaysia."

"Author of *Madame Bovary?* Obviously, somebody playing a game with an alias."

"Obviously. That's dangerous. Talk about a name that doesn't blend. By itself it wouldn't mean much, but Jean Valjean is using the same mileage number now. I still can't imagine Gaudet would risk the connection with Grace."

"Could be Gaudet. Could be one of his henchmen using the names and number," Sam speculated. "Gaudet using the name offends me. Jean Valjean epitomized a man of great character and I was moved when I read the story."

"This morning Jean Valjean left New York for Eureka, California. Bought his ticket at the gate."

"Oh, crap. I knew I shouldn't have let Grady go."

"Remember, we don't know that Valjean is Gaudet himself. Could be an accomplice."

"No point in thinking that way. I gotta get there fast!" Harry looked startled. Sam petted him. "Tell Grogg and the investigators good work."

"How would Gaudet know where Michael Bowden is?" Jill wondered.

"I don't know. But consider this. The French government is in this up to their eyeballs. If Gaudet didn't have Raval followed, or didn't have Bowden followed, then maybe the French did or maybe Gaudet found him by getting a tip and then calling the realtors in five counties. Right now the French need Raval, and telling Gaudet where to get him wouldn't be beyond belief."

"You're right," she said. "Shit."

"Devan Gaudet is beyond any redemption in this life."

"Sam," she called behind him as he walked out.

"Yeah?"

"Take the part of you that is your grandfather and let it loose. See what happens."

"Yeah, well, while I'm getting in touch with my spiritual side, you move heaven and earth to find Benoit Moreau. She could be in one of those warehouses along the waterfront."

The canyon descent had been difficult, to say the least. It had appeared so formidable late the first afternoon that she slept in the car to get an early start in the morning. Near the highway the trail had begun fairly benignly in a mixed conifer forest with oaks and madrona under the evergreen canopy. From there it quickly changed into steep, rocky terrain. In places Grady found sheer faces, but most of it was slightly less than vertical, with rock protrusions, manzanita, and scrub oak passing for handholds. Every step of the way the wind rushed through the canyon, making a background murmur like the sound in a seashell, the river with its tumultuous stepladder falls adding its own ghostly rush.

Nothing looked touched by the hand of man and most of it looked like the work of a furiously creative God who loved drama and vast plunges and steep pinnacled rises interrupted by vibrant splashes trailing down mountains. It had a kind of awe that glass and steel could never put in human imagination. But it was also a foreign and inhospitable place. Even a frightening place.

The trail had been narrow and full of switchbacks and had traversed cliffs, where the drop-offs were deadly. Halfway down the slope to the river, occasional, light snow flurries started in and Grady began to chill. Here the trail became less steep and she could walk upright most of the time. The next major obstacle was a steep stretch, where she had to turn and crawl facing the hillside while grabbing exposed roots. She noticed hoofprints and couldn't imagine someone taking a horse down this trail. She'd have to ask Michael about that. Below her the river roared, mostly churning white water with occasional pools. Wind-whipped sleet pounded her poncho and soaked her pant legs from the thighs down. It was cold, but the vigorous climb, even going down, kept her from chilling completely through.

The mountain on the far side of the river directly opposite was laden with conifers all the way up, except for deep scars of raw earth where she supposed water ran and pushed the loose rocky soil down the hill. When she got to the bottom and the cable car, it felt like a full-blown storm, the clouds wrapping madly around the mountain peaks.

Grady wondered how long she would have to sit under her poncho, staring across the chasm at the little car on the other side. Smoke still curled cheerily up from the log house.

As they pulled her across, they watched the opposite hillside with guns at the ready. Nobody showed and the crossing was uneventful.

Grady hopped off the cable car, scarcely looking like herself. Her face was shadowed under the hoods of the poncho and overcoat. From beneath the hoods her blond hair hung sopping wet, and was surprising brunette. Amazingly, the blue eyes had turned brown. Her face had its usual life, but at the same time she seemed tentative. Nervous maybe.

Her lips were curved in a soft but sensuous smile; Michael wanted to kiss them, and nearly did so before catching himself.

He hugged her instead.

"You probably didn't expect to see me so soon." Grady gave him a smile that made him stand a little straighter without meaning to. She was shaking a bit from the cold, but she seemed to find something amusing in her own plight. "I needed to borrow some detergent. And I needed a lot, so I brought my suitcase."

They began the walk to the cabin, Yodo lagging behind.

"You look great. Different, though, I think."

"Natural hair color. For some reason I wanted it natural."

"Then previously you did an amazing job of dying it. I'd have never known. I don't get the eyes."

"I wore colored contacts to turn them blue."

In the log house they hung their ponchos in a vestibule. Under her poncho Grady had worn a distinctive long brown coat that was apparently made of softened cowhide. She unbuttoned it and hung the drenched garment on a hook, where it could drip harmlessly onto some plastic. With her hood off, Michael could see that she wore earrings and a matching choker, the choker having a wooden emblem about the size of a quarter; it looked Native American. He liked the style and mood of the jewelry and of the leather coat, and now he definitely felt a different side of Grady emerging, a side even more pleasing than any he'd seen so far.

The next layer of her clothing was a sweater, which was suds white, and had the look of something made by hand. She seemed content to leave it on.

He reminded himself of her figure and how it pleased him—slender and solid, with a little muscle on her frame. They stood gazing at one another long enough to be noticeable, and intensely enough that Yodo remained absolutely still.

"Maybe you would like to unpack your bag and freshen up. I could show you to your room."

Michael picked up her suitcase and directed her ahead to the hallway at the far end of the great room. The hall was about six feet wide and twenty feet long, with replica medieval tapestries and gargoyles left over from the prior owner. On a pine table lay an old bear skull. Michael cringed. He'd been meaning to remove it.

"This stuff's not mine," he said. "Last guy left it."

"Likely story," she teased.

They turned to the right, where the hallway formed a T. There were two bedrooms to the right and two to the left.

"I'm sure you'll want to take a shower and warm up. We have a power plant on the Wintoon that gives us electricity. But we also have a wood-fired boiler that makes very hot water, so we have great showers. You can soak in it as long as you want."

"Sounds good," she said.

"Turn right through that door and we're at your room."

"Great. I came for a little laundry detergent and now I have a room." As they walked through the door of what was to be her room, he glanced around, hoping that it was in order, and he was reassured. There was handmade wood furniture: a couch made of an oak frame, with cushions in greens and browns, a coffee table, two chairs matching the sofa in design and materials, and a small writing desk with a wooden chair. When she was about five feet inside the door, she turned and looked down at her clothing, the black jeans, the handmade sweater, and the soggy tennis shoes.

"I guess you noticed my clothes. No time to pack and frankly I thought rural was like the Dixie Chicks. Out here is like . . . you know . . . *National Geographic*. I understood that we were leaving the civilized world when we went to the Amazon, but across this river, man, this place is right out of Edgar Rice Burroughs. GORE-TEX would have . . ."

"Don't worry about it."

She had a half smile that was delicious and it asked all sorts of questions that only a poet could define, and in the smile was mischief and secret knowledge and sexual stirrings too deep to describe. Michael's throat caught and he knew she was made for him. It was in the sound of her voice, in the bow of her lips before she laughed, the quiet mirth in her eyes, the way she took a small breath before she started a sentence. It was found in the way her body was formed to fit some strange hollowness that was a need he couldn't put in words, the way her eyebrows curved, the way her lips formed words and the way her mind strung them together. It dwelled in her sense of humor, her essence, the things that formed her soul. He wanted to inhale her through every pore. Her eyes looked larger than before, but also delicate, and he knew her intent could be easily dissuaded if he returned passion with uncertainty, and so he took great care to meet her stare with equal boldness, daring her to continue.

She glanced away, then back at his eyes, as if testing him. He tried not to waver.

"What are you thinking?"

"Sometimes in the jungle, where there is a very dark canopy, a single tree falls to make a perfect hole. Right after a heavy rain, when the sun first breaks out and shines down through that hole, it pours in and lights the droplets all around and there are rainbow colors everywhere, and it gives you a feeling like you are in a magic place made for just that moment. Right now I feel like I'm in one of those moments." Michael could be devastatingly poetic.

She stepped forward and took his hand. He kissed the back of it and moved into her.

"Uhm, I would like to say that just as a for instance, I wouldn't mind going to the Amazon sometimes. I mean to visit you."

Michael knew that she was getting at something more than the Amazon. He tried to think over the top of his desire. Then it struck him.

"You know I would not have to be in the Amazon all the time."

"Like if you had kids or something?"

"Yes. That is a good example. But I would have to make a lot of trips to Peru and Brazil."

"Sure, and I imagine that kids with the proper shots and everything could go to the Amazon."

"You know, I have been told that I could get a position at a university."

"You have? Just as a for instance, do you think you could fall in love again?"

"I think I already have. Is it the custom to talk about everything? Do we need to go out for dinner or something? The nearest restaurant—"

"No. No, Michael, are you joking?"

"Will you ever stop planning world history before it happens?"

"Okay. Okay. But there is one more thing that is important."

"Yes?"

"I was what some people call a stripper. I did it for a living."

"In Brazil there is lots of sex like that."

"Not sex. Basically you take off your clothes and get naked while men watch, and then you dance for them and you touch them. They have their clothes on, but you tease them."

"Why did you strip?"

"For money."

"Ah." His mind sought to focus. "You did not have sex with them for money?"

"No. No. Not what I think of as sex. I undressed while I danced. Sometimes I sat in their lap, but they couldn't touch me."

"So you just get naked and men pay you money?"

"I used to. Now I work for Sam and I've left that behind. But I wanted you to know, in case it matters."

"Did they pay you a lot of money?"

"Yes."

"You are very beautiful. It is worth it I suppose."

"No. No. You and me . . . that's not about money."

"You want laundry soap instead?"

She punched him. "Now you're teasing me."

"Yes. I know about strippers. I don't care."

He put his hand in the small of her back, as if they were going to dance. The slight smile increased and they began kissing, and he put both his arms around her middle and pulled her to him. There was a rush in his mind and body, and they began pressing themselves together and he could feel the energy in her body and the strength of her supple back. They kissed deeply and hard, and their tongues explored without hesitation.

Michael closed the door with his foot. Grady began to unbutton his shirt. Taking her pullover sweater by the bottom, he pulled it up and she allowed it to slip over her head by extending her arms. Michael tossed it on the bed. Her blouse was a reddish orange, the color of a jungle vromillius. It was far from wilderness clothing, but he liked it.

Putting his fingers at the top of her neck, he began a massage and, at the same time, looked in her eyes.

"You are beautiful," he said.

Concentrating on her neck muscles at the base of her skull, he worked his fingers while he smiled at her.

"That feels so good."

"I have wanted to touch you."

And he tugged her to the bed, where she fell down, and he with her, and he continued on her neck and after a moment her shoulders.

She kissed him again and wrapped her leg around the outside of his thigh to draw him closer.

In order to facilitate the work of his fingers, he began with the buttons on her blouse while they each played with the ways of kissing. He succeeded with most of the buttons but popped one when pushing the blouse back over her shoulders and then down over her arms. Her skin was smooth and slightly browned and there were a few light freckles like cinnamon sprinkles above her white satin bra. Her cleavage was noticeable and inviting, but he moved his fingers back to her shoulders as they kissed.

It did not seem possible that he could ever tire of putting his hands on her. She moaned, as if reading his mind. Gently he ran his fingers over her shoulders, neck, and chin, as one might feel the texture of silk or touch an object of veneration. He kissed the freckles on her back and slid his fingers lower, feeling a tightness unwind in her. Soon he sensed that the small of her back had some connection of sensation to her thighs, and he pressed in as she pressed herself to him. He could feel her start to breathe heavily as if finding a subtle rhythm. Her thighs wrapped around the meat of his leg while his fingers pushed in smaller circles.

She wanted to kiss again and they played with their tongues. When he left her lower back, they unzipped the front of the pants so that he could work his hands over her buttocks. He sank his hands into the flesh of her bottom and pressed her close and she breathed deeply in his ear and he knew it was good for her. He kissed her above her breasts and waited until she moved the bra to expose her nipples. Her breasts were brown in the areola and slightly rounded in their shape, and for him they were perfect.

Kissing her breasts, he let his lips feel the texture of them and of her nipples. She didn't finish with his shirt before moving to his belt.

As she loosened it, he willed her to slow down, playing his tongue over her ears. She shivered and laughed and he stroked her scalp, kneading it with a gentle touch, then smoothing her hair.

"You make love like you know me," she whispered.

"I make love like a student," he said, and she drew him in.

"I want to talk to you," Grady said as she lay with Michael in the quiet after their lovemaking.

"Yes. I want to talk to you too, but when you are naked like this for the first time . . . well . . ."

"I know. I know. You are ready for more. This will just take a minute. Do you think that you would be open to actually getting married?"

"I thought we just discussed that. I'm getting a job at a university and you're going to make babies."

"You're supposed to ask me."

"Okay. How many babies do you want?"

"Are you teasing me again?"

"Yes. But I'm not going to ask you until we go to the restaurant."

"You don't care about my dancing?"

"Is there some disease associated with dancing naked?"

"Will you be serious?"

"Okay. I will be very serious." And he rolled on top of her and began kissing her again.

"I want to show you something the shaman taught me."

"If you do that other thing again with the panties, I may need a shaman."

Chapter 23

The great mountain roars before the rocks tumble.
                                        —Tilok proverb

Sam looked at the hard rock of the mountains, the jagged, knife-edged ridges that plunged near vertically and the dull gray and black of the clouds that swathed their peaks, the dormant plants vying for life, the barren trees whose sap had receded into the roots, withering the leaves, the rust on the needles of tired conifers. It was a cold day. The animals would be gaunt with the miseries of winter, the songbirds gone to a better place. Most of the mountain seemed dead or struggling. It all brought to mind Russian peasants on the frozen steppe and the precious vodka that helped them to flee the pain. It was enough to make him weep.

Jill had called on the satellite phone and told him that the doctors had evaluated Anna and she was no better. That was a blow, but he insisted to himself that she was also no worse and prayed that she would recover. The miscarriage still haunted him. They still had no word from Benoit Moreau, but Jill was coordinating a massive private search, this in addition to an earnest government effort.

Sam had arrived one day behind Grady.

It felt like a path that Sam had walked before—dead or

dying people that could not be mourned because live people could still be saved. Every time it took something from him, and every time he knew he got a little worse for the wear.

He was waiting for the right moment to tell Grady about Anna.

Standing by the cabin, he tried to let anger displace his sadness.

He watched Michael and Grady through the window holding each other on the couch. Grady had always seemed alive, but now her smiles were deeper, and he had also observed the angelic patience of new love. He had seen it in others with marriage and pregnancy and engagements, and it was always followed by realism—a necessary but unfortunate end to infatuation. Living alone allowed for a certain frivolity, a good scotch, a wink and a nod at the Devil. It also allowed one not to worry about making someone else miserable. It avoided any analysis over whether Indian blood would ultimately be a turnoff for a celebrity like Anna, or whether someone like her could live with someone without celebrity status. If he lived out his days alone, it would be okay, but he had to quit thinking about it because thinking about life and meaning and that stuff would send him into despair. Right now he had to focus on keeping these people alive, finding Benoit, and eliminating Gaudet.

For some reason thoughts of death on a mountain brought on this kind of thinking. He wished Grandfather were here. Something was about to happen.

He imagined Anna again as he had left her, lying in a coma, and tried to shake the thought off. Shouldn't he be at her side while she struggled for her life? The thought was interrupted by a second premonition of the sort he had now come to accept. At that moment Sam felt sure he could feel Gaudet. He looked up at just the visible edges of the vast expanse of the surrounding terrain. He saw countless places to hide, then dismissed the feeling as superstition.

Sam had asked the government to come in with an infrared-sensing helicopter and look for people on the nearby mountains. It was how they would catch Gaudet and then use drugs to pump him for information about Cordyceps. What the government would not dare try, Sam would do without hesitation. The helicopter was coming, he was told, but to date it hadn't arrived and now it was too late. The growing snow flurries would prevent them. Sam had tried to impress on Ernie the logic of waiting in the mountains, but the FBI was convinced that Gaudet was orchestrating Cordyceps from a Manhattan warehouse. They agreed to come to the California outback only if anybody showed up.

Mother Nature had other ideas about that.

Grady and Michael appeared at the cabin door with Georges Raval. They had donned stocking caps, obviously preparing for a walk around the compound.

"It's not a good idea to go far," Sam said.

Michael nodded.

"There's nothing but wilderness up that mountain and it goes for miles. The artillery is down here."

The wind was whipping and a chime near the porch dropped to the ground with a final metallic tinkle that was choked off on impact. Black clouds hung everywhere; it appeared as if the forecasted blizzard were about to cut loose. Chandler jogged up, looking like a man with something on his mind.

Just then, Sam cocked his head as he heard a cracking sound reverberate through the mountains, followed by a rumble and a vibration that he could feel in his feet. It grew in intensity until the sound was deep and rolling, perhaps a volcano or a massive landslide with the vibration filling the air and literally shaking their bodies. Suddenly it stopped.

"What was that?" Michael asked.

"Shit," Chandler said as he reached the group.

"What in the world was that?" Grady murmured. "An atomic bomb?"

"Look." As Yodo pointed toward the river, Chandler's head exploded in a burst of blood. Sam shoved Grady and Michael to the ground, urging them to crawl to a small rock wall. Yodo ran for a rock fortification and the machine gun it housed, apparently more concerned with fighting back than with getting shot.

Bullets smacked into rock and occasionally ricocheted with a whine. Sam's men were returning fire and the opposite hillside was pocked with puffs of snow, dust, and rock. Someone on Sam's team fired a rocket and a small patch of trees on the opposite mountain was upended and a body came tumbling over the lip of a cliff. It slapped its way from one rock protrusion to the next, the body bending and breaking in a gruesome display.

After depositing Grady and Michael in the rocks, Sam belly-crawled through the brush to the bluff edge, where he could see whatever might have excited Yodo. He looked down at the river and saw its flow had ceased and that it was shriveling to a series of tiny pools, the green rocks exposed, the car-size boulders surrounding what had once been a vibrant river now standing like monuments over ancient graves. Cascades of heavy rapids became trickles even as he watched. And there was something else. Men in white camouflage were coming across the river bottom, spread out, one at a time. Yodo was firing virtually nonstop, pinning down one member and then another of the enemy team. It was an assault—too many to fight off. Looking at the force, Sam wondered whether Gaudet had actually managed to enlist the French. Raval was still a French citizen and they would do everything possible to take him back to France. It was crazy, but maybe they saw it as their only hope of getting what they thought they had purchased.

"Count on the government to be someplace else when you need them," Sam muttered. The snipers were not going for Michael or Raval. That explained why Chandler had his head blown off, with Michael and Raval standing close by, but it didn't explain why Sam still breathed. Probably the first bullet was a premature shot by an overanxious sniper; probably Gaudet would be boiling that shooter's balls before daybreak next.

Sam kept low and ran back to Grady and Michael. "Get to the base of the mountain," Sam said. "We're gonna climb."

"Supplies?" Michael said. "I have to get the '98 journal anyway." Sam looked at the spacious log house thirty yards distant across mostly open space. If they tried to make it into the house and back out, at least one of them would probably die.

"Over there, through the trees, there's a rock house. Inside, there are two guns and a little ammo. Run like hell. I'll be right behind."

"First the journals." Michael sprinted off through a hail of bullets without awaiting an answer.

Sam took out his radio. "Everybody up the mountain now. High ground."

Sam looked again at the main house. By some miracle Michael had made it inside. Sam waited to see if he would emerge. Between the front door and his current hiding place were several oaks, trimmed up and offering little cover. There were some benches cut from logs, a chain saw sculpture that formed the likeness of a walking bear, and an old hammock strung between two of the oaks. Unfortunately, his M-4 was on the porch. He set out in a run, his boots sinking in the soft earth and throwing up black soil as he zigzagged to make himself a tough target. Shots cracked in the cold air and bullets spat mud around him. Just as he reached the porch, he heard a rushing sound—something like the sound following a jet fighter's low pass at an air show. Michael passed him at a dead run. Grabbing his rifle, Sam fled as the rocket vaporized the back of the cabin and the concussion sent him flying. Hitting the dirt, he was moving instantly with hands and feet flying, and his gun slung over his back in an unconscious motion guided by reflex.

Food would have been good, but they would have to make do without.

Sam found Grady, Michael, and Raval huddled, Grady with red eyes.

"God, I thought you were both dead." Her voice cracked, but she held back any tears.

"Let's go," Sam said, grateful at least for his gun.

They ran through the densest clumps of trees toward a corner of the property, where there was a pump house and a cache of M-4 ammunition. Sam's body sung with adrenaline, his mind working out how he could get his charges up the mountain.

They ran at a full sprint, except where rough ground or tree branches slowed them. They bulled their way through a heavy stand of fir saplings and into a small opening. For a second Sam had difficulty locating the small doghouse-size structure that he had seen only once. Then he located an old madrona tree that had been partially burned at the base, and he knew right where to look. Upon finding the rickety, grayed pump house, he yanked the door off its hinges and grabbed ten clips, stuffing them in his pockets. In a war it wasn't much. Michael, Grady, and Raval grabbed handfuls, he didn't know how many each.

Grady, Michael, and Raval were running behind Sam, while Yodo was running through the trees about thirty feet to their right, as were Martin, Gunther, Kenneth, and the rest. Yodo had a rocket launcher; Martin was lugging the BAR. They were taking one heavy piece of armament each and he hoped it wouldn't slow them down. They were all headed across a forested stretch of the plateau that was dotted with sixtysomething-foot conifers. As they neared the corner of the plateau and the mountain, they tightened into a single-file formation.

The snow began falling in windblown sheets. Almost immediately it became difficult to discern angles and slopes; "down" became the white ground and "up" the white sky. Beyond that, there was little visible of anything. It even made it hard to balance. They began running through what seemed a white tunnel with snow-laden branches whipping them and the *whoosh* of snow underfoot. The cold air poured into their lungs in odd juxtaposition to their sweating bodies. Soon they were laboring in the heavy branches.

Sam had on shooting mitts. The thin leather of the trigger finger was cold against the metal of the M-4. As he ran, he peered into the blinding snow and the dense white and green of a tree-choked forest in winter. Then from the murky landscape a form suddenly took shape—off to his left—then shots were pounding in his ears.

A man had burst through the trees, firing. Gunther hit the ground as Sam and the others fired back, turning the attacker's white camo into red-splotched laundry.

They ran on for a few seconds until more deafening muzzle blasts tore through flesh and forest. This time Martin and Kenneth were down, writhing in the snow, their wounds hopeless, their bullet-riddled bodies nearly empty of life.

Sam ran the thirty feet to Grady, Michael, and Raval.

"Run as fast as you can. Stay in the main branch of the creek at the end of this trail. We'll catch you when we can."

Grady grabbed his neck and kissed him on the cheek, then quickly gave him a peck on the mouth.

"You gotta live" was all she said.

Yodo remained while the three others ran after Michael, Grady, and Raval. Sam had killed the shooter, but he waited for more. Yodo squatted with his M-4 ready to fire and the rocket launcher cast beside him on the ground. They heard the cracking branches of men in a hurry to kill and Sam decided on a strategy.

"Yodo," Sam whispered. He pointed up the trail and began to move with Yodo following. When they left the plateau, it was on a steep, snow-covered sliver of a trail, which soon became a faint tracing on the ground. Under the snow-coated oak lay loose rock and acorns rotting from winter. Douglas fir and slightly smaller white fir canopied over the oaks, diminishing the light greatly. Sam and Yodo followed the route of the others until they came to a spot fifty yards up the white-foamed creek. It was steeper than any city street but did not require traveling on all fours, although just ahead the smaller branch of the Y moved up steeply in a couple of near-vertical drops. Quickly they lay track in the earth and the old snow, and they broke branches, making it appear that the larger number of the group had taken the small fork. Next they used tree branches to obliterate as best they could the prints going up the main fork.

"Yodo, you need to go after the others and be the rear guard."

"But the larger force, if not all of them, will follow after you."

"Yes. But I know these mountains. I'll be going fast. Very fast."

Yodo's frustration showed, but Sam knew that he would not disagree.

Yodo nodded. "Take the rocket."

"No. I will make my point another way. This is partly a mental war."

Yodo nodded and took the artillery.

Sam turned and began scrambling, carrying only the M-4 and his backpack. As he went, he slowed a moment to feel for the satellite phone that created a reassuring bulge in a pocket at the bottom of the pack. As soon as he was several hundred yards up the hill, he took out the phone and called Jill.

"We're being chased up the mountain into the wilderness by thirty men, maybe more. I'm guessing they're rogue French SDECE or mercenaries trying to take Raval back to France. Gaudet may be leading the attack. They've created two large rock slides into the river, one above us and one below. I imagine that a huge lake is forming above. It's only a matter of time before the dam bursts. When the second one breaks, there'll be an amazing debris torrent for miles downriver."

"In that case, anyone near that river is dead."

"Call the authorities just to make sure they are evacuating people. I know it's obvious but it is the government . . . and don't worry, we won't be near the river."

"I'll call the authorities." She paused. "You're pretty much on your own, Sam. Be careful."

"Uh-huh. Look, I've got to move. Any word on Benoit?"

"No."

"Do everything you can to find her, Jill."

"We've got men combing the warehouses. We're trying to get permission to go inside. It's slow work."

"I know. How many atomizer-equipped helicopters have they found?"

"Only three so far. There must be many more. We're running out of time. I figure twenty-four hours max."

"What about Grogg?"

"Government is showing no signs of letting us release the Internet antivirus."

"That's nuts. If Grogg gets into the Quatram server and gets a read on Gaudet's virus, call me before anyone else."

"Even the government?"

"Especially the government."

* * *

Benoit Moreau stretched her body as far as she could. Lying in a fetal position, she could not straighten anything but her back. It was becoming excruciating. The space was perhaps a foot high, but much wider. There was a water bottle and she could obtain water by sucking on a plastic tube. Gaudet had put her there and was holding her as an asset. He didn't care if she suffered, but he wanted to keep her alive. There would be many questions to answer about why the French didn't get Chaperone, and she was still valuable with respect to Chaperone and the French laboratory, and Gaudet might need all the bargaining chips he could get. Surely, he'd gone after Raval and Bowden now. A couple of Gaudet's guards came every so often to give her a little food and to let her use the toilet. One man reminded her of Saddam Hussein in appearance. She had taken to calling him "Hussein," and the other guard she had dubbed "Napoleon" because he was a short strutter.

Last time Hussein had come to let her out, he had looked at her too long for a man with no interest but his job. Of course she immediately thought about how she might use it. Although Gaudet had dropped her into the box with her hands cuffed behind her back, she had since managed to pass her wrists under her feet by turning on her side. The flexibility for the maneuver was the result of her Pilates and stretching. Strangely, Hussein, the more attentive of the two, did nothing about rearranging the cuffs. He underestimated her, and that was her first break.

As she waited, she thought about what she would do if she could escape. Sam might be the only person, aside from Raval, that she trusted. She had a phone number of his committed to memory. That was step one. Another number she remembered was one that Trotsky had used to access the mainframe with the laptop. She needed to get that info to Sam, including a warning about the cement trucks, before it was too late.

It had been hours since the guard's last visit and her bladder was bursting. If she had even the slightest chance, she would risk everything.

No sooner had she thought it than Hussein came. He was alone, no doubt with ulterior motives. This was her second break. He pulled up the boards, allowing a pinpoint of light into the hole. Then shining a bright flashlight, he was obviously perusing her. This time she made sure that one of her breasts was nearly exposed. For a long time he just looked and she didn't move, feigning near unconsciousness. Finally he reached down and felt her forehead. Then his hand drifted to her shoulder, caressing it and tugging at her dress. Making no move and not acknowledging him, she waited. It was instinct. Every man required a slightly different seduction. Finally he grabbed her arm.

"Stand up."

She made as if to stir and struggled to her feet while she remained hunched over. She hoped he wouldn't think about her hands. In the near darkness she fell against him, making sure that her arm and even her hands rubbed his crotch. He took her by the shoulders to try to draw her to him.

Violently snapping her head up, she hit him hard under his chin and knew instantly she had hurt him badly. Blood spurted from his mouth and he half screamed, half moaned. Then she found his face and drove her thumbs into his eyes, trying to squish them like vintners' grapes. When he grabbed her wrists, she kneed him in the testicles as hard as she could. He wore a shoulder holster and she grabbed the gun. Then she ran.

She was terribly stiff and she stumbled as she went, nearly falling. It was a huge warehouse full of drums in the area of her captivity. Two more men came running; they were shooting, and almost unconsciously she shot back. Then she ran down an aisle, turned, and was out of sight. She found an alcove and went in it, trying to get her wits about her, to stretch cramped muscles, to clear her head.

Looking around, she could see that she could easily reach another aisle by crawling over some barrels. She moved quickly across barrel tops on her hands and knees. In the next aisle she ran and took the first turn. Then she stopped. Running footsteps approached the next intersection. She leveled the gun. The steps slowed. She leaned into a small space between the barrels so that she would not present an obvious target. As she watched, she saw the barrel of a hand-gun; then a hand came slowly around the edge. The man was no more than twenty feet away. Weakness paralyzed her arm and it shook. The sights wobbled. Part of a man's head came into view—too small to hit. She waited. In the dim light he hadn't seen her. He kept coming. His face was full on. It was a wide face, with a big nose. The snarl in his soul was captured in the lips. He was squinting over his gun. She fired. Flesh blew out the back of his head in the instant before he dropped.

Benoit shuddered and nearly collapsed, but she forced herself to run past the body, around the turn, and perhaps a hundred feet more to the next four-way intersection. As she approached, she slowed. There was another alcove, where barrels had been removed.

Her chest heaved, her legs still cramping from confinement. A headache behind her eyes made her nauseated and she knew she had to get away. She had no more fight in her.

A man burst into the aisle, right into her sights. She started shooting at the same time he did. He dropped. She felt a stinging in her shoulder. She reached and felt blood. Her head spun. Footsteps, running. She tried to raise the gun, but her arm was crazy. The ceiling spun and she fell. For some reason the floor felt soft.

* * *

Sam scrambled up the mountain through the oaks and then into the timber, careful to watch the lay of the land for the formations he had studied through the binoculars. Some ravines ended in vertical faces high on the mountain, where water tumbled down over bare, smooth rock. In these areas the rock was harder and the water's etchings were displaced to areas where the stone was softer and more easily worn away. It was one such ravine that Sam had in mind and it was the watercourse that he now followed. About two thousand feet up it ended in a waterfall on a stone face that only a rock climber could scale. To either side of the face there were ridges that could be scaled, but they were widely separated. It would be very difficult for climbers to take an alternate ridge, get above him, and then come back down. At night he would use the terrain. When his grandfather had taught him, it was to stalk deer, but it would serve equally well for hunting men.

Sam turned after forty minutes of rapid climbing and looked down the mountain. The snow had abated briefly. He saw many following him—maybe twenty or so. No doubt most of Gaudet's force.

It was growing dark and Sam resumed his climb. A few minutes later, he veered out of the ravine onto the ridge, broke a few branches, and made the trail ridiculously obvious. After he had gone high on the razor-sharp ridge near the head of the rock wall, he found the deep chasm that would stop the climb of Gaudet's men, even assuming they could reach it before nightfall. He dropped off the ridge and went down its shoulder, leaving no trace. If he were being followed by Tiloks, they would laugh, go down the mountain, and take a different route, but these men were from the city and they would not laugh, nor would they double back in darkness. They would be trapped for the night with Sam below and impassable terrain above.

Meandering down into a forested hillside, he stayed away

from loose rock to avoid slides and broke no branches. Stepping on the balls of his feet, as Grandfather had taught him, he avoided making deep heel imprints that would be easy to spot. Where he could, he walked on hard rock. After twenty minutes of rapid downhill progress he moved back near the ridge and waited. It was only minutes until he heard the heavy, labored breathing of men who were not in shape to climb mountains. They were noisier than a herd of elk. Rocks bounced down the mountain; branches were fractured; they tried to whisper, but their voices were nearly shouts when they found his sign. They would stop for the night, spread out along the shoulders of the ridge.

When Benoit awoke, her mouth felt dry as dust. The first thing she saw were plastic tubes hanging all around her. As she turned her head to the left, she noticed her arm and shoulder in a giant cast and her hand above her, off the bed. The terrible ache came from her shoulder. By her bed stood a woman she did not recognize. The room was unsteady. She still had the awful headache. At once she remembered the box in the floor; then she was running and they were shooting. She felt so tired—exhausted, really. She closed her eyes.

When she next opened her eyes, she tried to put things together. There had been a hamper and a large crate in a store. She had been with Gaudet and in the river. Somehow it didn't seem to fit. The woman next to the bed was still there, although now she was asleep. It must have been a long time. As she lay there, things began to become less elusive in her mind, and suddenly she remembered coming from France and prison, the government job, Baptiste and the admiral, the meeting with Sam and Spring. Georges.

"Cordyceps," she whispered.

The woman by the bed jerked and her eyes flashed open.

"It's okay," she said. "I'm Jill. I'm with Sam, but officially

I'm your sister. Outside are the French SDECE and the FBI. Sam's people found you in the warehouse. During the shootout."

"Jean-Baptiste Sourriaux. Is he here?"

"No, a René Denard seems to be in charge."

"Don't let him in!"

"Yes. I understand."

"We have to get out of here."

"That will be tough."

"Cement trucks. Tell Sam that Cordyceps is cement trucks and helicopters."

"Got it."

"Did you get the laptop?"

"Yes."

"There is a code. Let me see. The year of the French revolution, 1789. Then the telephone city code for my sister in Bordeaux, fourteen. Next one year after I was born, but one decade off. So 1977. Next it is . . . let me see . . . oh yes . . . it is BMW backward so WMB . . . then it is Gaudet's age transposed, so it is fifty-four instead of forty-five. Next it is the number of my driver's license. Gaudet did that because he used to be fond of me. I don't remember the number on my driver's license, but you should be able to look it up. Last it is Trotsky's birthday. He was born in 1959 on the day before Christmas. Put those numbers together, and if I have remembered correctly, you can enter a folder on the laptop where you will find another much more complicated code. Use that to get into Gaudet's computer, if he hasn't shut it off. I doubt he has because it's about to release a major computer virus."

The woman called Jill pulled out a cell phone.

"Grogg, take this down. There is a password to a folder in the laptop." Benoit helped Jill repeat what she had told her. "Call me back when you've cracked it. . . . Tell us your assessment of what we can do and we'll call Sam." Then there was a pause. "I don't care what you have to do to hide it. Tell them you have to take a shit and smuggle it into the restroom." Another pause. "Okay, well, if that won't work, then take advantage of their boredom. But just do it." Another pause. "Yes, you can bring in gourmet food. Anything. Wine, whatever. Get it downloaded to Big Brain, give them the wrong code, and get back to our offices."

Jill hung up and dialed again.

"Ernie, it's cement trucks and helicopters." A pause. "Yeah, good. That's a hell of a lot of helicopters, but she says definitely also cement trucks." Then after a moment. "I have another call. Yes?" A pause. "That's all the French know? Shit, Figgy, you'd think they'd know more than *that*. What the hell good does it do to know Gaudet is going to do something in the next sixty hours?" A pause. "No. Benoit's still unconscious." She gave Benoit a wink. "We'll call you the minute she wakes up." A pause. "Figgy, of course we'll let the SDECE interview her, but only when the doctors say she's ready." Another pause. "I can't promise that. Hell, I probably won't even be here." A pause. "I gotta go, Figgy. Can't talk now. Sam's calling." A pause. "He's in New York looking for Gaudet. Where else would he be?" Jill disconnected. "Lying bastard."

Next Jill dialed Sam's satellite and left a message.

Chapter 24

If the wolverine chooses the fight, it will defeat the bear.

—Tilok proverb

Sam turned on the sat phone every thirty minutes on the half hour when he could. This time he got an immediate incoming call.

"What's happening?"

"We got her. She's alive and awake. The vector is to be delivered in cement trucks and helicopters. The FBI found more helicopters painted like state police choppers and fitted with atomizers. A lot more. They've arrested some pilots. Now they're going after the cement trucks."

"Good."

"Benoit also gave us a way into Gaudet's server. Grogg's working on it. He's gotta get around the government guys."

"I'm gonna cover us the best I can. Tell him to call me when he gets it figured. If I'm unavailable, then release the antivirus."

"The government has forbidden us."

"I've cleared it with the vice president and the head of the FBI."

"Is that true?"

"For you it's true. Do what I say."

Thankfully, Jill didn't argue.

Next Sam did call the office of the director of the FBI and spoke to an assistant director with connections to Homeland Security.

"I need something."

"Go ahead."

"If I do something brilliant that works, I want you to say that the director gave his approval. Likewise, Homeland Security."

"Take credit for something brilliant that's already worked? What are we talking about?"

"Saving the free markets."

"This is the antivirus for the Internet, isn't it?"

Sam said nothing.

"We'll look into it. You got that?"

"Got it."

That meant they would more than likely do it. They wouldn't call him back or discuss it further.

With that business done, he turned his attention to the mountain. It was nearly dark and snowing hard. Fortunately, the wind had picked up and it was creating a blizzard. The hunters would try to bed down or get under cover, probably under the big trees. Now was the time to start back up the hill. Without a light he crept along, weaving back and forth across the ridge. Most of them would be just below the ridge on the leeward side—all but Gaudet, who would see the mistake in doing the obvious. Sam was certain they hadn't made it to the chasm; they would still believe that the task was to climb and to catch the group high on the mountain.

Sam kept low to the ground and moved at a snail's pace. In the dark and these conditions he would have to feel whoever was ahead. Then he saw the first fire. It surprised him. Yes, it was bitter cold on the mountain and these men weren't up to the elements. But to lose the advantage of surprise? He could smell the overconfidence.

As Sam crept to within thirty feet, he tried to figure how he might take out all five men around it without being shot. They sat close to their guns and looked jumpy.

Sam settled down and waited, the cold penetrating his clothes, making him miserable. First his ears started to ache; then things started tingling like they were going to sleep. A bit of a snowbank began building next to a log and he tried crawling into it and under the log for some insulation. Under the log he found moss and leaves and packed it in his clothing. It helped to insulate and cut the cold further. The part of him that was in the snowbank was 32 degrees Fahrenheit outside of his clothing. Inside his clothing, with the leaves and moss, it was considerably warmer. The part of him that was outside the snow was subject to windchill and below-freezing temperatures, so he did all he could to get himself covered in the white powder. After an hour the men near the fire were nodding off, but they frequently stirred because of the bitter cold and the need to throw on more wood. One man had his back near the fire and he appeared to be in a deep sleep.

Shooting all five didn't appeal to Sam. Carefully he searched the ground beneath him, digging down with his fingers and a large skinning knife. The ground was very hard, frozen, and without the heavy knife it would have been nearly impossible. After twenty minutes he had located ten small stones. Waiting until they all appeared asleep, he came out from his shelter and belly-crawled near the fire. He went to the man farthest from the fire, whose gun leaned against a log. Reaching carefully, he slowly picked it up. Moving back into the shadows, he pushed the barrel into the icy snow and plugged it. For certainty he poked in a rock. Then he returned it to the log, just as it had been. After waiting a moment and satisfying himself that they all still slept, he crawled to a second man whose gun was leaning against his leg. This was more tricky. He removed three small stones from his pocket and put them quietly down the barrel. With the third man, who had his hand wrapped around his gun, he did the same. Getting to the other two men was too dangerous, but perhaps the problem would solve itself.

On his hip he had the large skinning knife, which he once again removed from its sheath. Its blade was still razor sharp. Two of the men lay with their feet within a foot of one another. Very quickly he lifted the first boot and sliced clean through the leather and into the Achilles tendon. There was a split-second reaction time and, with the first scream, he had cut the second man as well and then leaped back behind the log.

Three guns literally exploded in rapid succession. The men farthest up the hill hadn't fired. The other three were wounded from metal fragments. The men who were cut were yelling and so were the wounded. It was pandemonium.

"Stand with your hands up," Sam shouted.

The two men with unfired guns hesitated but didn't seem interested in testing their weapons.

"I can't stand," one of the men said. He had been cut.

"You can stand if you wanna live," Sam said. "Step away from the fire. Hands behind your head and kneel."

They did as they were told, even the men with the bleeding heels.

Sam kicked snow over the fire.

"Take off your coats."

"We can't survive without coats."

"You won't survive with them because I'll shoot you."

"We are French diplomats. We have diplomatic immunity." The man had a Spanish accent.

"Take off your coats, run down the mountain, and call your embassy."

Sam collected the two functional weapons, the coats, and all the radios.

Suddenly there was a huge roar down the river canyon and Sam knew the upper dam was gone, with the lower dam soon to follow.

"Take off. If you hurry, you might make it to the landing where the cabins were and start a fire and stave off frostbite. If you don't get a fire going down there, you'll lose body parts from the cold. Don't forget matches." One of the men fumbled through a pack. "Now *go!*"

Without waiting they hurried down the mountain, the un-injured helping the injured.

Sam got on the radio.

"Mr. Gaudet. Do you hear me?"

"I hear you. What do you want?"

"Same thing you do, only it's you I want to kill and not me. But I'll make you a deal. If you want to live in a prison, you can surrender yourself. Call off Cordyceps. It's failed anyway. I'll turn you in to a country that doesn't allow capital punishment."

"We can make a different deal."

"Oh yeah?"

"I will trade you Benoit Moreau and the girl you call Grady for Raval."

"Good luck, chum. Benoit's safe in a Manhattan hospital and Grady's back at the office."

"Grady is on this mountain."

"Five of your guys are headed back down. They're dis-couraged. Your plan is falling apart. FBI's all over the heli-copters and cement trucks. Your underworld investors are gonna be pissed off. They'll hunt you harder than I can. Hell, I'll give you to them."

"You aren't listening. Do you want Grady back alive?"

"You've been whupped by Benoit Moreau, and you don't even know it yet."

Gaudet had no response for that.

"You've defrauded the French government. You. Not Benoit Moreau. Did you read the fine print in those papers you signed?"

Again, no response, but Sam heard Gaudet's breathing.

"You screwed your investors and the French. You're done, Gaudet. Fish food."

"No," Gaudet said simply. The line went dead.

"Hey," Sam spoke into the radio, changing from channel to channel. "The rest of you on the mountain should know your boss is losing it. Gonna be a Tilok war party up here and we'll be taking scalps. Go ahead, stick around. We've done five; we can do more."

On one channel Sam heard calls go out to the five men he had neutralized. The calls got no response.

"Told you. They're running down the mountain without scalps. Bad deal."

"Stay in your places." It was Gaudet again. "I have Sam's woman."

"Sam . . ." It was Grady. She was crying.

Sam ran through the dark, paying little heed to the noise of his movement.

It took only a few minutes to get down to the Y, where he and the others had split up. There were the tracks of many men, even though the bulk had gone up the mountain on his trail. Even as he went, he knew he should call in, so he forced himself to stop.

"What's happening?" he said to Jill.

"Thank God you called. Grogg got into Gaudet's computer and got the virus file. His antivirus, with a little tweaking, will probably do the trick."

"Release it."

"Against the government's orders?"

"I told you I spoke with the director of the FBI. And the vice president. They know, so just release it."

"You got it. Benoit's doing well, but she's desperate to know about Raval."

"I think he's fine, but somehow Gaudet has Grady."

"Oh no. No. No."

"I'm sorry. I'm going after them."

He signed off and resumed his run. To improve his progress he popped on the light. At this point he didn't care about the risk. He scampered over the rocks, banging his shins occasionally, but managing most of the time. Finally he was out of the creek and on a tiny, steep trail. It was the trail to the high mountain meadows, where the berries were thick in summer. Damn it. He should have known Gaudet would take the other trail.

Ahead he heard a laugh—an incongruous sound if there ever were one. Light from a campfire followed, and Sam shut his own light off. Slowly he crept forward. Soon he saw the fire and a big canvas lean-to. They had Grady tied spread-eagled on two poles that formed an X. She was close to the fire, nearly close enough to burn. Although she still had on her panties and bra, it was easy to see what was coming. Below her, also tied, sat Michael Bowden. The wound in his leg had reopened and bled freely. That explained how they were able to catch him in a forest. Fortunately, they didn't seem to have Raval. There were six men, all armed, all looking around, but all clearly distracted by Grady.

Gaudet was nowhere to be seen. Sam guessed that Grady and the men were bait. Nearby Gaudet would wait with more men. Sam moved back in the forest, blocking from his mind what was going on with Grady. He moved inches at a time, slowly circling the fire and the men. Soon they would begin the torture and the rape.

He had to focus.

Gaudet would be sick with anger and even fear. For a few minutes in this forest Gaudet might be on top, but in the larger scheme his world was crumbling.

Sam's radio crackled. Quickly he dialed down the volume and hunkered down to listen.

"I just wanted you to know that there are also boats along the Manhattan waterfront. Just about now they are releasing the vector." Gaudet paused, breathing heavily. "My investors will be fine."

Sam had to call Jill. That's what Gaudet would be counting on—to slow him down, maybe to give himself away. Sam walked deeper into the forest.

Grady screamed and it nearly undid him inside.

"Jill," he whispered. "There may be boats along the Manhattan waterfront. That's from Gaudet; he could be full of it. Pass it on to Ernie."

"Okay. They've cleared people away from the waterfront just in case."

Ernie was a smart guy.

Sam wanted to call Gaudet and get in his face about the boats, but he knew it wouldn't help. Slowly he made his way back near the fire and began again to circle. If he touched branches, there would be a dusting of snow that would fall. The wind was his ally, for it too moved the bushes and made it difficult to discern what might be coming or going. After another thirty or more paces he saw a dark spot standing out against the forest hues. Grady screamed again. He could feel her anguish in his bones, but he couldn't see what they were doing to her. Tears were running down his cheeks and he wanted to kill like never before.

He waited. For a minute nothing moved. He took another step. Then he saw it. The dark spot moved. Then another moved, and another. Soon he could make out people facing the fire. From their vantage point they could see what was happening to Grady. He could not. Grady screamed again in pure agony. They watched the torture like cows watch a hay truck.

"Put her down on the ground," someone near the fire said.

Sam heard himself groan.

"You bastard," he muttered. "You miserable piece of shit."

Flipping the M-4 on automatic, he leveled it at the men hiding in the forest. Without caring who saw him, he walked forward. Grady screamed. His angle ensured his gunfire wouldn't hit the campfire area. He pulled the trigger. Shadows moved, men screamed; he marched on, spewing death. Five or more were down. A new shadow jumped into the forest. Without hesitation he sprinted, crashing through the snowy bushes. A massive-caliber gun roared behind him. Yodo must have shown up. The forest filled with thunder from all sides, but Sam kept after the one. He stopped. Everything was black. Then he heard something running through the trees. Without thought he ran and flicked on his headlamp. A head moving through six-foot huckleberry electrified him. He knew it was Gaudet.

Sprinting, he tried to hold the beam of light on the target. He filled his lungs and ran with huge strides. Then he was on him and grabbed him by the neck, pulling him down. Sam let out a guttural cry and Gaudet turned. They clawed at each other in wild combat. His teeth snapped at Sam's head, even as his knees churned, trying to find the groin.

Sam's light wobbled crazily, filling the forest with a weird shadowy half-light. He swung with an uppercut, connecting to the ribs. Gaudet growled and gouged at Sam's eyes and face, ripping the skin off his cheeks and bruising his eyes. For once, Sam fought not with deliberation but with rage. He clawed back at Gaudet and grabbed his throat. In turn, Gaudet's hands clamped on Sam's throat and they were staring into each other's eyes.

As they squeezed one another for death, Sam's years of training took over. He released Gaudet's neck and brought his joined hands up under Gaudet's chin with a fierce strike, breaking Gaudet's hold. Sam used a palm to splinter Gaudet's nose, which sprayed blood and had him wobbling. He threw an elbow into the floating ribs, intent on piercing a lung.

Gaudet fought like a man possessed, hitting Sam in the head and body, fighting back only to be pounded in the solar plexus.

The blow crumpled Gaudet, but before Sam could move in, Gaudet managed to rise and free his knife. Blood ran down his face, covering him, but Sam saw life in his eyes as he held the knife in front of him expertly.

Sam waited. Gaudet lunged but missed. Once again Sam waited, and Gaudet jabbed, nicking Sam's arm. With lightning speed Sam grabbed the knife hand at the wrist and struck the back of the elbow with an open hand, breaking it clean. Gaudet screamed and Sam took out a knee. He threw the knife into the trees. Gaudet crawled on the ground like a cornered animal.

"Hold it." It was Figgy. A light shone from his hand. "I'm afraid I need to take him for the French government."

"I don't think so, Figgy."

"I'm taking Raval too. The French got screwed in this deal."

Sam shook his head at the audacity of the allegation.

"You and Baptiste and Admiral Larive, and nobody else, screwed the French government and the Free World. You were going to let Cordyceps happen and reap the profits. This isn't about governments. It's about a few crooks. I'll prove that."

"No. I don't think you will." Just before Figgy shot, Sam leaped at him. Figgy shot probably at the head but missed. The second shot hit the Kevlar vest dead center. Sam slapped away the gun, which tumbled into the darkness. Gaudet and Figgy came at him at once, both desperate. Sam went for the uninjured Figgy first. A kick to the knee connected. Then both men were on Sam, trying to take him down. They hit the ground in a tangle, fighting like animals, tearing, biting, going for anything vital.

Sam struggled to roll free of the melee. Somebody had a hand on his throat. He didn't have long. Sam found a throat, grabbed the Adam's apple, and pulled with all his strength. Someone gasped, and the hand on his throat loosened. He punched blindly where the throat had been and connected with a face. Lifting his right leg over Gaudet, he caught his head and squeezed with a scissor lock. Gaudet bit into his thigh, and it became a contest of pain and endurance. Sam yanked on Gaudet's neck once, then twice, then clamped down viselike once more. At last, like a dying dog, Gaudet let go with his teeth and sank back.

Figgy was still choking. He didn't seem to have any fight left.

"Think about the upcoming throat surgery. It'll be a bitch."

The gunfire on the mountain had long since ceased. Sam shouted for Yodo, got up, and found his emptied M-4. Then he slapped Gaudet awake, yanked him up on his crippled leg, and did the same for Figgy, who couldn't stop choking. Carefully Sam checked Gaudet for weapons.

"So, you take me down. I got thousands or millions of your fellow citizens. I'm going to an American jail until the appeals run out."

"Would you like to hear the bad news?"

It took hours to get everybody that hadn't escaped back to the cabin site that was now covered with snow-frosted debris from the torrent. Both cabins were obliterated. Yodo and three men were left, plus Raval, Michael, Sam, and Grady. Raval, who had managed to escape into the woods, had taken up arms during the firefight. Grady was okay, but for a couple of nasty burns on her thigh and a badly bruised breast. Gaudet was a mess, his face swollen nearly beyond recognition, one broken elbow, a broken knee, and a badly sprained ankle. Figgy couldn't eat and could barely drink and would need an IV soon.

As soon as they were at the cabin site, now a mess of mud and wood, Sam called Jill.

"We're all okay."

"Grady too?"

"They abused her, but no rape. She's tough and she'll heal."

"Thank God."

"What happened with the vector?"

"We got all the copters and all the cement trucks. It was a miracle and took three thousand law enforcement personnel, but that did it. There were some boats. They tried to evacuate everybody, but there were stragglers and some homeless that remained. It wasn't pretty. The homeless murdered each other in gruesome ways. Lost maybe fifty to a hundred people. Still counting. Those that survived the fighting died from the immune response. It could have been a horrible disaster involving millions."

"The antivirus on the Internet?"

"They say it worked."

"Benoit?"

"Doing okay. She's going to need your help, Sam. A lot of angry Frenchmen here."

"I'm coming as fast as I can."

"We're waiting."

It was twenty-four miserable hours later that the sheriff and National Guard and FBI made it to the hillside. They used inflatable rafts to cross the river—the cable across the river was gone—and then rope ladders and lines for gurneys to retrieve everyone. With the storm raging, helicopters remained impossible.

Sam went with everyone to the hospital. Just before leaving he got a call from the director of the FBI.

"Pretty damn gutsy of me, approving that antivirus without any testing."

"That's real leadership," Sam joked. "Maybe you should write a book."

"How come you never want to take credit for anything or be associated? It might be good for business."

"I like my privacy. And I'd appreciate it if the Bureau would support me in that. Tell the *People* magazine crowd and the rest that this was the work of my good friends, Ernie and Dennis."

Sam chose silver gray hair for the occasion, along with a mustache and horn-rimmed glasses. He watched from behind a one-way mirror. Benoit Moreau was present with her attorney, Jefferson Peakum, a Tennessee trial lawyer hired by Sam. They sat at a big table with about twenty other people.

"This is an informal get-together to try to mediate an agreement," the fellow from the State Department began.

"We'll begin with Benoit's legal counsel, Jefferson Peakum."

"I'd like to say," he began in his Southern drawl, "that Miss Moreau has been granted asylum for her outstanding role in saving us from a considerable calamity with which you are all familiar. She's grateful for that, and I think no one quibbles that said asylum was well deserved. Initially we had some arguments about the rules concerning asylum, but we're here today to make our case to the French that the government of France should grant a pardon making asylum unnecessary. We are certain that once the fair-minded French have fully considered the matter, such a pardon will be granted."

He looked pointedly at the French, who suddenly all looked like their neckties might be too tight.

"There has been some concern that the French bought a pig in a poke from a French citizen of ill repute by the name of Devan Gaudet. Now a pig in a poke is a Southern term for a farmer's acquisition of unknown livestock. And that's like the French. They didn't check the pedigree. Chaperone, which is the pig in my little analogy, is a process centered on

a molecule, and this process was developed by one Georges
Raval, another Frenchman, at a time when he was an independent contractor for Grace Technologies. Now, in your
notebooks I have supplied you with a copy of that contract
with Mr. Raval that specifies his independent contractor status at the time of his discovery of Cordyceps and at the time
of his development of the process, and I have also verified
with the French trustee that, in fact, this document is in the
official minute book of the corporation duly attested by the
secretary, Benoit Moreau. It is dated 1999. The Grace
Technologies corporation took back a royalty-free license to
use the invention when it executed the independent contract."

"That was all done by Benoit Moreau," the French diplomat interrupted in a shout.

"It was done in 1999 and the full board signed off on it."

"I doubt the board even understood. . . ."

"Were you there? Benoit was there. Why not ask someone who was there?"

The Frenchman was red-faced but did not continue the
debate. "Also attached are the notes of the American attorney wherein he records that Benoit Moreau raised the issue
of Raval's employment and further indicates that the French
bankruptcy lawyers represented that they would look into
the matter of Raval's employment status at the time of the invention."

"Yes, we know this now. She fooled us," the senior French
diplomat said. "The French bankruptcy lawyer was tricked.
He did not understand the significance, so he overlooked the
investigation, but Moreau knew all of this. She knew he was
failing in his duty."

"You opened an escrow with an impeccable Swiss escrow
agent. It says in the instructions that there are no promises or
covenants between the parties, except those expressed in the
escrow documents. Is that agreed?"

The French were silent.

"I take your silence to be similar to that of Pontius Pilate."

"It says that in the instructions, but that is no license for fraud," the French diplomat shot back.

"Certainly. Let us go further. It says in there, does it not, that Georges Raval was the inventor?"

More silence. "I won't keep referencing the murderer of our Savior in the same breath with the French position, but once again I take your silence to mean agreement."

"It says that, but once again—"

"It is not a license for fraud, and we would agree. Neither is it a license for stupidity, is it? So, if we continue to follow the beauty of logic and undertake the glories of wisdom, we get to the affidavit of Georges Raval. It says that this description of Chaperone is from the official records of Grace Technologies. And then Raval says that he cannot personally vouch for the efficacy of the science, as presented in these papers, but only that these are the official documents of Grace Technologies."

"This is merely legal jargon to protect him in case, for some reason, it doesn't work as expected."

"Precisely. And as I understand it, this doesn't work as expected."

"But he held back the real thing."

"No, he held back the version that he kept personally as the inventor. He states he is the sole inventor. Had he given you his version, he would *not* have met your demand. Your demand was for the *official* Grace Technologies documents."

"You're saying that Grace paid for all of this and has nothing."

"Absolutely not. They have a license by contract and Mr. Raval, or rather the foundation to which he has transferred the patent, will honor that perpetual royalty-free license. The French can use the Chaperone recipe without royalty. You obtained all of the vector technology from Gaudet. And I might add you got most of your money back."

"But this foundation can also sell Chaperone to the world and reap all the benefits," the French countered.

"Yes. That sometimes happens when you buy a pig in a poke. Now I agree that Mr. Gaudet as the seller could have done more to research the matter, but he did not, and you allowed him to close and dropped your demand to review the matter and voluntarily gave up your opportunity to ensure that you understood the species in your poke. One would think that you would be grateful that the foundation is going to honor your royalty-free license and actually give you the right pig."

"We are not happy with the asylum. Benoit Moreau knew what she was doing."

"She knew that she was being lied to about a pardon by Messieurs Baptiste and Larive. She suspected those men were taking kickbacks. She knew that they planned to profit from Cordyceps. So, in her words, she used devil bait and caught some devils. She couldn't stop the atrocity of Cordyceps unless she got to America. To get to America she had to lie and convince these French devils that they could acquire Chaperone. All the while she knew, of course, that they had only a license, so she would get them what was rightfully theirs. And then"—Jefferson Peakum drew himself up and paused—"Benoit intended to stop the transaction before French dollars were transferred. This has been documented. But it could not be stopped because at the time set for closing she still had not learned enough about Cordyceps to save American lives. So she risked her own life and a few French dollars to save millions of lives. Now, that might not please a devil, but it should be good enough for an angel. You get what is rightfully yours under the law and she saves the free markets from a calamity and potentially millions of lives. Only a devil would quibble with that. So which are you? Angels or devils?"

Sam could see that Jefferson was going to do just fine. He nodded to Harry and they left.

Epilogue

It was billed as an engagement party. Sam had seen Anna five times since she'd emerged from the coma. In keeping with the doctor's advice he had kept the conversation to light topics: her family, her pets, her upcoming scripts, celebrity news, and who was winning in sports. Nothing had been said about the loss of their child. In fact, Sam had been told by her doctor that her memory of the days preceding the shooting were unclear. They had the party at the home of a friend of Anna's in the Hollywood Hills. Below the house was a large pool, with a pool house at one end and gardens going up the opposite hillside. Sam had been there before but chose not to think about it. There was a spacious patio by the pool and that was the site of the party.

It was an eclectic group. Agent Ernie Dunkin was present, along with several other FBI types, including an assistant director as well as officials from Homeland Security. There were officials from the CIA, politicians—such as the mayor of Los Angeles, folks from the publishing industry (but no journalists allowed), a goodly number of celebrities—many of whom had read Bowden's books, producers, and directors.

All in all, it was an important party for people who wanted to be in the know about the near-miss terrorist attack that wasn't publicized until a few days after it was thwarted. The Dow had risen two hundred points with the news that the government had done it right.

Jill was present, acting as bartender, and Sam was chief of security, his usual cover. Harry was in charge of cleaning up—when people dropped their hors d'oeuvres and such, he took care of it with his long pink tongue. Then sleep seemed to overtake Harry, since there were too many droppings and not enough help.

Guests of honor, Georges Raval and Benoit Moreau, billed as the medical wizard and the spy who loved him, were mingling and had lines of people waiting to meet them, as did the other guests of honor, Michael Bowden and his gorgeous girlfriend. The engagements giving rise to the party were, of course, those of Michael and Grady and Georges and Benoit. For a band they had landed a group that Grady loved and no one had ever heard of—their career was launched.

Anna wandered over and stood next to Sam. Just like Sam, she had an earpiece. Sam saw it and smiled.

"Working security today, huh?"

"Figured it was the only way I could stand by you."

"I tell you what. If you'll drop your earpiece, I'll drop mine."

"Really?"

"Yeah. This once. And if it works out, we might try it again."

"Deal," she said.

"Let's have some wine and then maybe we'll actually eat hors d'oeuvres. I don't know if I've ever really eaten in quantity at a party."

"Me either. But you realize it's not cool to actually eat food. It's cool to nibble and waste it."

"Tell that to Harry." They shared a moment of comfortable silence. "We're going to Benoit's wedding?"

"Absolutely. And you're going as my security guy, right?"

"That would be one way we could do it."

Anna left the answer alone.

After some more banter they sat down under an umbrella, amazingly getting a few moments to themselves.

"You know, Sam, I seem to remember that we were discussing marriage. . . ."

"Yes. We were."

"I'm a little unclear on the details. But neither of us seems quite there right now. If I could just be blunt about it."

"We were at a point there . . . one of those crossroads in life . . . and whatever decision we had made, I believe it would have been good. But we somehow got pushed right through that crossroads."

"And now maybe we need a new crossroads."

"Right."

"Have I ever told you that one of the things I really like about you is that you are a wonderful contradiction. You're very physical, but you have none of the baggage of your typical macho man. I love your heritage and your family. Did you know that I appreciated that about you?"

"I guess not."

"You're strong and you're sincere. To me that's macho. Not drinking beer and swearing a lot."

"I haven't been much on humor lately."

"Harry is your sense of humor."

"I'm kind of a loner to be paired up with."

"Rugged individualists are fascinating. Everyone wants to get to know them if they have a chance."

Sam didn't say anything but thought about his conversation with his mother.

"I have a question for you," she said.

"Yeah?"

"So, tell me, Kalok Wintripp, would you be my boyfriend?" Sam nodded and looked in her eyes. "Take me to a football game? Leave the earpiece at home?"

"Yeah. No problem."

"I'd like to buy you a new tux for Benoit's wedding."

"No problem."

"No one will tell me what happened with the shooting and all that was going on. I think it's your duty as my boyfriend."

"I'll tell you, but I don't want to spoil the afternoon."

"Would you tell me just one thing?"

"What's that?"

"What about Gaudet? Seems we'd all sleep better if we knew he was out of the picture." Anna was truly concerned.

"Oh, he is. I got permission off the record to transport the prisoner. I was told by the spooks that I could accidentally deliver him to the wrong part of San Francisco International Airport, where a jet happened to be waiting. The idea was that first he would be worked over by some less-sensitive ally of the U.S. with the CIA present. I guess there were a couple of Saudis on that plane that had lost a few hundred million when Gaudet's plan didn't work. It wasn't clear whether they would eventually get to minister to Gaudet after the first debriefing. If I were Gaudet, I certainly wouldn't want to bet that I wouldn't end up in a little torture chamber with these guys and the other investors. So, I took him up to that plane, and when he saw who was waiting, he started screaming and begging for me not to do it. I swear this is true, Anna. Devan Gaudet sat right down on the pavement and defecated. I have never seen a human being so afraid in my whole life. I guess what his former investors would eventually do to him, if they ever got hold of him, would be unimaginable to us, and it should be. Anyway, as I was dragging him toward the stairs and to the waiting arms of his tormentors, I thought about Benoit Moreau, one of our guests of honor here. I'll tell you all about her later. She is a woman who has come from the dark side to the light side, with amazing results. And I thought about all my hate, how this man had killed my friends and people I loved, and about all the misery he'd brought to the world. And I realized that in dragging him up those steps I was crossing into the dark side. So I didn't do it."

Anna waited for a moment, rapt. "Well, what did you do?"

"I guess I'll never know whether I gave him back to the FBI because he wanted a bullet in the head so badly or because I wanted to stay on the light side. Anyway, they kindly took him back, saying it probably wasn't a good idea to work through the CIA anyway. He's still getting amazing drugs for inspirational purposes and I guess he's singing away. He knows a lot of dirt. And he's a terrorist, so they can hold him forever it seems."

Anna didn't say anything for a while.

"I'm glad you gave him to the government. . . ." She turned to the party, picking out the celebrated couples. "I guess in view of all this we should think about young love."

"Look at them now," Sam said, watching as they slow danced.

"I guess Grady and Michael are rebuilding his log house," Anna said. "She loves it . . . dirt and trees and sky and mountains and, of course, Michael. She says she'll be going to the Amazon part of the time."

Sam smiled. Anna gave him a look.

"You'd laugh too if you'd seen her in the Amazon."

Anna sipped her wine. "I think she loved you, Sam."

It came out of nowhere, but Sam showed no surprise.

"But now she loves Michael, and he's younger, and he's hot."

Anna laughed at that.

"At least Harry thinks I'm hot."

That got Anna laughing again.

Sam's mother, Spring, came over.

"Anna, I'd like to invite you to the Tilok festival of new beginnings. We bless the whole earth and try to start the good things over again. Being incognito, Sam hasn't gone in years. But he's going this year. I have great faith."

Sam thought about that. A lot was changing very fast. Maybe he should consult Benoit for butterfly lessons.

"I'll be there," Anna said. "I'm guessing Sam won't leave me unescorted. Will you, Sam?"

Sam nodded, then looked back to the party. Benoit Moreau and Georges Raval seemed to be having a kissathon, along with Michael and Grady. People were clapping and the band was cranking up.

"Did Sam tell you that he's going to start working with his cousin on a program for the Tilok teenagers?" Spring asked.

"No, I meant to tell her about that," he said.

"That's great," Anna smiled, obviously pleased.

Spring wandered off and they sat in silence for a while.

"You know," Sam began choosing his words carefully. "Maybe it was about the baby. But now it isn't. It's about you."

Anna reached out and took his hand. It was the first time in public. She looked over the top of her sunglasses the way she usually did. "Would you like to go get some smoked salmon? I made sure they would have it at the buffet."

"I believe I would. And let's make sure we eat it in front of everybody and start a lot of speculation."

Sam dropped his earpiece in the trash barrel.

For a sneak preview of David Dun's next thriller,

THE EDGE OF ETERNITY—

coming from Pinnacle in 2005, just turn the page.

Beware the bears of the night—
put the camp meat in the tree.
—Tilok proverb

11:00 A.M. Saturday

Ben Anderson had worked alone through the holiday weekend, feverishly setting huge flasks of nutrient broth, inoculated with strains of genetically altered bacteria, on an orbital mixer, and watching three timers, keeping the manufacturing process moving to optimize the production and complete the project by the wee hours of Monday morning. He worked like someone's life depended on it—which in fact was the case.

On the bench in front of him were priceless molecules, one of which was the first of its kind in the known world.

He had just pulled two more flasks off the mixer when the air vibrated with the sound of the pump alarm. It sounded like the dive warning in a World War II submarine movie, and it meant that the Sanker Institute's sea creatures were at risk and the lab's valuable experiments jeopardized. With his mind going over the possibilities, Ben set down the flasks and ran for the sea water pump system control panel to see what needed to be done.

On the panel down the hall, a blinking light indicated that only one seawater intake had failed. The sea creatures in tanks fed by this particular intake were in peril, but the situation was salvageable. In theory. Today, on the Saturday morning after Thanksgiving, no one would be on duty except for a half-blind caretaker who couldn't scuba dive, much less replace a broken pump. Although there would be researchers and their student assistants catching up on projects, none of these would be familiar enough with the problem to fix it.

Ben had helped design the Sanker facility and knew the basic plumbing of the place, including the pumps feeding the various labs and tanks, and what might go wrong with them. He reached up and flipped a switch that would electronically control a large valve. For the moment, water would be shared between the tanks, but the overall flow would drop by at least one-third throughout the system. It was important to replace the pump with a small emergency pump as soon as possible and get any necessary parts on order. If the problem were a simple obstruction, Ben might be able to solve the problem himself. But it would require a scuba dive.

Ben hurried back to the lab to check the mixer. Three minutes and he could remove another two flasks to the workbench and the contents to the test tubes. Quickly he checked the centrifuge. There would be some lost time as that batch would be ready for the sonicator before he got back from the dive. While he waited for the flasks, he glanced out the window observing the calm harbor, the blue of the water, the sea gulls wheeling in the November breeze at the ferry approaching the dock across the bay, and the boats in their slips. Even without the pump failure, his hurried effort to make molecules without the Institute's knowledge had his mind in turmoil. He was at once attracted to the extraordinary and revolutionary work, and at the same time repelled by nearly everything else about the Institute in which he did his science. The plan was to replenish his supply of five life-saving organic molecules before he left the Institute forever. Although he cared about his fellow scientists and their work, he was convinced that those who controlled Sanker were corrupt.

Even more important than his work was Jamie, a young woman whom he and his wife had effectively adopted in 1981 when she was nine years old. She was his personal legacy and had followed in his footsteps obtaining her PhD in 1996. For financial reasons, the Institute's primary bene-factor, the Sanker Corporation, had destroyed her career and brought her to the brink of mental collapse. For that he would never forgive them and for that reason alone he would have left immediately. Now he kept things from her to pro-tect her, but it was eating away at his guts and he could see that his silence and secrecy brought added disappointment to her eyes. If not for the production of the molecule. . . .

Decisions, decisions.

By the time the timer went off, Ben had poured another batch of broth into two flasks. He removed two other flasks from the orbital mixer, put on the two new flasks and then ran to the dive room. It was almost one hundred and fifty yards, and a couple of flights of stairs, but Ben made it in less than a minute. Diving kept him more physically fit than one might think after seeing the marks of his age—bushy gray brows, leathery age-spotted skin, and what Jamie called "Einstein hair."

He carried the diving gear outside and toward the sea pens. The Sanker Institute occupied 100,000 square feet of offices and laboratories with vast tanks of raw seawater built to hold all manner of sea life. The buildings had been de-signed to blend with the madronas and conifers on the steep rocky hillside around it. Like the University of Washington invertebrate lab facility next door, it was populated by jean-clad, flannel-shirted, science types who on the whole were pretty much liberal, vastly cerebral, and simple in their pleasures. This group could not have been more different from the ruling class at the Sanker Corporation.

Ben arrived at the sea pen containing the broken pump and, with the practiced ease of an experienced diver, sat on a bench near the edge of the redwood-planked dock, put on a dry suit, mask, fins, snorkel and diving tank, and surveyed the water below him. In addition to the errant pump, the meshed-net enclosure housed "Blue Blood," the world's largest known North Pacific octopus. Blood, as the staff called him, had a leg span of more than thirty-eight feet and weighed more than 700 pounds. Octopi of his species only had a four-year life span even in captivity. Blood was six. Like his relatives, Blood had light-blue blood, and he had been named for a student's *faux pas*. A sincere and enterprising young woman, noticing the color of the pigment in the blood, believed she had found an extraordinary specimen, and upon her announcement of the discovery, Blue Blood received his name.

Ben clipped the emergency pump to his weight belt and let himself slip from the edge of the dock into a weightless world of endless intrigue. A swallow of seawater contained millions of bacterial cells, hundreds of thousands of phytoplankton, tens of thousands of zooplankton, and, to date, only-God-knew how many viruses. There was another ingredient, and that was the bit of magic that gets in a man's blood and draws him back to the ocean again and again. The sea was a part of every other sea on earth, all interconnected like a single, giant organism. Containing far more species than the land, the sea was the mother of all species, the sustainer of all life, and the arbiter of the planet's climate and weather. If that weren't enough, it contained 99% of the earth's living space. Ben thought the planet never should have been called

Earth. Rather it should be Water, for it was water with its many wonders that made DNA-based life a possibility.

Ben punched the button on his buoyancy compensator and let out just enough air to create slight negative buoyancy. Then he punched a similar button on his dry suit and pushed a bit of air out from the area of his chest. Gently, with his arms folded and in a slightly facedown position, he sank, turning slowly, taking in the world around him and gradually picking up speed in his descent as the air inside his suit was compressed. He felt the familiar chill from the seawater and shot a quick burst of air from his tank into the suit to create a thin layer of warming insulation.

He estimated the visibility at a little more than twenty feet. Just beyond him was a kelp forest rich in sea life, the giant leafy ropelike material rising from its anchors in the rocks below. Kelp was the fastest growing plant in the world and grew by as much as two feet a day. At the stony bottom, he used the compressed air from the tank in one tiny burst to create neutral buoyancy. He was weightless, and his existence was as close to effortless as it would ever get. Ben listened to the sound of his breath captured in liquid medium, each inhalation another moment of life. Like the yoga practitioner he was, Ben let the rhythm of it relax him and transport him. Moments like these, of late, provided his only mental escape from the extraordinary pressures of his new discoveries and the related troubles facing him at Sanker.

The broken intake happened to be at the seaward end of Blood's pen. Ben let his eyes travel over the bottom, looking at Blood's various dens and crannies. Littered on the bottom were the leavings from Blood's meals in the form of crab, clam, and mussel shells. Seeing Blood himself was another matter: At thirty feet below the surface, the sun still penetrated, its color a reality, an important component of life in the sea. Blood changed his colors with his mood: red for fear, white for anger, and a camouflage brown for workaday normalcy.

Ben was pretty certain that Blood knew, as much as an octopus could know, that he need not fear a diver. But Blood could hold a man down tight and inflict vicious damage with his beak, so it was best to exercise caution. Especially lately. Blood had been strangely aggressive with the staff and was hanging onto divers, even pecking one with his beak hard enough to puncture the wet suit and require stitches for a laceration. This diver swore that he saw a look in the creature's eye, even claimed that Blood had tried to hold him down while wedging himself under a boulder. A new lab tech had been hired recently, and Ben had heard that he was spending a lot of time with Blood. Perhaps something he was doing was having an effect on the normally shy and docile creature.

Ben neared a large rock that housed Blood's favorite cave. Still no sign of the octopus. That puzzled him. If not hidden there, Blood should have been readily visible elsewhere in the pen.

A cloud passed overhead, blocking the sunlight streaming through the water. Glancing up and out in front of him, Ben thought he saw a shadow, and then it was gone. Something or someone was in the water, in this pen, in fact. He swam upward, but the figure had disappeared, leaving Ben wondering whether he'd seen anything at all. It was odd—no diver, no Blood, and no amount of reasoning that could remove the mild sense of apprehension inhabiting him.

Ben picked his way through the kelp patch, approaching the area that housed the broken pump. Fish schooled around him, then moved on, black snappers hoping for tidbits. At the outside of the pen he spotted a scattering of dogfish, harmless members of the shark family three to four feet in length. Outside the mesh wall lived stone crabs and even a dungeness or two. Those were the only crabs a person would find. Blood would quickly turn any in the pen into crab salad.

Staring at the enclosure's edge, Ben was struck by a new thought: Blood might have climbed the netted sidewall. There were, after all, those crabs just outside the pen, and Blood was smart enough to solve the puzzle. Ben began swimming up the net, the sunshine brightening as he neared the surface.

Directly over his head something hit the water with a splash. Looking up he saw Blood descending. Instead of jetting through the water, Blood spread wide like a parachute, blocking the bright of the sun.

Ben bled air from his buoyancy compensator, or BC, and tried to move to the side. More quickly than he'd imagined possible, Blood wrapped all eight tentacles around him in a giant octopus hug. The pressure was shocking, but Ben's first thought was that someone had taught Blood to do this, using food—some thoughtless student playing games. Ben let his body relax, hoping it signaled an end to the game and an absence of threat to the giant sea creature.

At about twenty feet down, something yanked the mouthpiece from Ben's teeth. The shock of having no air hit him. His diver's mind instinctively began a countdown: He had two minutes.

Forcing himself to stay calm, he reached up to grab the hose and to follow it with his fingers to the mouthpiece. With Blood's massive tentacles wrapped around his chest and over his arms and through his legs, it was much more difficult than usual. After a few seconds of fumbling, he realized the regulator was gone. Oxygen pumped into the water over his head, just out of reach of his pinned arms. He wiggled and reached for the air button on his BC to inflate and ascend, futile as it might be. Instead, a torrent of bubbles escaped the BC at the back of his neck. Something had punctured it. Freezing cold water entered his dry suit from behind, preventing his next move, which would have been to inflate the dry suit.

Panic began to set in. Ben's weight belt was covered in octopus, and he couldn't reach the buckle. Almost unconsciously, Ben's fingers moved toward the backup mouthpiece velcroed to the BC at his chest. It was the only available air, and Blood's massive suction cups had it trapped. Shoving the fingers of his right hand beneath Blood's tentacle, Ben finally touched the backup air, but he couldn't move it.

Something tore Ben's diving mask away from his face. His vision immediately went blurry, and his mind became strangely calm. Reaching up with his left hand, he felt for the mask. It was gone. It had been perhaps thirty seconds since his last breath. It occurred to him that he might die in the arms of an octopus.

Using all his strength, Ben tried to move Blood's tentacles off the emergency air. He couldn't do it. Blood's massive head hung near Ben's chest. Ben rammed his fingers down Blood's gills. The sensation shocked the octopus; in response the creature shot ink and used his sharp beak to peck him in the chest. His dry suit punctured and he felt the ripping of skin, then the more painful burn of saltwater in the wound.

As Blood attacked, he also readjusted his tentacles. Ben was able to get hold of the emergency air and get it partially released. By bringing his head down and pulling with his hand, he was able to get it in his mouth. One good breath, and then Blood tugged on the hose and the mouthpiece was lost again. Ben struggled to retrieve it, barely able to accept what was happening to him.

Something grabbed his leg and pulled it tight to the mesh wall of the pen. That wasn't the octopus. It had to be another diver.

Of course. The splash. The shadow. The BC. But who?

Ben had no time to consider it. The octopus was everywhere. And he was moving up Ben's body. The beak could easily get to his face, to his eyes. Fear was overwhelming Ben, ugly thoughts passing through his head as the air in his lungs dissipated.

The emergency air brushed Ben's hand. He siezed it and sucked. The air gave him strength and hope. Vigorously he shoved at Blood. He thought he felt Blood loosen his grip.

Ben forced himself to breathe. And think. *Deep breaths, relax, relax, relax.*

A face flashed in his mind. *Frick.* The realization: *Frick wants it to look like an accident.* And the solution: *Play dead.*

More Books From Your Favorite Thriller Authors

HORRIFYING TRUE CRIME
FROM PINNACLE BOOKS

Body Count
by Burl Barer   0-7860-1405-9   **$6.50US/$8.50**CAN

The Babyface Killer
by Jon Bellini   0-7860-1202-1   **$6.50US/$8.50**CAN

Love Me to Death
by Steve Jackson   0-7860-1458-X   **$6.50US/$8.50**CAN

The Boston Stranglers
by Susan Kelly   0-7860-1466-0   **$6.50US/$8.50**CAN

Body Double
by Don Lasseter   0-7860-1474-1   **$6.50US/$8.50**CAN

The Killers Next Door
by Joel Norris   0-7860-1502-0   **$6.50US/$8.50**CAN

Available Wherever Books Are Sold!

Visit our website at **www.kensingtonbooks.com**.